GET

WITH JUST ONE PROOF OF PURCHASE:

$50 VALUE

◆ **Hotel Discounts** up to 60% at home and abroad ◆ **Travel Service** - Guaranteed lowest published airfares plus 5% cash back on tickets ◆ **$25 Travel Voucher** ◆ **Sensuous Petite Parfumerie** collection ◆ **Insider Tips Letter** with sneak previews of upcoming books

You'll get a FREE personal card, too. It's your passport to all these benefits—and to even more great gifts & benefits to come!

There's no club to join. No purchase commitment. No obligation.

HPT-PP6A

Enrollment Form

☐ **Yes!** I WANT TO BE A *Privileged Woman.*
Enclosed is one PAGES & PRIVILEGES" Proof of
Purchase from any Harlequin or Silhouette book currently for
sale in stores (Proofs of Purchase are found on the back pages
of books) and the store cash register receipt. Please enroll me
in PAGES & PRIVILEGES". Send my Welcome Kit and FREE
Gifts -- and activate my FREE benefits -- immediately.

More great gifts and benefits to come.

▼ DETACH HERE AND MAIL TODAY! ▼

_____
NAME (please print)

_____
ADDRESS   **APT. NO**

_____
CITY   **STATE**   **ZIP/POSTAL CODE**

PROOF OF PURCHASE

**NO CLUB!
NO COMMITMENT!**
*Just one purchase brings
you great Free Gifts and
Benefits!*

Please allow 6-8 weeks for delivery. Quantities are limited. We reserve the right to
substitute items. Enroll before October 31, 1995 and receive one full year of benefits.

Name of store where this book was purchased_____

Date of purchase_____

Type of store:
   ☐ Bookstore   ☐ Supermarket   ☐ Drugstore
   ☐ Dept. or discount store (e.g. K-Mart or Walmart)
   ☐ Other (specify)_____

Which Harlequin or Silhouette series do you usually read?

_____

Complete and mail with one Proof of Purchase and store receipt to:
U.S.: PAGES & PRIVILEGES", P.O. Box 1960, Danbury, CT 06813-1960
Canada: PAGES & PRIVILEGES", 49-6A The Donway West, P.O. 813,
         North York, ON M3C 2E8

HPT-PP6B

Dear Reader,

Welcome to Harlequin's latest volume of
Regency romance. This month you'll meet
Serena Calvert, a woman with a mysterious
past, in *Serena* by Sylvia Andrew, and her male
counterpart, Kirk Thorburn, in *Debt of Honour*
by Gail Mallin. As you will find, in fiction as well
as in life, things are not always what they seem.
There are lots of twists and surprises as well as
two romances to keep you warm on these cool
autumn days.

In 1996 we have more surprises in store.
Keep an eye out for the latest romance from
Georgina Devon. *Scandalous* is a sizzling
sequel to *Untamed Heart* and will hold you
spellbound from start to finish. But for now,
enjoy *Dalliance & Deception*. There's some
wonderful reading ahead!

The Editor

Dalliance & Deception

SYLVIA ANDREW
GAIL MALLIN

Harlequin Books

TORONTO • NEW YORK • LONDON
AMSTERDAM • PARIS • SYDNEY • HAMBURG
STOCKHOLM • ATHENS • TOKYO • MILAN
MADRID • WARSAW • BUDAPEST • AUCKLAND

DALLIANCE & DECEPTION

Copyright © 1995 by Harlequin Books S.A..

First North American Publication 1995.

ISBN 0-373-31220-2

The publisher acknowledges the copyright holders of the individual works as follows:

SERENA
Copyright © 1994 by Sylvia Andrew

DEBT OF HONOUR
Copyright © 1993 by Gail Mallin

Printed in U.S.A.

CONTENTS

About the Author

Sylvia Andrew taught modern languages for several years, ending up as vice-principal of a sixth form college. She lives in Somerset with two cats, a dog and a husband who has a very necessary sense of humour and a stern approach to punctuation. Sylvia has one daughter living in London, and they share a lively interest in the theatre. She describes herself as an "unrepentant romantic."

Books by Sylvia Andrew

Harlequin Regency Romance

95—Perdita

Darling Amazon (in *Reluctant Bridegrooms*)

Serena

Sylvia Andrew

CHAPTER ONE

THE LATE AFTERNOON sunshine pierced the blinds over the veranda, dazzling in its intensity. Reluctantly Serena moved to close the slats. It was very hot, and the breath of wind coming off the sea had been welcome. She returned to her seat and waited for her visitor's reaction to her plan. "Well, Lady P.?" she asked finally. Very few people on the island were permitted to use this mode of address for the governor's lady, but Serena, a Calvert of Anse Chatelet and one who had known Lady Pendomer for most of her life, was one of the privileged. However, Lady Pendomer, normally the most placidly optimistic of creatures, said firmly, "You will never manage it, my dear! You can have no notion of the cost of a London Season—it was more than enough for us, I assure you, and, sad though I am to have to say this, your circumstances are not such that you could afford anything like the amount needed!"

Serena lifted her chin, and the look she gave her guest was slightly cool.

"You needn't give me one of your father's stares, either, Serena. I would be doing you a disservice if I did not speak plainly now, rather than later. The project is doomed from the start—you simply do not have the resources to carry it through properly. And unless you do the thing in style it is better not to do it at all."

Serena said with a teasing smile, "You are suggesting that we lack the necessary style, Lady P.? I am surprised."

"You lack the necessary funds, my dear! If you wish the *ton* to take note of you, you will need to hire a house with an impeccable address, and have an extensive and fashionable wardrobe—shoes, fans, shawls and all the other bits of nonsense. And then you will need servants, a carriage and horses. It's not as if you have any sort of base in England—you would be arriving with everything to find! When we launched Caroline we were at least able to stay at Rotherfield House with Henry's cousins. You have no one. No, no, it is quite beyond your means! Unless Lord Calvert left some secret Eldorado which I know nothing of?''

This time Serena's smile was bitter. ''No, there were no pleasant surprises in my father's will. The family fortunes are quite as you describe them. The estates bring in just about enough to keep us and to repay a little of the mortgage each year.''

''You are surely not contemplating raising more money on the plantation?''

''I doubt we could.''

''Well, then . . . ?''

''I have managed to put a little aside. And I have some jewellery—''

''No, Serena! You must not! If and when you ever agree to marry anyone, that jewellery will be your dowry! And if you do not marry it will be your only safeguard for the future. You must not spend it on Lucy!''

''I wouldn't have to sell all of it, Lady P. Possibly just the Cardoman necklace—''

''The Cardoman necklace! Sell the Cardoman necklace?''

''Why not? It's not even particularly beautiful—''

''But it's a priceless heirloom! Serena, I really think you are not yourself. It may not be beautiful to modern eyes, I grant you—it is, after all is said and done, over a hundred and fifty years old—but how many families can boast of a necklace made for one of their ancestors by a king? There are those who say that King Charles would have married Arabella Cardoman if he could. No, no, you must not let it go out of the family. Besides, you would never find a purchaser.''

''Now there I fear you are mistaken. I have one already. And as for the family . . . have you forgotten that Lucy and I are the last Cardoman Calverts? The name will disappear when we marry—or die. And Lucy must be given a chance to . . . to escape, before it is too late. The loss of the necklace is a triviality compared with that.'' Serena walked over to the edge of the veranda, released one of the blinds, and gazed out over the sea. The dying sun had laid a path of golden light across the waves, which rolled lazily into the cove below that gave the estate its name. ''You seem surprised that I have never married. Tell me, if your Caroline had been forced to stay on the island, or if she

had not met Lord Dalcraig during her Season in London,
would you wish to see her accepting an offer from one of St.
Just's 'eligible bachelors'?" She turned back to look at her old
friend and, without waiting for a reply, she continued, "Of
course you wouldn't. You were wise enough to see that both of
your children left the island while they were still young. This
climate seems to bring out the worst in the men who stay here.
They are either weaklings, sapped of energy, lacking any kind
of enterprise, content to let others direct them ... or they become self-indulgent, vicious—" She broke off suddenly, and
turned away again. After a small pause she said, "Lucy is a
lovely, high-spirited girl. I will not see her married to someone
who would break that spirit, nor yet to someone whom she
would eventually despise."

"You are very harsh in your judgement of island society,
Serena."

"Have I not good cause?"

There was another, longer silence. Finally Lady Pendomer
sighed and said, "I know the importance you place on seeing
your niece safely established, and I cannot deny that the pos-
sibilities here on St. Just are few. But the cost of such an enterprise as a Season in London for the two of you—"

"Oh, but I should not go!"

"Not go? Why not? Who would look after Lucy?"

"Lucy would take Sheba with her to England, and my Aunt
Spurston would chaperon her. I could not leave the management of Anse Chatelet in the hands of anyone else for such a
length of time. The situation is precarious enough."

"But you must go!" said Lady Pendomer, quite forgetting
that she had been protesting just one moment earlier that the
whole scheme was impossible. "If there is to be a trip to England at all then you must go too, Serena! You are so concerned for Lucy's future—surely you should be thinking of
your own?"

"Oh, come, Lady P.! Who would look twice at me—a middle-aged spinster, with no dowry to speak of? No, we must
concentrate on happiness for my niece."

"Serena, I could become very angry with you if I did not
know how hard you have fought to keep Anse Chatelet in the
family. You are twenty-six, not middle-aged. You may be
somewhat thin, but that is because you do not look after yourself. You could be a very handsome girl if you bothered to dress

properly. And, whatever fears I may have had for you when you were a child, they have now disappeared—"

"Fears? Surely you mean disapproval, Lady P.?"

"No, Serena, I was afraid for you. Wild, hot-headed, lacking any kind of discipline or self-control—faults I lay completely at your father's door, I may tell you." Serena's chin lifted again and she stiffened. But Lady Pendomer swept on, "And you were both so completely dazzled by Richard... Everyone was, if it comes to that. But even after the rest of us knew your brother for what he was, you and your father still idolised him. Your hero-worship I could understand—both your brothers were so much older than you—but your father... he should have known better—"

"He was cruelly punished for his blindness. We all were."

"Yes, Serena." Lady Pendomer bit her lip. "Forgive me. I did not mean to remind you of the past." She returned to her former theme. "I should not be at all surprised if you were to find a match for yourself as well as for Lucy in London! You rate yourself far too low."

"You are mistaken! It is rather that I rate myself too high!" Serena smiled at Lady Pendomer's exclamation of disbelief. "Let me explain. My brothers almost ruined Anse Chatelet before they died, and you know as well as anyone how we have fought to save it ever since—I am still fighting. I never had the sort of girlhood I have tried to give Lucy—"

"You could have had one with your great-aunt in England, Serena. She invited you to live with her long ago."

"I know, and I was grateful to her. But you must know how impossible it was. There was Lucy... and as my father grew older he depended on me to run the estate—there was no one else. And indeed, I think I have done as well as any man—better by far than my brothers would have done. I assure you, I wouldn't marry and give up control of Anse Chatelet, not after all these years, unless I found a husband I could trust to manage it better than I can myself. And if such a paragon existed—I say if—he would surely find a better match than a spinster of uncertain age with a run-down estate in the West Indies!"

"Yet you say you rate yourself too highly?"

"Yes. I rate myself too highly to accept less. In any case, what man could tolerate less than total control of his wife's estates? Would I respect him if he did?" She smiled at Lady

Pendomer. "No, I am doomed to die an old maid. And now let us talk of something else. Lucy may come in at any moment."

But Lady Pendomer was not to be deflected. She said obstinately, "Whatever rubbish you talk, Serena, I will tell you that I still consider you eminently suitable to be a dutiful and loving wife to any man fortunate enough to win you."

"You make me sound such a dull creature!"

"Nonsense, my dear! In fact, I think you might well make a very good match. And I might just be persuaded to help in this ridiculous scheme of yours if you were to accompany Lucy to London. Surely Will Norret could run Anse Chatelet for one year? Pendomer will keep an eye on him. And there are other ways in which I could be of some assistance—your wardrobes, for example. I fancy Maria might be of some use..." Serena's eyes lit up at this. Lady Pendomer's maid had at one time worked for Madame Rosa, the noted London *modiste*. If she would make some dresses for Lucy there would be a great saving. But Lady Pendomer was continuing, "And, most important of all, I shall be very surprised if you can persuade Lucy to go without you. Think it over, Serena. Your mad scheme will very likely fail in any case. But if you force Lucy to go alone—"

"Sheba would be with her!"

"A slave!"

"Sheba is a freedwoman, Lady P. We have no slaves on Anse Chatelet."

"That might be so, Serena, but slave or not, Sheba is as ignorant of England as Lucy herself. A former nurse is not quite the company Lucy needs! If, as I said, you force her to go without you, then you are being quite unnecessarily cruel to the child. And I will not help you in that."

AFTER LADY PENDOMER'S departure Serena was left in a most unusual state of indecision. For years she had practically run the estate, for her father, the nominal head of the family, had been a sick old man, and there had been no one else to shoulder the burden and make the decisions which affected all their lives. Now her father too had died, and Anse Chatelet was hers—hers, that was, except for the massive mortgage which had been raised years before to pay off the family's creditors. She lived in constant fear that she might one day, through mismanagement or some oversight, fail to pay the instalments as they fell due. The agent in Barbados had left her in no doubt that the creditor for whom he was acting would foreclose. It would be folly to risk such a disaster by leaving Anse Chatelet to the care of someone else, even for one year.

On the other hand...Lucy was growing up fast. She was now well past her seventeenth birthday, and if she was to be prepared for presentation to London society then a voyage to England could not be long delayed. And go to London she must! It was unthinkable that her beloved niece's beauty and vivacity should be wasted here on St. Just. If Caroline Pendomer, who was a girl of very moderate charms, could capture a gentleman of such breeding and fortune as Lord Dalcraig in her first London Season, then Lucy's success would be certain, and her future secure. And at least one of Serena's private worries would be set at rest.

At this point Lucy came running on to the veranda. "Sasha, Joshua and the others are having a crab race on the beach—do come and watch it!" She grabbed Serena by the hand and attempted to pull her back through the house.

"Wait, Lucy! I have something important to discuss with you. And how many times—"

"Must I tell you to call me Aunt Serena?" finished Lucy in chorus with her aunt, adopting a disapproving frown. "Lady Pendomer has been here."

"If you know that, why weren't you here to speak to her?"

"I didn't know—I just guessed it from your expression—you've got your Aunt Serena face on. And you're not often stuffy, Sasha. Do come down—Joshua won't wait much longer!"

"Lucy, my love, you're no longer a child." Serena hesitated, then went on, "You know I've always tried to do what is best for you..."

"Goodness, Sasha, what a Friday face! What has Lady P. been saying?"

"Nothing that need concern you. But I think it's time we talked about your future. I have been thinking of a Season in London for you."

Lucy's eyes grew large, and she sat down rather suddenly on the stool by Serena. "We can't possibly afford it!"

"Yes we can, with a little planning and management. I shall sell the Cardoman necklace."

"But, Sasha, that's a Calvert heirloom!"

Serena said innocently, "Oh, forgive me, Lucy, I thought you didn't like the necklace? But, of course, if you wish to keep it, then there's no more to be said..."

"I think it is hideous! But it's been in the family for such a long time, Sasha—"

"Too long! Your grandfather was considering whether to sell it when he died. It would fetch a pretty little sum—enough to pay most of our expenses, at least. What better use can there be for it?"

"It's yours, Sasha. You mustn't sell it for my benefit."

"Why not, pray? Let us talk no more about it. We are the last of the Calverts, Lucy, and if you do not wish me to keep the necklace in trust for you, then it will be sold—in an excellent cause," Serena smiled lovingly as her niece's anxious scruples gave way to excitement and she threw her arms round her aunt.

"Oh, thank you, thank you! I hadn't thought...I never imagined I would ever see England! Oh, Sasha! It would be beyond anything! I've always dreamed of London, but I never thought I should go there! And to make my come out...I can't believe it! London! Oh, how soon are we going?"

"Wait a moment! I'm not sure that I can come with you." Serena put her hand over her niece's mouth. "No, listen to me, Lucy. Our resources are not great even if we sell the necklace, and it is important that they are wisely spent. You will need clothes, lessons in deportment, a suitable background, and lots more besides. If I came I should also need clothes and the rest. It's not as if you would be alone in England. Sheba will go with you, and I am sure aunt Spurston could sponsor you in society better than I could. And you know the estate needs my attention here."

"*I* need your attention, Sasha. How could I manage without you? Can't you forget Anse Chatelet, just for once?"

"Anse Chatelet is our only real asset, Lucy. It is a far greater part of the family heritage than the Cardoman necklace. I dare not forget it." Serena watched as the bright hope on Lucy's face faded.

"Of course. It was stupid of me. But if we cannot go to England together, then I do not wish to go." Lucy walked out on to the veranda and Serena's heart sank. This was worse than she had bargained for. She started to follow her niece but then changed her mind. She would avoid further confrontation for the moment. Lucy was impulsive, but essentially reasonable, and when she had had time to consider the advantages of a Season in London she would probably agree to the plan.

In the weeks that followed Serena was able to judge how wrong she had been. Lucy remained adamant in her refusal to go to London without her. Reason, persuasion, threats—all failed. Lucy merely said that she could enjoy nothing without the company of her aunt, and that they could perfectly well be two old maids together on St. Just. When Serena turned to Lady Pendomer for support, her old friend merely replied, "I have never been one for saying 'I told you so', Serena, but did I not warn you that this would happen? And much as I disapprove of Lucy's refusal to obey you, I do in fact agree with the girl. I'm afraid you must reconsider your position. Either you both go to England—and I have already expressed my doubts on that head—or Lucy must make do with St. Just!"

So Serena was already weakening when a letter arrived from England which took the decision out of her hands. Aunt Spurston offered to accommodate them in Surrey, and to help in preparing Lucy for presentation to society. However, for Aunt Spurston herself, a London season was out of the question, her doctor would not hear of it. Serena, as Lucy's guardian, must accompany her niece.

Serena was resigned, Lucy was overjoyed, and Lady Pendomer exerted herself on their behalf. She wrote to her friends in London, she spoke to her husband to engage his help in overseeing Will Norret's work on the plantations, and, best of all, she commissioned her maid to make some dresses for them. The necklace was sold and preparations were soon under way for a voyage to England.

LUCY'S DÉBUT was of enormous importance to herself and her aunt, but they would both have been very surprised to hear that four thousand miles away someone else was looking forward to their departure from Anse Chatelet and their arrival in London with an eagerness that almost equalled their own . . .

CHAPTER TWO

TO THE DISCERNING EYE the gentleman striding through Grosvenor Square in the direction of Upper Brook Street was unmistakably wealthy. His buckskin pantaloons and dark blue superfine coat were plain, but superbly cut, and his starched muslin cravat was secured with a very fine diamond pin. His cane was discreetly mounted in gold, and his boots were of the finest quality and polished to gleaming perfection. His dark hair was fashionably dishevelled under his beaver hat. This was no fop, however. There was a suggestion of power in the broad shoulders and lithe figure, and he had an air of one accustomed to command. Many would have called him handsome, but there was an indifference, a coldness even, in his ice-blue eyes, and a hardness about the well-shaped mouth which was not prepossessing.

The gentleman turned in to one of the houses at the nearer end of the street, where he was met by Wharton, his butler, and two footmen.

"Bring a bottle of Madeira to the library, Wharton. I am expecting Mr. Bradpole," was all the master of the house said as one of the footmen reverently received hat and cane.

"Yes, my lord. Your lordship may wish to read this before Mr. Bradpole arrives."

Lord Wintersett, for that was the gentleman's name, took the card which the butler offered him and looked at it impassively. "When did Mr. Fothergill call, Wharton?"

"Shortly after your lordship went out."

"If he calls again, tell him I'm not at home."

As Lord Wintersett closed the library door behind him and Wharton disappeared to the wine-cellar, the two footmen retreated to the rear hall. Here they lost their professional stiffness and became more human. "Cold fish, ain't 'e?" said the younger one. "Wonder if old Fothergill will call 'im out?"

"Not if he wants to live, he won't. And you mind your tongue, Percy. If Wharton hears you, you won't last long in his lordship's service, even though you are my own sister's boy."

"I'm not sure I'd mind. A proper frosty-face 'is lordship is, no mistake. I don't know what all those gentry females see in 'im."

"His wealth, that's what they see. And as for you—let me tell you, Percy, you don't know a good place when you see one, you don't. His lordship may be a touch cold in his manner, but he's fair. You could do a lot worse, a lot worse. Anyway, what makes you say that Fothergill would want to call his lordship out?"

"I thought you'd know. They're saying 'e seduced old Fothergill's daughter." Percy looked in astonishment as William burst into chuckles.

"Not another one!"

"What do you mean?"

"I'll bet you a tanner it's a try-on. The Fothergills aren't the first aristocratic coves who've had an eye on the Wintersett gelt and attempted a bit o' genteel blackmail. But they'll be like all the rest. They won't get far with him."

"You mean—"

"I mean it's time we cut the gabble-mongering and did our jobs. Off you go, young Percy, I can hear a carriage. That'll be Bradpole."

"Oo's that?"

"The lawyer, you nocky!" Once through the door to the entrance hall they resumed their air of stately indifference and went to stand by the door to the street.

AFTER MR. BRADPOLE had been received with dignity he joined Lord Wintersett in the library. First they spent some time clearing up odd bits of family business, and then the lawyer was offered a glass of Madeira and a seat in a more comfortable chair by the fire. These he accepted with pleasure, saying as he sat down, "I have something further of interest to your lordship."

"What is that?"

"News from our agent in the West Indies." Lord Wintersett frowned.

"And?"

"Lord Clavert is dead. He died at the end of May."

There was a pause during which Lord Wintersett got up and poured some more Madeira. Finally he said, "I'll drink to that. Damn him!"

"My lord!"

"Oh, we're all damned, Bradpole, but he, I fancy, more than most. Who inherits?"

"His daughter."

"Sasha Calvert. Or has she married?"

"Not yet."

"She's unlikely to do so in the future. Whatever her attractions were in the past, they must have faded by now—the tropics are notoriously hard on women, and she must be nearly forty. Over thirty, anyway. And her fortune is small enough. I'll drink to her damnation, too."

"My lord, I must protest. You do not even know the lady."

"But I know of her, Bradpole. Oh, I know of her."

"Lord Wintersett," said the lawyer gravely, "have you never considered that Mrs. Stannard, your sister-in-law, might have been influenced by her own very natural feelings in presenting the circumstances of your brother Anthony's unfortunate death. It all happened so long ago—some thirteen years, I believe. Would it not be better to... to forget the past? After all, Lord Calvert and his sons are now all dead."

"But Sasha Calvert is still alive, Bradpole—and has inherited everything, you say?"

"There's also a granddaughter, Rodney Calvert's child—but she has no share in the estate, merely a small sum of money. I understand that Miss Calvert is her guardian."

Lord Wintersett said swiftly, "I have no quarrel with the granddaughter." He sat down on the other side of the fireplace. "So... Sasha Calvert is now mistress of Anse Chatelet—but for how long? Now that the father is dead, surely the estate cannot survive?"

"I understand from our agent in Barbados that Miss Calvert has been running the estate herself for some years now. Indeed, he is full of admiration for her courage and spirit—in the past year or two Anse Chatelet has made some recovery—"

"A lady of many talents, it seems. But I don't believe she can keep it up forever. And the estate will survive only as long as the mortgages are paid, Bradpole—paid on the day they fall due

and not a second later. Do you understand me?'' Lord Wintersett's lip curled. ''There is to be no extension of time, no
soft-hearted response to appeals from a lady in distress.''

Mr. Bradpole looked at his client in silence. Finally he said,
''Am I to understand that you wish to deprive Miss Calvert of
Anse Chatelet if you can?''

''I not only wish to—I shall, Bradpole, I shall. One of these
days she will make a mistake—and then I shall have her.''

''Before that time comes you will have thought better, I
hope,'' said Mr. Bradpole soberly. ''I very much doubt that
your lordship could take pleasure in such a victory.''

''Pleasure! No, there isn't much pleasure in the whole damn
business. When the Calverts drove Tony to his death they ruined the lives of half of my family—you know that as well as I
do myself.''

''And in return your lordship has done his best to ruin the
Anse Chatelet estate ever since. Yes, I know the story.'' The
lawyer chose his words carefully when he next spoke. ''Lord
Wintersett, do you think what you are doing will improve the
state of your mother's mind? Or make Mrs. Stannard happier? Or give your nephew the use of his legs?''

Lord Wintersett's voice was glacial as he replied, ''Bradpole, your family has served the Wintersetts for many years.
You are one of the few people in this world in whom I have
confidence. But I will not tolerate further doubts on this matter. Do I make myself plain? I intend to deprive Sasha Calvert
of her home and her happiness.''

Mr. Bradpole started to put his papers together in silence.

''God's teeth, Bradpole, why do you feel the need to defend
the woman? She's a harlot, a Jezebel. My poor brother was so
ashamed of falling victim to her that he—'' Lord Wintersett
swore and turned to the window. His back to the room, he said,
''On the whole I do not admire my fellow creatures, and with
few exceptions remain indifferent to them. But Tony was...
unique. A gentle scholar who loved the world—when he noticed it, that is. I would have sworn that his honour and integrity were beyond question. That's why he shot himself, of
course,—having betrayed his marriage, and with such a
woman, he could no longer bear to live.''

Mr. Bradpole started to say something, then stopped as Lord
Wintersett swung round.

"I wish to be kept informed of every circumstance on St. Just, do you hear?"

"Of course, Lord Wintersett. I will see to it. Er...there is something else, in fact. I understand that Miss Calvert is thinking of bringing her niece to London—to present her during the next Season."

"Sasha Calvert in London, eh?" A most unpleasant smile on his lips, Lord Wintersett added, "Good! Not only will Anse Chatelet be left in less watchful hands, but Miss Calvert will be within my reach at last—and on my ground. Excellent! Let me know as soon as you hear of her arrival in London."

Mr. Bradpole's face was impassive as he left the room, but once outside the house his expression revealed his worry. He had long known Lord Wintersett's feelings on the subject of his brother's death, and, convinced as the lawyer was that the true facts had yet to be established, he had frequently attempted to argue his client into a more temperate frame of mind. In everything else, Lord Wintersett was scrupulously fair, capable of objective judgement—almost inhumanly so. But in this one matter he was unapproachable. Mr. Bradpole returned to his chambers filled with foreboding.

It was unfortunate that Mr. Bradpole's departure coincided with Mr. Fothergill's return, for that gentleman took advantage of this to force his way into Lord Wintersett's presence. William and Percy would have removed him, but with a resigned wave of the hand Lord Wintersett took him into the library and shut the door.

"I've come to demand satisfaction, Wintersett."

"Pistols or swords, my dear fellow?"

Mr. Fothergill stammered, "No, no you misunderstand, by gad. I mean that I...we—my wife and I—expect you to make an offer for our little Amabel—after the situation you placed her in last night, that is. She was very upset."

"You surprise me, Fothergill," murmured Lord Wintersett. "I quite thought that it was the lady who had placed herself in the 'situation', as you call it."

Mr. Fothergill shifted uncomfortably under Lord Wintersett's cynical gaze, but the memory of his wife's words as he had set out, and even more the consciousness of what she would say if he returned without result, spurred him on. "Amabel wouldn't compromise herself—for that is what being found in a private room with a man of your reputation must mean—without encouragement! My daughter knows what's expected of her!''

''Now there I am in complete agreement with you, Fothergill,'' said Lord Wintersett with a sardonic smile. ''She does indeed—a very able pupil. Who coached her? Your wife?''

''What do you mean by that?''

''I mean that I am far from being the flat you think me. If I were green enough to be taken in by the kind of trick employed by your wife and daughter last night, I would have been married long since. Do you think they are the first to have tried? Believe me, the ladies find me almost irresistible.''

''You take pride in that, do you?''

''None at all. I find it excessively tedious—what tempts them is my wealth, not my person. I assure you, Fothergill, whatever your wife may have said, your daughter's good name has not been damaged by me—I have learned to be far too wary a bird. At worst she might be accused of a slight indiscretion— which will be forgiven because of her youth and high spirits. But her chance of making a respectable match will be much reduced if society hears how you have pursued me this morning. Bad losers are never admired.''

''But the private room! My wife said ... and your reputation—''

'' —is not for seducing young and innocent girls. You may be assured of that. Your daughter followed me into Lady Glastonbury's winter garden—which can hardly be described as a 'private room'—without my knowledge, let alone my encouragement. I think she realises that now. Go back to your wife— tell her that I am neither worthy nor desirous of Miss Amabel's attentions. She is a pretty enough girl, and should look elsewhere.''

''But—''

''My man will see you out. No, really, I have had enough. And Fothergill—'' He waited till Fothergill turned. ''I am indifferent to what society thinks of me. But I should warn you that you will only make yourself even more ridiculous if you persist in these accusations.''

AFTER FOTHERGILL had left Lord Wintersett found himself unable to settle. He was conscious of nothing so much as an overwhelming sense of boredom. The scene that had just been enacted was not the first such. London was full of pretty, empty-headed little dolls, whose chief, if not only, ambition was to marry a wealthy man. The thought of marriage to such a one appalled him. Yet he ought to find a wife before long. He could not in all conscience let the title and all the responsibilities of the estates fall to young Tony—delicate since his birth and now confined to a wheelchair. He frowned as he thought of his nephew. Perhaps he should take more of an interest in him. The boy was intelligent, but hopelessly spoiled. Alanna was far too indulgent . . .

His gloomy thoughts were interrupted by another unexpected, but far more welcome, visitor. A warm smile transformed Lord Wintersett's face as Lord Ambourne came into the room.

"Ned! What are you doing in town? Is Lady Ambourne with you, or can you dine with me tonight? I need you, dear fellow, how I need you! I was rapidly falling into a melancholy."

"I can and shall dine with you. Perdita is down at Ambourne, supervising the packing. We are off to France in three days."

"Well, then, where shall we go? Or would you prefer to dine here? Albert has a way with a capon which I think you would find acceptable. And I have a very fine white burgundy . . ."

After it had been decided that Lord Ambourne should dine in Upper Brook Street, and orders to that effect had been sent to the kitchen, the two men settled down with a bottle of wine in the most comfortable chairs by the fire.

"What's wrong, James? Or can I guess? Fothergill?"

"You heard? No, that's nothing. I'm used to it."

"From what I hear, you were not very kind to the young lady."

"I should think not, indeed. If I were, she'd have cast herself on my bosom and matters would have been much worse. The chit will recover." His tone was indifferent.

Lord Ambourne's face was troubled. He hesitated, then took the bull by the horns. "Probably. However, there have been others who have not found it easy to recover from the public set-downs you have given them. I dare swear they have deserved them. But do you have to be quite so brutal, James? Perdita and I do not enjoy hearing what society says of you."

"I am indifferent to what society says of me. You should try not to care, too." James glanced at Edward's set face. "I mind what you and your family think of me, Ned. Am I such a monster?''

Edward sighed in exasperation. ''You've always been the same! The best friend a chap could have, but the coldest fellow in creation towards anyone else. Why don't you find a wife?''

James smiled derisively. ''You think that would cause me to love my fellow creatures more, Ned?''

''Perhaps not. But at least these poor girls would stay away from you. Though I'd feel sorry for your wife. Unless . . .''

''Unless what?''

''Unless you found someone like Perdita.''

James laughed, a warm, human sound. ''Impossible! Perdita must be unique. If you can find me her double I'll marry her on the spot. Now, you've done your duty, let's change the subject. Tell me what you've been doing.''

Later that night, after Lord Ambourne had returned, with a certain deliberation of movement, to Rotherfield House, James thought over what his friend had said. Ned was right, he ought to get married. He promised himself that after he had settled the affair with the Calverts once and for all he would seek out some amenable débutante, the least stupid he could find, and beget some heirs. Meanwhile he would wait patiently for Sasha Calvert to walk into his parlour . . .

CHAPTER THREE

SERENA KEPT HER expression of polite attention firmly in place as she wondered for the third time in as many minutes how much longer the visitors would stay. They were sitting in her great-aunt's drawing-room, a somewhat dismal apartment made gloomier by the heavy grey skies outside. She and Lucy had been staying with Lady Spurston ever since their arrival in England two weeks before, and it seemed to Serena that she had not seen the sun in all that time. In spite of the large fire the drawing-room was chilly, though Mrs. Galveston and her daughter seemed not to notice. For the moment Serena was free to follow her own thoughts, for Mrs. Galveston, an imposing dowager in plum silk and an amazing hat, had finished with her, and was now quizzing Lucy. Miss Eliza Galveston was timidly displaying her velvet reticule to Lady Spurston, her fingers twisting the strings nervously as she explained how she had painted it. Mrs. Galveston was one of her great-aunt's closest friends, and a member of one of the first families in the county. Aunt Spurston had said it was important to please her for a number of reasons, the chief one being that she had an elder daughter, Maria, married to a peer of the realm, whose own daughter was about to make her début...

Though Serena herself had been amused rather than intimidated by the dowager's trenchant remarks, she was anxious about Lucy. But her niece had so far done well, answering Mrs. Galveston's questions with charming deference and remembering not to put herself forward. This was not easy, for some of Mrs. Galveston's remarks would have been considered impertinent even among "colonials." The constant guard on tongue and behaviour which her great-aunt deemed essential for Lucy and Serena were not apparently necessary for this dreadful old woman. The corners of Serena's mouth lifted in a hint of a smile as she listened. Lucy was not giving anything away, for all her pretty ways.

"Serena?" Lady Spurston's voice was reproachful. "Miss Galveston was asking about the flora of Jamaica."

"I must tell you, Miss Calvert, that I positively dote on Nature. I have quite a collection of pressed flowers at home, have I not, Mama? Perhaps you would like to see them?"

Before Serena could reply Mrs. Galveston cut in tartly, "Do not encourage her, Miss Calvert. She spends far too much time as it is with her collections. But there, what else is there for the poor fool to do—unless it's daubing paint on velvet!" She turned to Lady Spurston and pronounced her verdict. "Miss Lucy has a pretty way with her, and once she acquires more polish might well take. But it won't do for Miss Calvert to be her niece's sole chaperon."

"Why not?" asked Serena in astonishment. "I'm Lucy's guardian."

Mrs. Galveston eyed her with scorn. "Whatever they might do in the colonies, Miss Calvert, it is still necessary here for a chaperon to be married! You are not married, I take it?"

"No, but I have surely reached the age of discretion."

"No spinster, of any age, not even Eliza here—and she is well into the age of discretion, one might say almost beyond it!—can be a young girl's sole chaperon—not in the kind of circles I imagine you wish to move in. It is unfortunate that your great-aunt's indisposition makes it impossible for her to be with you in London, but without a chaperon to assist you you may as well abandon the whole scheme."

Serena looked at her in some consternation. Was her beautiful plan for Lucy's future to fail after all? Mrs. Galveston looked speculatively at Lucy, and then back at Serena.

"Perhaps Miss Lucy should meet my granddaughter and her mother, Lady Warnham. Maria's as much a fool as Eliza—I am singularly unfortunate in my daughters—but at least she married well. Isabella is the same age as your niece, and is making her come out at the same time. We might be able to arrange something... I will see." She looked with disapproval at Serena's sober dress. "It would not be impossible to find you a husband, too, Miss Calvert... Some respectable widower, perhaps. But you are sadly brown—I'll send some Gowland's lotion round. You won't find it here in the depths of Surrey, but I have a supply from London. Applied nightly it might repair some of the damage done by the tropical sun." She cast another speaking glance at Serena's dress, but decided to say no more and got up to go. She took her leave of Serena and Lucy, then kissed Lady Spurston's cheek. At the door she stopped and said, "See that Miss Calvert takes some of Dr. Massinger's beef extract, Dorothy. She's far too thin. Come, Eliza!" She sailed out with supreme assurance.

After Mrs. Galveston had gone Lucy said passionately, "I would rather die than spend another second in that woman's company! Do not, I beg of you, Sasha, have any more to do with her!"

"That will do, miss!" said Lady Spurston sharply. "It is kind of Mrs. Galveston to take such an interest in you. She is extremely well connected, and you might consider yourself fortunate indeed if she decided to help with your début. You must curb that unruly tongue of yours, Lucy. Pert young ladies are not admired."

"My dear aunt," Serena said swiftly before Lucy could reply, "After this afternoon I am sure you must agree that we may have every confidence in Lucy's ability to behave well, whatever the provocation."

"Provocation? What provocation, pray?"

"Surely Mrs. Galveston's questions passed the bounds of discretion?"

"Serena, you do yourself no credit in taking exception to Mrs. Galveston's very natural interest. She must satisfy herself that you are both worthy, before assisting a young girl from the colonies with little dowry and only a maiden aunt to protect her."

"We are nevertheless Calverts of Anse Chatelet, Aunt Spurston," said Serena, always sensitive about her family's name. "I should have thought our credentials were sound enough for anyone, however well-connected they may be."

"Besides, Mrs. Galveston is so unkind!" Lucy cried. "Sasha doesn't need her Gowland lotion and . . . and . . . beef extract!"

"How many times must I tell you to call your Aunt Serena by her proper name, Lucy? Mrs. Galveston may be somewhat blunt in her pronouncements, but she knows the world as you do not!" She looked at Lucy's downcast expression and said more gently, "I am sure you are fond of your aunt and would not wish her to have wasted her efforts in bringing you to England. So you must exert yourself to conform—I cannot tell you how important it is. And now I would like to have a word in private with your aunt."

Lucy glanced at Serena, saw her nod, and reluctantly went out. Serena waited calmly for her aunt to speak. Finally Lady Spurston began, "Why are you here in England, Serena?"

"You know why. I want Lucy to meet the kind of man I would wish her to marry."

"Have you any matrimonial ambitions for yourself?"

"Oh, no. Mrs. Galveston may confine her good offices to Lucy. They would in any case be futile—I cannot imagine who would be interested in me. I have too small a dowry to attract a man in search of a rich match, I have neither youth nor looks to attract a romantic, and I'm afraid I lack the docility required by a man simply looking for a wife to run his household. No, my ambition is purely to see Lucy settled, after which I shall return to Anse Chatelet."

"And die an old maid. Not a very attractive prospect."

"I fear that is the only prospect left for me."

Lady Spurston considered this for a moment. Then she said briskly, "I am not yet convinced of that, Serena, but at the moment I wish to discuss your niece's future, not your own. Lucy is very pretty, and her liveliness will do her no harm in the eyes of the young men. She will take, no doubt of that. But the world in general will judge her as much by your demeanour as her own—you are her guardian, after all. If you wish her to move in the very best circles, you must pay more attention to your own dress and behaviour. That slave you brought with you from St. Just—Bathsheba—"

"Sheba is a freedwoman, Aunt Spurston. She could have stayed behind on St. Just, but came with us because she can't believe we could manage without her," Serena said, smiling.

"Well, whatever she is, she seems to manage to dress Lucy well enough. Why does she not do the same for you?"

"I suppose I don't ask her to!"

"Exactly so! At the moment you are careless, dowdy even, and there is altogether a want of ladylike formality about you. These colonial manners will not pass in London. Try for a little elegance. Learn what is acceptable behaviour for a lady. Lucy looks to you for her example, and never forget that you are on trial as much as she."

Serena coloured, but forced herself to remain silent. Her aunt was probably right. If only she knew how hard it was, how

Serena longed for the sunshine and freedom of her life on St. Just! The weeks she had so far spent here in this damp, cold climate, hemmed in on every side by strictures on "acceptable behaviour for a lady", had seemed like a year—a century. The trouble was that for too long she had been her own mistress. For years she had ranged the plantation in complete freedom, exercising the authority her father had given her. If truth were told she knew that the English inhabitants of St. Just were not so very different from their London cousins. Her independent ways had more than once shocked them, though the Calvert name kept them silent. But at least there she answered to no one. Here she felt stifled—"cabin'd, cribb'd, confin'd".

"You are silent, Serena. I hope you are not indulging in a fit of the sulks."

"No, no, Aunt Spurston. Forgive me, I was . . . I was thinking. You are quite right of course. I will try to mend my ways."

SERENA DID HER honest best in the weeks that followed to meet her aunt's exacting standards. Whereas before she had always hurried Sheba along when dressing, now she was patient with her maid's attempts to dress her properly. Together with Lucy, Serena stood docilely while they were fitted for morning dresses, walking dresses, carriage dresses, ball dresses; they learned to walk elegantly, sit elegantly, eat elegantly, converse elegantly; they practised the quadrille and the waltz, though Serena had no intention of dancing in London. They learned the subtle differences of curtsying, bowing the head and offering a hand, how to encourage welcome approaches and how to depress pretension. Lady Warnham proved to be as amiable as Lady Spurston had said, and Lucy struck up a most unexpected friendship with her daughter Isabella. In fact, Lucy seemed to be enjoying every minute, but to Serena the endless trivialities to be learned by a lady who aspired to Society's approval were stifling. She wanted to be alone, to feel free, to rid herself of her resentment in a burst of energy. At home on St. Just she would have taken off on her horse for the day, but here that was impossible. A tame stroll round the dank gardens, a gentle trot with a groom round the park, were the only available forms of exercise. The very notion of a lady walking or riding out unaccompanied was unheard of.

But just when she was at her most desperate, salvation appeared—a course of action that was highly risky, unquestionably not "acceptable behaviour for a lady," but all the same a perfect answer. It came in the unlikely form of Mrs. Galveston, who one day brought with her a bundle of clothes which her grandchildren had outgrown.

"They're for your wretched charity, Dorothy. The Society for the Relief of Indigent Gentlefolk, or whatever you call it. Improvident, more like. However, Isabella hardly has room as it is for her clothes, and now Maria has ordered more for the chit. It's all quite unnecessary, as far as I can see. One or two pretty evening gowns and a presentation dress are all Isabella requires, but there, Maria was never noted for her common sense. Some of Michael's things are in the bundle as well. They're quite old, but too good to give to the villagers—they would not appreciate them. No, do not thank me. I am glad to find a use for them." She turned to Serena. "By the way, Miss Calvert, it is rumoured that the Cardoman necklace has been sold. Surely that was part of the Calvert heritage?"

Serena was ready with her answer. "My father always disliked the necklace, Mrs. Galveston. It is notoriously unlucky. But I wonder where it has been since he decided to get rid of it? I thought it had been sold in the West Indies, I must confess. Can you tell me more?"

Much to Serena's relief, Mrs. Galveston was unable to enlighten her, for apparently the purchaser had remained as mysterious in England as he had in the West Indies. As for the clothes, they were taken to a closet in one of the unused bedchambers where such items were housed until they were bundled up and sent away. But Serena sought them out, for an audacious idea had formed in her mind as soon as she had seen the boy's garments. She tried them on behind locked doors—breeches, frilled shirts with one or two cravats, a waistcoat, and a warm jacket. A large forage cap in a military style successfully hid her hair, and there were even some boots which almost fitted. She secreted her treasure trove in the West Lodge—a cottage which had fallen into disuse since the drive to the western side of the park had been permanently closed after Sir George Spurston's death.

When her aunt and Lucy next went visiting Serena pleaded a headache. She waited till Sheba had stopped fussing and had gone to the kitchens, then slipped out to the stables. They were deserted, except for the stable lad and Trask, the elderly hunter. Saddling him presented no problems, and she was soon in the cottage, feverishly changing. She had left her petticoats in her bedroom, and it was simple to replace her dress and light slippers with shirt, cravat, breeches, jacket and boots. One other thing she had brought from her bedchamber—something which she had kept hidden away in a special pocket in her valise, for her aunt, if she had known of its existence, would have most strongly disapproved. This was a small pistol. On St. Just she had carried it whenever she went any distance away from the house, for the danger of poisonous snakes or renegade slaves was very real. Now she slipped it into a pocket in her jacket which could have been made for it. She had no idea what dangers she might meet in England—but it was better to be sure.

Once Serena's hair was bundled into the cap she made a very fine boy, helped, no doubt, by the lack of curves and the brown complexion so displeasing to Mrs. Galveston. She would be safe from detection in any casual encounter, she was sure. And she did not intend to meet anyone at all!

Half an hour later she was enjoying the wide views and invigorating air of the North Downs. The ground was too hard and Trask too elderly for her to let fly as she would have wished, but the sense of freedom was intoxicating. After a good run she paused on the highest point for miles round. Far away to the north she could see the smoky haze of the city, but up here...up here the air was clean and the hills empty of any visible dwelling. For the first time since leaving St. Just she felt happy. It was a far cry from the tropics, but it was beautiful. Away to the south the slanting winter sun exaggerated the folds and furrows of the land, and the fields below formed a patchwork of black and brown, russet and green. Something tugged at her mind, a line of poetry she had recently read and not fully appreciated till now. It was about hedgerows... "'Once again I see these hedgerows—'" she murmured slowly. "'Scarcely hedgerows—'" She frowned and tried again. "No, that's not right. 'Hardly hedgerows...hardly hedgerows...' but what comes next?"

"'Hardly hedgerows—little lines of sportive wood run wild,'" said a voice behind her. "And who the devil are you?"

Serena nearly jumped out of her skin, and Trask took exception to the sudden tug on the rein and took off. After the initial surprise Serena knew she would have no difficulty in bringing her horse under control—she had dealt with horses of greater mettle than this. But she allowed him his head for a while—she had no desire for closer contact with the stranger, and she just might escape. It was annoying therefore to hear drumming hoofbeats behind her and to see a lean hand stretch out to take hold of the reins and bring Trask firmly to a halt.

"Let go! I don't need your help!" she said furiously.

"I think you do, you ungrateful whelp!" said the stranger looking at her in lazy amusement. "And unless you express yourself more gracefully I'll take it upon myself to teach you some manners." His voice was still amused but there was steel in it, and in the hand that held the reins. "We'll start again. Who are you?"

She remained silent.

"Are you playing truant? Is that it?"

A fugitive smile touched the corners of her mouth and she nodded.

"You may safely tell me who you are. I'm no tale-bearer."

She looked at him, unable to hide a lurking amusement in her clear amber-gold eyes. If he only knew!

The gentleman saw the amusement. His face was suddenly cold, the eyes diamond-hard. He tightened his grasp on the reins. "I warn you—I intend to find out who you are, one way or another. What are you doing on my land?"

Serena tried to pacify him. "How did you know what I was trying to say—about the hedgerows? You must be pretty clever. I've been trying to think who wrote it . . . ?"

"Wordsworth—William Wordsworth. And I'm still waiting for an answer to my questions."

He was not to be put off, it seemed. Serena realised that if she were not to be discovered on her very first outing she must satisfy him, somehow. She cleared her throat, and adopted the sulky tone of a schoolboy. "I'm sorry. I didn't know it was private land. I didn't do any harm, just enjoying a ride. It was boring at . . . at home."

"Gave your tutor the slip, eh? Where do you live?"

Serena waved her arm vaguely. "Over there."

"And what is your name? You shan't go till you've told me, you know."

"It's . . . it's William."

"Shakespeare or Wordsworth?" There was scepticism in the gentleman's voice. He wasn't so easily deceived.

Serena let herself look puzzled. "Neither. It's . . . It's Blake. May I go now?"

The stranger laughed in genuine amusement—and Serena gazed in astonishment at the change in him when he did so. He was suddenly altogether more approachable, more human. "You mean the 'Tiger, tiger, burning bright' Blake? The golden tiger eyes match it, but I'm not so sure about the rest."

"What do you mean, sir?"

"I mean that there's a whiff of poetic fishiness about you! Blake indeed!"

Serena said with dignity, "My family is connected to the other Blake, sir—" which was no more than the truth "—Robert the Admiral, not William, the poet." She hesitated, then pleaded. "They'll soon be looking for me. Keeping me here is almost as bad as telling."

"Very well, William Blake. We can't have the truant caught. But you will promise me not to do it again, if you please." He held her eye until she reluctantly nodded. "And in future keep your wits about you when you're riding. You could have taken a nasty toss. Off you go!" Serena was about to protest again that she had not needed his help, but he said softly, "'Waste no time in words, but get thee gone'—and that's by the other William."

She smiled impishly, replied, "I believe the correct reply is— 'Sir, I go with all convenient speed'—that's by Shakespeare, too!" and rode off followed by the sound of his laughter.

FOR A SHORT while Serena stayed circumspectly within the grounds of her great-aunt's house. Much as she had enjoyed her encounter with the strange gentleman it had brought home to her the enormous risk she had been running. She could not imagine what Lady Spurston would say if her great-niece were discovered to have been masquerading as a boy, but Mrs. Galveston would surely wash her hands of them all. Lucy's future might be at stake.

So Serena contented herself with pleasing her aunt. This was not always easy, for Lady Spurston had grown so set in her own ways since the death of her husband that the addition of two young ladies to the household often made her irritable. She enjoyed talking of her youth, however, and Serena would spend hours with her great-aunt looking at old pictures and souvenirs of the past. Lady Spurston was appreciative of her audience and one day said, "You are a good girl, Serena. And very good to Lucy. I dare swear the greater part of your dress allowance for London was devoted to her. Well, I have a surprise for you. In that bureau over there you will find a small box. Be so good as to bring it over to me, if you please." Serena did as she was asked. The box though small was heavy. "Put it on the table here. Thank you." Lady Spurston opened the box and took out a small picture. "This is a portrait of your mother when she was Lucy's age. It is for you."

Serena examined the heart-shaped face with its large blue eyes, delicate colouring and blonde hair wreathed in roses. "I'm afraid I am not much like her. She must have been much admired."

"She could have been a duchess. But, though your father was so much older than she was, she fell in love with him and his stories of the tropical islands, and nothing would move her."

"Othello to her Desdemona," murmured Serena.

"I beg your pardon?"

"It's a Shakespeare play, aunt. Desdemona fell in love with Othello for the same reason."

Her aunt looked at her disapprovingly. "You run the risk of being thought bookish, Serena, if you continue to quote Shakespeare on every occasion."

"The Bible, my mother's edition of Shakespeare, and a few books of poetry were all we had to read on St. Just, Aunt Spurston. I think I know most of them by heart! Did my mother ever come back to visit you?"

"No, we never saw her again after your father took her to St. Just." Lady Spurston paused, then said, "We didn't want your mother to marry Lionel Calvert, you know—a widower with two boys not much younger than she was herself. The older one—Richard, wasn't it?—was a charming rogue. I don't remember the other one—he would be Lucy's father. What was his name . . . ?"

"Rodney."

"That's it. Rodney. He was a very quiet boy." There was a short silence. "She had always been so biddable, such a loving, obedient child. . ." said Lady Spurston, gazing into the fire. "But she would not be dissuaded, and in the end your grandfather was forced to agree. And then she died when you were born. . ." Her voice faded away again. Then she suddenly raised her head and said sharply, "There was some sort of scandal later, wasn't there? Not enough to damage Lucy's chances, I hope?"

"No, no. The scandal was all over long ago, Aunt Spurston. Thirteen years, in fact. And my father saw to it that the affair was all hushed up at the time. In any case, Rodney was not involved—he was already an invalid."

"Good!" said Lady Spurston and then added, "The other things in the box are also for you."

Serena carefully put down her picture and looked inside the box. In it were some jewels and a fair number of gold coins.

"I haven't much to leave you, Serena. When we saw that there were to be no children of our own, Sir George arranged an annuity which will die with me. These baubles would have been your mother's had she lived. They are of more use to you now, I think, than after I am dead. And you may spend the money on clothes for yourself—yourself, mind, not Lucy."

Serena got up and embraced her great-aunt warmly. "I . . . I don't know what to say, Aunt Spurston. Thank you."

Her aunt's expression softened, but she said sharply, "Control yourself, Serena. A lady does not display excessive sensibility in public. Oh, if only my stupid disability did not prevent me from accompanying you in London . . . but there. Maria Galveston—or Lady Warnham, as I suppose I should call her, she's been married these twenty odd years—was a good girl, and I have no reason to suppose she is very different now. Her mother will see that she helps you. We still have a little time before the season begins, and I will spare no effort to see that you are prepared."

Serena managed to amuse herself well enough with these conversations with her aunt and other rather tame pastimes, but finally the lure of another ride proved irresistible. It was for consolation, more than anything else. To Serena's mingled pleasure and regret Lucy, who had always been so close, was at the moment increasingly deserting her aunt in favour of her new companions. It was not surprising. For years Lucy had been denied the company of young people of her own age and class, and here in England she was not only learning the manners of the young ladies of English society—she was learning from Isabella and Isabella's brothers and sisters their amusements and interests, too. The preparations for their forthcoming début, which Serena found so tediously dull, were viewed by Lucy and

Isabella with happy anticipation. Even Sheba seemed to have
settled into an English household better than Serena herself,
and spent much time in the kitchens, gossiping, regaling the
other domestics with gruesome stories of voodoo and the like,
and incidentally keeping warm. In short, Serena was lonely, and
when she found that Lucy had apparently forgotten that it was
her aunt's birthday, she grew very low in spirits.

Serena had always despised people who felt sorry for themselves, and she decided to take action. So once again she took
out her boys' clothes and made her way to the top of the
Downs. Here she dismounted, tied Trask to a tree, and walked
to the edge of the ridge. The weather seemed to reflect her
mood, for the sky was heavy with rain clouds and the fields
looked dull and grey. A most unaccustomed feeling of melancholy overcame her in which the battle for Anse Chatelet hardly
seemed worth the effort and her own future looked as dread as
the fields below. With a heavy sigh she turned to go back. The
tall gentleman was standing by Trask.

"Well, if it isn't my young friend William!" he said ge-
nially. "Which one are you today?"

"Sir," said Serena, trying wildly to remember what she had
said her name was.

"Wordsworth, I think you said."

"No, sir," Serena replied in relief. "Blake. My name is William Blake."

"Ah, yes, forgive me. My memory occasionally fails me—"
a slight pause "—too."

Serena could not resist it. She said gravely, "I expect it's your
age, sir. My grandfather was very absent-minded."

He glanced at her sharply, but she managed to return a look
of limpid innocence.

"Hmm. I am not yet in my dotage, however. And I clearly
remember letting you go in return for your promise that you
would not do this again."

Serena started to enjoy herself in spite of the risk she was
running. She looked injured. "I am not sure what you mean by
that, sir. A Blake does not break promises, I assure you."

"Oh? So you are not playing truant again? Tutor broken his
leg, has he?"

"His arm, sir. A most unfortunate fall." Serena looked
sideways at the gentleman, and what she saw caused her to say
hastily, "I was only joking. I've been given a holiday—today

is my birthday." She lowered her head as the memory of Lucy's defection returned.

"That has the ring of truth. But why aren't you celebrating it at home? Where are you parents?"

"They're dead."

"I see." There was a pause. "May I join you on your ride?" Serena looked at him suspiciously, but he was serious. She eyed his bay mare, cropping the grass a short distance away.

"Could you ride her?" The gentleman's voice broke in on her wistful thoughts. She turned to him, her eyes glowing.

"Oh, yes!"

"Sure?"

"Oh, please let me try! I'll go carefully, I promise."

He laughed at the eager face before him, and then he frowned.

"What is it? Aren't you going to let me, after all? I'm sure I can manage her."

"I believe you can—and anyway, Douce is like her name, although she's so fast. I was just puzzled for a moment... Where have I seen those eyes? No matter. Come, I'll help you up."

But Serena had already mounted the mare, who was pawing and nodding playfully. "She's beautiful! Do hurry!"

The stirrups were adjusted and, while he was occupied in fetching Trask and mounting, she furtively checked her cap to make sure it was secure. They set off along the ridge. At first Serena was careful to hold Douce to a steady walk, getting the feel of the animal's responses. But then they came to a piece of open land and she gave way to temptation. She let the mare have her head.

Serena had never experienced anything like it. The mare fairly flew over the soft, springy English turf, and the air rushed past, intoxicating in its cool, damp freshness. For five minutes she was in heaven. When she finally slowed down, Trask and the gentleman were nowhere in sight. It was as well. Her cap was thoroughly askew and her cravat was flapping wildly. Both had to be restored to order before she returned, somewhat apprehensively, to look for her companion. When she came into view he pulled Trask up, and sat waiting for her in silence. He was, quite understandably, very angry.

"You deserve a whipping, my boy," he said unpleasantly. "Get off that horse."

"I'm . . . I'm sorry," Serena faltered. She thought of flight, but dismissed the idea. Riding off with the gentleman's horse would only make bad worse.

He saw how her hand tightened on the reins, though, and said menacingly, "Don't even think about it."

"I wasn't, not really." Then, pleadingly, "I'm truly sorry, sir."

He dismounted and came towards her. She quickly jumped down and clutched his arm. "Please don't be angry! You've just given me the best birthday present I've ever had. Don't spoil it!"

The gentleman looked down at the hand on his arm with a frown, and then, surprisingly, stepped back. He turned to mount Douce, but stopped with one foot in the stirrup. "Perhaps it is I who deserve the whipping," he said harshly. "You might have broken your neck. When you disappeared I was afraid for a moment that you had."

"Oh, no! It was . . . it was magnificent! I cannot thank you enough! I felt as if . . . as if . . . as if I was 'an angel dropp'd down from the clouds, to turn and wind a fiery Pegasus—' "

Once more he completed her quotation, " 'And witch the world with noble horsemanship.' So you're acquainted with the history plays as well. And I think you're right. You certainly know how to ride. Well, I'll overlook the fright you gave me—this time. Come, we must get back. It looks as if it will rain before long."

The clouds were gathering fast as they rode back down into the valley, and by the time they reached the high road it was raining heavily. The gentleman was apparently absorbed in his own thoughts, and Serena was cold and wet, her elation of a short time before quite vanished. Suddenly he said, "We'll stop here till the rain eases. Old Margery will give us shelter—and perhaps even something to eat—though it won't be quite a birthday feast. In here!"

They turned into a narrow lane, at the end of which was a tumbledown cottage. Serena was seized with apprehension.

"No, I . . . I must get back—"

"Don't be ridiculous boy! You cannot go on in this downpour! What would your guardians say? The cottage may look decrepit from the outside, but Margery always keeps a good fire going. We'll be dry in no time."

Nervously Serena dismounted and followed him inside. The cottage was empty, though a fire was laid ready.

"She must be working at the farmer's down the road. She won't mind if I light this, however. We can reset it before we leave. Now I'll get this going, and you can fetch more kindling and wood from the shed. Then we'll take our wet coats off and dry them. It won't take long..."

He was busy with the fire. Serena slipped out, tiptoed to Trask, and led him quietly to the end of the lane. Then she leapt up and rode for her life along the high road.

CHAPTER FOUR

THE FIRE WAS burning brightly. In a few minutes the cottage would be warm and they could get dry. Not before time—the rain had penetrated his thick riding coat and the boy must be chilled to the bone. He heard a step outside. "You've been a time! Could you not find any?"

"Whatever are you doin', my lord? Oh, I beg y'r lordship's pardon. But if I'd a knowed y'r lordship was comin' I'd 'a made sure things was ready! 'Ere, let me do that!"

James Stannard, sixth Baron Wintersett, straightened up and surveyed the newcomer. "Good day to you, Margery. We took the liberty of sheltering in your cottage while the rain was so bad. What were you doing out in it? When you weren't here I thought you must be at Rufford Farm for the day."

"I 'ad ter go down the road a piece after the goat. She'd gotten loose, the bothersome thing. Y'r lordship's welcome to whatever 'e can find. There isn't much, though. I'll fetch some more wood in for the fire, shall I?"

"Where's the boy? He should have brought some in by now."

"There's no boy 'ere, my lord—just the two of us."

"What? Of course there's a boy!" He strode outside. The rain had stopped as quickly as it had started. Douce was placidly sheltering under the lean-to shed. Of Trask and the boy there was no sign.

"I see'd a boy ridin' off down the high road as I came up the lane," offered Margery, who had followed him out. "In a terrible 'urry, he were. Ridin' as if the devil 'imself were arter 'im."

"In which direction?" Lord Wintersett's first instinct was to leap on Douce and ride in pursuit, but then he changed his mind. Let the ungracious whelp go! "No, it's of no consequence. I expect he had to get back." He looked at the cottage. "I'll send someone round to repair this roof, Margery. It's leaking yet again. You should move into the village. This hovel isn't fit to live in."

"I'll end my days 'ere, thanking y'r lordship," said Margery, her face settling into obstinate lines.

"Very well. But if you should change your mind, let Rossett know. He'll find you somewhere to live." And, slipping some coins into Margery's hand, Lord Wintersett mounted Douce and set off for home. As he rode his mind was puzzling over the boy's behaviour. An odd mixture, William Blake—if that was his name, which he doubted. It was strange to have this conviction of the boy's integrity, when so much of what he said was open to question. Whoever was teaching him had managed to instil a love of poetry, that was clear. But they were undoubtedly careless in their supervision. He was too often left to his own devices. The lad was probably lonely—he had certainly been unhappy when they had first met today. The slender figure standing at the edge of the ridge had had a melancholy droop to the shoulders. It had been that more than anything which had resulted in his own impulsive offer of a ride on Douce. James Stannard smiled grimly. He must have been mad! How his London acquaintance would stare if they had seen it! Frosty Jack Wintersett, for he knew what they called him, giving way to a kindly—and ill-considered—impulse! And then to be rewarded with such cavalier treatment . . .

In spite of his efforts to dismiss the boy from his mind, the thought of "William Blake" continued to plague Lord Wintersett, and one particular aspect more than the rest.

THAT EVENING they were three at dinner, for his mother had appeared just before the meal had been announced. At first James had been delighted, but Lady Wintersett had acknowledged neither her son nor her daughter-in-law, and was now lost once more in a shadowy world of her own. Alanna Stannard sat between them, dressed in a very pretty lavender gown which enhanced her Irish colouring—black hair, speedwell-blue eyes and a wild rose complexion. It was difficult to believe that she had been a widow for so long, the mother of a child who had never known his father. James wondered briefly why she had never remarried. She looked very little older than the girl of nineteen who had most unexpectedly captivated his brother

Tony—Tony, who had never looked twice at any woman before, Tony, who had always been immersed in his books and his plants, gentle, unworldly Tony, who had been a near genius. What had there been in Alanna to attract such a self-sufficient man? And what had Alanna found in Tony? It had been a most unlikely match, for behind her pretty face Alanna was an empty-headed butterfly—or so James had always thought. He had wondered at the time of Tony's marriage whether Alanna had made a mistake—had she been seeking a rich young man who would give her the social life she wanted? But he had misjudged her—she had remained in retirement here at Wintersett since her return from the West Indies, a widow with a tiny, delicate baby, born prematurely after Tony's death. James's face saddened as it always did when he thought of his brother. He glanced at his mother, still sitting silently. She had been a lovely woman, too. Now she was like a ghost.

Alanna had kept up a flow of inconsequential chatter throughout the meal, but she now interrupted it to ask what was wrong. "For I have asked you twice whether you can obtain some French lace caps for your mama and me, and you have made no reply."

Lord Wintersett glanced at the figure at the other end of the table. "Would you like a new lace cap, Mama?"

A sweet, infinitely sad smile was the only response. Lady Wintersett slowly rose and left the room. With a little sigh Mrs. Stannard got up to follow. "I think you should come down more frequently, James," she said. "You seem to be the only one of us who can get any response from Mama."

"A smile? Before she slips away?"

"It's more than anyone else gets, I assure you. She spends hours at little Anthony's bedside, but her face never changes. She is like a doll sitting there. I would be so obliged if you could procure the lace caps."

"Isn't my nephew any better? Why is he in bed this time?"

"The winter is always bad for Anthony. He is very listless, and his limbs ache, he says."

A sudden picture of a face glowing with eagerness as the boy on the ridge, who called himself William, pleaded for a ride, an image of Douce and the boy flying off into the blue, poetry in motion, filled his mind. He dismissed it, and said, "Well, of course Tony's limbs will ache, damn it! He never has any exercise! You'd do better to get him out and about instead of mollycoddling him. In a chair, if necessary."

Alanna's blue eyes looked at him reproachfully. "Your mama would not like to hear you swear, James. I am sure she would prefer you to keep your oaths for your club. And, forgive me, but how can you possibly judge what is best for my darling? You hardly ever see him! Dr. Charlesworth—"

"It is my considered opinion that Dr. Charlesworth is a quack! All he does is echo your own wishes! What's wrong with Galbraith?"

"Oh, no! Dr. Galbraith is impossible! I have tried him and he is quite unsuitable. He would kill little Anthony in no time at all with his fresh air regimes—"

"Little Anthony! He is nearly thirteen, Alanna! You are far too protective of him—"

"And why shouldn't I be? Is he not all I have left?"

Alanna's eyes were large with tears. James got up and went to the fireplace. He had lost interest in this argument. It was one which frequently occurred between them, and always ended in Alanna's tears. Since tears irritated him, and since he was in any case not prepared to stay at Wintersett Court to see any reforms carried through, discussion was fairly pointless. Mopping her eyes, Alanna made to leave the room.

"Wait! If you please, Alanna, we must talk. Come and sit down." His sister-in-law came back to the table, her head drooping, and waited while James carefully closed the dining-room doors. Then he poured two glasses of brandy and, ignoring her shake of the head, put one of them in front of her. "You might need it. I have something to tell you which might upset you." He paused, then said abruptly, "Sasha Calvert is coming to England." Alanna's head jerked up, her hand at her throat. Her face was suddenly colourless.

"What did you say?" she whispered.

"Have a sip of brandy, it'll do you good. Sasha Calvert is bringing her niece to England. It seems that the girl is now of an age to be presented to Society." His lip curled. "The society of St. Just isn't good enough for Miss Calvert's ambition."

"She mustn't come to England, she mustn't!" Alanna's voice rose hysterically. "James, you must stop her!"

"Oh, no, my dear. Even if I could, I would not dream of doing anything of the sort. It suits my plans quite well to have her four thousand miles from Anse Chatelet."

"Be quiet, James! Be quiet! You don't understand!"

"Pull yourself together, Alanna!" he said coldly. "It shouldn't matter to you whether Sasha Calvert is in England or in the Antipodes. You have no need to meet her. Indeed, it's better that you shouldn't. You never come to London, so any encounter is very unlikely. You could even spend the summer in Ireland if you wish."

Alanna looked at him with haunted, terror-stricken eyes. He forced himself to speak more kindly. "I do understand your feelings, believe me. I hate the Calvert name as much as you— and with nearly as much reason. Thirteen years have not diminished the memory of their infamy. But this time I will deal with its last member once and for all. Have confidence in me, Alanna."

In spite of his reassurances she remained unconvinced, pleading with him again and again to prevent Sasha Calvert's journey to England, refusing to believe he could not prevent it even if he wished. She became quite distraught, and in the end he sent one of the servants for her maid, saying that Mrs. Stannard was unwell and should retire to her room.

THE THOUGHT of the boy continued to haunt him that night and throughout the next week. Several times he took Douce up on the Downs, and found himself scanning the area for the slight, quaintly dressed figure on horseback. "William Blake" nagged at his mind like the toothache. There was something elusively familiar about him, and yet James was convinced they had never met before. And then—he had to face it, to bring it into the open—when the boy had put his hand on James's arm, James had felt a totally unfamiliar sensation, one which was strangely agreeable. He had been profoundly shocked at the time, and had wondered if he was going mad. The obvious explanation had been so ridiculous that he refused to entertain it for one moment. Nothing in his past had ever suggested anything of that nature. There must be another reason. He went over their meetings again and again, recalling every detail. Slowly an incredible suspicion began to take root. He grew impatient to see the boy once more, so that he could test his theory. But though James stayed at Wintersett Court for much longer than he had originally intended, the landscape remained empty of both boy and horse.

SERENA HAD MADE UP her mind that her excursions were too dangerous to be repeated. She could hardly bear to think of what might have happened in the cottage. What excuse could she have found for keeping her soaking jacket on? What would have been the gentleman's reaction on finding out how she had deceived him?

Even after she reached the comparative safety of the Lodge her difficulties were not over. It took some time to remove her wet things and drape them over whatever she could find in the Lodge. When she arrived in the house, dressed but without her petticoats and with wet hair, Sheba was waiting for her.

"Where you been, Miss Serena? Your hair's all wet, and you got no petticoats! Shame on you!"

Serena hurried to her room with Sheba in close attendance. If her great-aunt saw her now she really would be in trouble. She was only halfway through changing when Lucy came in.

"Goodness, Sasha, where have you been? Out in the rain, I imagine—your hair's wet. I've been looking everywhere for you. What have you been doing, aunt of mine?"

Serena tried not to say anything, but Lucy would not be put off. Finally the fear that Lucy would continue questioning her in front of Aunt Spurston caused Serena to confess that she had been out riding on the Downs. The gentleman was not mentioned. Lucy was highly amused.

"And to think I thought you had become totally stuffy, Sasha! Oh, my dearest aunt, I do so love you!" She hugged Serena tightly, saying, "And I will never breathe a word, I swear! Now, I have something for you."

She ran out of the room and soon returned with a very pretty reticule, wrapped in silver paper. "It's for your birthday!"

Serena was unable to speak. The reticule was exquisitely painted with poinsettias, delicate orchids and ferns. The work must have taken Lucy hours to do.

"Serena?" Lucy's voice was uncertain.

"I . . ." Serena cleared her throat. "It's beautiful. Thank you." She looked at Lucy's anxious face. "Lucy, it's the most beautiful thing I've ever seen! Thank you, oh, thank you, my love."

"That's all right, then. I thought for a moment you didn't like it. Now tell me about your rides."

"Not at the moment," said Serena firmly. "Great-aunt Spurston will be waiting downstairs. I don't want her to start asking questions—they might be difficult to answer!'' So Serena brought the boys' clothes back into the house and put them with the other things for her great-aunt's charity. She returned her pistol to its special place in her valise and applied herself resolutely to her duties, determined to forget her new acquaintance. In the days that followed this proved to be more difficult than she had imagined. She was surprised how sharply she regretted the thought that she would never see him again.

One reward for Serena's concentration on improving her behaviour was Lady Spurston's approval.

"You are growing more presentable by the hour, Serena! I'll swear the lotion Mrs. Galveston sent is doing your skin a vast amount of good. You will never be a beauty, but your complexion is much less sallow—and I do believe you are filling out a little. Certainly your new dresses are most becoming! And that woman of yours is learning fast.''

Serena privately thought that it was lack of sun which was causing her tan to fade, but in accordance with her new mode of life she smiled, and when she next saw Mrs. Galveston she thanked her gracefully.

Alas for Serena's good intentions! Her great-aunt forgot to have the charity clothes ready when the agent next called, and they were left for another month. The weather improved, and the fresh scents of an English spring proved too enticing. Once again the clothes were rescued from their storage place, the pistol was tucked into the jacket, and, after a lively argument with Sheba, Serena stole away to the stables. With the assistance of a friendly stable lad, Trask was saddled and removed unseen to the Lodge. Excited, her heart beating nervously, Serena set off through the country lanes towards the Downs.

TRASK HIMSELF also seemed to be feeling a springtime renewal of energy. Together Serena and he had a good run, until they both ended up on the ridge, panting. The advancing season had turned the patchwork of fields into a medley of greens. The air was brilliantly clear—Serena could see for miles. Entranced, she slipped down from Trask and stretched voluptuously, breathing in the scents of the countryside. The tropics had their own beauty, but this air was like champagne. She felt quite warm, but did not open the jacket or remove her cap. It was most unlikely that the tall gentleman would appear again after all this time, but she dared not risk it . . .

It was as well. Douce and her rider were emerging from the trees, almost as if they had been waiting for her. A warm glow of satisfaction spread through her veins, astonishing her with its intensity. She suddenly felt exhilarated. It was worth any risk to feel like this. "Hail, Caesar!" she cried gaily.

His face was inscrutable as he dismounted and stood beside the horse for a moment.

"Hail to thee, blithe spirit! Bird thou never wert—"

Her eyes grew intent. "I've not heard that. Where is it from? I don't think it's Shakespeare, is it?"

"Not Shakespeare. Nor Wordsworth. Nor Blake, my boy."

He spoke with a curious inflection. What was wrong? He even looked menacing. For a moment she felt frightened and thought of flight, but he suddenly smiled and she was reassured. She must be imagining things! "Then who, sir?" she asked.

"It's by Shelley—Percy Bysshe Shelley. Have you heard of him?"

"No." He was now quite close. He was menacing—he seemed to loom over her, and she suddenly felt breathless.

"How . . . how does it go on?"

"Hail to thee, blithe Spirit! Bird thou never wert—"

His face and voice were hard as he added, "Or should it be 'boy thou never wert'?" He put out a long arm, pulled off her cap, and breathed a long sigh of satisfaction as her dark hair tumbled out over her shoulders. "I thought so," he said. He regarded her in silence while her face flamed and she stared back at him, mesmerised. Finally he smiled and, drawing her to him, he kissed her hard. "I thought so," he said again with satisfaction. "You've been haunting me, my little changeling," he murmured, covering her face in little kisses. "I've had some sleepless nights over you. Now you must pay." His fingers were undoing the buttons of her jacket.

Serena came to life. "Stop! Stop it, I say!" She tried to get free, but he held her easily, laughing at her struggles.

"Don't bother to pretend. You've led me a pretty little dance, my dear, but it's over now. The game is over. I'm willing to admit you're an original. Unlike most of your sisters, you've at least succeeded in catching my interest." He bent his head again, whispering against her lips, "We'll discuss terms later."

He pulled open her jacket, took her even more firmly into his arms and started to kiss her again, more passionately than before.

Serena was in a state of panic. She had never felt so helpless. No man had ever kissed her like this before, held her so roughly, talked to her in such a manner. But soon her pride and spirit came to her rescue. She managed to kick Trask, who snorted and jibbed in surprise, and, taking advantage of a momentary relaxation in the man's grip, she tore herself free and backed away. Before he could catch her again she pulled her pistol out of her jacket pocket and cocked it. "Don't take another step!" she said. He made to move, and she pointed the pistol at his knees. "I mean it! I'll shatter your kneecap."

They regarded one another in silence, Serena's eyes watchful and her hand steady.

"The devil!" he said then with a laugh. "I believe you would, too."

"You may count on it," Serena said grimly.

"Hmm. Perhaps I was wrong after all. Does this mean—forgive me if I seem somewhat obtuse—that all this was *not* part of a plot to become—er—more closely acquainted with me?"

"I would rather have a closer acquaintance with a boa constrictor. Whatever made you think I would?"

"What the devil else was I to think? Oh, point that pistol somewhere else. I give you my word you're safe from me."

"I'd rather keep it where it is for the moment. So far I have no reason to take your word for anything."

"In that case we're quits, William Blake—or is it Wordsworth? What *is* your name, girl?"

She hesitated, then her lips began to twitch. "It's Serena. But that's all I'll tell you."

He gave a great shout of laughter. "Serena! I refuse to believe it! You've made it up!"

"No, it's my real name."

"Serena! Oh that's rich, that's really rich! Wait! Er...do you expect to ride Trask back?"

Serena turned her head to see Trask moving slowly out of sight. She gasped in dismay and moved to go after him, but before she had taken a step an iron hand had caught her wrist and forced her to drop the pistol. An exclamation of pain escaped her and she looked at him with a fear she could not con-

ceal. But though he did not release her, he made no attempt to
kiss her again.

"If you promise not to point it at me any more you may have
it back," the man said quietly, holding her gaze. "I intend you
no harm. Do you believe me? Will you promise?" Serena nodded and he picked her pistol up, made it safe, and handed it to
her. She hesitated, then put it carefully away. Her wrist was
aching and she furtively rubbed it. He saw the movement, and
stretched out to take it. She backed away nervously. The gentleman raised his hands and smiled. "I mean no harm. I'm
sorry I hurt you, that's all. And I apologise for my behaviour
a moment ago. I think we owe each other an explanation, don't
you?"

"Trask?" she croaked out of a dry throat.

"Douce will soon overtake him. In fact, if you wait here I'll
fetch him for you now."

Trask was brought back and tied up, while Serena restored
herself to order.

"Now, Serena!" His lips twitched and he said, "A less suitable name would be difficult to find—"

"Prudence?" suggested Serena. He burst into laughter. She
went on, "I may not be very serene, but I have been even less
prudent, I'm afraid. But you have no notion how stifling it is
to be a woman."

"Tell me," he said. "Why did you have to turn into a boy?"

She looked at him uncertainly. How far could she trust him?
He said, returning to a colder manner, "I have given you my
word, Serena. I do not in general force myself on unwilling females, once I am sure they are unwilling, that is. Not many of
them are. But you have convinced me of your reluctance in the
plainest possible way."

She made up her mind. "You misunderstand. I was wondering how much to tell you, not whether you were about
to... to attack me again. I accept your word on that. Though
why the discovery that I was not a boy should lead you to the
conclusion that I would be... would be... a woman like that,
willing to be treated in such a way, I am at a loss to understand!"

"Dammit, how could I think otherwise? Modest young females don't normally roam the countryside with no one to
protect them! And modest young females don't normally dress
like boys—or ride astride, if you'll forgive my mentioning it."

"But why should you assume that I was doing all this just to attract you? Or do you take that for granted? I have to tell you that I find you guilty of a fault worse than any of mine."

"What? What fault?"

"Your conceit!" She was pleased to observe that this remark had struck home. A faint pink appeared in his cheeks, but then he drawled,

"I have been pursued by the fair sex, Serena, ever since I was old enough to notice. But I am not so green as to believe that they love me for myself. My family's fortune is famous. It's only too obvious where my attractions lie."

"If your riches are your only attractive feature, that may well be true!"

"Is that your opinion? That my wealth is my only attraction?"

"We have agreed, have we not, that attraction is not a question between us?" said Serena loftily. She spoilt it by adding, "In my case, I had no idea—still have no idea—who you are, so how could your riches appeal?"

He bowed. "I am Wintersett."

"Well, Mr. Wintersett—"

"Lord Wintersett. And my given name is James. So now we have settled the question of our relationship—or rather the limitations to our relationship, shall I say?—isn't it about time you told me why you had to be a boy? So far we have only established that being a woman is stifling." He indicated a fallen tree-trunk at the edge of the track, and they sat down. Serena in spite of his assurances, took care to keep her distance.

"Till recently," she began carefully, "I have led a less restricted life than I have to at the moment. Don't misunderstand—my former life was completely respectable, just more . . . perhaps 'independent' is the word."

"You're not old enough to be a widow! Are you?"

"You may speculate as much as you wish. I will not tell you anything more than I choose. But I was able to go much my own way."

"And now?"

"Now I have to set an example to someone younger than myself."

"You're a governess. I find that incredible, too."

"Perhaps. Perhaps not. And sometimes, just sometimes, I cannot stand the restraints any longer. I have to get free."

"But why the disguises?"

"You ask that! When you have just demonstrated—and so roughly, too—what happens to women who—what was your phrase?—'roam the countryside with no one to protect them.' Can you imagine the disgrace if it were discovered that the very person who should be setting an example was breaking every rule in Society's book? No," she continued bitterly, "I thought my disguise would give me the freedom I longed for without hurting people I—" she looked at his intent face—"to whom I owe my loyalty. As for not riding side-saddle—have you ever seen a boy who did?"

"That's true! Yes, I can see that one followed from the other. And now?"

"And now I shall have to confine myself to 'acceptable behaviour for a lady.'" She sighed deeply. "Walks round the garden, morning calls, which are *always* paid in the afternoon, polite conversation, in which one never, ever says anything worthwhile. Do you know that I am thought 'bookish' because I enjoy Shakespeare? I shall probably finish by pressing flowers and painting on velvet."

His laugh rang out again. "May heaven preserve you from such a fate! I must confess, you intrigue me, Serena. It's clear that you are no governess—you occupy a superior position in society than those unfortunates—and I'm fairly sure you're no widow, either. What possible circumstances have combined to give rise to such a life as yours?"

Serena looked at him in alarm. He was too intelligent. Before long he would learn everything from her. "I must go!" she said hurriedly, and went to pick up her cap, which was still lying where Lord Wintersett had dropped it.

"Oh, no!" he said and calmly appropriated the cap. "You don't escape so easily. Like you, I spend much of my life with people who bore me beyond measure—'

"I didn't say that! I love my—" she stopped short. She had almost told him more. His face changed, and he looked like a stranger. His voice was icy as he said,

"Have I been mistaken yet again? Can it be that you seek relief from a boring lover in these . . . escapades?"

"No, no!" His face remained cold, so she said desperately, "I'm . . . a kind of chaperon. The person I love is my charge."

"You're not old enough!"

"I am seven and twenty."

He looked flatteringly astonished. "I will not express disbelief," he said. "You must know how old you are, and can have no reason to exaggerate your age. But I would not have guessed it." Then a new thought occurred to him. "If you are a chaperon, then you must be married—or a widow?"

"Neither. That is why I must be so circumspect."

"Of course. As you are. Indeed. I have seen it myself."

Serena chuckled. "You, sir, have seen my alter ego. It is unkind of you to mock me. Now, if you will give me my cap..."

"I did not finish what I had to say, Serena." He looked down at the vivid face lifted to his, the golden eyes half laughing, half anxious. "I have found more amusement in half an hour of your company than in a year of most of my acquaintance. I do not intend to do without it."

"But... but I cannot spend more time with you now!"

"Why not?"

"You must see it is impossible! Pretending to be a boy so that I can have some time to myself is one thing. Slipping out in disguise to an assignation is something very different—indeed, it would be shameful! And I will not do it!"

"I would never have thought you so poor-spirited. Or so conceited!"

"Conceited?"

"Yes, Serena. How can you be so quick to accuse me of conceit, when you suffer from the same fault yourself? What makes you think I want an assignation with you? Those I can have whenever I choose."

"Of course," she murmured. "That wealth of yours... What would you want of me?"

"Companionship, friendship—call it what you will. I enjoy your company, and do not wish to lose it."

"I'm afraid you must. I cannot agree to meet you clandestinely."

"I fear, dear Serena, you will have to!" She started to make an angry protest, but he overrode her. "For if you do not agree to ride here in your boy's clothes, let us say once a week, when I am at home—" he held her gaze "—I will seek you out where you live and reveal all. It would not be difficult to trace you if I really tried."

Serena looked at him in horror. "You wouldn't do such a thing!"

"I agree I probably will not. You will have seen reason before it become necessary."

"But that's blackmail!"

"Quite. I am glad your understanding is so quick." When he saw that she still didn't believe him he said slowly and clearly, as if speaking to an idiot, "I will find out who you really are, and you will be disgraced, unless you agree to continue our acquaintance."

It was obvious that he meant every word.

"You . . . you scoundrel!"

"Come, you are disappointing me, Serena. What am I asking you to do that you were not doing already? I have told you that I have no wish for an alfresco love-affair. And I would not suggest for a moment that we meet anywhere but here on this open ridge. No, it will be as if you are the boy I first thought you. I will even call you William if you desire me to."

She looked at him uncertainly. "But you know I am not a boy. It is. . . it is embarrassing to be in br. . .breeches, when you know I am a woman."

His voice quivered as he said, "I promise never to look at your br . . . breeches."

"You will call me William?"

"All the time."

"And not help me, or coddle me as you would a woman?"

"I will be as severe on you as on the toughest of the members of my own club."

"And you won't think badly of me for this masquerade?"

"I'm beginning to think badly of you at this very moment, Serena—"

"Ha!"

"I shall call you Serena while you continue to act like a woman. At the moment you are suffering from a totally feminine inability to face the inevitable. If you wish to be thought a man, then you must begin to think like one—logically and clearly." He held up one hand and counted on his fingers.

"One: for no reason other than your own pleasure, you chose to dress as a boy and ride out on the Downs. Am I right?"

Serena nodded reluctantly.

"Two: at the risk of being accused of conceit, I will say that you have enjoyed our conversations as much as I. Correct?"

Serena nodded again and he looked satisfied.

"Three: if you do not agree to continue these very pleasant activities, you will suffer some very unpleasant consequences. Where is the choice?"

Serena was going down fighting. "How can I possibly enjoy something I am doing under constraint?"

"Humbug! You want to, you know you do, constraint or no. But it's time to put an end to this unnecessary discussion. Are you to be Serena or William?"

"If I agree, you won't attempt to find out where I live or who I am? I can only carry this out if I feel my two lives are totally separate."

"Hand on heart!"

"You'll let me ride Douce occasionally?"

His face, normally so cold, was transformed by his smile. "Of course you may, my boy! Now, if you wish."

Serena took a deep breath and said, "Done!"

THAT WAS THE FIRST of several outings. Aunt Spurston, whose health improved as the weather got better, decided she would visit Mrs. Galveston every Friday in Reigate. Here Lucy could join Isabella in a dancing class with other young people of the district—all under strict supervision, of course—while Aunt Spurston herself renewed old acquaintances. Serena was excused from these excursions as the carriage was really only comfortable for two, and Aunt Spurston so much enjoyed the opportunity to gossip with her cronies.

"You will have time to yourself for a change, Serena. There will be little enough occasion for that once the season starts."

It was as if everything conspired to smooth the way for Serena's meetings with Lord Wintersett. Sheba scolded, but helped her. Her great-aunt, naturally, always took the coachman and groom with her, and Tom, the stable lad, became one of Serena's staunchest allies. Trask enjoyed the exercise after several years of neglect. As for the outings themselves—they soon became the focus of Serena's week.

CHAPTER FIVE

SERENA'S LIFE had till now been active and rewarding, but not really a happy one. Her childhood had often been lonely, in a household dominated by two strong-willed males—egomaniacs, both of them—her father and her brother Richard. Looking back, Serena could see now that Richard had always been selfish and unscrupulous, but she and her father had worshipped him, blinded by his charm and reckless courage. "The looks of a lion, with a lion's heart," her father had said of him. Richard and her father had both bullied Rodney unmercifully, and had at the same time despised him for allowing it. For a while Rodney had managed to escape them through his marriage with Lucy's mother. But when she died he had returned to Anse Chatelet with his little daughter, and in the end he had found another, more dangerous way to forgetfulness. Serena had been so anxious to avoid the same contempt that Anse Chatelet had been haunted by her tiny figure fiercely determined to win Lord Calvert's approval or Richard's admiration by acts of reckless daring. By the time she was fourteen she had learned to shoot, to ride, to sail almost as well as they did themselves.

Later, in a sadder and wiser time, she had worked unceasingly to keep Anse Chatelet out of the hands of the creditors. The work had been rewarding, but very demanding, and the consciousness of her twin responsibilities—for Lucy and for the estate—had weighed heavily on her.

Now, here in the heart of the English countryside, she learned what it was to be unreservedly happy. Together she and Lord Wintersett explored the hills, valleys, lanes and fields of Surrey. They seldom met anyone, for they kept to the unfrequented paths and byways. But her favourite place was still the top of the ridge, for there she could feel as if they were on the roof of the world, far removed from the restrictions of life below.

They explored each other's minds, too. The love of poetry they already shared, but Serena, conscious of her lack of other knowledge, listened avidly to her companion's accounts of his journeys in Europe, of the people he had met and the sights he had seen. New worlds were opening up before her, and she soaked up knowledge as a sponge soaked up water.

For his part, James talked more freely than he had ever done in his life before, and he waited with a quite unaccustomed interest for anything she might say or ask in response. She never disappointed him. Her quick intelligence, her strong sense of humour, the freshness of her views, were a constant source of pleasure to him. He delighted in the mobile features, golden eyes now sparkling with laughter, now wide with wonder, the generous brow wrinkled in concentration, the sensitive mouth soft with compassion or set in determination. Almost the only barrier between them was her fixed resolve to keep everything about her other life completely hidden. He sensed that this was her defence against any stirrings of conscience about her behaviour, and respected her wishes, never seeking to trap her into betraying herself. Any indications he gleaned from things she said he stored up in his mind, but he gave them little importance. He, too, liked the feeling of isolation from the rest of society, in the world which they had created for themselves on the top of the hill.

They had differences, of course. Serena had already experienced Lord Wintersett's ruthlessness in pursuit of something he wanted. She was occasionally repelled by his coldness, his indifference to the feelings of others—even of those he liked. And he soon found that Serena was touchy about her independence and very fond of her own way. Worse than that, she had a temper. He could see that years of discipline had taught her to control it, but once it was released it blazed like a furnace, leaving her with no thought for the consequences.

On one memorable occasion he actually had to use force to save her from catastrophe. They had wandered further afield than usual, and came upon an isolated cottage in front of which an ugly scene was being enacted. The cottagers—an elderly couple—were being forcibly removed from their home. Two men were throwing pathetic scraps of furniture out on to the grass in front of the cottage. The woman was wailing, and her husband had a bruise on his forehead—graphic evidence of the treatment they had received. Serena rode forward and said imperiously, "What are you doing there? Stop what you're doing immediately!"

The two bailiffs looked round in surprise, but when they saw a mere boy confronting them they turned back to resume their activities.

"I told you to stop, you hog-grubbers!"

One of the men thus addressed turned round swiftly and said, "You saucy young buck! Be off and stop interfering with what don't concern you! This here lot has to be got out by tonight or else! We don't need you to teach us our jobs." He turned round. "Here, you!"

The old woman had scrambled to the pile of furniture and was trying to take it back inside. The bailiff went over to her and pulled her away so roughly that she fell into the mud. Serena, her eyes flashing molten gold, jumped down from Trask and ran to pick the woman up. This was the point at which James thought it prudent to intervene before "William" ran into disaster. He rode into the clearing and interposed Douce between the bailiff and the boy.

"What's the trouble?" he asked coldly.

The bailiffs took off their caps. "Pardon, sir. We was just doin' our duty when this young gentleman appears."

"And your duty consists of throwing a woman old enough to be your grandmother to the ground?"

The men flushed darkly, and one of them muttered, "The old biddy must 'a tripped. She wouldn't do what we told 'er. Troublemakers, that's what they are."

"Can't they pay their rent?"

"It's not that, sir. The master wants the land for another purpose. And the cottage ain't fit fer man nor beast to live in. They've been offered somewhere else."

"But this is their home!" cried Serena. "Why do they have to leave if they don't want to?"

"If the landowner wants the land and has offered them an alternative they have no choice," said James. He turned to the men. "But see that you go gently with the old people. Come—William!"

"I'm not going till I'm certain that they're all right," said Serena hotly. "Where is their new home?"

"In the work'ouse, young maister!" shouted the old man. "And Sal and me are goin' to 'ave to live apart!"

"Well, what's wrong wi' that? You ain't much use to a woman at your age, old man," jeered the other bailiff.

"That's monstrous! How dare you!" cried Serena. She dodged round Douce and kicked the unfortunate bailiff in the shins.

"'Ere!" he roared, and grabbed Serena by the scruff of the neck.

James was there in a flash, almost breaking the man's arm as he knocked him clear. "You," he snarled, "lay another finger on my nephew and you'll be the worse for it. Who is your master?"

"Sir Oliver Camden," muttered the bailiff resentfully, picking himself up. "You'd best be careful—Sir Oliver don't like interference with his concerns. And he's a magistrate, as well!"

"I know Sir Oliver. I don't believe he would wish this. I'll speak to him about it. Meanwhile leave the old people alone, do you hear? William—get on your horse. We're leaving."

"But—" Serena started to protest.

"I said get on your horse!" When she would have argued James picked her up under one arm and carried her, kicking and protesting, to where Trask was patiently waiting. Here he threw her up on to the horse, called Douce to him, and they were soon riding away, with Trask's reins firmly held in James's hand.

Serena was furious. "Let go! I said let go! You're every bit as bad as they are!"

James rode on in grim silence. Ignoring Serena's worst efforts, he guided them both until they were well clear of the wood. It was a superlative display of horsemanship. But as soon as he stopped Serena immediately wheeled Trask around and urged him back the way they had come. She was quickly overtaken, and this time James forced her to dismount. They stood facing one another in the quiet lane. Serena was still angry. "How dare you treat me as if I were a child? Those people needed my help! I shall go back. You cannot stop me!"

James was every bit as angry as Serena, but he was in control of himself. He said coldly, "You're a fool, Serena! Do you wish to make a public spectacle of yourself? You were within an ace of discovery back there! If I hadn't stopped him that bailiff would have found he'd got more than he bargained for when he held you by your collar! Pull yourself together!''

"But that old man—and the woman!"

"Forget them! Sir Oliver is within his rights, you know he is!"

"But he's going to separate them—after all those years together!"

James regarded her curiously. "Why are these people so important to you?"

"It's not that—it's just that it's wrong to deprive anyone of their . . . their dignity like that. If you have people in your care you have to treat them with humanity. I've met people like them. Separate them and they'll die without each other, I've seen it happen."

"They'll die anyway soon enough. Forget them!"

Serena looked at him in disgust and turned away. They stood in silence for a while.

"I'll speak to Sir Oliver," he said finally. "He can probably find some cottage in the village for them, though he might well wonder what business it is of mine. Still—will that satisfy you?"

In an instant she had turned round, her face glowing with gratitude. She came close and clutched his arm. For a moment James thought she was going to kiss him, and he experienced such an unexpectedly strong surge of feeling that, before he could stop himself, he had put his hand over hers, clamping it to his arm. "Serena!" he said fiercely. She looked up, startled. For a moment they stared at each other, and then they both took a step back as if they had reached a sudden abyss.

"You . . . you promised always to call me William," she said uncertainly.

James strove to regain mastery of his feelings. He knew that this next moment would be decisive. If Serena even suspected how powerfully she had affected him she would refuse to see him again, he was sure. If that happened . . . his mind shied away from the possibility. Her friendship and trust had become more important to him than he had realised. He must not lose them because of any transitory feelings of desire. Those could be satisfied cheaply. The value of this relationship with Serena was beyond price.

She was waiting for his response. He took a deep breath.

"As I think I've said before, when you behave as irrationally as you have just done with those men, I shall call you by your woman's name," he said coldly. "Act sensibly and you will be William again to me."

Serena was reassured by this. In all their other meetings, apart from the one when he had discovered her to be a woman, Lord Wintersett had behaved impeccably. He had treated her and spoken to her like the boy she was pretending to be. If he had ever hinted at a warmer feeling she would have been forced to abandon her excursions, even if he carried out his threat to expose her. A moment ago she had been afraid that this might be the case, but his reply had hardly been that of a lover! She must have been mistaken. She was surprised how passionately relieved she felt, that she was free to continue with this strange friendship.

It was astonishing that such a brief moment could have such a profound effect on both James and Serena—the very opposite of what might have been expected. Each had recognised the danger of the moment. But each had also realised the value of their relationship, the importance of preserving it. So an incident which might have led to a reserve, a wariness between them, in fact served to draw them closer.

But the disadvantage of their precarious relationship was brought home to Lord Wintersett when Serena did not appear at her usual time the following week. The trust between them was now so absolute that he had no thought of carrying out his threat of finding her if she refused to meet him. But he was worried. Had she had an accident? Had she reached wherever she lived safely after the last expedition? Was she ill? He had no means of knowing without exposing her—the last thing he wanted. When she did not immediately appear for the second week he was so anxious about her that he was debating whether to set off to look for a clue—anything—as to where she might be. His relief therefore was enormous when she appeared over the hill, and he strode to meet her.

"Serena! What happened?"

"Last week? I must say I was quite relieved not to see you riding up the drive to... the place where I live, like Nemesis. I suspect you are a humbug, Lord Wintersett. I should have tested your threats before now."

"What happened, Serena? Did you have an accident? Were you waylaid?"

"No. My...the person I live with was unwell. I could not leave her."

They suddenly realised that James was holding Serena's hands, and she moved away self-consciously. "You promised to call me William, Lord Wintersett!" she said almost angrily.

"I know, I know!" he replied. "It's sometimes damned difficult to remember that. I've been worried about you. You may dress like a boy, but you are a woman when all is said and done. And vulnerable."

Serena laughed as she flourished her little pistol. "Not while I have this, my friend."

"Much good that toy would have done you had you fallen off your horse and broken your leg."

He was obviously seriously upset, and Serena, not without some secret amusement, set herself to coax him into a better mood.

THE WEEKS FLEW BY, and Serena was aware that she would soon have to think of removing to London. She had received a letter from Lady Pendomer saying that Sir Henry's cousin, Lord Ambourne, was prepared to sublet a small house in Dover Street at a very moderate rent for Serena's stay in London. Serena had written to Lord Ambourne, and had had a very civil reply offering her the house, together with its staff, as soon as she needed it. He regretted that he would be unable to make her acquaintance as early as he had hoped, since he and his Countess were spending the early part of the summer on his estate in France.

Lady Warnham and her family were leaving Surrey within the month to open up the Galveston mansion in Portman Square, and Lucy was growing impatient to be gone. Her and Serena's wardrobes had long been ready. The small finishing touches, such as shoes, fans, shawls and the like, would be bought in the warehouses and shops of London. Little remained to be done in Surrey, and yet Serena lingered. She was sure she would meet Lord Wintersett in London, and was fairly certain that their friendship was secure enough to withstand the transition, but it would not be the same. In London she would be "Miss Calvert," or "Serena"—never "William."

When she mentioned her imminent departure to Lord Wintersett he seemed to feel regret, too. "I take it you are going to

London for the Season—your 'charge' is no doubt to be presented? Oh, don't look at me like that, William! I have not pried into your affairs all this time, and you have no reason to suspect me of doing so now! Well, it is perhaps as well. This could not continue forever, much as I have enjoyed it. *Will* you be in London? Shall I meet you there?''

She nodded.

"It will seem strange," he continued. "I feel I know you better than anyone of my acquaintance, and yet we shall have to appear to be strangers. Do you realise that I have never seen you in a dress?"

She looked at him doubtfully. "Don't expect too much, my friend. Remember my position as a chaperon."

"Now that really will be a piquant situation! The thought of seeing how William the Turbulent is transformed into Serena the Respectable Chaperon almost consoles me for the loss of our present meetings. Almost. But not quite."

They had ridden up to the ridge and were looking down on the bright green fields and sprouting hedges. "Hardly hedgerows..." Serena murmured.

"'Little lines of sportive wood run wild'. I shall miss William, Serena."

"He has to go, Lord Wintersett. But he will always treasure the memory of how good you have been to him."

"Serena—"

"No! I shall be Serena in London," said Serena quickly. "Wait till then. When do you plan to move to the town?"

"I live most of the year in London. My home here is not a very happy place, I'm afraid, and I am not often to be found there. This spring has been quite exceptional." He smiled down at her. "I think you know why, William."

But Serena was thinking of what he had said before. Breaking her own rule, she asked, "Why is your home not a happy one?"

"My nephew is confined to a wheelchair when he is not actually in bed. My mother is also an invalid, and recently she has been getting worse."

"Can she be cured?"

"Who knows? Her illness is not physical, but the result of two shocks, the one rapidly following on the other. Both my father and my younger brother died within a month of each other. She has never been the same since." Then he added abruptly, "But don't let us spoil a beautiful afternoon with such gloomy thoughts. It might be one of our last. Come—is Trask fit for another gallop—or do you wish to ride Douce?"

Serena smiled. "What an unnecessary question!"

SERENA TOLD JAMES the next time they met that this was their last meeting. He looked at the wide view below and wondered why the devil it all had to look so bright. Rain would have been more appropriate. He forced himself to speak calmly.

"You told me last time that you were soon going to London, so it comes as no surprise. And I will soon in any case be unable to spend much time here in Surrey—I have business of my own in London." Serena shivered. "You're cold?"

"No. Someone walked over my grave, I think." She looked at him with troubled eyes. "Or was it because of stories I've been hearing about a certain Lord Wintersett?"

"Stories?"

"I haven't been prying. I respect your privacy as much as you have respected mine. But now that our London début is so near, my charge and I have been subjected to a great deal of advice and gossip...I have heard your name mentioned several times. The Lord Wintersett I hear of then does not seem to be the man I know."

"No?"

"No. I hear that Lord Wintersett is cold, heartless, indifferent to others. That any lady who attempts to attract him runs the risk of a severe set-down. That even his paramours—forgive me, I am still speaking in the character of William, so I can mention these things—never know when his interest will wane and they will be discarded."

He said harshly, "They are right, Serena—you see, I have already said goodbye to William, so you must now be called by your right name—I do not deny these stories." Serena looked at him gravely and something in her eyes made him continue, "You once said that I could have no notion how stifling it was to be a woman. But you have no notion of what it is like to be a very rich man. You once called me conceited because I assumed that you were pursuing me. My experience would never have led me to think otherwise. I will not bore you with other and different stories. But I think every trick known to woman has been tried to trap me—not my person, you understand, but my wealth. As for my paramours—they run the risks of their calling. They are well rewarded.''

Serena swallowed and looked away from him and down into the broad valley.

"What is it, Serena?"

"In one breath you excuse your lack of concern for others because you think they seek you only for your wealth. In another you use your wealth as a substitute for concern. 'They are well rewarded,' you said. It does not reassure me, Lord Wintersett.''

He took her by the shoulders and turned her towards him. "The stories may be true. But one thing my critics have never been able to say. Look at me, Serena, for this is important to me." She looked up, her golden eyes serious. "No one has yet been able to say that I have broken any promises.''

"I suppose that is something. But it is not enough. I think you lack . . .''

"What?"

"I don't know. Kindness?"

"Is that important to you? Universal kindness, I mean?'' he asked in surprise.

"I think it is.''

"Strange. It is not a quality I have sought to cultivate. One is kind to idiots or well-meaning fools. I have always avoided them where possible." Serena was still looking troubled. He felt a sudden urge to remove the worried frown from her brow. "Do you wish me to make promises to you? Is that it?"

"No!" she said vehemently. "No! Now is not the time to be promising anything. This situation between us . . . is too artificial—"

"I sometimes feel it is the only real thing in my world," he said whimsically.

"But the world you talk about is here, on this hill. It isn't real, either," she said sadly.

"Serena, believe me, the world of London society is infinitely more artificial than any make-believe world we have here. You will be flattered and cozened, as I have been—"

" 'Taffeta phrases, silken terms', Lord Wintersett?"

"Exactly! 'Words, words, mere words, no matter from the heart.' What a splendid thing quotation is! But please, Serena, don't change when you get to London." A small frown creased his brown. "I am strangely afraid that I am going to lose you. Can we not take some kind of vow? I am willing, if you are."

"Lord Wintersett, if, when we meet again in London, you still wish to make a promise of any kind—for friendship, for loyalty or...of any kind—then I will listen to you. Not till then. And now I must go."

"Then farewell till then, Serena. But first there's something I must do." He drew her gently to him and kissed her, and was jubilant to feel her total response, untutored though it was. "Whether you realise it or not, you have just made a promise all the same, Serena," he said as they drew apart again. "Serena, my 'bright, particular star.'"

Serena, still looking at him with wonder in her eyes, said nothing.

"Till London, then," he said, holding her chin in his hand. She nodded silently. He kissed her once again, then let her go, and stood watching as Trask carried her away from him down into the valley.

As James returned to his home he had the unpleasant feeling that an idyll had just ended. What would take its place he had no means of knowing, but he feared the effect of London on their relationship. Serena had called their situation artificial and he supposed it was, but they were able to be more natural with each other here than in any conceivable situation in the city. Would Serena be different when she put her skirts on? He couldn't imagine her fluttering and twittering like the rest of society's vapid females, but she was almost certain to lose that wholly natural spontaneity which so delighted him. Especially as she was a "kind of chaperon." Who was her charge? Among the local families he rather thought the Warnham girl was of an age to be presented—but she had a perfectly adequate family, including the Gorgon figure of Mrs. Galveston. Speculation was useless—he would find out soon enough.

ALANNA'S HYSTERICAL outburst when she had heard that Sasha Calvert was coming to England had not been repeated, but she was pale and tense and feverishly active. James had offered to send her to her parents in Ireland for the summer, but she had refused, especially when he told her that young Tony would stay in England where he belonged.

"You would not separate us, James!" she exclaimed.

"I'm beginning to think it might be the best thing that could possibly happen to the boy," he said brutally. "Tony will never make the attempt to be normal while you are constantly hovering over him assuring him he is delicate. Where is he now?"

"He's up today," she said eagerly. "In his room. He has even been working with his tutor."

James went along to Tony's room. It was a sunny room on the ground floor, with a large window which opened on to the garden. But the windows were always closed, sometimes even shuttered, and the child often lay in darkness for hours on end. James hated visiting him. This boy was all that was left of his beloved brother, yet he could see nothing of the older Tony about him. Born at seven months, the infant had grown slowly from a puling, sickly baby into a pale, lethargic invalid. There was nothing of his father's gentle courage, none of Tony's eagerness to learn of the world around him. He remained confined to his bed or a wheelchair, watched jealously by an overanxious mother. Of all the casualties of the tragedy on St. Just this was the most pathetic.

Tony was sitting in his chair, but his tutor was missing. The boy looked up as his uncle came in.

"I've been ringing the bell for ages. No one came."

"Where's Mr. Gimble?"

"He's gone to look for some book in the library. Uncle James, would you pass me that box of comfits from the table by the bed?"

"The wheels of that chair—they can be pushed by hand, can't they?"

"Yes."

"Push them, then. It's not far to the table."

The boy opened his eyes in astonishment. "But . . . but—"

"Go on. If you can do it I'll bring one of Flossie's pups to see you." The boy's face brightened and he leaned forward to grip the wheels. His frail hands whitened as he pushed.

"It moved!"

"Of course it did," said James, surreptitiously moving the chair a fraction further with his foot. But then Alanna, who for some reason could never bear to leave James alone with her son for long, came in. When she saw Tony straining to turn the wheels she shrieked in horror and ran forward to stop him.

"No, Mama! I must do it! Uncle James says he'll bring a puppy for me if I can."

"A puppy! You must surely be mad, James! Anthony would be coughing and wheezing half the night if an animal came in here. Come, my darling, Mama will get you what you want. This box, was it?"

James gave an exclamation of impatience and left the room.

THE NEXT MORNING there was a note from Bradpole, requesting an interview with Lord Wintersett. Sasha Calvert was expected about the middle of April, and would be staying in a house rented from the Earl of Ambourne in Dover Street. James gave a twisted smile at the thought. It was ironic that Ned should give shelter to a Calvert, for Ned and he had been at school together and the Earl was one of James's few close friends. Not that Ned knew anything of the events on Anse Chatelet so long ago, for the story of Tony's suicide in the West Indies had remained a well-kept secret. Alanna had wished it so for the sake of her son, and the Calverts had had their own reasons for hiding the truth. The world at large had been allowed to think that Tony had succumbed to the tropical climate.

When they met, Mr. Bradpole's manner was grave. "I have been unable to ascertain which packet boat Miss Calvert and her niece took from the West Indies. The passenger lists are most inadequate. But numbers of people are arriving in London every day for the season, and I have learned from Lord Ambourne's man of business that he is expecting his tenants to move in next week. Are you still as adamant, Lord Wintersett?"

James hesitated. In truth he had recently had occasional feelings of distaste for this vendetta against the Calvert family. But it was not in his nature to reveal weakness or lack of decision, so he evaded a reply. "What about affairs on Anse Chatelet?" he asked.

"News travels slowly between England and the West Indies, and even more slowly between Barbados and St. Just. I do not expect to hear for some time."

"Tell me when you do. I'll decide then what action to take."

Soon after that he tried to persuade Alanna to talk about the past. "Believe me, Alanna, I am far from wishing to raise any ghosts. But the time is approaching when I must decide what to do about Sasha Calvert, and I need your help. I need to know what really happened."

Alanna's blue eyes filled with tears. "I have told you over and over again," she whispered brokenly. "It was a nightmare, James. Why do you force me to remember?"

"Try. Were you and Tony happy before you went to St. Just?"

"Oh, yes!" she cried. "We were deliriously happy! And on the island, too. Right up to the moment it happened. Yes, we were happy."

"You were living at the house—Anse Chatelet?"

"Yes. Lord Calvert had invited Tony to stay there while he explored the island and sought out new plants."

"Who else was living there at the time?"

"Let me see . . . Lord Calvert was there, and Sasha, and Rodney—but he was an invalid. And the elder brother—Richard, I think he was called. And little Lucy."

"And what happened?"

"That woman—Sasha. She hardly ever spoke to us in the house. But she followed Tony everywhere on his expeditions."

"Where were you during these expeditions?"

"I stayed behind at the house, at Anse Chatelet." She said defensively, answering his unspoken criticism, "I suppose it would have been better if I had been able to go with Tony, but it wasn't what I was used to! I found the heat too much."

"What about Tony? Surely the climate was new to him, too."

"He was so fascinated by the plants out there that he didn't seem to notice it. Or me." She added forlornly, "He was always out."

"When did you learn that Tony was having an affair with the Calvert woman?"

"She was so clever, James! She never went near him in the house. And when they were out everyone thought she was just guiding him through the forests. It never entered my head that she would appeal to him, for she wasn't at all like me. She was not at all feminine. But all the time . . . My poor Tony! My poor darling Tony!" She began to sob.

James set his teeth. "I've nearly finished, Alanna," he said as gently as he could. "Tell me, if you can, what happened before Tony died."

"I will, I will, James. But not now. I must go to see Anthony—"

"Mr. Gimble is with Anthony. Tell me what happened, Alanna."

She sat down again. "I . . . I wasn't feeling well. I told Tony about . . . about the baby, and . . . and that's when he confessed. That he was in love with Sasha Calvert, and he wanted to leave me. There was a dreadful scene. I was distraught after it. Perhaps I should not have done what I did."

"What did you do?"

Alanna paused and wiped her lips with her handkerchief. Then she continued, "I went to Lord Calvert, to tell him how badly his . . . his daughter had behaved. He didn't believe me at first, but finally he said he would confront them. We were waiting on the terrace when they came in. When her father accused her Sasha just laughed." Alanna was white to the lips, and she closed her eyes as she said, "I shall never forget that laughter. It is still ringing in my ears." She said this with such genuine anguish in her voice that James was moved to pity. He was about to suggest that Alanna should rest for a while, but she was already continuing,

"Can you imagine how Tony felt when she said . . . she said— Oh, James, with such an expression of scorn!—she said she despised him, that she had no intention of taking him away from me, however besotted he might be. That one lover more or less made no difference to her, she had plenty, and any one of them was more thrilling than a tame little botanist. That I was welcome to him and could take him home with her good will."

With a muffled exclamation James got up and brought his fist down on the mantelpiece. "Go on!" he said harshly.

"Lord Calvert was beside himself with rage. He must have known what sort of woman his daughter was, but he pretended to blame Tony. He swore to ruin him, to throw him off the island, and to see that he was never allowed back anywhere in the West Indies. I don't think Tony heard any of it. He was . . . he looked like a ghost, a zombie they call them out there. Then he went to our rooms. I followed him a few minutes later but . . . you know the rest."

"And Richard Calvert?"

"Richard? What about Richard? What has Richard to do with this?"

"Didn't he die about the same time?"

"Later—after Tony. But the deaths were unconnected, I think." Alanna swallowed. "Richard fell off a cliff on his way back to Anse Chatelet. He was drunk. I believe he usually was."

"They were a pretty lot! But now only Sasha is left. What shall I do about her? Anse Chatelet may be said to be mine if things go as planned. Is that enough?"

Alanna's pretty face showed her distress as she pleaded, "I don't want you to take Anse Chatelet! Leave Sasha Calvert where she belongs, where we will never see her again. Send her back, James! Don't even try to see her! Send her away!"

"You are talking nonsense! How can I send Miss Calvert away? And why should I?"

"You do not know her! She is a wicked liar—she casts a kind of spell over her victims till they do not know what to believe. They said on the island that she had learned the arts of voodoo. Look at the way she dazzled my poor Tony until he was driven to his ruin."

"She is surely not such a Circe now! She must be well into her thirties."

Alanna ignored him. She was becoming hysterical again. "Send her away! Make it impossible for her to remain in England. She ruined our lives once and she will do so again unless you get rid of her!"

"I suppose there is one way," said James thoughtfully. "To disgrace her somehow in the eyes of society so that she has to leave England. It would be a kind of poetic justice, after her father's threats to Tony. But it would not be easy to do anything like that without involving the niece, too. And that must be avoided, for neither she nor her father were involved in this sordid affair."

"Why are you so scrupulous about the niece? The Calverts are all the same."

"Lucy Calvert is innocent and must be protected," said James firmly. "But have no fear, Alanna. Sasha Calvert will pay for Tony's sufferings—and yours."

"I like your idea of poetic justice, James. If you destroyed the Calvert woman's credit in the eyes of the world, then no one would believe her stories," said Alanna slowly. She smiled for the first time that evening. "Oh, yes, James! I think that would be the best idea of all! If you wish, I'll help you in that. In fact

I think I have the beginnings of a plan already. Why don't you leave it all to me!"

"Alanna, you are too impetuous! Sasha Calvert is not yet in England. When she arrives she should be given time to become known in society, and to establish her niece. Then we shall see."

CHAPTER SIX

SERENA AND LUCY, together with Sheba, were carried to London in a hired post-chaise. The chaise was comfortable, and the journey not long, so they arrived in Dover Street in reasonably good order. The Earl's agent was waiting for them. He introduced himself as Etienne Masson, and they found to their surprise that he was French. "Though I prefer to describe myself as Norman, *madame,*" he said with a smile.

He introduced the footman, John, and the housekeeper, Mrs. Starkey. Mrs. Starkey curtsied and said in a soft, West Country voice, "Your rooms are ready, ma'am. Shall I lead the way?" While John supervised the unloading of their many valises and had them carried up to the rooms, Masson gave them the directions for the best shops and the sights he thought they would like to see.

"John knows London very well, madame. He will accompany you anywhere you go."

"Always?" asked Lucy in astonishment.

"It is the custom, *mademoiselle,*" the agent replied apologetically, with the smile that Lucy always seemed to attract.

"And I for one am grateful for it," said Serena. "From what I have seen of it so far, the size and bustle of London appals me."

"Forgive me, *madame.* You have only just arrived. You will soon see that London is in fact very small—the part of it which you will need to know, that is. Er...Lord Ambourne seemed to think that since you are a small household Mrs. Starkey might combine the services of steward and housekeeper. She is experienced in both kinds of work. She has a number of domestics to help her in the house, but if you would prefer to engage maids for yourself and Miss Lucy Calvert I will arrange it."

Serena was secretly relieved that the household expenses would be so much lighter, but simply replied, "It is kind of Lord Ambourne to take such trouble. We have brought our own maid with us from St. Just, and I think she will be enough, but I will let you know a little later what we decide."

"Then I will take my leave. I hope you will enjoy your stay here."

After Monsieur Masson left, Serena and Lucy explored the house. It was delightful.

"How can Lord Ambourne bear to let it out? Does he not use it himself?" Serena asked.

"The Dowager Countess occasionally stays here when she is on her own. But when the Family are in London," said Mrs. Starkey, and Serena could hear the capital in her voice, "they stay in Arlington Street—at Rotherfield House. They are all in Normandy at the moment, but I believe they will be here later in the season."

"I hope so," said Serena, "for I should like to thank Lord Ambourne in person for his kindness."

Mrs. Starkey smiled. "It's probably her ladyship you ought to thank, Miss Calvert. Very particular, Miss Perdita is, about her house. Lady Ambourne, I should say. She lived in it before she was married, you see, and his lordship kept the lease on because she likes it so much. But I'm forgetting my duties. Would Miss Lucy and yourself like a refreshment?"

Serena had wondered somewhat apprehensively about the domestics in Lord Ambourne's establishment. The servants at Anse Chatelet had all known her since she was a child. Betsy, the housekeeper there, had been Serena's nurse, and Sheba had been Lucy's. For many years Serena had relied on all of them to help her in keeping Anse Chatelet viable, so the relationship between household staff and mistress had been more informal than was usual. She had heard dreadful stories from Mrs. Galveston and her friends of maids who were more conscious of position than their mistresses, of footmen who despised anyone who did not know his place. It had been impressed on her that she must always keep her distance with London domestics, otherwise they would "take advantage." Another source of worry had been Sheba's position in the household. Would London domestics accept Sheba? But the stories were all proved false as far as the servants in Dover Street were concerned, and Sheba, with her tales of magic and her warm grin, quickly made herself as popular in the servants' quarters here as she had been in Surrey. Mrs. Starkey had known Lady Ambourne before her marriage and admired her enormously. Indeed, she was devoted to the whole Ambourne family, and was prepared to extend her good will to any of their friends who happened to be staying in Dover Street. It was impossible not to like her, for she was a sensible, kindly woman, who soon took the interests of both her young ladies to heart. "But Mrs. Starkey," cried Serena when she heard herself thus described, "you mustn't call me a young lady! I am supposed to be Miss Lucy's chaperon!"

"If you'll forgive my saying so, Miss Calvert, it's hard to believe that, when you're looking so handsome." She regarded Serena admiringly. They were standing in front of the cheval mirror in Serena's bedchamber, where Mrs. Starkey had been helping Sheba with the final touches for her two ladies' first appearance in society. Whether it was Mrs. Galveston's lotion, or the new wardrobe, or something quite different from all of those, Serena was blooming. Her dark hair was now fashionably cut and arranged, her dark-fringed, amber-gold eyes glowed with well-being, and her skin was pearl-like. A conventional beauty she would never be, but she was striking. Too striking. With determination Serena took off her topaz-yellow silk dress, undid her hair and, while the bewildered housekeeper looked on, ordered Sheba to plait it into a tight chignon on the back of her head. Mrs. Starkey might have disapproved of the freedom with which Sheba voiced her objections, but she heartily agreed with her sentiments.

"Sheba, that is enough! You have had your say, now do as I tell you!" said Serena. "And fetch the green dress, the one with the high neck, if you please."

Still grumbling under her breath, Sheba brought out a dress in a dull, greyish-green, and helped her mistress put it on.

"Sasha! What are you doing?" cried Lucy when she saw her.

"Looking like a chaperon," said Serena grimly. "We came to England to give you a London Season, Lucy, not to make a spectacle of me. It's you who must shine."

"But I do!" said Lucy, twirling gaily round. "Apart from you in your yellow dress, I'm the most beautiful thing I've ever seen! I'll swear this creation by Maria is more exquisite than any to be found in London! Lady Pendomer is a trump!"

"Lucy! Wherever did you pick that up?"

"Oh . . ." Lucy blushed. "I beg pardon, Sasha. It's something Isabella's brother says."

"Good God! About you?" asked Serena, looking at her niece in amusement. Growing even redder, Lucy nodded. "Well, I'm sure the sentiment is admirable. But the word itself should not be any part of a young lady's vocabulary!"

"I'm sorry, Aunt Serena. I should have said that Lady Pendomer possesses the attributes of a very good friend!" She laughed and danced away, then came back to ask mischievously, "Is it all right to say 'Good God'?"

LUCY AND SERENA joined Lady Warnham at Mrs. Galveston's mansion in Portman Square, prepared for the culmination of all Serena's plans—Lucy's introduction to London society. Lucy was nervous, but this merely gave a sparkle to her eyes and a becoming colour to her cheeks. At the rout party which followed Serena sat firmly with the chaperons, and only with difficulty did she disguise her pride. The daughters of most of the best families in London were there but, in Serena's eyes at least, not one of them could hold a candle to her niece. She noticed with some amusement that there was at the party a sort of magic circle of Lucy's Surrey friends, who tended to regard intruders with uneasy suspicion and were ready to see them off. But Lucy handled them all as if born to it. The girl was a credit to her training. When the two Misses Calvert returned to Dover Street that night they were both extremely satisfied with the evening.

Serena had not looked to see Lord Wintersett at Mrs. Galveston's. The party had been specifically for the younger section of society, with the purpose of giving Isabella and Lucy some experience before they were launched into the deeper waters of a full-scale ball. It was hardly an occasion which would be graced with his lordship's presence! But he was never far from her mind. However busy she was, matching silks, trying on shawls, walking in the parks, occupied in the hundreds of activities which made up the London Season, she was always aware that he might suddenly appear round the next corner. She grew increasingly nervous of seeing him again. What would he think of her? Each time they went to a ball or some other grand affair she took out the topaz silk dress, wondering whether Lord Wintersett would be there. But each time she put it away again and put on something more modest. She was Lucy's chaperon.

It was Lucy herself who was instrumental in persuading Serena to change her mind. Lucy's nature was sunny, and here in London she was having the time of her young life. But one day she came in from a walk in the park with a face like a thundercloud. Serena was unable to find out what was wrong, but was even more concerned when Lucy refused an invitation to spend the next afternoon with Isabella. When she finally extracted the cause of Lucy's displeasure she didn't know whether to be relieved or annoyed.

"I've quarrelled with them," said Lucy.

"Why?" asked Serena in astonishment. "You've always been such friends with Isabella. Whatever was it about?"

"It wasn't Isabella. It was the other girls. They were being unfair."

"To you."

"No, about someone else."

It was clear to Serena who this was. There was only one other person who could rouse Lucy to this passionate defence. "About me?"

"They called you a dowd, Sasha! They said you had spent all your money on me, and had none left for yourself. They started to make fun of you. It's not true, is it?" Lucy was worried.

"Of course it isn't! I have lots of dresses, you know I have."

"Well, why don't you wear them?"

Lucy was seriously upset. Serena remembered that Great-aunt Spurston had told her that Lucy would be judged by Serena's appearance as well as her own, had even given Serena money and jewels for this purpose. Had she been selfish to ignore her great-aunt's advice? Was it protection that she had sought among the quietly dressed chaperons? Serena started to get angry not only with herself, but with those who had made her darling niece unhappy.

"Spend the afternoon with your friends, Lucy. Try not to let what they say about me make any difference. They don't understand. But just between ourselves—just between ourselves, Lucy, my love—I think they might be in for a surprise . . ."

So that night Serena put on her topaz silk dress, together with the diamond drop earrings and bracelet which her great-aunt had given her. Her black hair was swept into a knot on top of her head and secured with a diamond pin, and loose waves and curls framed her face. Her slender throat rose proudly from the low-cut neckline of her dress. Sheba's face was one big grin, and Mrs. Starkey was very impressed. Lucy was ecstatic. "You'll eclipse everyone there, Sasha! Oh, indeed they will be surprised!"

"Tonight, Lucy, I want you to exert yourself—as I shall. You will call me Aunt Serena, and we shall both remember all our lessons in the manners of the *ton*. We shall be very grand—true Calverts of Anse Chatelet. Do you agree?"

"Oh, yes," breathed Lucy, her eyes shining.

THE OCCASION ITSELF was also grand—a ball at the Duchess of Stockhampton's, no less. Serena was aware of curious eyes on her as they mounted the huge, curving staircase, but she put her chin up a touch higher and ignored them. Her blood was up, and generations of Calverts marched with her. A chaperon she might be, but Lucy's aunt was no dowd!

Mrs. Galveston greeted her in typical manner. "Good evening, Miss Calvert! How well you look! I was beginning to wonder whether you would have been happier left in Surrey, but now I see I was mistaken. We may well find you a match, after all. Indeed, I doubt a respectable widower would have a chance with you tonight! Perhaps we should look higher?"

"I am not," said Serena coolly, "in search of a husband, Mrs. Galveston. But I am touched by your compliments. May I return them? Town life obviously suits you."

Mrs. Galveston almost smiled. "Your great-aunt would be proud of you. She always said you'd repay dressing, and there's no doubt you have an air about you tonight."

Serena smiled and moved on. One of Lucy's beaux, a handsome, well set-up young man who was looking rather nervous, came up to ask if Lucy would stand up with him for the country dances.

"Thank you. May I first introduce you to my aunt? This is Michael Warnham, Aunt Serena. I believe you are acquainted with his mother?"

Serena hastily disguised her involuntary laugh with a cough and inclined her head slightly. As the young man took Lucy off with a sigh of relief, that maiden gave her aunt a very arch look.

Serena was soon besieged by various ladies with requests to be allowed to introduce Lord This and Sir That. She smiled charmingly at her admirers, and answered their eager questions willingly enough, but refused all requests to dance.

ABOUT HALFWAY through the evening Lord Wintersett came into the room and gazed casually round. His eye lighted as if by accident on the chaperons' corner, and then moved on. Serena was not there. He surveyed the scene before him. She was not dancing, either. He had hardly expected it. Perhaps she had gone with her charge to the supper-room. He was about to leave the ballroom when an animated group on the other side of the room caught his attention, and he glanced at the central figure. She was surrounded and her head was bent. But he knew instantly who it was, and at that very moment Serena looked up and their eyes met. His widened as he saw the proud lift of the head and recognised the sparkle of diamonds in her ears. He looked briefly in the direction of the winter garden, and she closed her eyes once. No more was needed. A few minutes later he was standing at the end of the path, half hidden by the lavish arrangement of plants, when he saw Serena coming towards him.

James had not known what to expect—he had imagined everything from a sedate, quietly dressed ladies' companion, to a girl/woman uncomfortable in society and ungraceful in skirts. But he had never imagined anything like this cool, poised beauty. The diamonds in her ears and at her wrist, the pin in her hair, the exquisite dress—these were merely the trappings of a most unusually lovely lady. He was almost afraid to speak to her, almost afraid that he would find that his Serena had gone forever. Then she smiled, her eyes glowing with happiness, and he knew he had not lost anything. Nothing at all. He had gained more than he could ever have imagined.

"Lord Wintersett? You are shameful, sir! We have not been introduced, and yet you invite me to an assignation in the Duchess's winter garden!" Her amber-golden eyes were brimming with laughter. "I dare swear you will even say I took it upon myself to follow you!"

"Serena! I am overwhelmed!" He took her hands in his. "William was never as lovely as this!"

"Alas, poor William in his hand-me-downs! No! I am wrong. Fortunate William!" She gently released herself. "At least in the short time allowed him he was free from observation and criticism—except by you, of course. Here in London it is very difficult to escape at all.''

"From your admirers, no doubt."

"From my critics, rather! I must not stay long. The chief function of a chaperon is to prevent her charge from behaving as I am doing at this very moment! I must not be found out!''

"You! A chaperon? I know you said you were, but I find that impossible to believe. How can you possibly look after some-one else when you so obviously need protection yourself?"

Serena looked at him mockingly. "What, Lord Wintersett? 'Taffeta phrases, silken terms' from you, of all people? You have no need to pay me pretty compliments, sir. I know you for what you are."

"Do you, Serena? Do you? Then I must congratulate you, for I no longer know what that is myself. I know what I was in the past."

A faint rose appeared in her cheeks. "I must go," she said, "I have already been out here too long."

"William was not so cowardly."

"William was an invention, a dream. The reality is Serena, and Serena is bound by the conventions of society. I heard you have always avoided situations like this in the past, Lord Wintersett—indeed, that you have severely punished the poor la-dies who have enticed you into them. Why do you wish to prolong this one?"

"You ask that? After our . . . tacit vow?"

The colour rose in Serena's cheeks, and she said hurriedly, "I must return to the ballroom."

"What if I refuse to let you go?" He took hold of her hand again.

She shook her head. "Oh, no! Here in London you cannot blackmail me or force me to do your bidding—I have too much to lose."

He tightened his grip and said softly, "I think I could per-suade you."

"But you will not attempt to do so. It would not be kind. And who knows? The great Lord Wintersett might suffer a re-verse. I might prove adamant!" She took her hand away and moved towards the door. The orchestra was striking up a waltz.

"Dance with me, then!" When she hesitated he swept her into the ballroom and on to the floor. He put his arm at her waist, and at her warning look he laughed and said, "Strict propriety, I swear, Serena!'' Decorously they circled the room, but there was that about them which drew all eyes. The young bloods admired Lord Wintersett's conquest, the young ladies envied Serena for her daring capture, for the duration of the evening anyway, of society's most eligible and most dangerous bachelor. The matrons and chaperons whispered behind their fans and shook their heads. Wintersett was beginning another of his flirts! It was a pity that it should be quiet Miss Calvert. Perhaps her success tonight had gone to her head.

But the two who were dancing were oblivious to all this. They were lost in each other. James held Serena with the lightest of touches, but they could not have felt closer if he had embraced her. A curious feeling of certainty mixed with a dangerous excitement ran between them, surrounded them, isolated them from the rest of the room. Watching their mutual absorption, society wondered and gossiped.

At the end of the dance Serena made to return to her seat, but her partner refused to let her go. "No! Come to the supper-room—I want to give you champagne, Serena. I wish to discuss a promise."

"A promise?" she echoed, flushing again.

"You would not listen to it in Surrey. You told me to wait until we met in London. Now we have met, and I will not wait any longer to claim what you must know is mine."

"Aunt Serena!" Lucy's voice broke the spell. "So this is where you are! You decided to dance after all?" Lucy looked curiously at Lord Wintersett.

"Lucy!" Serena was blushing in real earnest now. "I...I..." She glanced at Lord Wintersett and took hold of herself. "Lucy, I wish you to meet an...an acquaintance of mine, Lord Wintersett. Lucy is my niece, Lord Wintersett. And my charge," she added with a warning in her voice.

Lucy's eyes were huge. "Wintersett?" she asked. "Lord Wintersett? But Aunt Serena—"

"Lucy—"

"What your aunt means to say, Miss Lucy, is that it does not do to believe all the stories you hear. Am I right?" James was enjoying himself. He had little doubt that this charming girl would discover in a very short time what sort of acquaintance he intended to have with her aunt, but was content to leave it for the moment. "May I escort you both to the supper-room? We might discuss these stories over supper."

Still looking slightly puzzled, Lucy allowed herself to be ushered to the other side of the ballroom. Here they were met by Michael Warnham.

"Lucy! Oh, good! You've found your aunt." He looked curiously at Serena and Lord Wintersett, but decided to continue. "Have you asked her yet? No?" He turned to Serena, with a charming smile. "Isabella and some of the others are making up a party to go to Hampton Court tomorrow. We should like Lucy to come." Lucy's expression made it clear how much she would like to go. "Do say she may, Miss Calvert! My mother has agreed to act as chaperon."

Serena was distracted as Lord Wintersett narrowed his eyes and turned his head swiftly towards the young man. She hesitated.

"Oh, Sasha, do say yes!" pleaded Lucy.

"*Sasha!*"

Serena smiled at Lord Wintersett's interruption. "It's what Lucy calls me when we're alone," she explained. "A pet name from my own childhood. Very well, Lucy, my love. I'll see Lady Warnham later and arrange things with her. It's very kind of her." She glanced at Mr. Warnham and added, "I suppose you wish to join Isabella now, Lucy? Perhaps Mr. Warnham would escort you to her?" Lucy nodded, and Mr. Warnham bowed and took her off.

"*Sasha!* That cannot be your name! But she called you Sasha. And he . . . the boy—he called you *Miss Calvert! Sasha Calvert?*"

Serena looked at Lord Wintersett in some concern. He was very pale, and he spoke jerkily.

"I had forgotten that we had not been formally introduced! How shocking!" smiled Serena. "But if you don't like 'Sasha,' I am happy to answer to Serena. In fact, I prefer—"

"Why did you tell me your name was Serena?" he rapped out.

"Because that's what it is! Serena. But Lucy has called me Sasha since she was a baby."

"Why did you not tell me this before?"

Serena looked at him as if he had suddenly become deranged. "Why should I? My proper name is Serena. And you forget that until recently I was always 'William' in Surrey." She put a tentative hand on his arm. "Are you not well, Lord Wintersett?"

"I am perfectly well, thank you," he replied. As if to bely this he put his hand to his head and ran it through his hair. "Sasha Calvert," he murmured. "You're Sasha Calvert!" He looked down with distaste at her hand, resting on his arm. "Your solicitude is excessive, I assure you," he said coldly.

Serena flushed, then grew pale. "Forgive me," she said withdrawing the offending hand. A thought seemed to strike him.

"Where do you live, Sasha Calvert?"

Serena looked at him in amazement. He seemed to be speaking against his will, and his tone of voice was peremptory, even angry. He might have been able to speak to William like this, but not to Miss Calvert of Anse Chatelet! She replied stiffly, "I fail to see why that should concern you, sir, but while in London I live in Dover Street. My home is in the West Indies."

He turned away from her, and she thought she heard him say "Oh, God!" but could not be sure.

Serena began to feel she was in some kind of nightmare. Though no one else was near enough to overhear their conversation, she could see that they were arousing a great deal of speculation. She said quietly, "We are being observed, so it is difficult for me to speak. I am not sure what I have said or done to offend you, Lord Wintersett?" She paused a moment, looking up at his averted face with a plea in her eyes. When he remained silent she took a step back and said, "Forgive me. I must have misunderstood your feelings. Or perhaps you are as capricious as your reputation would suggest. I will bother you no longer."

He seemed to pull himself together at this, and turned again to face her. She was astonished at the change in him. His eyes were empty of feeling and his face was like stone. He eyed her up and down with a curl to his lips, then cast a glance round the room, "You are right, Miss Calvert. We are being observed." He smiled and raised his voice as he drawled, "No, it is you must excuse me. I must admit I can hardly tear myself away—especially after the idyll in the winter garden, which you so…hopefully arranged. But, alas! I must. However, you look so delightful that I am sure there are many others here who would be only too glad to take my place. Your servant, ma'am." He bowed and strode out of the room.

By exercising every ounce of self-control Serena pulled herself together and kept her head high as she walked back to the bench where Mrs. Galveston and Lady Warnham were sitting. She would not give the assembled company the satisfaction of seeing the extent of her shock or of watching her scuttle to some convenient alcove or cloakroom to hide herself like a hurt animal. When one of the Warnham sons offered to fetch her some refreshment she accepted gratefully, and took care to drink the champagne he brought slowly and with appreciation. After a short while the trembling in her limbs stopped, and she began to grow very angry. Her pride would not have allowed her to cut the evening short, but it was this anger which helped her to endure it.

It was obvious that the massive snub Lord Wintersett had delivered her so publicly was the chief topic of conversation among the mothers and chaperons present, and though some of them regarded her with sympathy there was a certain amount of head-shaking and shrugging of shoulders. They all knew that Lord Wintersett was a dangerous man to tangle with, and, in the opinion of some, Miss Calvert had been foolhardy in showing her feelings so openly. They had all watched that waltz.

Criticism and sympathy were equally intolerable to Serena, and, since she did not lack partners, she escaped both by accepting every invitation to dance. She dazzled them all. The diamonds in her ears glittered with no greater intensity than Serena herself, but she could not have said afterwards who had danced with her, or how long they had danced with her, or what they talked about while they were dancing. At some time in the evening Lucy joined her, obviously having heard some of the gossip, but Serena said softly but fiercely, "No, Lucy, not now. Tell me of your outing tomorrow, tell me what you had for supper, or what Mr. Warnham was saying, or anything you like, but do not, I pray you, mention . . ." She stopped. She found it impossible to say Wintersett's name.

The evening eventually came to an end and Serena was at last able to escape to the haven of Dover Street. She could not avoid Lucy's anxious questions, but told her very little. She did not know herself what had happened to cause Lord Wintersett to change so rapidly, so how could she explain it to Lucy? After a short while Lucy gave up asking questions and set herself to restoring her aunt's spirits. For perhaps the first time in their lives Lucy was the one who gave comfort that night, and Serena was the one who needed it.

Serena's behaviour in the next week did much to reestablish her in the eyes of society. Mrs. Galveston had arrived in Dover Street the day after the ball and, though she gave Serena a hard time herself—harder than she realised—she also gave her some excellent advice. After this Serena went about her usual visits and outings with composure, warding off all impertinent questions and comments by admitting, apparently frankly, that she had roused Lord Wintersett's anger and had had to pay for it. "As a colonial," she would say with a disarmingly rueful smile, "I'm afraid I still have to learn what is done and what is not done. I think the gentleman in question—" she still could not say his name—"took my lack of formality for something more than I intended. Tell me, is he always so concei... er... so quick to assume that the ladies are in love with him?"

While there were still some who looked knowing when they heard this, most people were so impressed by Serena's quietly confident manner that they began to think that Lord Wintersett had indeed been too hard on a newcomer from abroad, that his well-known aversion to being pursued had in this instance misled him, and soon Serena was generally held to have been treated ungallantly. All the same, society looked forward with interest to see if there was to be another encounter between Lord Wintersett and Miss Calvert.

IT WAS A WEEK before this happened, and in the meantime Serena made a new acquaintance. Lord Ambourne's mother had returned earlier than expected from France, and had arrived in Rotherfield House the day after the Duchess of Stockhampton's ball. She called on Serena after that. When she was told that the Dowager Countess of Ambourne was in the carriage outside and wished to know if she were at home, Serena's heart sank. Of course she must receive her—it was very gratifying that the Countess should take the trouble to call. But another Mrs. Galveston was not a pleasing prospect, and this high-born lady would be even worse, she was sure. Serena was due for a surprise! John ushered in a tiny figure in a pelisse and bonnet in the very latest mode, who came forward saying in a charming French accent, "My dear Miss Calvert! How agreeable to meet you! Forgive me for calling on you so early, but Lady Pendomer's letter was written in such terms that I felt I had to see the paragon she described as soon as possible! And my son asked me to visit you, also." She surveyed Serena. "But *alors,* you are much better than I expected."

Serena smiled her first genuine smile since the ball as she indicated a chair and they sat down. "It's very kind of you to call, Lady Ambourne, but I'm afraid Lady Pendomer is overpartial. I am no paragon. Paragons are perfect, and I am far from that!"

"That is just what I meant! Perfection is very boring, don't you agree? Now you must give me news of Lady Pendomer, and then tell me about yourself. I wish to know everything!" The Countess settled comfortably in her chair, accepted some refreshment from a beaming Mrs. Starkey, and proceeded to delight Serena for the next half-hour. Though Lady Ambourne had the indefinable air of a great lady, she was not at all haughty or reserved. She talked freely of her son and daughter-in-law, of whom she was clearly very fond, and had Serena laughing at her descriptions of her grandsons' antics. "You will think me a doting grandmother, Miss Calvert—but how can I help it when the children are so clever and so good? Well, perhaps not 'good' exactly—but so charmingly naughty!"

At the end of the visit the Countess asked Serena to call on her soon in Rotherfield House. "Bring Miss Lucy Calvert with you—I am sorry not to have met her. Perdita and Edward will not be back from Normandy for a few weeks yet and I miss them very much, so you will be doing me a kindness. In fact, I should like to arrange some kind of evening party for you both, for it's time we had something to brighten up the family mansion—a barn of a place, Miss Calvert, but it does very well for balls and the like. Living in it is less agreeable." She departed, leaving behind a faint breath of a perfume and a strange feeling of comfort. Though Serena had said nothing, of course, about Lord Wintersett, she had found the Countess warm and sympathetic. She would be a good listener if Serena ever needed one.

CHAPTER SEVEN

FOR A WEEK after the Duchess's ball Lord Wintersett was not seen at any of the drums and assemblies held in the evenings, nor was he observed riding in the parks or walking in the gardens of London during the day. This surprised no one. It was said that he had recently been in the habit of disappearing to his estate in Surrey for days at a time. Though Serena secretly gave a wry smile at this, she was grateful for the respite. When she and Lord Wintersett next met she wanted to be in command of herself. Keeping composed in company in general was one thing. Coming face to face with a man she could have loved—for, lying awake in the hours of darkness, she had faced that fact—and a man who had treated her so inexplicably was quite another. However, they were both present in the Assembly Rooms exactly one week after the ball. Though Lucy was not there, having gone with Lady Warnham to another gathering, Serena stayed by Mrs. Galveston, for she took care nowadays to behave with utmost circumspection.

He came in late with a lady on his arm, a ravishing blonde with a startlingly good figure. It was a pity, perhaps, that the lady was wearing pink, thought Serena critically; blondes should not wear pink. Nor was it perhaps in the best of taste to choose a dress which, in spite of its elaborate trimmings, so clearly revealed the lady's ample charms. Serena's own dress of pale blue zephyrine caught up over a slip of white sarsnet silk, which she had thought so pretty, suddenly seemed very tame.

"The devil!" exclaimed Mrs. Galveston, startling Serena into turning round to her. "Look at them! His lordship, looking as cool as you please, and Amelia Banagher. I thought that connection was finished some time ago, I must say."

"Who is the lady, ma'am?"

"It is better for you not to know, Serena." This was said with pursed lips. "Indeed, if Miss Lucy were with us I should most certainly take you both home immediately." Then, as her love of gossip got the better of her, she leant forward and said confidentially, "Amelia Banagher comes of a highly respected Irish family. She married Lord Banagher when she was seventeen, but they haven't lived together for years, and her mode of life since has shocked everyone—though not quite enough to have her totally ostracised. Everyone knows that she was Wintersett's mistress last year, though they were discreet enough about it. They say she took it very hard when he discarded her. I wonder how she persuaded his lordship to bring her tonight? And how did she wheedle that magnificent necklace out of him?" The couple had been advancing up the room and both Serena and Mrs. Galveston could now see them more clearly. "He paid a fair penny for that, I dare say, if those rubies are real."

The sight of Lord Wintersett had given Serena an unhappy pang, but now the anger which had never been far below the surface since the night of the ball began to burn again. "They are real, and he did indeed pay a pretty penny for it, ma'am. I fancy you will recognise it when—if—they come any closer. The lady is wearing the Cardoman necklace."

Mrs. Galveston looked suitably shocked, and turned to Serena with an expression of sympathy. When she saw Serena's face her look changed to one of apprehension. Her young friend was flying flags of anger in her cheeks, and her eyes were glowing like those of a cat. "I think we should leave now, Serena," said Mrs. Galveston, sounding nervous for the first time in years.

"I would not think of it, ma'am," said Serena between her teeth. "That would carry the flavour of retreat. And I am in no such frame of mind."

It was too late in any case. Lord Wintersett was upon them and at his most urbane.

"Mrs. Galveston, your servant, ma'am. I believe you know Lady Banagher?" Unsmiling, Mrs. Galveston inclined her head by no more than a millimetre. Lord Wintersett turned to Serena. "Amelia," he said, without taking his eyes, which were glittering with malice, from Serena. "May I present Miss Calvert of Anse Chatelet? Miss Cardoman Calvert."

The two ladies exchanged what hardly passed for a curtsy. Lady Banagher raised an eyebrow. "Cardoman? Isn't that the

name—'' She fingered the ruby hanging in the cleft of her
breasts and gave Lord Wintersett a slow smile.

He took her fingers and kissed them lingeringly, then with a
sideways look at Serena said, ''I believe it is called the Cardoman necklace, my dear. Miss Calvert, was it not at one time a
valued possession of the Calvert family?''

''Hardly,'' drawled Serena. ''It belonged to us, certainly, but
the family has wanted to sell it for years. Like so many other
things, Lord Wintersett, its history is somewhat . . . tar-
nished.'' With totally spurious concern she asked, ''Oh, dear,
am I to understand you were the mysterious purchaser?''

Lady Banagher looked startled. ''But I thought it was a gift
from a king? From King Charles?'' She turned to her companion. ''You said—''

Serena swept on. ''King Charles had it made for his mistress, Lady Banagher. But there have always been so many of
those, have there not? However, I think the necklace looks
charming on you. Just right.'' Mrs. Galveston made a strangled sound and Lady Banagher at first looked uncertain, and
then her brow clouded as she began to wonder whether Serena's compliment might not be all it seemed. It was clear that
Lord Wintersett was in no doubt. His face, which had been
somewhat pale, darkened, and he said curtly, ''Come, Amelia. It's time we danced. Mrs. Galveston will forgive us. Miss
Calvert.'' He bowed and removed Amelia, who was still looking puzzled.

Mrs. Galveston regarded Serena with admiration. ''Your
great-aunt was always telling me what a spirited girl you were,
Serena—I hope you will allow me to call you Serena?—but I
must confess that when I first met you I was disappointed. But
no more. I have never seen Lord Wintersett at such a loss. My
felicitations. I think you may consider his unkind behaviour at
the duchess's ball well returned.''

Serena, still angry, said, ''I'm afraid it was ill done to involve Lady Banagher, however.'' Mrs. Galveston said something regrettable, which Serena ignored. Instead she continued,
''But you are wrong to think I was taking revenge for Lord
Wintersett's behaviour at the ball, Mrs. Galveston. That would
have been better forgotten. I am convinced that for some reason which I cannot fathom Lord Wintersett means to injure me
in any way he can. I believe he bought the necklace and put it

on his mistress in order to bring the Calvert name into disrepute."

"Oh, come, Serena. The necklace is too expensive a bauble to play with like that! It must be worth five thousand pounds at least! You must not let your imagination run away with you!"

But Serena remained unconvinced, and her suspicions were confirmed later in the evening. During one of the country dances she found herself partnered with her adversary—for that was how she now regarded him. She faced him across the set. He was pale again, and she saw now that he was thinner than he had been in Surrey. But his eyes were diamond-hard and his mouth set in ruthless lines. She remembered that she had once accused him of a lack of kindness. Now he looked . . . pitiless. They joined together to move up the room.

"I congratulate you on your rapier wit, Miss Calvert. But, for all your brave words, I think you did not enjoy seeing a necklace worn by your mother and grandmother round the neck of a harlot for all London to see," he said.

"Conceited, mad, and no gentleman, either! Fie, fie, Lord Wintersett!" she replied mockingly. "Have you forgotten that the lady is your partner for the evening, sir, when you call her such a name?" They swung away from each other, then as they returned she added, "But you may hang the necklace round all such ladies in London for all I care. It makes little difference to me. My mother died when she was not much more than twenty, so I never knew her. As far as I am aware she never wore the necklace." She smiled sweetly as they parted again, then said, as they came back together to move up the set, "So if your ambition was to cause me chagrin, your ruse has failed. An expensive mistake. Oh, but I was forgetting—the *rich* Lord Wintersett does not consider such things."

"By God, ma'am," he said in a voice of suppressed fury, "if the necklace is to be worn by a harlot, then it should be round your own neck!"

Serena was so shocked by the term he had used and the very real animosity in his voice that she stumbled and nearly fell. With relief she realised that they had come to the end of the set and she could escape.

In bed that night she lay awake asking herself over and over what had provoked that last remark. It had not been idle abuse,

she was sure. For some reason Lord Wintersett regarded her as
a Jezebel. But *why?*

JAMES RETURNED from the Assembly Rooms to Upper Brook
Street with his mind in a most unaccustomed state of turmoil.
He had planned the evening knowing that Sasha Calvert would
be at the Assembly Rooms that night. He had relished the
thought of Sasha's humiliation when the world realised that the
Calverts were being forced to sell their most prized possessions. How her Calvert family pride would resent seeing the
precious Cardoman necklace paraded before the world on such
an unworthy neck! For this he had engaged the help of his former mistress, Amelia Banagher, who had now become notorious for her numerous affairs. She was always hopelessly in
debt, and a suggestion that her ex-lover might settle some of her
more pressing bills had been enough to persuade her to accompany him, and to wear the necklace. Indeed, after the evening was over and James had escorted her back to her rooms,
there had been an awkward moment when she had made it clear
that she was ready to do more—for love. James was relieved
that he had managed to extricate himself without offending her,
for he had found the idea surprisingly repugnant. And, for all
his planning, the evening had been a failure. He had no sense
of triumph, felt no satisfaction.

He knew why. In spite of the discovery that Sasha and Serena were one and the same, he still felt a strange kinship with
Serena. He had such a strong sixth sense about her that he was
sure that his insults tonight and on other occasions had struck
home. But only once had she lost her self-possession and revealed her distress—when she had stumbled in the country
dance. And instead of being triumphant he was ashamed. His
savage outburst to Serena during that dance had not been
planned. It was the result of an unexpected surge of anger at her
steady refusal to be daunted. Since his was a nature which
needed to remain in command of himself as well as others, he
was furious at this loss of control. And then, worse still, when
she had nearly fallen he had experienced an overwhelming desire to catch her, to protect her. It was enough to drive a man
mad!

He sat now in his library, looking at the necklace. Its huge
cabochon rubies gleamed dully in the firelight—a pool of blood

in his hands. He smiled reminiscently as he thought of Serena's reaction to the sight of the necklace. It was impossible not to admire her. Few women would have responded with such spirit and wit to his insults, his attempts to diminish her in the eyes of society. She had never allowed herself to be diminished. Far from becoming discredited, she had gained society's sympathy and admiration, including his own. But what was he thinking of? How the devil could he possibly admire Sasha Calvert?

In the days that followed James was no nearer to finding peace. The thought of Serena/Sasha was like a canker, a goad, which kept him awake at night, and unable to rest during the day. He hated Sasha for her treatment of Tony, and he hated Serena for being Sasha. He despised himself for being so confused, for wishing to punish Sasha, while taking pride in Serena when she frustrated his efforts.

He went back to Surrey, thinking that his determination to discredit Sasha Calvert would be strengthened if he had another talk with Alanna, if he reminded himself of the unhappiness the Calvert woman had caused his family. But in Surrey he found himself going for long rides on the Downs, taking Douce on to the ridge, where he was haunted by the memory of "William", of their talks, their arguments, their shared laughter. He remembered with bitterness his fears that he would lose Serena in London. As he had. He was tormented by the two contrasting pictures—on the one hand Serena, a woman of intelligence and compassion with an integrity he had never questioned, and on the other Sasha, the destroyer, the wanton. And this visit to Surrey, far from strengthening his determination, seemed to be undermining it, for doubts began to creep into his mind. In his initial shock and blind anger at discovering that Serena and Sasha were one and the same he had not attempted to set one against the other—Serena's good against Sasha's evil. But was it *possible* for the Serena he had known to have done the things Sasha was said to have done on the island? Perhaps she had changed? Perhaps Tony's death had caused her to reform? She must have been very young... in fact, *very* young! He must talk to Alanna again. But he could not bring himself to mention Serena to Alanna—only Sasha.

"Sasha Calvert told me recently that her mother was only twenty when she died, Alanna. However I try, I cannot recon-

cile this with the age of her brothers. Surely Richard Calvert
was older than Tony?''

''Yes. Yes, he was.'' Alanna's voice was nervous. ''Did I not
tell you? I thought I had. Lord Calvert was married twice. The
Sasha woman was the daughter of the second marriage.''

''So how old was she when you were on the island?''

''Why are you asking me? What are you trying to do,
James?''

''Merely to establish some facts. How old was she?''

''I don't know! What does it matter?'' said Alanna petulantly. ''Old enough! Sixteen or seventeen, I think.''

''She once said she was now twenty-seven. That would make
her fourteen.''

''Fourteen, fifteen, seventeen! Am I a mathematician?
You've been spending too much time with Miss Calvert! I told
you what would happen. She's such a liar, she will bewitch you
as she bewitched Tony... Oh, Tony, Tony!'' Alanna burst into
loud sobs.

James waited until she was quieter, then said, ''Fourteen is
not much more than a child, Alanna. I find it difficult to
imagine Tony deserting you in favour of a child.''

''You don't know what they're like in the tropics, James!''
Alanna said between further sobs. ''The women mature at a
ridiculously early age. Many of the natives have children at
thirteen or even less! And she—Sasha—ran practically wild all
over the island—she must have had her morals from them.''
She burst out, ''Why are you asking these questions? I tell you
she never left him alone! Poor Tony had no chance. Dear God,
why do you remind me?''

Alanna was now very distressed. She clutched at James,
pleading, ''Get rid of her for me, James! Have nothing more
to do with her, but get her sent back to where she belongs, I beg
you!''

Disguising his distaste for her melodrama, James said patiently, ''Be calm, Alanna. It takes time.''

With an exclamation of despair Alanna ran out of the room,
leaving James with the feeling that, if she had enacted these
tragedies thirteen years before, he for one did not blame his
brother for seeking consolation elsewhere. He told himself that
women were often temperamental when they were breeding—
had Alanna chased Tony into the arms of Sasha Calvert by her
own irrational behaviour? With an exclamation of impatience

he realised that even now he was seeking excuses for the unhappy business. Alanna was probably right. Sasha Calvert had power to make a man believe anything!

BEFORE THE incident in the Assembly Rooms, Serena would have been content to go through the rest of the season accepting that Lord Wintersett no longer wished to continue their friendship, and learning to live without it. She had reluctantly concluded that the fact that she came from the Colonies, and her irregular conduct at the outset of their acquaintance—dressing as a boy and roaming the countryside—had caused him to have second thoughts when they met in more formal circumstances. The explanation was not completely satisfactory. The charm with which he had first greeted her, his compliments in the winter garden—these had seemed real enough. And that dance... Her thoughts shied away from the dance. But his behaviour afterwards had been so extraordinarily cruel! Then she heard more stories of Lord Wintersett's summary dismissal of females who pursued him, his heartlessness in other matters, too, and she finally accepted his treatment of her as not untypical. What she found impossible was to reconcile the man in London with the man she had known in Surrey.

But now the situation had changed. That he or anyone else should dare to insult her by calling her a harlot was not to be borne! Not without some action on her part. She had no male protector to call on—the nearest approach to that was Lord Ambourne, and not only was her claim on him too slight, but he was also on the other side of the Channel. Besides, she had no wish to create further scandal by calling on an outsider for protection. However, the thought of Lord Ambourne brought the Dowager Countess to her mind. She would see if she could consult Lady Ambourne.

Accordingly Serena took the Countess at her word and called on her in Arlington Street. As Lady Ambourne had said, Rotherfield House was imposing rather than homelike, but Serena was led through the huge state-rooms to the back of the house, where there was a small garden-room. Here her hostess was sitting on a comfortable sofa and she insisted that Serena should sit by her side. They talked for a while, but finally the Countess sat back and, putting her head on one side, said, "I have enjoyed our chat, Miss Calvert, but you shall now tell me what is exercising your mind. If I can be of any assistance to you, you have only to ask." Serena looked amazed and the Countess laughed. "You look just like my daughter-in-law!" she said. "Perdita swears I have second sight. But it isn't so. It was obvious to me that you were not entirely happy when we last met. Today you are angry, too. What is it, child? Begin from the beginning."

Serena found to her astonishment that she was telling Lady Ambourne everything—her restlessness in Surrey after the freedom of her life on St. Just, her expeditions to the Downs disguised as a boy, and her meeting with Lord Wintersett. She took care not to mention his name for she had decided that no purpose could be served by revealing it. And she had, besides, this ridiculous inability to say it! Her voice, which had been soft and warm as she had talked of her relationship with the gentleman in Surrey, grew more agitated as she went on to describe the gentleman's behaviour since. She omitted to say anything about the necklace, but told her listener the substance of the insult during the country dance. "I am at a loss to explain it, Lady Ambourne. The gentleman's animosity is real. But he called me . . . called me . . ."

Lady Ambourne said the word for her. "A harlot."

"And he has no reason to suppose that I am anything of the kind!" cried Serena angrily. "Our relationship on the Downs was totally innocent—more that of a boy and his mentor. I just don't understand! What am I to do?"

Lady Ambourne sat in thought for a moment. Then she said gravely, "It is obvious to me that there must be more behind Lord Wintersett's behaviour than you have told me." When Serena gasped she added, "Please do not misunderstand, Miss Calvert. I do not believe for a moment that you are wilfully hiding anything of substance from me."

"It's not that," said Serena faintly. "How did you know I was talking of . . ." She exclaimed impatiently as she once again found herself unable to say his name.

The Countess smiled. "My dear child, I have known London society these past thirty years or more."

"I suppose everyone is talking about us." Serena's voice was bitter.

"There is naturally some gossip, yes. But I have heard nothing of what you have told me this afternoon—of Surrey and so on. And on the whole, you know, opinion in general is in your

favour—if that is any comfort. Lord Wintersett is not univer-
sally liked.''

"Do you know him?''

"I'm afraid he is a great friend of my son's. They were at
school together.''

In some confusion Serena started to gather herself together.
"In that case, you must forgive me, Lady Ambourne. I am
sorry to have caused you embarrassment. I . . . I must go.''

"What are you thinking of, child? Edward's friendship with
Lord Wintersett does not mean that I am blind to that gentleman's faults—any more than I am blind to Edward's faults. In
some ways they are very similar. Oh, yes. I assure you they are!
They can both be completely ruthless when it suits them—and
they can be cruel. But Edward has been more fortunate than
James. He was surrounded in his youth by a loving family, and
he now enjoys a very happy marriage. James, on the other
hand, had a tyrant for a father, and his family circumstances
since his father's death have been most unhappy.''

"Is there no one he loves?''

"There are, or were, two. One is his mother, whose devotion was divided between her husband and her younger son. I
have always thought that it says much for the basic soundness
of James's nature that the other person he loved was this same
younger brother. But he is now dead.''

"What happened to him?''

"He died abroad some years ago at about the time James
came into the title. His mother has never properly recovered
from her double loss.''

"Do you like him, ma'am?''

"I think I do. Edward is a good judge of men, and though
James is generally held to be coldhearted I think this is not really so. But it would certainly not be easy to find out. Of one
thing I am certain. He is a just man.''

"Then why is he so cruel to me?''

"I do not know, but there must be some reason which he
thinks justifies his behaviour. Are you sure, quite sure, you
cannot think of anything?'' Serena shook her head. "No. Well,
I shall do my best to find out. Will you allow me to make some
discreet enquiries?''

Serena took her leave a little later, after arranging to call on
the Countess again in three days' time.

WHEN SERENA CALLED at Rotherfield House again three days later she found the Countess in an unusually grave mood.

"Miss Calvert, I think I have at least found a previous connection between your family and Lord Wintersett. If you remember, I mentioned a younger brother who died abroad some time ago." She looked penetratingly at Serena.

"Yes?" Serena was puzzled.

"I am somewhat surprised that you do not seem to know that he died on St. Just."

"Oh, no! Forgive me, Lady Ambourne, but that cannot be so. If it were true I would have known of it. Nothing ever happened on St. Just without my knowledge!"

"His name was Tony," Lady Ambourne continued. "Tony Stannard."

In a voice that was almost unrecognisable Serena said, *"Tony Stannard* is—was—Lord Wintersett's brother?" Lady Ambourne nodded. "Oh, God!" Serena buried her face in her hands.

There was a silence. Finally Serena lifted her head and whispered, "I had no notion . . . I simply did not connect the two names."

"That is obvious, my child. However, the link is as yet slight. There is little in the fact that Mr. Stannard died on St. Just to account for Lord Wintersett's enmity."

Serena drew a long shuddering sigh and said, "What have you learned of his death, Lady Ambourne? What does London say?"

Lady Ambourne was still grave. "It was reported that he fell victim to a tropical disease."

Serena got up and moved restlessly about the room. "Tony Stannard! Poor, poor Tony! And a Wintersett! Oh yes! I understand now." She stopped in front of the Countess, who was looking as if she had more to say. "What is it, Lady Ambourne? Why do you look like that?"

"There are rumours that the circumstances of Tony Stannard's death were not as reported." Serena turned away, but the voice with its charming French accent continued relentlessly. "Rumour says that the young man killed himself. No one seems to know why, however."

Serena remained silent.

The Countess appeared to be choosing her words carefully as she said, "You came to me for help and advice, Miss Calvert. I would not normally press you to reveal anything you do not wish, but it seems to me that the cause of Lord Wintersett's enmity must lie in his brother's death. You have already confided a great deal of your story. Do you feel able to tell me anything more? I think I have no need to assure you of my discretion."

Serena thought for a moment. "I cannot discuss Tony Stannard's death, Lady Ambourne—not even with you," she said slowly. "But if it will not weary you, I will tell you something of the events which led up to it. They might well go towards explaining Lord Wintersett's enmity, for they reflect little credit on the Calverts. Though I should have thought it would be directed rather towards my family than to me . . ."

"My memory is very accommodating. I shall remember only what I need to know in order to help you. I should be extremely surprised if there is anything to your detriment in the story."

"There is one aspect of which I am ashamed. But I will tell you, all the same."

The Countess sent for some tea and told Purkiss that she was not to be disturbed for an hour. Serena was soon launched into the unhappy story of the Stannards' visit to St. Just.

"My father had heard through a Cambridge friend that Tony Stannard wished to study tropical plants, so he invited the Stannards to St. Just, and offered them the hospitality of Anse Chatelet. Tony Stannard was newly married when he came to stay. His wife, Alanna, was quite young and very pretty—I think she was Irish—and at first they seemed to be devoted to each other. But after a while she started to complain—she didn't like the heat, she didn't like the insects, she was afraid of what the sun would do to her complexion. It wasn't what she had been used to, I suppose. Perhaps even more, it wasn't what she had looked for in marrying Tony Stannard. I gathered that the family was quite rich, and she had hoped to play a leading role in society."

"It was natural, I suppose. A young girl, pretty, married to a rich man. Surely she could reasonably expect a fashionable life?"

Serena shook her head. "I was still quite young at the time, but even I could see that the study of plants was Tony's life. He was a brilliant botanist, you know. It was obvious that the fashionable world was not for him. But Alanna Stannard was not really at all interested in Tony's work, and she soon gave up accompanying Tony on his expeditions into the rain forest. I must confess I was secretly glad.''

"Why?" asked the Countess, opening her eyes wide. "What had it to do with you?"

"I used to guide Tony on his expeditions. I knew the island better than anyone. If Mrs. Stannard came with us we were constantly having to stop—to rest, to help her across a stream, to clear a wider path ... And we had to carry all sorts of extra supplies—creams and lotions, cushions and rugs, water, wine. We were always having to stop for picnics. You can imagine how impatient a child would get with all this."

"So Alanna stayed at home?"

"Yes. She remained all day on the veranda, feeling, no doubt, that she was being treated very ill. You will observe," said Serena with an apologetic smile, "that I was not particularly fond of the lady."

"I had noticed," said the Countess with a smile. "But tell me—now that you are older and have more understanding, do you not feel some sympathy for her?"

Serena thought for a moment, then said, "I don't know. What happened afterwards makes it impossible to judge."

"Pray continue."

"First I need to digress a little, to give you some background. What do you know of the West Indian islands, Lady Ambourne?"

"Not very much. St. Just is one of the smaller ones, is that correct? As you know, Henry Pendomer is a second or third cousin of Edward's, so all my knowledge comes from him. He's the Governor of St. Just. But doesn't he look after some other islands as well?"

"Yes. Sir Henry governs a number of the smaller islands together. In fact, he only spends about four months a year on St. Just."

"And?"

"Thirteen years ago, when the Stannards came to stay at Anse Chatelet, my father was still strong and active. The Calverts have lived on St. Just since the days before there was a Governor there at all, and until very recently they have always regarded the island and its people more or less as their own. The islanders looked on my father as a sort of uncrowned king, and my ... my ... brother Richard regarded himself as the Crown

Prince." Serena was finding this more difficult than she had thought, but the steady, sympathetic gaze of the Countess encouraged her to carry on. "We all loved Richard. We were dazzled by him. I was his shadow, his slave, always trying to ride as well as Richard, to shoot as well as Richard . . . I had no other friend, wanted no other companion." She sighed. "He was always causing trouble, yet he would charm his way out of it all. He had such an infectious smile—you would find yourself laughing when a minute before you had sworn you would never speak to him again. And women . . . they were fascinated by him. It's difficult to explain . . ."

"You have no need. I have met someone quite like him, Serena."

Serena looked doubtful, but carried on. "It ruined him. The adulation, the feeling that he could do anything...anything at all, the lack of any restraint . . . I think that if he had had to struggle for what he had, if there had been a war he could have fought in, a cause he believed in, he might have been saved. But there wasn't. And finally he was overtaken by his demons . . . Even my father rejected him in the end..." Her voice faded and she paused. Then she squared her shoulders and said in a clearer voice, "I was telling you about the Stannards. About Alanna Stannard. A pretty, new face on St. Just was just the sort of challenge Richard enjoyed. He was never satisfied until he had conquered, and Alanna Stannard was instantly an object of desire."

"And she . . . ?"

"I think you must know the answer to that, Lady Ambourne. Mrs. Stannard was lonely, bored, and feeling resentful towards her husband for his neglect of her. She spent long hours alone. Whenever Richard set out to charm anyone he was irresistible. In this case the end was inevitable, I suppose."

"Was there no one to stop them, to talk to Alanna?"

"No one. The Pendomers had just left St. Just for their tour of the other islands. By the time they returned it was all over."

"And no one else? What about your father?"

"Until the final, dreadful end, my father could never see any wrong in Richard. And I was a child—I didn't even realise what was going on until father told me later, when he thought I was old enough. Apart from that, I was out most of the time with Tony Stannard. I knew the island and its inhabitants so well, you see. I knew where the interesting plants were."

"Poor Alanna!"

"Why do you say that? Alanna at least returned alive to England. Richard and Tony are both dead."

"But Alanna's baby was born prematurely, and the child is still an invalid even now. Alanna never sought the gaiety of London life, but has lived in retirement in Surrey, looking after her son, ever since she returned. But you say your brother Richard died, too?"

"He fell two hundred feet from a cliff path near Anse Chatelet. We found his body the next day on the rocks below." Serena shut her eyes and when she opened them again they were full of anguish. "I blame myself for his death," she said in a whisper.

The Countess put a sympathetic hand out and would have spoken, but Serena continued, "Did you...did you say that Alanna had a child, Lady Ambourne? After she came back from the island?"

"Of course. He is Wintersett's heir."

"But—" Serena stopped abruptly. "No. No matter." She got up again and looked out at the gardens. Then she added bitterly, "I wish I had never come to England! If it were not for Lucy I would return to the West Indies tomorrow!"

"Come, come, this is no way to talk!" The Countess led her back to the sofa. "We have now accounted for Lord Wintersett's unfriendliness. It is, I suppose, natural that he should dislike the name of Calvert, but I think I can talk him into a more reasonable frame of mind. He might even call later this afternoon."

Serena said slowly, "I am not sure we have quite accounted for it. What he called me was specific, not a slur on my family as a whole."

"Then he must explain himself," said the Countess briskly. "Unless... No, he is surely not such a fool! Can he believe perhaps you...er...consoled Tony for his wife's disloyalty? You were with him a great deal, were you not? No, no! It is too absurd!"

"Indeed it is, I think—even for him! I was fourteen years old—a child! Probably even younger than most girls of that age. I regarded Tony simply as a wonderful source of knowledge—no, of marvels. He was a born teacher, and I was thirsty for anything he could tell me about the plants and trees of my own home."

"Of course, of course. There must be another explanation."

CHAPTER EIGHT

WHILE SERENA'S conversation with Lady Ambourne was taking place Lord Wintersett was making his way to Rotherfield House in response to an invitation from the Countess. He had arrived in London two days before and had found Lady Ambourne's note, together with a letter from Bradpole requesting an interview. The lawyer had arrived the next day with a folder of documents and the news that the substitute manager on Anse Chatelet had indeed defaulted on the payments, and that the agent in Barbados had foreclosed as ordered. "I have the documents here. They only require your lordship's signature." He spread some legal papers out on the table. "Er... Norret, the manager, has pleaded that he was unaware how important it was to get the quarterly payment in on the exact day, and further, that unfavourable winds and tropical storms delayed his journey to Barbados. He is supported in his plea by Lord Pendomer, the Governor of St. Just. I am aware that I risk your anger in saying this, Lord Wintersett, but I will say it just the same. It can do you no credit to foreclose on what is in effect a technicality. I hope you will consider changing your instructions to the agent, and restoring Anse Chatelet to its former owners." He waited, but James was deep in thought. The lawyer sighed and continued, "However, if you remain obdurate, the documents are here."

James was in a quandary. For years he had sought possession of Anse Chatelet with the sole aim of evicting the Calverts. The estate was now his, if he insisted—but he could not quite bring himself to let the axe fall. He thanked Bradpole brusquely for his news, and told him to come back in a week for his decision. Bradpole's face, which had been very serious, lightened when he received this indication that his client might be reconsidering his course of action.

James was still pondering this question as he made his way to Rotherfield House. But as he drew nearer to Arlington Street he began to speculate on the reason for Lady Ambourne's invitation. Ned, he knew, was still in France, so it was not to meet him. Strange! He was however very willing to visit the Dowager Countess, for he had always found her a sympathetic and amusing hostess. He arrived promptly at the appointed hour and was received by Purkiss.

It was at this point that Purkiss, the Ambournes' elderly and experienced butler, made his worst mistake in all his years of service. The lapse occurred when the visitor presented himself at the door of Rotherfield House, gave Purkiss his hat and cane, and said easily, "You needn't bother to announce me, Purkiss. Is Lady Ambourne in the garden-room? Right, I'll go through."

Normally the butler would have frozen such informality on the spot, but Lord Wintersett had been a familiar figure in the house since he had first arrived in an Eton jacket many years before. Purkiss also knew that her ladyship was expecting him, and that she wished her two visitors to meet. It was true that she had told the butler when he had taken refreshments in earlier that she was not to be disturbed for an hour, but that had been almost an hour and a half before. So Purkiss allowed Lord Wintersett to carry on, without first making sure that her ladyship was ready for him . . .

JAMES STRODE confidently through the state rooms, but went more slowly as he drew nearer to the garden room. He could hear voices—the Countess had a visitor, it seemed. He stopped short, astounded, when he realised that the voice was Serena's. What was the Countess up to? She had been in London for some time now—she must know something of the situation between Serena and himself! Was she trying to effect some sort of reconciliation, perhaps because of Ned's position in this? Was that why he had been invited?

Then he heard Serena say, "It's true that I pursued Tony Stannard relentlessly. All over the island." There was a smile in Serena's voice. "I suppose I had a bad attack of hero worship! At first he didn't take much notice of me. I was just an importunate child, a nuisance! But then, as time went on, he learned to tolerate my company and even to enjoy it! In the end we became surprisingly close. I think you could even say that I loved him, after a fashion.''

James's first impulse was to turn on his heel and stride back the way he had come. His second was to continue into the garden room and demand to know why his brother was being discussed. He was on the point of doing this when he stopped abruptly. The Countess had just asked ''I suppose you were missing Richard's company?''

''I suppose it might have begun like that. But at one time Tony seemed as important to me as Richard.''

''You haven't told me why you felt responsible for his death?''

James found himself holding his breath. What would Serena say?

''It was what I said to him shortly before . . . before he d . . . died. I was in a rage—I've always had a hot temper and this time I was in a fury. I told him . . . I told him I despised him. That he'd be better dead.'' Her voice dropped so that James had to lean forward to hear. ''And he was dead, very soon after that.'' There was a silence. Then Serena said unevenly, ''Why did I say such things to him?''

There was a rustle of silks, and Lady Ambourne's voice was soft as she said, ''But you were little more than a child! How were you to know that your words would have such a catastrophic effect?''

''He no longer saw me as a child. What I said affected him mortally. He had heard my father telling him he had no future on the island or anywhere else, and he looked to me, sure that I would comfort him. We had been so close! But suddenly I felt I hated him and wanted him to know it. It is my belief that my rejection of him that night caused his death.''

''My dear! How can you blame yourself? You surely did not really wish him dead!''

''Lady Ambourne, please do not misunderstand me. I regretted his death and still regret it . . . the Calverts do not seem to have had a happy hour since that dreadful time. But even now I cannot feel that there was any other way out for him. I only wish that I had never uttered the words which drove him to it. I think they will be on my conscience forever!''

James turned and went back the way he had come. When he reached the entrance hall he gave Purkiss a message to deliver to Lady Ambourne, something about urgent business elsewhere. The message was confused, for his mind was on what he had just heard. Sasha Calvert was a self-confessed adulteress, a woman who had driven Tony to his death, and whose chief regret was that this had made the Calverts unhappy! That and her uneasy conscience! It was enough to remove any doubt about Anse Chatelet—and more! He sent for Mr. Bradpole that night.

ALANNA STANNARD sat in the window of the drawing room and gazed out resentfully at the green lawns and flower-filled rose-beds of Wintersett Court. The London season was now at its height. How she would have loved to be part of that colourful parade! For thirteen weary years she had lived here in retire-ment, miles away from any kind of amusement. She had de-voted her energies to looking after her son, with only a half-witted mother-in-law for company and an occasional visit from her formidable brother-in-law to enliven the monotony. She sighed. At first it had been easy, for it had seemed a suitable atonement for her sins. Then she had grown discontented. She still was, but now she was feeling more nervous with every day that passed.

For years she had lived with the lies she had told of her so-journ on St. Just, and, though she had never been really happy, she had at least felt secure. Her word had never been doubted by her husband's family. Not only were the West Indies thousands of miles away—far enough to discourage casual communication—but it had been in the interests of both fam-ilies to hide the truth as each had seen it. The Stannards had believed they were protecting Tony's memory from the shame of betraying his pregnant wife, and the Calverts had probably wished to protect their own family from the scandal of Rich-ard's seduction of a guest. The facts surrounding Tony's death had therefore been well concealed by both families. All this had worked to Alanna's benefit.

But now, with the advent of Sasha Calvert in London, Alanna's world was suddenly threatened. She was living on a precipice. She had done her best to prevent any meeting be-tween James and the Calvert woman, but her efforts had failed. James had clearly been talking to her in London, and had re-cently shown signs of doubt, had even come down to Winter-sett Court to question Alanna further. Any day now he might ask Sasha Calvert directly about the events on St. Just thirteen years before, and what would happen then? Alanna shifted in her seat uneasily. Surely he would take the word of his own sister-in-law, the mother of his heir, against that of a Calvert? Of course he would!

Alanna got up, fetched her hat and parasol, and went outside. But though the sun was warm, she shivered. What if James didn't take his sister-in-law's word? Her old friend from Ireland, Amelia Banagher, had told her how well society regarded Serena Calvert, as she now called herself, in spite of James's efforts to discredit her. Amelia, who had not enjoyed the débâcle with the necklace, had also hinted that James was more impressed than he admitted. How stupid men were! These small tricks with necklaces and suchlike were useless! Something outstanding was needed, something to ruin Sasha Calvert once and for all! Then no one would believe her, whatever she said, and she would go back to her West Indian island and be forgotten! Alanna already had a half-formed plan in her head. It required a little more thought, for failure would be disastrous, and then she would see what could be done. But she would need help . . . Alanna decided to write to Amelia.

WHILE ALANNA Stannard was plotting to do mischief to Serena, Serena herself was doing her best to promote Lucy's interests. She had never before put into words her feeling of anguish and guilt about her brother's death. Now, though Lord Wintersett's dislike was still only half explained, she felt better for having unburdened herself to the sympathetic ear of the Countess, and felt ready to put her own problems aside for a while and concentrate on Lucy. Michael Warnham had become most particular in his attentions, and Serena was taking pains to get to know him. He was certainly an eligible candidate—twenty-three, heir to a barony, and certain to inherit a large share of his grandmother's considerable fortune. Isabella, his sister, was Lucy's great friend, and the Warnhams appeared to approve of a possible match. Serena found him pleasant and amusing, but she was not yet certain that he had enough strength of character to retain the respect of her high-spirited niece. If he had not, it would be a sure recipe for an unhappy marriage. So for the moment Serena was keeping an open mind. Lucy seemed to find much to admire in Mr. Warnham, and Serena was amused to see how willing her niece was to defer to his judgement. There might be more to this young man than she had thought!

Her efforts on Lucy's behalf had led her into attending more balls, concerts and assemblies than she would otherwise have wished. She had always intended to keep in the background, leaving Lady Warnham and Mrs. Galveston to chaperon the two girls. But in order to meet Michael Warnham, to observe him in company with Lucy, she had to take an active part in society. She was aware that Lord Wintersett's eyes were frequently turned on her, sometimes brooding, sometimes with an unaccountable gleam of satisfaction, but she never allowed herself to be put off. Serena was proving to be a minor success.

One evening, at a reception given by the French Ambassador, Serena was delighted to see the Countess of Ambourne approaching. The Countess was accompanied by an extremely handsome man in his thirties, dark-haired and grey-eyed.

"Ah, Serena!" she cried. "I have such a pleasant surprise for you! I wish you to meet my son Edward."

Lord Ambourne smiled quizzically as he bowed. "My mother has her own quaint way of putting things, Miss Calvert. You must forgive her. The pleasant surprise is mine, I assure you!"

Serena laughed and curtseyed. "Lord Ambourne, I would forgive your mother anything. She has been so kind to me—as you have, too. I find your house in Dover Street delightful."

"The house belongs to my wife. I am pleased you like it."

"Then I must thank her. Is she with you?"

"She is in London, but not with us tonight. She was a little tired after the journey."

"I am sure Perdita would wish to meet you as soon as possible, Serena. I shall arrange it," said the Countess. "But have you yet spoken to the Ambassador? Come, let me take you to him—he will be intrigued to meet someone from the West Indies. He has estates on Martinique, you know."

"Ma'am," protested Serena. "His Excellency surely has more important people to speak to tonight?"

"That shows you do not know him! Now me, I have known him since we were children, and I assure you he will always take time to talk to a beautiful woman." The two ladies, escorted by Lord Ambourne, made their way through the crowded rooms into the Ambassador's presence. His Excellency received the Countess with cries of pleasure, and they talked rapidly in French for several minutes. Then he turned to Lord Ambourne and asked most kindly after his family and his estate in Normandy. Finally he turned to Serena, who was amused to find that the Countess could perform rigorously correct introductions when she chose.

"Miss Calvert," said the Ambassador, "I am enchanted. Is it too much to hope that you will dance with me? We could talk about Martinique and St. Just."

Serena looked somewhat apprehensively at the Countess, who nodded encouragingly. "I am honoured, Ambassador," she replied with another curtsy.

The Ambassador proved to be an excellent dancer and an amusing companion. Serena was enjoying herself enormously when halfway through the waltz an aide came up to him and said something discreet. The Ambassador pulled a face. "Miss Calvert, I am desolate. Duty spoils my pleasure. But do not worry, I shall leave you in good hands." He looked round to the gentleman who had been standing by them. "Ah, yes! May I present the gentleman who has been described to me as the best dancer in London, Miss Calvert? Lord Wintersett! You are more fortunate than you deserve, milor'!" With a smile and a graceful bow the Ambassador was gone. Serena and James were left facing one another on the edge of the floor.

James bowed. His face was cold. "Miss Calvert?"

"Please forgive me, Lord Wintersett," said Serena, equally coldly. "It was kind of the Ambassador to think I wanted to carry on dancing. But I find I am tired, and I must return to my companions. They will be looking for me—" She turned to go, but was held firmly.

"I think you do not understand, Miss Calvert. A request from an ambassador is the equivalent of a royal command. You must dance with me, however repugnant the idea is—to either of us."

They set off in silence. For a while they circled the room carefully, avoiding anything but the slightest contact, but as time went on they each relaxed. They drew imperceptibly closer, James's hand more firmly at Serena's waist, Serena's hand resting more confidently on his shoulder. Serena shut her eyes. It was like the first time she had danced with this man— the same strange mixture of excitement and certainty, the same feeling of wordless communication. What James Stannard thought about her she could not begin to guess. But whatever it was, it had no effect on what she, deep down, had come to feel for him when they were in Surrey. It was astonishing, but nothing that had happened since had changed that. It seemed to have become part of the fabric of her being. Unwilling to continue with this melancholy train of thought, Serena opened her eyes. James was looking down at her with a bemused look in his eyes, as if he, too, was remembering their idyll.

Encouraged, Serena smiled, tentatively at first, then as his gaze softened she said hesitantly, "Our friend William—Blake the poet, not Blake the boy from the hill—has words for this situation, I think. Will you listen?"

"What are they?" he said, still looking at her with a smile in his eyes. She began, "'I was angry with my friend, I told my wrath—'" But she was interrupted before she could go any further.

"'My wrath did end'?" The smile vanished. His face changed once more to that of an implacable enemy. His hand gripped hers cruelly as he said softly, "I think not, Sasha! You do not escape so lightly, for all your wiles! And recalling our relationship in happier times will not help you, either. You deserve no privilege of friendship."

"But *why* do I not deserve it? Why will you not discuss it with me?" In spite of herself her voice had risen.

"I suggest that you control yourself, Sasha Calvert. Unless you wish us to be the subject of yet more gossip? That would suit me better than it would you, I believe."

The waltz came to an end, and the other dancers started to leave the floor. Serena began to follow them, but then stopped, turned to Lord Wintersett and said with determination, "I *will* have it out with you! Here, if you will not find a more suitable place!"

He looked at her with a twisted smile on his face. "Why is it that you can rouse my admiration, even though I know you for what you are? You are unique!" He took her arm and led her off the floor. "Come!" he said, and opening the door of a small salon he ushered her into it. Serena just had time to see Lady Ambourne's troubled gaze before Lord Wintersett shut the door. "Now?"

Serena turned and faced him steadily. "Lord Wintersett, I will not refer again to our 'relationship in happier times.' That

period of my life shall be forgotten. I claim no 'privilege of
friendship,' either—indeed, when we first met in London, and
you behaved so...in such an ungentlemanly manner, I believed that my behaviour in Surrey had given you a disgust of
me. I could not account for the sudden change in your conduct towards me in any other way! But there must be more to
it. This antipathy, no, it is much more than that—this personal animosity puzzles and distresses me. I cannot account for
it. I wish you to tell me its cause!''

''Bravely said! If a little disingenuous. You already know
why.''

''You hold the Calverts responsible for your brother's
death?''

''The other Calverts are all dead themselves. I hold you responsible, you alone, Miss Calvert.''

''But this is prejudiced nonsense! I loved Tony! I never
meant him any harm!'' When he turned away from her with an
expression of disgust, she cried desperately, ''Help me to understand! They call you a just man—hard, but just. Why are
you going to such lengths to punish *me*?''

''You do not yet know to what lengths I am prepared to go,
Sasha Calvert!'' The expression in his eyes as he turned back
to face her was so malevolent that she took a step back.

''You hate me!'' she whispered. ''I believe you really hate
me. Oh, God! How could I be so deceived? To think I once
imagined I could actually love you!''

''Love! I would sooner be loved by a loathsome toad! What
could you possibly know about love? I've heard you talk of the
kind of love you offer! A love that tells a desperate man that he
is despised! A love that drives a man to his death!''

For a moment Serena was taken aback. The words were so
familiar. Then it came to her. ''You were there! At Rotherfield
House. You must have been eavesdropping! Eavesdropping on
my conversation with Lady Ambourne. How dare you?'' Serena was fast losing her temper. The thought that this man had
listened unseen to the confession of her deepest, most painful
feelings about her brother's death outraged her.

She lost control altogether when she heard him say, ''This
moral stance sits ill on a harlot, Sasha!''

Something inside Serena exploded and she slapped Lord
Wintersett with the full force of her arm behind the blow. He
instantly grabbed her to him and kissed her hard. She tried to

scream, but he held her mouth to his, so that she could hardly breathe. Her struggles to escape were futile, for his arms trapped her in an iron grasp. She felt sick. This kiss was worse, much worse than the first embrace on the hill, for though that had lacked any respect, this had not the slightest element of more tender feelings in it. Anger, a desire for revenge, a primitive lust, but no regard for her, not the slightest hint of any feeling for her as a person. When he finally released her she was so dizzy that she was unable to stand, and he had to hold her again to save her from falling. She stood rigidly, staring at him in horror, unable to hide her fear and revulsion. His face was white to the lips, a dazed look in his eyes.

"I...I...I don't know what to say, Serena. I don't know what came over me..."

She managed at last to move away from him, to walk to the door like a sleepwalker.

"Serena!" She stopped, but did not turn round. "Serena, it was never my intention to attack you in that barbaric manner. I am sorry, deeply sorry."

"I believe you," Serena said harshly. "You would rather kiss a loathsome toad, you said. But you k...kissed me just the same. Do you think that saying you are sorry can wipe it from my memory?" She put her hand on the doorknob.

He continued desperately, "If you go out of the room now, looking as you do, the whole of London will be scandalised."

Serena turned round then and looked at him ironically. "Do you not think London should be scandalised at the punctilious Lord Wintersett behaving like a savage, a wild beast?"

"I am ashamed of my behaviour, Serena. I deserve your scorn and theirs. But even you must agree that I was provoked. Do you not think London would be equally scandalised at Miss Calvert using her fists like an untamed gipsy? No, wait! I am not concerned for myself in this instance. It is you I wish to spare. Wait a short while, please. Give yourself time to recover. You cannot wish to arouse the sort of comment I am sure would otherwise follow."

She looked at him incredulously. He meant it! "What are you at now, Lord Wintersett? I was under the impression that that was precisely what you wanted!"

"Not in this instance. This was no part of my plan. I...I do not know what came over me. I will say once again that I deeply regret what I did, and ask you to forgive me—"

He stopped as Lord Ambourne and his mother came into the room, leaving the door open. The Countess went quickly over to a door in the wall on the right and unlocked it. A maid entered. Then Lady Ambourne took Serena by the hand, and said in a slightly raised voice, "Gracious, Serena, you look ill, child. How thoughtful of Lord Wintersett to bring you in here when you felt faint! I am sure Marie was a help until I managed to come. I am only sorry that Lord Wintersett's message did not reach me sooner. I have informed Mrs. Galveston that I will take you home, and she will stay with Lucy and her friends. Thank you, Marie, you may help Miss Calvert to her feet." She whispered, "Forgive the French farce, Serena! It's the best I can do to prevent scandal. You have been closeted with Lord Wintersett for some minutes, and the tongues are wagging outside. We need not tell them that Marie has only just arrived! I've told her to swear she was here all the time."

Lord Ambourne was giving his friend a long, straight look. As the little party made its way to Lady Ambourne's carriage he said coolly, "Shall you be at home tomorrow evening, James? May I call on you? I think we have things to discuss."

THE NEXT DAY was sunny, but there was a cool breeze which sent the remaining blossom on the trees in Green Park drifting over into the garden of Rotherfield House. The Ambourne family were sitting in the garden room. The window doors were wide open to let in the air, while those sitting on the pretty sofas and chairs were protected from the wind. The younger Lady Ambourne was laughing up into her husband's face as he spread a shawl over her knees.

"Stop, Edward!" she protested. "I am not cold, not in the slightest. Nor am I any longer tired! There is no reason on earth why I should not visit Miss Calvert as soon as I am respectably dressed! I wish to meet her!"

Serena heard this as she followed Purkiss through to the garden-room and she thought what an attractive picture they made. Lord Ambourne's dark head was bent over the sofa on which his wife was lying, and she was stretching her hand out towards him. The expression on his face belied his next words.

"Perdita, I am already angry with you for coming downstairs while I was out! Dr. Parker expressly forbade it."

"Pooh! You are tyrants, you and Dr. Parker both, and it will do neither of you any good to be pandered to. Do you not agree, Mama?"

"Yes, but you know Edward will have his way, Perdita. Except . . ."

"I knew it! What are you plotting?"

"I believe my plot is already here. The mountain has come to Mahomet," said the Dowager Countess, rising with a hand stretched out in welcome to Serena. She dismissed Purkiss with a nod and brought Serena forward to her daughter-in-law's couch.

"My mother surpasses herself. The metaphor is not even apt yet for Perdita. But now you may have the pleasant surprise of meeting my wife, Miss Calvert," said the Earl with a grin. Serena looked down at a woman of about her own age with eyes of the darkest blue she had ever seen. The younger Lady Ambourne was as beautiful as her lord was handsome, and together they made a striking couple. It was easy to see the reason for the Earl's concern, for Lady Ambourne was clearly in what was usually called an interesting condition.

"Surprise? What do you mean, Edward? The surprise—and the pleasure—are mine, Miss Calvert," said Lady Ambourne, adding as her husband gave a laugh and even Serena smiled, "What have I said? Why are they laughing, Mama?" When they explained, she said, "Well the thought may not have been original, but is none the less true. Welcome, Miss Calvert. As you see, I find it a trifle difficult to get up at the moment—"

"You will not attempt to do so, Perdita," said the Earl firmly, and when she looked rebellious he smiled and added, "Please?"

"Then, Miss Calvert, you must sit down next to me and amuse me," said Lady Ambourne. "You see how I am beset with despots and conspirators. Now, I have a hundred things to ask you. You must tell me what you think of London, you must tell me about Miss Lucy and her début—I hear that Michael Warnham is growing most particular in his attentions, by the way—and you must tell me about Lady Pendomer and her family."

The Dowager Countess left them together, and Lord Ambourne soon excused himself too. Serena spent a very pleasant half-hour at the end of which she could see that Lady Ambourne, in spite of her brave words to the contrary, was getting tired. She rose to go.

"I hope you will come again, soon," said Lady Ambourne. "We are not here in London for long. Edward has some affairs in London to see to, but we shall return to Ambourne as soon as he has finished. I miss my children, and, though I wouldn't say so to Edward, I must own that I find London tiring. But I should like you to come again before I go."

"You are very kind, Lady Ambourne. And so is Lady Ambourne...er...the Countess...I mean your mother-in-law."

"Confusing, is it not. Well, the Ambournes do not stand on ceremony when it is inconvenient to do so. I think you had better call me Perdita. I notice Mama calls you Serena, and I propose to do the same. We may not have known each other in person for very long, but Lady Pendomer's letters have made me feel you are an old friend. Bring Lucy with you when you next come. I should like her to talk to me about young Mr. Warnham, if she will. I am glad to hear you say that you quite like his grandmother. I enjoy Mrs. Galveston myself, but there are many who find her a tartar! Goodbye, Serena!"

Lord Ambourne appeared as Purkiss was ushering Serena through the state-rooms. "May I speak to you, Miss Calvert?"

They went through to a study. Here the Earl gave her a small glass of wine and saw her comfortably seated.

"I hope you will not consider me impertinent, but I am curious to know a little more of what happened last night. Do you wish me to take the matter up with Lord Wintersett?"

Serena grew pale. "I...I think it is better forgotten, Lord Ambourne. No harm came of it, I think, and...and..." Once again she had this curious inability to say Lord Wintersett's name. "The gentleman had already apologised to me before you came in."

"For what?"

Serena pulled herself together. She raised her chin. "It is kind of you to concern yourself, Lord Ambourne, but I consider the matter settled. Lord...Lord W...Wintersett embarrassed me, but, though I am ashamed to admit it, I had provoked him."

"You are sure that you are satisfied?"

"Yes. Quite sure."

"I must confess I am relieved to hear you say so. James is an old friend of mine, and I am not anxious to pick a quarrel with him."

"Oh, you must not think of it!" Serena cried. Then after a pause she said, "Lord Ambourne, you say you are old friends. Has he ever spoken to you about his brother?"

"Tony? Not a great deal. I never really knew him. He was younger, of course, and rather a quiet person. James used to talk a lot about Tony's work—he was very proud of it. Tony was already making a name for himself even before he left Cambridge, and we all thought he was sure to go into academic life. He was a bit of a monk at Cambridge and his marriage took everyone by surprise, James most of all, I'd say. Why do you ask?"

"What was . . . your friend's reaction to his brother's death? Was he unbalanced by it?"

"What an odd question!" Lord Ambourne stared at her, but though Serena grew pink she said nothing. He shrugged his shoulders and went on, "He was certainly not unbalanced by it. I've never met any man saner than James Stannard. But it did have a strong effect on him, and he never mentioned Tony afterwards." He sat thinking for a moment. "I suppose he became more . . . inaccessible, though he was always a bit cool, especially to anyone he didn't know. They called him Frosty Jack at Eton, you know. He was never so to me—we have been very good friends for years." He eyed her curiously. "Why are you asking me all this? Is there more to Tony Stannard's death than the world knows? Did he in fact die of a fever? Or is it true that he committed suicide?"

"I . . . I cannot tell you that. I was a child at the time." She began pulling on her gloves, and they both rose. Then almost involuntarily she added forlornly, "He blames the Calverts for it all, and I suppose there's some justification for that. But I find it strange that he blames me in particular. I really don't know why."

"Are you asking me to find out, Miss Calvert?"

Serena's thoughts raced. The idea was a tempting one, but the two men had been friends for many years. What if that friendship was destroyed because of her? Lord Wintersett's apology the evening before had seemed sincere—she doubted he would attempt more tricks. Also, the season was more than half over, and Lucy was now so well established in society that

Serena could reasonably take the less prominent role that she had always wished for herself. If she could avoid meeting Lord Wintersett for the short time left he would forget her. Quite soon she would leave England to return to the West Indies, and after that it was most unlikely that they would ever meet again. No, the mystery was better left alone.

She sighed and said, "Thank you again, Lord Ambourne. You are very kind. But I think not. Instead, I shall try to avoid meeting your friend. Goodbye."

THAT EVENING over dinner Lord Ambourne asked his ladies what they thought of Serena Calvert.

"She's a lovely woman, Edward. Not altogether in the usual manner... but those eyes! They are quite extraordinary—such a clear golden amber."

"I would like an opinion on her character, Perdita, not her appearance. I can see her beauty for myself, and I agree with you. She is not completely to my taste—my preference is for sapphires, as you are no doubt aware—but very lovely."

"She is unhappy, I think. Her face is sad in repose."

"That is hardly surprising!" said the Dowager Countess. "Serena's family history is far from being a happy one. She is quite alone in the world except for Lucy. And she has worked like a Trojan to keep the family estate going. Alicia Pendomer's letters have been so ecstatic on the subject of Serena's dedication to duty and other boring things that I was not at all looking forward to meeting her. But she is absolutely charming. I am quite baffled by James Stannard's behaviour—and very disappointed in him."

"How can we judge, Mama? We hardly know anything of the matter. You tell me Serena Calvert is charming, but what value has that? She may even have been hardworking—but is she honest?"

Both ladies were quite clear on this point, and were incensed that Edward should think it necessary to ask.

After Perdita had gone to bed the Countess sought out her son. "I don't want to worry Perdita with this matter, Edward, but I heard you tell James last night that you would like to see him."

"Yes, I thought I would go in a few moments."

"You wish to speak with him about his behaviour, I suppose? Are you and James about to fall out over this matter?"

"You may rest your mind, Mama. Miss Calvert has said that she has no wish for me to take the matter further, so I am not about to challenge him, thank goodness. I'm glad she's so sensible. I cannot say I understand James's behaviour, but I shouldn't wish to lose his friendship over it. However, I think I would like him to be aware that Miss Calvert is a friend of the Pendomers and so entitled to some protection from me. I shall do it tactfully, so you need not look so worried. Do you know more than you have said about the affair?"

The Countess then related as much as she thought she could about the Stannards on St. Just. It wasn't easy. She had given her word to Serena, so much of the story remained untold.

CHAPTER NINE

JAMES WAS NOT looking forward to this forthcoming meeting, any more than Lord Ambourne. He was not so rich in friends that he could afford to lose one, and Ned and his family had been good friends indeed. During the dark days of his school-days, when nothing James did ever pleased his father, when his mother treated him with indifference, and Wintersett Court was like a prison to him, a visit to Arlington Street or Ambourne had been like coming into light. Damn Sasha Calvert! Wher-ever he looked she was there, destroying everything he had ever valued.

When Lord Ambourne was announced the two men greeted one another cautiously, like fencers. But, to James's astonish-ment, it gradually became clear to him that Ned was not there to challenge or condemn. Unlikely though it was, Serena seemed not to have told Ned what had actually happened. It had been obvious the night before that his friend was willing to take on the role of protector, but Serena had apparently not desired him to do so. With a sigh of relief James produced a bottle of wine, and the two men sat down to chat more easily. One bottle led to another, until the candles were guttering in their sockets and the fire was almost dead. Ned asked idly, "What *did* you do to Serena Calvert, old fellow?"

"She didn't tell you?"

"No, she said you'd apologised and that she had provoked you, and that she wished the matter to be forgotten. I'd give a lot to know what you did, though. It's my belief that Serena Calvert is a cool enough character, but she was certainly in a flutter last night."

"I kissed her," said James abruptly. "And you're wrong about her being cool. She has a fiendish temper." He fingered his jaw.

"Well," said Edward, with a large gesture which betrayed how much wine the two friends had consumed. "Well, the ladies often make a fuss about a kiss, but it can be a pleasant experience for all that. No harm done. She said so."

"She said it had been a pleasant experience? I don't believe it."

"Not that, no. But she said no harm had been done."

"I wish I could believe that was true. I frightened her, Ned. And I'm ashamed of myself." He burst out, "That woman seems to bring out the worst in me. Sasha, I mean. Not Serena. No, not Serena." He filled his glass and drank deep.

"You're foxed, James! Who's this Sasha woman?"

"She killed my brother."

Edward sat up, reached for the bottle and poured some more wine into James's glass and some for himself. "You're wrong, James, old fellow. Your brother killed himself, unless I'm much mistaken."

"Who told you that?"

"Never mind. He did, didn't he?"

"Yes. Yes!" James got up and stood by the fire, kicking it with his boot. "But *why* did he? You cannot imagine what it's like to live with that question, Ned. I don't suppose we shall ever know the answer now. I try to forget—I even succeed for a while, and then I go back to Surrey and see my mother and Tony's boy, and the question returns to plague me, together with the sense of waste, the bitter waste! You know what he was like, curse it! Why did he have to kill himself over a confounded woman?" James turned away from the fire and roamed restlessly about the room. "He had his work—the Calverts couldn't have kept him out of it for long! God knows, the Wintersetts are a match for any damned colonials. And for Tony—Tony of all people—to do that to my mother... The devil take it! *Why*?"

"What makes you so sure that he killed himself over a woman?" asked Edward carefully.

"What else could it possibly be? Anyway, I have proof. I've even heard her admit it. Oh, for God's sake, let's leave it!" James looked moodily down at his glass and drank again.

Edward said slowly, "I'll tell you something you might like to think over, James. A while back I almost made the biggest mistake of my life, just because I was too blind to see the truth. I could have lost Perdita because of it. Mind you don't fall into the same trap. Now tell me exactly what it is that you have against Serena Calvert?''

James stared at Edward and then he started laughing helplessly. ''Nothing at all, Ned, nothing at all!'' Then he dropped down on his knees beside Edward, and whispered solemnly, ''But Sasha—now that's another question. Oh, what a surprise I have for her!'' He slipped slowly down the side of the chair to lie in a heap on the floor.

Edward saw with regret that nothing more could be got from James that night. He called that gentleman's valet, and walked, somewhat unsteadily, back to Arlington Street.

The next morning Edward took one look at Perdita's wan face, called Dr. Parker, ascertained that his wife would be able to withstand the relatively short journey to Ambourne if it was taken in easy stages, and declared that he and his wife would leave London that afternoon. The Dowager regretted their departure, but agreed with her son. Her daughter-in-law smiled ruefully, wrote numerous notes, including one to Serena, and then lay back thankfully in the chaise and was carried away.

Thus it was that Lord Ambourne was unable to pursue the mysterious question of Sasha Calvert and the surprise in store for her. His overriding concern for his wife caused all such thoughts to vanish from his mind.

THE FOLLOWING DAY James sat for most of the morning gazing moodily into space. The meeting with Ned had gone better than he had hoped. James was aware that, had she wished, Serena could have caused a rift between Ned and himself which would have been difficult to heal. If Ned had heard the whole story of James's behaviour at the French Ambassador's reception he would have been obliged to tackle his friend about it. But Serena had not told him the whole story. Why not? She had no reason to spare James. He had insulted her, had attacked her, had even frightened her. He frowned at the memory of the look in her eyes when he had held her after that shameful kiss. She was usually so dauntless, so spirited—the golden eyes did not often hold such a look of fear, he was sure. He got up impatiently. Why was he worrying? For whatever reason, his friendship with Ned had been preserved, and if all went well Sasha Calvert would soon be out of Anse Chatelet and out of his life. So would Serena. The thought did not make him feel any better.

James was relieved when a visitor in the form of Mr. Bradpole came to distract him from his gloomy thoughts. But the damned lawyer brought with him the papers which completed Lord Wintersett's possession of Anse Chatelet. Neither gentleman felt particularly cordial. There was no comfortable chair for Mr. Bradpole, no glass of Madeira, nor did the lawyer seem to wish it. Instead he gave the impression that he saw no cause for celebration.

"What do I do with these now?"

"The copies should be delivered to Miss Calvert, Lord Wintersett. Does your lordship wish me to retain the originals?"

"Of course. I'm not sure why you ask, Bradpole. Nor do I understand why you have brought the copies here instead of delivering them to Miss Calvert. You have her address."

The lawyer said colourlessly, "I thought your lordship might wish, even at this late stage, to reconsider your decision. Or, alternatively, you might wish to deliver them in person."

"What the devil do you mean by that?"

"The acquisition of the Calvert estate has been an object with you for some time, Lord Wintersett. I believe the reason to have been personal rather than a matter of business. But if your lordship wishes me to deliver the papers I will, of course, do so."

"Then do so, Bradpole," said Lord Wintersett curtly. "Now, if you please—and damn your impudence!"

Mr. Bradpole bowed and went out. James threw himself into a chair and wondered why the devil he was feeling so out of sorts. His head was aching, but that could easily be accounted for by the amount of wine he had drunk the night before. He had had hangovers before now. It was not that. He smiled sourly. Bradpole never gave up. "Even at this late stage!" Perhaps he should have ignored the lawyer's implicit criticism and taken the papers round to Dover Street himself? But truth to tell, he had been afraid. After the scene at the French Ambassador's he could well believe that Serena would refuse to see him again. He got up and walked restlessly about the room, reminding himself of the events on St. Just, holding them like a shield against the wave of desolation which swept over him at this thought. After a while he managed to subdue this ridiculous feeling and sat down again to consider the lawyer's visit.

Serena would soon have the papers about Anse Chatelet. How would she react to its loss? She would probably be devastated, a thought which gave him surprisingly little pleasure. This was Sasha's loss, Sasha Calvert's loss, he reminded himself fiercely, but it was no good. Thoughts of Serena were filling his mind—regret for the pain he was causing her, a wish that it had not been necessary. What the devil was wrong with him? This was the culmination of years of planning and waiting, and he should be feeling pleased that they had borne fruit, not jaded and weary! The trouble was that he seemed to be living in two worlds at once, neither of them happy. He sat there brooding for a while and then decided that a good dose of fresh air would clear his head and possibly raise his spirits. A ride in the park was called for.

On his return he found a note requesting him to call on Miss Calvert in Dover Street at his earliest convenience. He was astonished at the sudden feeling of elation. The reason for her request mattered not at all. What was important was that Serena was at least prepared to face him again!

SERENA WAS PACING UP and down in the drawing-room of the house in Dover Street. The fateful papers lay where she had thrown them, scattered over the table in the window. Lucy sat wide-eyed and pale on the sofa.

"What does it mean, Sasha? We've always lived at Anse Chatelet. It's our home! He cannot take it from us! Can he?" Lucy's lip quivered as she spoke, and Serena stopped her pacing to take Lucy in her arms and attempt to comfort her.

"Don't cry, Lucy! Hush, my love! I'll get it back, I swear! Come, dry your eyes. He might come at any moment, and we must not let him see any weakness. He's a no-good—" Here Serena used some island patois which shocked Lucy out of tears and into laughter.

"Sasha! Whatever would Lady Pendomer say?"

Serena grinned at her niece. "She wouldn't say anything, Lucy. She wouldn't know the words. I'm surprised you do!"

"I was brought up on the island, Sasha. You can't play with Joshua and the others without learning some of the things they say. How I miss Joshua and Betsy and the rest! Oh, Sasha, are we never going to see Anse Chatelet again?"

Lucy's mercurial spirits were descending once more. Serena said hastily, "Of course we are! But Lucy, if you marry here in England, St. Just would surely be less important to you than it has been till now. You like it in England, don't you?"

"Oh, yes, I love it! In fact, I'd miss Isabella and... and the others even more than I miss my friends on St. Just. It's not that I don't love the people on Anse Chatelet, Sasha! I do, still! But... it's different here. Some of the people here are very important to me." Serena looked quizzically at her niece, who blushed and added, "I think I'd miss Isabella's brother most of all. He's... he's fond of me, too, I think. But what would you do if he... if I... were to marry?" Serena saw that Lucy was thinking for the first time what marriage in England would entail, realising for the first time that it would mean parting from her beloved aunt. Lucy's face brightened. "I know, Sasha! When I marry we can live in England together!"

Serena smiled wryly. Now was not the time to point out that she had no intention of living with her niece once Lucy was married. From the beginning Serena had made up her mind that she would see Lucy safely established, and then return to St. Just to spend her energies on Anse Chatelet. Now, it seemed, this consolation was to be denied her. But she would not give up without a fight!

One result of this conversation was that Lucy was able to face the arrival of Lord Wintersett with composure. He came in dressed in impeccable linen under a dark green coat and riding breeches tucked into shining Hessians, his face impassive as usual. He gave a cool bow. Serena greeted him in an equally businesslike fashion and said, "You know my niece, I believe, Lord W... Wintersett."

"I do indeed. Your servant, Miss Lucy." Lucy got up, curtsied modestly and sat down again. He went on, "Though I am surprised to see her present on this occasion. I thought it was to be a business meeting, Miss Calvert. I assume you have had the papers concerning Anse Chatelet?" He took his glass and eyed the chaos on the table. "Yes, I see you have."

"It *is* a business meeting, Lord W... Wintersett." Serena was glad that she could at least say his name, though she wondered impatiently why she couldn't say it without stumbling! "The estate is Lucy's home, as well as my own. And you can hardly blame me for wishing for a companion in your presence."

A faint red darkened Lord Wintersett's cheeks, but he drawled, "*Your* home, Miss Calvert? I think not."

"That remains to be seen," replied Serena swiftly. "The manner in which you acquired my estates was doubtful, to say the least."

"It was legal, Miss Calvert."

"A minimal claim, I should have thought. Most men of honour would not have stooped to such measures. And though I am fully aware that an appeal to your sense of honour would be like asking a hyena to stop scavenging—" There was a gasp from Lucy, which she hastily suppressed, Serena ignored it and continued, "I am persuaded that the courts might view an appeal with sympathy—especially as the Governor of St. Just would support it."

Lord Wintersett smiled mockingly, "'A hit', William, 'a very palpable hit'!"

"Then may you be 'justly killed with your own treachery'!" said Serena, her voice full of feeling. "And we will omit further quotation, if you please. I enjoy that game only with my friends."

"Well, then, my case might be destroyed, though I doubt it. But it will certainly not be destroyed by you! Believe me, your weapons are puny. Anse Chatelet is mine by every law in the kingdom, and I defy anyone to take it from me."

"Of course! I had forgotten. The *wealthy* Lord W... Wintersett can afford the best lawyers in England!"

"I haven't won Anse Chatelet with my wealth, Miss Calvert, but by your own family's prodigality in the past. If I hadn't taken up the mortgage, someone else would have!"

"Pray do not attempt to defend yourself—"

"I am not," said Lord Wintersett grimly, "trying to defend myself. I see no necessity to do so, not to a Calvert. God's teeth, you squander a handsome and profitable heritage and then come whining to me when it is taken from you—"

Lucy jumped up and faced Lord Wintersett, her cheeks scarlet.

"How dare you? How dare you talk to my aunt in such a way? What do you know about it? Sasha has worked hard and gone without for years—all to save Anse Chatelet! She has never squandered a thing in her life—"

"Except my brother's life."

Lucy swept on, ignoring the interruption "—and she has something you will never have, not for all your money. She has the love of everyone who knows her. You can keep Anse Chatelet! Sasha will live with me when I am married!"

His icy gaze swept Lucy's face. "Married? That is good news, indeed, Miss Lucy. May I ask who the fortunate young man is?"

A cold shiver went down Serena's spine at this question. Lord Wintersett was a dangerous and vindictive man and he must not be allowed to threaten Lucy's happiness. She put a hand on Lucy's arm. "You may not, sir. It is none of your business. Lucy, thank you for your defence, I am touched. I think Lord Wintersett's visit is almost over, so would you now leave us?"

Lucy looked doubtfully at them both, but Serena forced a smile and nodded her head, "It's all right, Lucy, really! I wish you to go, please." Lucy gave their visitor one of her best curtsies, every line of which conveyed disdain, and went out. When the door was shut once again Serena said urgently, "She is young. And devoted to me. You must forgive her." She was aware that she was pleading with him, but could not help herself. "Her father was already a sick man when your brother and his wife were on St. Just. He took no part in their affair. Do not . . . do not spoil her life."

"You think I would harm a girl who can't have been more than five years old when my brother died?"

Serena said spiritedly, "I could well be forgiven for thinking so! You have just annexed her home!"

"Not hers, Serena. Yours. I understand that Miss Lucy has a fortune of her own, and that you intend her to marry in England. Losing Anse Chatelet should mean nothing to her."

"Nothing? Nothing! Why, you heartless, vindictive scorpion, how can you judge what a home means to a child. The feelings of love and comfort, the happy memories of childhood!"

He grew white and turned away from her. After a pause he said harshly, "Lucy is fortunate if she has such happy memories of her home. But she is about to be married, she said, and she will soon forget the loss of Anse Chatelet when that happens. I repeat, I mean her no harm. You may believe me, Miss Calvert."

Behind his words she sensed a feeling of unhappiness, of deep loneliness, and angry though she was it gave her pause.

She said uncertainly, "Though I have not experienced it, everyone says you are a just man. Hard, but just. It would not be just to punish Lucy."

He said abruptly, "If your niece marries in England, will you in fact live with her?"

Serena shook her head. "No."

"What will you do?"

"I had always intended to return to St. Just in order to run Anse Chatelet. It was my ambition to carry on building it up again." She looked up defiantly. "It still is!"

"And if your appeal fails? As it will."

"I . . . I might return to Surrey. But it would be hard, I admit. My aunt is elderly and set in her ways . . ."

"You might be forced to seek refuge with William!"

He seemed to regret the words as soon as they were spoken, as did Serena. They were both reminded of the companionship they had known and lost. He frowned, then seemed to come to a sudden decision. "Miss Calvert, if you will promise to go back to St. Just immediately I shall accept Sir Henry's word that the payment should have arrived on time and cancel the foreclosure. Anse Chatelet would be returned to you on the old terms. But you must leave England and not come back again, not ever."

Serena was suddenly aflame again. "'You must not'! 'You must promise'! Who the devil do you think you are, Lord Wintersett, to suggest that I should never visit Lucy in England—or even come for my own pleasure? I am a Calvert of Anse Chatelet, and would not be one of your pensioners—not for the world! If I cannot win my estates back with my own efforts, you may keep them! I am damned if I will accept your charity or your restrictions!"

He gave a reluctant smile. "Forcefully, if not conventionally expressed. That temper of yours will dish you one of these days, Serena. You know, I find you an enigma. You would almost persuade me of your integrity, except that I have heard you condemned out of your own mouth."

"Integrity? How could you possibly judge integrity? Where is the integrity in the low, cheating ruse you have employed to steal Anse Chatelet? And how can I have condemned myself out of my own mouth? I simply don't understand what you mean. Why did you say I had squandered your brother's life?"

"Because you drove him to his death, that's why!"

Serena looked at him blankly. "*I* drove him to his... But that is nonsense!"

" 'I loved him,' you said."

"Yes, but—"

" 'I pursued him relentlessly,' you said."

"Yes, but—"

" 'I told him I despised him, that he'd be better dead,' you said."

"No! That I did not say! Not to Tony!"

"Then to whom?"

Serena was about to answer him, then she stopped short. Why should she betray Richard to this monster? "I will not tell you," she replied. "But it was not to Tony." He raised a sceptical eyebrow, but she ignored him. "You are wrong about me, Lord Wintersett. I loved Tony, and I would never have willingly harmed him."

He looked at her, confident of his case, scornful of her attempt to plead her innocence. "It had to be you," he said. "There was no one else."

Serena's eyes widened as the implication of what he was saying hit her. "I . . . I . . ." she stammered.

"Please continue!" he jeered. "Tell me that Tony did not kill himself! Or that if he did, it was not because of a woman!"

"It was not because of me," she said quietly. "And that is all I will say. You must believe what you will. You have done your worst to the Calverts. It is now time to forget. But I warn you, I will fight for Anse Chatelet. And if you harm a hair of Lucy's head I will cause you more anguish than you have yet known, Lord Wintersett. Goodbye."

WHEN ALANNA heard that Sasha Calvert had been taken up by the Ambournes and was enjoying a modest success in society, her fears for her own safety reached breaking point. She had to rely more and more on Amelia Banagher for her information—a not altogether satisfactory source, for Amelia was no longer received in the very best houses. Though James had paid them frequent visits in the earlier part of the year, he seemed now to have tired of the country and was spending much more of his time in town. There was a greater risk, therefore, that he would become more friendly with the Calvert woman than was healthy, and Alanna was in daily expectation of a visit from an irate James demanding to know the truth about St. Just. She bestirred herself to complete her plans.

It was towards the end of June and Alanna was holding a council of war. To a casual eye this was a tea-party in the garden, given by Mrs. Stannard for some Irish friends—a natural enough occasion. But the lady sitting gracefully by the sundial was one of the most notorious courtesans in London, and the distinguished-looking gentleman who had brought her was Fergus O'Keefe, an Irish soldier of fortune and a man of parts, all of them bad. Alanna was anxious to disgrace Sasha Calvert, and the other two were eager to get what money the rich Mrs. Stannard would pay them to help her—though in the case of the lady there was a certain amount of personal ill-will as well. Amelia Banagher had not forgotten Serena's remarks at the Assembly Rooms.

"But how can you be sure that Sir John and Lady Taplow will be staying at the Black Lion, *acushla*?" asked Captain O'Keefe.

"Don't be stupid, Fergus! Do I not know where all of them have their favourite inns? Have I not seen the Taplows many a time at the Black Lion at Hoddesdon when they've been on their way back to London from Huntingdon? They haven't seen me, mind!" Amelia gave a rich laugh. "They take good care not to. They might soil their disapproving eyes!"

"I dare swear you are seldom alone." Captain O'Keefe accompanied this remark with a wink.

Amelia's laugh was scornful. "Hardly! I've even been there with one of the Taplows' closest acquaintances. That was a lark! They almost twisted their heads off their necks in their efforts not to see either of us that time!"

"But Amelia, how will you see that word about Miss Calvert's fall from grace spreads through society? From what I've heard the Taplows are so upright that they don't believe in scandalmongering either, do they?"

"Alanna, pray stop worrying! I've set up an assignation myself in the same inn on the same night with Harry Birtles. He's the most notorious rattle in the town. I'll make sure he sees what he needs in order to make a juicy tale. It will get round, never fear. So with Harry to spread it, and the Taplows to confirm it, the plot can hardly fail. Be easy!"

"Very well. But I hope you are right. And the plot will only succeed if the rest goes well, too. Captain O'Keefe, what about your part?"

"Well I still think it would have been better for me to use my charm on the lady—it doesn't often fail, eh, Amelia? But you said not to try, so I've hit on the idea of hiring a coach and putting the Ambourne cipher on the panels for the night. Then I can have a message sent, supposedly from Lord Ambourne himself, asking her to visit him."

"No, no! You must ask her to visit the Dowager, not Ambourne! She would never come out at night to meet him."

The gallant captain pulled a face. "She sounds a damned dull fish to me—I can't see much fun for myself in this business, and that's a fact!"

Alanna said coldly, "You are not being paid to have fun, Captain O'Keefe. The woman is not to be harmed while she is in your power, do you hear? It's her reputation I wish to be damaged, nothing else."

"You may rest easy, Alanna," said Amelia. "I'll make sure he behaves. We'll be together most of the night. He'll just appear when it's necessary in the morning."

"What about Sir Harry? Won't you be occupied in . . . er . . . entertaining him?"

"Not if I slip a little something into his wine. He drinks like a fish. No, I can manage both of them. Miss Calvert's virtue will be safe, if that's what you want—though I think you're being a mite overscrupulous."

"I will not pay either of you if Miss Calvert is harmed, Amelia."

"Well that reminds me, Alanna, my dear," said Amelia. "When will you pay us, and how much?"

"We agreed five hundred pounds—"

"Each?"

Alanna looked at the faces before her. They were suddenly hard and watchful. She nodded. "Each. I will pay you each a hundred and fifty pounds beforehand, a hundred and fifty immediately afterwards, and two hundred when Sasha Calvert is finally disgraced. But pray finish telling us what you plan to do, Captain O'Keefe."

"Once the lady has entered the coach she'll be taken to the inn. The landlord has been primed—you did say you'd pay expenses, didn't you, Mrs. Stannard?"

"Reasonable expenses, yes. Afterwards."

"Beforehand," said the Captain softly.

"Very well. Carry on."

"She'll not like being abducted, of course. Amelia here will give her some womanly sympathy, and offer the lady something to drink. Miss Calvert will be out for the night after she drinks it."

"You're sure you can gauge the dose accurately?"

"Mrs. Stannard, once she has it in her, I could tell you to the second when she'll wake up again! Was I not once assistant to a doctor?"

Alanna looked doubtfully at Amelia, who nodded reassuringly. "It's all right, Alanna. I've known him to do that kind of thing before."

Still looking doubtful, Alanna asked, "And when she wakes up?"

"Before she wakes up," Captain O'Keefe corrected her. "When she's still half asleep, I'll make sure she's on display to the world through the open door of the bedchamber. If Amelia does what she's supposed to the world will include the Taplows and the chatty Sir Harry. By the time she wakes up properly her reputation will be like the seeds on this dandelion head." He blew on the dandelion clock in his hand, and the seeds vanished on the wind.

After they had gone, Alanna was uneasy. Necessity was driving her into this plot, but she did not enjoy the association with Fergus O'Keefe. He was charming enough, but she felt he could be dangerous. She must consider her plan a little more carefully, for she had a lot at stake. If O'Keefe did misbehave and the plot were discovered then nothing would save her, not even her relationship to the Wintersetts. The Ambournes would see to that, especially as they were to be involved, however indirectly.

SERENA WAS BUSY during the next few days. She was disappointed that the younger Ambournes had returned so unexpectedly to the country, but was consoled when she found that the Countess was intending to stay on for some time. She sought the lady's advice on a suitable lawyer.

"Our family lawyer is Bradpole. He is very good, but I believe the Stannards use the firm as well. But Perdita had an ex-

cellent lawyer. Let me see…the name was Rambridge, I think.
I shall send one of the men to make enquiries at Lincoln's Inn
tomorrow, Serena!''

Mr. Rambridge called at Dover Street almost immediately.
He was cautious on the question of Anse Chatelet, saying,
''The firm of Bradpole, Chalmers and Bradpole is highly respected, Miss Calvert. I would find it hard to believe that they
would be involved in anything of a dubious nature.''

But after Serena explained the circumstances, including the
role played by Sir Henry Pendomer, the lawyer promised to
look into it. Serena thanked him, gave him the papers and various addresses, and stressed how urgent the task was. At this he
smiled and said, as all lawyers did, that one could not hurry the
processes of the law, but then he became more human and assured her that he would not waste any time.

Serena also went down to Surrey to visit her great-aunt. Lady
Spurston demanded to know the whole story, which was impossible. But Serena told her enough to rouse her indignation
at the injustice, and she promised to give Serena all the help in
her power.

Feeling she had done as much as she could for the moment
Serena then devoted herself to Lucy's interests. It was now more
important than ever that Lucy should be established, and
though Serena still had private doubts about Michael Warnham she suppressed them. Lucy seemed to have made up her
mind in his favour. She spent some time with the Warnhams,
who were obviously pleased with their son's choice. Considering how modest Lucy's fortune was, this was a great compliment. They were a pleasant family, and Serena rather thought
that her niece would be happy with them. She willingly agreed
to allow Lucy to go down to Reigate with them for a few days.
London was getting very hot and dusty, and Mrs. Galveston
had expressed a wish to spend some time in the country.

Serena felt quite lonely when Lucy and the Warnhams had
gone. The depression which was never very far away these days
came down like a black cloud on her spirits. What if she did not
succeed in her attempt to save Anse Chatelet? What would she
do with her life? The prospect of living with Aunt Spurston was
not an alluring one, and she suspected that her aunt would not
view it with much joy either. After the death of her husband the
old lady had become used to living alone. She had been willing
to support her great-niece for a few months, but after Serena

and Lucy had gone to London Lady Spurston had returned to her quiet life with relief.

Serena decided to try to forget her problems for the moment, and kept herself busy. Always with John, the footman, as her faithful follower, she paid calls, went shopping, buying small unnecessary things in order to cheer herself up, and visited the galleries and museums for which she had never till now seemed to have time. She went walking in the park, admiring the phaetons, the curricles and various other strange vehicles as they bowled along. The horses were beautiful. With a sigh she thought of Douce and Trask and the wonderful rides on the Downs.

"Good afternoon, Miss Calvert." With a start she looked up. Douce's master had just drawn up in a dangerous looking high perch phaeton with a pair of extremely handsome greys.

"Sir," Serena said coldly.

"You are alone? That is a rare phenomenon. Where is Miss Lucy?"

His tone was so affable that she regarded him with suspicion. "She is spending some days with friends," she said as curtly as good manners would allow.

"Come, a drive round the park will do you good. John will help you up."

"Thank you, but I would not dream of putting you to the trouble..."

"It's no trouble, Miss Calvert, I assure you. Are you afraid of the vehicle? There's no danger. John?"

John came forward, and before she quite knew what was happening Serena was high in the air on a narrow seat. With a word to John to wait where he was till they returned, Lord Wintersett drove off at a sedate trot. John was quite happy with the situation. Lord Wintersett was a friend of the Ambourne family, there could be no objection to him.

The two in the phaeton drove in silence for a minute or two. Serena was surprisingly at ease, and was enjoying the view of the park from her elevated position. She began to feel more cheerful. Suddenly Lord Wintersett spoke.

"Are you comfortable, Miss Calvert?"

"Thank you, yes," she said stiffly. "Why did you insist on taking me up? I find it very odd."

"I hardly know myself," he replied with a curious smile. "I saw you standing there—you were looking as you did on your birthday, on... on the hill. Miserable. I suppose I wanted to cheer you up. Why, I cannot say!"

"I am perfectly happy! Your sympathy, if that is what it is, is misplaced, I assure you, Lord W... Wintersett." She bit her lip in vexation. Curse that stammer! "But perhaps your reason is less charitable. Perhaps you wished to taunt me, to find out if I have changed my mind and am ready to accept your conditions?"

"I've withdrawn the offer," he said. "I've reconsidered, and have made other plans. But no, you misjudge me, Miss Calvert. I'm not here to talk about them. When will you manage to say my name without stuttering?"

"I don't know. But I'd prefer not to have to say it at all," she replied. "Pray set me down."

"What, here? I'm afraid that is impossible. You must wait till we are back with John—London is a dangerous place to a lady on her own. By the way, that's a fetching little bonnet. It suits you."

Serena was growing angry. She resented being forced to sit quietly while he said what he pleased. And she resented her enjoyment of this ride even more! "I cannot imagine why you think I wish for your compliments. Do you enjoy having me in your power like this? Please take me back! Immediately!"

He smiled—a long, lazy, utterly charming smile. "Well, you know, I rather do. But I shall take you back when you say my name again, Serena."

"Will you release me if I do? And my name is Miss Calvert."

"Only if you say it without stammering."

"I have your word? Not that that serves any purpose."

"You have my word."

Serena took a deep breath. "Then I wish that wealthy... witless... weaselly... Lord Wintersett would stop wearying me!"

He laughed. "What a woeful whopper, woman! I beg your pardon—I should have said 'Miss Calvert'. That's better—you almost smiled! I think I'll surprise you and keep my word. I have things to do. Good day to you!"

He drew up by John with a flourish, saw her safely on the ground, nodded and drove off, leaving Serena completely mystified. What was Lord Wintersett up to now? What were his

mysterious plans? Whatever they were, they seemed to have
made him look more favourably on her. For a moment he had
almost been the man she had known on the hills of Surrey.

CHAPTER TEN

SERENA HAD VISITED Lady Ambourne at Rotherfield House once or twice since the lawyer's visit. The Countess had seemed somewhat absent-minded, almost worried. So when Serena received a note from her that evening asking her to come immediately, and begging her to stay the night in Rotherfield House, she paused only long enough for Sheba to pack a small bag with necessities. Sheba was uneasy at letting her mistress go without her. She argued and wailed and prophesied doom until Serena became really annoyed. But Serena was determined to stick to what the note had asked. She could do no less for the friend who had been so kind to her.

> The matter is urgent and confidential, Serena. If I could impose on your discretion, I should prefer you not to discuss this visit with anyone. You will, of course, have to tell Mrs. Starkey you are spending the night with me, but say no more than that, I beg you. *Bring no one else.* Yours in haste, etc.

When she got to the door John was at her side, but she waved him away. "Look, the Countess has even sent the carriage for me. Stay here, John."

There was a maid in the carriage, but it was dark inside, and Serena couldn't see the woman's face. The groom helped her in and then they set off. Serena sat down and turned to the maid. "What is it? What is wrong with the Coun—'' Suddenly she was seized, then two people swiftly gagged and blindfolded her. One of her assailants was powerful and rough, and when she at first tried to kick him he twisted her arm behind her back and threatened to break it. The woman, presumably the one who had pretended to be a maid, helped to tie her bonds more firmly, but the only voice she heard was that of a man.

The journey seemed endless. They were travelling at a reckless pace, and she was thrown all over the seat by the jolting of the carriage, unable to save herself because of her bonds. She felt sick and faint—the gag was uncomfortable and it was almost unbearably hot. She must in fact have fainted for a while, for when she came to they were in the country, travelling swiftly along a turnpike road. Turnpikes had toll houses! She would listen for the next one. The keeper would surely hear the commotion she would make. But her captors had thought of that. As they approached the gate Serena felt the man in the coach pull her hood over her face and take her in his arms. The coach stopped. The driver and the gatekeeper exchanged a few pleasantries as the toll was paid.

"I shouldn't disturb the gentry inside, if I was you," said the coachman. "They're 'avin' a rare old time in there."

Serena heard with despair how the tollkeeper turned away and went back into the toll house.

The nightmare journey continued, but eventually they pulled up. From the scents and the absolute quiet Serena guessed they were deep in the country. Her captor removed her gag, but not the blindfold. "You wish to make a call of nature? The maid will go with you." Serena hesitated but her need was urgent. "Betty! Take Miss Calvert behind the bush. I'll whistle, my dear, so you can hear that I'm keeping my distance." He roared with laughter, but while Betty led Serena a little way off, he continued to whistle and talk loudly to the other men. Betty whispered hoarsely, "Make haste! The Captain's a devil when he gets annoyed."

"What does he want with me?" croaked Serena. Her throat was dry and her head ached abominably.

"Don't ask me! I do know it's not what you might think, though. Are you rich? Does 'e expect to get a ransom?"

Serena shook her head. "If he does, he's in for a disappointment. Can...can you untie the blindfold? If I could only see...Betty, won't you help me escape? I have jewellery at home I could let you have..."

"It's more than my life's worth, miss! Come on!"

Back at the carriage Serena could hear Betty having an argument with the man she had called the Captain.

"Oh, go on, Captain! Let 'er 'ave a drink. She can 'ardly speak! Just a little brandy won't do any 'arm! It's not 'uman to leave 'er to die of thirst. I could do wif one meself!"

"All right, all right. Not too much, mind!"

Betty returned. Serena could smell the brandy. The maid said, "There y'are! One fer me, and one fer you. I've put a drop of water in it, 'cos I expect yer thirsty." The cup was held to Serena's lips and she drank greedily. She heard the man say,

"Right! Off, my bonny fellows!" The last thing Serena remembered was being bundled into the coach again.

SERENA OPENED HER EYES slowly. The sun was slanting through the window. Was it evening or morning? She yawned. She was so sleepy... There was a horrible taste in her mouth, and her head felt thick. She wanted to close her eyes and sleep again but something told her that she must keep awake. Where was she? She tried hard to focus her eyes on the room. It was a bed-chamber, but not her own. She looked down. She didn't remember undressing, but she was wearing her night shift. That maid... Serena had a dim memory of the maid helping her off with her clothes. Not very expertly. She tried to sit up. Her head! She must ignore it—she must get up. She would get up in a moment...

Suddenly the door burst open, and a tall man came in, leaving the door wide behind him. He was half dressed, his shirt undone and hanging outside his breeches. Serena struggled out of bed and tried to run to the door, but she could only manage a few steps before she staggered. There were people outside, staring in, and she opened her mouth, ready to scream to them, for help. But the man was too swift. He held out his arms as if he were expecting her to run into them, and then caught her tight to him, her face hard against his chest. She couldn't say anything, indeed she could hardly breathe.

"There, there, my darling," he said loudly. "I was only away a few minutes. See? I'm back already. Oh, Serena, my love! Have you missed me all these months? St. Just was never like this, was it? There, there, Serena, be calm now!"

Serena's head was pounding. She tried to pull herself away, but his grip, in sharp contrast to his tender words, was cruelly tight. Her senses were swimming and she felt herself falling. From a great distance she heard him say, "Wait, Serena! I'll carry you back to bed, shall I?" Then he shouted, "What are you all staring at, damn you!"

The door was kicked shut and Serena was thrown on to the bed and held there, the man on top of her, his hand over her mouth. She was terrified. The man grinned, showing white teeth in a swarthy face. His eyes were black—he looked like the pictures of pirates she had seen in Jamaica. He whispered, "I've done you no harm, and will do none, though the temptation is very strong, me darlin'. You're a charmin' little bundle, for all your prim outside! But if you say a word, I swear I'll lose my control. Understand? There isn't a soul in this inn that doesn't believe you're willing, so none will come in unless I invite them. Now, if you wish to come out of this safely, all you have to do is to drink this drop of cordial. You'll fall asleep and when you wake I'll be gone. No, don't shake your head. You're going to drink it whether you will or no, so better to do it without getting hurt."

He stretched out, picked up a small glass, and put it to her lips. Most was spilled, but some of the bitter liquid passed through and was swallowed. It was enough to put her into a half-sleep. Some minutes later she heard him talking. There was someone else in the room.

"Stop your jangling, woman! None of your friends suspected, did they? How was I to know she'd come to as soon as that? However, all's well that ends well. My, but she's a brave one! It's a shame to do this to her, and that's a fact!" She heard them go out, and as the door was shut behind them she sank into unconsciousness.

When she next came to there was a chambermaid in the room, with a tray. It wasn't the girl from the night before. Serena's bag was on the chest by the bed, her clothes neatly folded beside it and on top was a note. The girl was looking at it. When she saw that Serena was watching her she blushed in confusion.

"Good morning, ma'am. I brought you breakfast."

Serena sat up. "Where am I?" she asked. The chambermaid burst into a volley of giggles.

"At the Black Lion, ma'am."

"But where?"

"At Hoddesdon, ma'am. Shall I fetch your shawl?"

Serena looked down. She had been mistaken. The night shift was not one of hers. It was a diaphanous affair which revealed more than it concealed. She went scarlet. "Please do," she said curtly. "Where is . . ."

"He's gone, ma'am. He left quite early. He left you the note, though." She giggled again. Serena snatched up the note.

My love,
You know I have to go, much as I hate to leave you. I'll arrange another meeting as soon as I can get away. Last night was even better than on St. Just. All my love—A.

Serena had had enough. She told the chambermaid to leave her and got out of bed. There was a bowl and a pitcher of hot water on the washstand. She scrubbed herself till she felt sore and hastily dried and dressed herself. The effort exhausted her, and she sat down for a moment to rest and think. What was she to do? She must find out what had happened the night before; she must speak to the landlord. She went in search of him. He looked at her stolidly as she approached.

"Landlord, did you see me arrive last night?" Serena asked.

"No, ma'am, I think I must have been busy in the bar. Your room was booked a week or two ago, so I didn't bother too much."

"Who carried the bags up?"

"I don't rightly know. I think you had your own people with you—"

"They were not my people! You must know! You're the landlord!"

"I'm sorry, ma'am. Last night was a busy one. We had a lot o' guests here. I can't remember seeing you arrive." Serena turned away impatiently. Then she had another thought.

"Where are the ostlers? I'd like to see them, if you please."

"Certainly, ma'am. Jem'll fetch 'em. Jem!"

But when the ostlers came they could tell her nothing. The coach had arrived, deposited three passengers, and then driven away. The maid had carried two small bags up. The gentleman had carried the lady, who had appeared to be asleep.

"The gentleman told us you were tired after the journey. Very thoughtful, 'e was. Very fond, like."

"Be silent! He was not fond! I was drugged!"

"Yes, ma'am. As you say, ma'am."

Their faces looked stupid and wooden. She would get nothing more out of them. Serena felt she would go mad. She returned to her room and sat down to think. There was a wall of silence in the inn concerning her captors of the night before. She was sure someone must know more, but who? And why had someone drugged her and brought her here to this inn, apparently only to put her in a large bedchamber for the night and then leave her? The sound of wheels caused her to run to the window and she saw a post-chaise turning into the yard. Serena watched as its passengers got out and stretched. The temptation to ask them for help was very strong. They were strangers, but surely they would understand? She had to get back to London. But as one of the travellers looked up at her window Serena hastily drew back. Perhaps it might be wise to consider her position. In view of the attitude of the innkeeper and his servants this was equivocal to say the least, and it might be prudent to avoid exposure, at least until she knew more.

There was a knock on the door. The landlord was there.

"Excuse me, ma'am. Were you thinking of travelling today, or do you wish to keep the room for another night? I need to know because of the chaise."

"The chaise?" asked Serena blankly.

"Yes, ma'am. There's one booked in your name for today—Calvert, that's right, isn't it? For London. At least that's what's paid for."

"Are you sure?"

The landlord looked as if he thought her weak in the head. Indeed, she almost felt it. He said patiently, "A well-sprung chaise and four, together with coachman and boys, hired for twenty miles, two guineas. I can show you the bill, if you wish."

"Yes, I'd like to see that, if you please. Immediately."

But the bill was unrevealing. It had been paid on the spot by the tall gentleman.

Further questioning of the landlord about the chaise produced nothing more than the conviction that this, at least, was above board. She would be safe to take it. But she was conscious of a touch of knowingness in the landlord's manner which went ill with his apparent stolidity. She became convinced that he knew more than he was acknowledging, and that he had probably been bribed.

"What is your name, landlord?"

"Samuel, ma'am. Samuel Cartwright."

"Well, Mr. Cartwright, I will take the chaise to London. It is clear I can do nothing more here. But, if you have taken part in this conspiracy, I warn you you may well lose more than you have gained by it.''

The landlord's expression did not change. "I don't know what you mean, ma'am. I keep a respectable house here," he said. "In fact, begging your pardon, I'd rather your friend didn't book any more rooms at the Black Lion."

Serena turned on her heel, and went out to the stable yard, where the chaise was waiting.

ON ANY OTHER occasion Serena could have enjoyed the journey back to London, for the countryside was pretty, and they passed through some places with famous names. But she pressed on, merely stopping once for a change of horses. The landlord of the Black Lion was a rogue, she was sure, but she dismissed him from her mind. The man behind him was more important. Her head still ached, and the drug had left an unpleasant taste in her mouth, but she ignored both of these and tried to concentrate on what her mysterious enemy was trying to achieve. Why Hoddesdon! Why the Black Lion, a coaching inn, and much in the public eye? If he had intended harm to her person he would have chosen a more out-of-the-way spot. So, if she was right, he had not intended harm to her person, he had merely intended her to be noticed. She vaguely remembered the open door to the bedchamber that morning. There had been faces in the doorway, she had tried to reach them. He must have left that door open deliberately! He had wanted her to be seen, not just in the inn, but in the bedchamber! With a blush she remembered the nightgown—there was no doubt about the sort of rendez-vous that garment was intended for! Serena's heart sank as she saw the scheme for what it was. It was no more or less than an effort to discredit her. And unless she could prove otherwise, that was exactly what it would do!

She walked in through the door of the Dover Street house as the clocks were striking five. Mrs. Starkey was waiting for her with a smile, but her expression changed when she saw Serena's face.

"Mercy me! What has happened, Miss Calvert? You're ill!"

"No, no. Just a little tired. But I am hungry. Could you bring some tea and a little bread and butter to the small parlour, Mrs. Starkey? I shall rest there for a while. And would you tell Sheba I have returned, please."

She lay on the sofa in the small parlour and when Sheba brought in the tea she asked her to close the shutters. Sheba tried to persuade her mistress to go to bed, but Serena's thoughts were too chaotic for sleep. And they were leading her to one inevitable conclusion. As far as she knew, there was only one person in London who wished her ill. One person who had tried to bribe her to leave England. One person who had told her just the day before that he had changed his mind and had other plans. One person who had taken her off her guard by his pretended concern for her. She buried her face in her hands and let the bitter tears flow unchecked.

But Serena was too much of a fighter to give in to tears for long. After a while she dried her eyes, and considered what to do. It all depended on those people in the door. If they had not recognised her then all might not be lost, and a great deal was to be gained by saying nothing. Perhaps her captor had made a mistake in hiding her face against his chest so closely? She would wait to see. Lucy was returning tomorrow and they would be out most of the time. She would not alter her plans for the moment.

Serena went upstairs and changed her dress. Lady Pangbourne was giving a dinner party and had asked Serena to come with an old friend of her husband's. Serena must be ready for him. Sheba used her skills, which were now considerable, to disguise the ravages of the past two days, and when General Fanstock called, Serena was waiting in the drawing-room as cool, as composed and as beautiful as ever. They arrived at the Pangbourne house in Grafton Street at exactly ten o'clock. They were received graciously by Lady Pangbourne, and soon found themselves among what Lucy called "The Pangbourne set," usually wrinkling her nose at the same time. It was true that the average age was high, and the average level of conversation worthy rather than scintillating, but Serena nevertheless enjoyed herself. She began to feel safer. Perhaps the people at the inn had either not recognised her or they did not belong to the very limited numbers which make up London society.

Halfway through the meal she found herself the subject of a penetrating stare from an elderly dowager some way up the table. She asked her partner who it was. "Hrrmph! Let me have a look. I think... Yes it's Valeria Taplow, my dear. Charmin' woman. A bit of a stickler, you know, but none the worse for that, none the worse for that! John, her husband, is a very nice fellow, too. Hrrmph! Great friends of mine.''

Serena was uneasy. That stare had not been one of approval. But the evening passed without incident, unless you would call it an incident that neither of the Taplows had come over to speak to their old friend.

Lucy arrived back the next day, glowing with happiness. She had had a wonderful week, with wonderful weather. The Warnhams and Mrs. Galveston were wonderfully kind! Serena smiled in spite of her own worries and waited. Eventually Lucy said hesitantly, ''Sasha?''

''Yes?''

''Sasha, you like Mr. Warnham, don't you? Isabella's brother.''

''I think he's charming.''

''If he . . . if he came to see you—to ask you if you would let him pay me his addresses—you wouldn't say no, would you?''

''Well . . . let me see . . .''

''Sasha!''

''Of course I wouldn't, you goose! You mean to tell me that he hasn't already 'paid his addresses'—or some of them, anyway?''

Lucy blushed. ''Not exactly. But he wanted to talk to you before we . . . before anything was made public.''

''He's a charming boy, Lucy. You are both fortunate.''

''He's not a boy, you know, Sasha,'' said Lucy seriously. ''He's a man—the man for me.''

She was shortly to be proved right.

LADY PANGBOURNE'S dinner party was followed the next evening by a rout party with dancing given by the Countess Carteret. Once again Serena was invited to go with a friend of the family who had been waiting for some time to escort the lovely Miss Calvert. Mr. Yardley was a lively bachelor and an excellent dancer, and Serena was looking forward to her evening. She was a little disappointed therefore that Mr. Yardley seemed to be somewhat subdued as he ushered Lucy, Serena and Mr. Warnham into the large ballroom in Marchant House. Lucy was immediately taken off to dance by Mr. Warnham, but Serena's partner seemed strangely reluctant. When Sir Harry

Birtles came up Mr. Yardley willingly performed the introduction he demanded, and then seemed to slide away.

"I hear you're a great sport, Miss Calvert," said Sir Harry with an engaging smile.

"I beg your pardon?"

"You know—the inn at Hoddesdon. I was there, too. A great lark, what?"

Serena felt herself growing pale. "I don't understand you, Sir Harry. What do you mean?"

"Oh, come! I won't tell, you know. Soul of discretion, give you my word."

Serena walked away without looking at him. She went upstairs under the pretence of repairing her dress and stayed there for as long as she dared. She must not lose her head! After a while she was calmer and came down again. Lucy and Mr. Warnham came over from the other side of the ballroom to join her. Lucy's face was stormy. Before they arrived, however, a man, a perfect stranger, came up behind Sasha and put his arm round her waist. She turned swiftly and took a step away from him. He smiled cynically and moved on, but his friend, who seemed to have drunk more than was good for him, lingered.

"Serena!" he whispered. "What a lovely...lovely name. Beautiful Serena! I could adore you."

"Sir!" said Serena. But she did not have to say more. Michael Warnham interposed himself in front of Serena and said coldly, "I think your friends are waiting for you in the card room, Dauncy. Miss Calvert is just leaving."

"Come, Sasha," whispered Lucy. "Come quickly!" Considerably shaken, Serena allowed herself to be taken away, Mr. Warnham in close attendance on them both.

The short journey back to Dover Street was accomplished almost in silence. Lucy began to speak as soon as they left Marchant House, but Mr. Warnham put his hand firmly over hers and said,

"Not yet, Lucy!"

"But—" She subsided when he shook his head at her.

Serena was shivering. The plot appeared to have succeeded all too well if the reaction of Mr. Dauncy and his friend was anything to go by. Now she was forced to face the problem of what to do about it. They reached the sanctuary of Dover Street, where Mr. Warnham suggested that they went into the small parlour. Here he said gently, "Now Lucy. Now you may talk."

"I know what you are going to say, Lucy," said Serena wearily. "Let me spare you what must seem an unpleasant task. London is buzzing with the story that Serena Calvert is having a secret affair. That she was seen in an inn outside London, having apparently spent the night with her lover."

Mr. Warnham made an involuntary movement towards Lucy, and Serena turned to him.

"Lucy and I have no secrets, and have never minced our words in speaking to each other, Mr. Warnham. However, if I *were* guilty of the behaviour I have just described, you may be assured that I would protect my niece from any knowledge of it."

Young Mr. Warnham relaxed. "I knew there must be something wrong with the story. It isn't true."

"There, I'm afraid, you are taking too simple a view. It isn't true, and yet it is." Lucy jumped up and ran over to kneel by Serena.

"Sasha! Oh, Sasha, don't speak in riddles like this, I can't bear it! I know you cannot have done anything wrong; why can't we just deny the story, threaten to go to the law. How can they say such things of you?" Serena gently drew Lucy to the seat beside her.

"Because people who don't know me as you do, Lucy, would find it difficult, if not impossible, to believe that I am the victim of a very carefully laid plot."

"A plot!"

"Yes, Mr. Warnham." Serena went on to give the two young people most of the details of what had happened the day before and at Hoddesdon that morning. She finished up by saying, "The conspirators were particularly clever in that they saw to it that the story would not only be spread—but believed, as well. I know now for certain that Sir Harry Birtles saw me there, and, unless I am mistaken, we will find that Sir John and Lady Taplow were also present at the inn, and also saw me."

Lucy flung her arms round Serena as if to shut out the dreadful picture her aunt had conjured up. But Mr. Warnham was silent. Serena said sadly, "It is an extraordinary tale, Mr. Warnham, I agree. Hardly credible, indeed."

At that he came over to sit on her other side.

"Miss Calvert, if I did not speak straight away, it was not, believe me, not in the slightest degree because I did not believe your account of what actually happened. I have known you for some time now, and Lucy has told me a great deal about you. To me, what you have told us is completely credible. No, I was thinking rather how one might best challenge the version going round London. Because you must! Your own good name, and Lucy's as well, are at stake."

Serena turned swiftly to Lucy. "Has anyone spoken to you . . . ?"

Mr. Warnham said grimly, "No gentleman has approached Lucy, no. They would hardly dare while I am there to protect her. But . . ." He seemed embarrassed.

Lucy finished for him. "The ladies are not always very kind, Sasha. I do not mean Lady Warnham—she is upset, of course, but she has been very sympathetic. She has suggested, however, that we—Michael and I—do not for the moment publish our engagement." She looked defiantly at Mr. Warnham. "And I agreed with her."

Serena looked towards the young man.

"I would publish it tomorrow, Miss Calvert, and so I told my mother," said Michael Warnham. "But Lucy is adamant. And perhaps she is right. It is better to postpone our own celebration until you are cleared, then we shall all rejoice together." He got up, went to Lucy's side, and took her hands in his. "You must not think that putting off the announcement of our engagement alters my determination to marry Lucy." The two smiled at each other. Then he turned back to Serena. "But, more immediately, I should like to help you in any way I can. Do you wish me to challenge Dauncy?"

"For heaven's sake, no!" cried Serena. "You would soon find yourself challenging half the men in London! No, we must look for evidence to convince London society that it is wrong!"

"What about Sir Harry Birtles!" cried Lucy. "Was he alone at the inn?"

"Most unlikely, I'd say." Mr. Warnham seemed to recollect himself. He turned to Lucy and suggested that she might like to leave her aunt and himself to discuss the matter. "I dare say you will accuse me of being stuffy, Lucy, but you really shouldn't be involved in discussing Lord Harry's behaviour and similar matters. You can support your aunt in other ways." Lucy looked mutinous, but he said firmly, "I am not discussing this unsavoury business in your presence, Lucy."

"Well, I shall go, but do not imagine I shall stop thinking about it. I wonder who Sir Harry was with?" With that she went, after hugging her aunt and giving Mr. Warnham a slightly cool curtsy. Serena smiled.

"I see I have no need to worry about Lucy's future happiness, Mr. Warnham. You will manage her very well. I cannot say how happy I am that you wish to marry."

"Lucy is a darling," he said simply. "I think I am very fortunate. But this is not solving your problem. You know, Lucy's question was an acute one. Your conspirators had to ensure that the necessary witnesses were there at the right place, and at the right time. The Taplows frequently travel to Huntingdon. It would be easy to find out when they would next be staying at the Black Lion. But Sir Harry... Who was Sir Harry's companion? You didn't see her, I suppose?" Serena shook her head. "Would you like me to try to find out?"

"Can you do so?"

"Easily, I should imagine. Sir Harry is not noted for his discretion."

"I would certainly like to know. And I think I will see Mr. Rambridge—my lawyer. He is dealing with another matter for me, and may have some suggestions to make about this one. But now, Michael—you see, I regard you as one of the family—I would like to ask you to do something more for me."

"Anything!"

"I wish you to make sure that Lucy and yourself are not seen in public with me for the moment."

"Miss Calvert!"

"Lucy calls me Sasha. Could you? In private, of course."

"I am honoured. Thank you...Sasha. But Lucy would never agree to desert you—nor would I."

"I know that you wish to show society your regard and support, and I am touched. But it is better for Lucy's sake that she should be kept away from this scandal as much as possible—at least for the next day or two until I find out what I have to do. Will you do this? From what I have seen you are the person to persuade her."

"Very well. But you must let me know if there is anything else I can do."

"I will." In spite of her weariness Serena smiled. "I feel we have a man in the family again, Michael. It is very comforting."

Mr. Warnham left, wishing he had a white charger or an army or two to defend Miss Calvert. Keeping Lucy safe seemed a small thing compared with all Sasha's other problems.

What he did not realise was that Serena was at least as anxious to keep Michael himself out of danger. In his eagerness to defend her honour he might well find himself picking quarrels with gentlemen more experienced than he in the art of the duel. And it was for this same reason that she had not mentioned her suspicions of Lord Wintersett.

But she had not forgotten them either. Thus it was that the next morning found her demanding to see Lord Wintersett at his residence in Upper Brook Street. Percy was alone in the entrance hall at the time, and found it difficult to deal with this totally unorthodox occurrence. He was only saved by Lord Wintersett himself, who came out of the library and invited Miss Calvert to enter.

"How can I help you, Miss Calvert?" he asked when the door shut behind Percy.

"You know how you can help me! Withdraw this rumour about me that you have set round London!"

"I have heard the rumour, of course. I have had no part in spreading it."

"You are too clever, and too cowardly for that," said Serena, her lip curling in scorn. "You, Lord Wintersett, stay in the background, merely pulling the strings for your puppets to hang me!"

Lord Wintersett looked down at the snuff box he was holding. His hand tightened, then relaxed. When he looked up again his voice was arctic. "If a man had said that to me, Miss Calvert, I would have knocked his teeth down his throat—as an alternative to killing him."

"I have no one to defend me, Lord Wintersett. It is easy for you to be brave with your threats."

"What about your mysterious lover? Is he not a man?"

Serena looked at him with loathing. "How can a creature such as you live with himself?" she asked, her voice quivering with feeling. "You have ruined me, Lord Wintersett, and yet you still taunt me with the creatures of your own invention. You know I have no lover!"

"Is there no foundation for this rumour, then? You were not at...Hoddesdon, was it? You were not seen by the Taplows?"

"Why are you fencing like this with me? There is no one else here. Why cannot you be open?"

"Tell me what you think I did."

"I will not waste my breath on such an exercise. But I warn you, I intend to expose you, if it kills me! You may have bribed that landlord with all the wealth in England, but one way or another, I shall rip your conspiracy wide open!" She went to the door.

"Serena!" He strode over to the door and put his hand on her shoulder. She wrenched herself free.

"Don't touch me!"

"Serena, what are you going to do?"

"Expose you for the villain you are!"

"And meanwhile?"

"Meanwhile I shall outface the scandalmongers and the gossips. I shall carry on as if they did not exist. I will not give in to your blackmail!"

"Serena, society can be cruel. It isn't wise—"

"You may save your efforts to dissuade me, Lord Wintersett. I will not let you win."

"Serena, what if I tell you that I had no part in any plot against you?" he asked rapidly.

"Who else wants me out of London?" Serena asked contemptuously. "Who withdrew the offer of Anse Chatelet and told me that he had 'other plans'?"

"But I only meant that I was going to St. Just myself! I am leaving in two days' time."

Serena whirled round. "To St. Just? You have wasted little time in your anxiety to review your new possession! I am sorry for the snakes on the island, for no viper, no fer-de-lance could rival your poison. Take care you don't bite one!" With that she pulled open the door and ran out.

CHAPTER ELEVEN

IT TOOK SERENA some time to calm down, but then she went to see Mr. Rambridge. He was not sanguine about the outcome of any action on the Anse Chatelet case, but promised to continue. When he heard the story of her abduction he was horrified. "Why, Miss Calvert, I have known only one other case like it. What do you wish me to do? As you say, it would be impossible to scotch the rumours without first finding the villain behind the plot. Who wishes you so much ill?"

When Serena tentatively voiced her suspicions concerning Lord Wintersett Mr. Rambridge was dismissive. "All things are possible, I suppose, and a lawyer hears more than most. But that Lord Wintersett should stoop to such dealings I find it impossible to believe!"

"But I know of no one else who bears me any kind of grudge!" cried Serena. "Mr. Rambridge, I should like to hire a trustworthy fellow to investigate the inn for me. I found it impossible to get any information at all from the landlord and his tribe. Perhaps a trained investigator, and a man, might be more successful. Do you know of such a person?"

Mr. Rambridge said he did, and if Miss Calvert wished he could present Mr. Barnet to her in a very few minutes. "He is just writing up the details of another case in the office next door. Can you wait? May I offer you a glass of Madeira or some other refreshment?" Within a short time Serena had engaged Mr. Barnet, given the particulars of the inn and everything she could remember which might be of use, rejected with scorn his suggestion that the Ambournes might have had anything whatsoever to do with it, and had taken her leave of both men. Mr. Rambridge's last words were, "I am glad you did not tell Barnet of your suspicions of your noble friend, Miss Calvert! I do not acquit the gentleman of ruining a lady's reputation. But that he should resort to such villainy to do so is quite out of the question.''

THAT EVENING Serena went to a concert in Northumberland House. She had taken a long time deciding what to wear. The temptation to put on a poppy-coloured India muslin dress was strong. Equally strong was the desire to wear stark white or discreet black. Each would make a statement to the world—but all had their obvious disadvantages. In the end she wore her topaz silk dress. Sheba brushed Serena's hair until it gleamed like silk, then twisted it into a knot high on her head. Aunt Spurston's diamonds glittered at her ears, throat and wrists, and the amber-coloured silk of the dress reflected the tiger gleam of her eyes. Lucy was spending the evening at Lady Warnham's, so she was not there to give her verdict on Serena's appearance. It was as well. She would not have recognised her loving, impulsive aunt in this creature of shining gold and ice.

Serena entered the great doors of Northumberland House five minutes before the concert began and started to walk up the wide staircase. Groups of people were standing on the stairs chatting and viewing each new arrival. As Serena passed silence fell on each group, and though the gentlemen eyed her, the ladies studiously avoided meeting her eye. Serena appeared not to notice. Her head held high, one hand holding the hem of her dress up, she mounted the stairs without haste, and without pause. The man standing at the top of the stairs looked down and thought he had never seen anything so graceful or so courageous.

"Cool customer, ain't she, Wintersett? Magnificent creature, though," said a young buck standing nearby, eyeing Serena through his glass. Lord Wintersett gave him such a glacial stare that he vanished, and avoided the noble peer's company for the rest of the evening. As he remarked to one of his cronies, there was no sense in looking for trouble.

Serena reached the music room at last and took a seat near the front. She was studying her programme, so did not apparently notice that several ladies sitting near her got up and moved to a different part of the room. But a faint flush appeared on her pale cheeks. The silence that followed was bro-

ken by the rustle of silk and the voice of Lady Ambourne
floating through the door.

"Serena, how pleasant to see you again! May I?" With a
charming smile the Dowager Countess of Ambourne sat down
next to Serena and proceeded to make light conversation until
the music began.

In the interval it was even worse. The two ladies made their
way to the supper-room, but, though the room was crowded, a
space appeared round them wherever they stopped. There were
smiles and greetings for Lady Ambourne, but no one offered
to join them or to fetch anything for them. Lord Wintersett,
watching from the other side, muttered a curse, and pushed his
way through the crowd. "Your servant, Lady Ambourne, Miss
Calvert? May I get you some refreshment?" he asked with a
low bow.

The Countess expressed her gratitude, adding, "Is it not
astonishing, Lord Wintersett, how very many underbred people come to these concerts nowadays? One might have thought
that a love of music would encourage courtesy, but the opposite appears to be the case." The Countess's voice was soft but
penetrating. A number of faces round them grew slightly pink,
and one or two people actually came up to join her. For a while
Lady Ambourne and Serena were surrounded. When Lord
Wintersett returned, carrying some glasses and a plate of delicacies, he had difficulty in reaching the Countess. Serena had
somehow been edged to the outside of the group. But when
Lord Wintersett presented her with a glass of champagne Serena looked at him expressionlessly, and emptied the glass into a
potted palm next to her. Then she turned and left the room.

LADY AMBOURNE was drinking her chocolate in the garden
room the next morning when Purkiss came in to ask if she
would receive Lord Wintersett. The Countess was surprised.
Only the most urgent business could excuse a call so early in the
day. She told Purkiss to show Lord Wintersett in and to bring
some more chocolate. Lord Wintersett, when he came, was
dressed in riding clothes.

"Lady Ambourne, this is good of you. I apologise for disturbing you at this early hour."

"Sit down, James, and share my chocolate."

Since Lord Wintersett's good manners forbade him to say that he disliked chocolate intensely, it was as well that Purkiss brought him some ale—"As it's so warm, today, my lord."

"Now, James, what is so important that you have to see me at this hour? I should think it is something to do with Miss Calvert?"

"Yes. She needs help."

"Why are you concerned, James? I thought that you disliked her. Why do you want to help her now?"

"I don't know! That's the devil of it. Forgive me, Lady Ambourne, I shouldn't have said that." He got up and went to the window. His back was towards her and his voice muffled as he said, "I seem to be doing everything wrong! The trouble is that I don't know what to think or what to believe."

The Countess looked at him with surprise. What had happened to self-sufficient, self-possessed Frosty Jack? She said thoughtfully, "But you wish to help Serena all the same. Why do you not speak to Serena herself?"

"I...I cannot. She would accept nothing from me—not even a glass of champagne! Certainly not any kind of advice." He came back and sat down. "I'm doing what I can. In a few minutes I shall set off for Hoddesdon, to do a little investigating. My time is limited, however. I leave for Falmouth and the West Indies tomorrow night."

The Countess's eyes widened. "You're going to St. Just?" James nodded. "Then we must not lose any time. How do you wish me to help Miss Calvert? I would have done so in any case, you know."

James came to sit opposite her, leaning forward in his chair. "She's so obstinate, so fixed in her determination to defy society, and she will be badly hurt if she continues. You saw what happened last night." He paused and looked down at his hands. "She would not listen to anything I might say. Could you use your influence to persuade her to live quietly until this business is cleared up one way or the other?"

"I have already resolved on that. Indeed, I have been laying plans this very morning. But James, am I to understand that you believe her to be innocent?"

"Yes, I do! That is—"

"Is that your heart or your head speaking?"

"It certainly isn't my head. The evidence is almost overwhelming."

"Good! Then it is your heart. Trust it. Are you in love with her?"

"At one time I thought I was," James said sombrely.

"In Surrey?"

"She has told you about the time in Surrey?" The Countess nodded. "I didn't know who she was, of course. Then when we came to London I found out she was a Calvert. Sasha Calvert. Since then my life has been in turmoil."

"Why?"

"Tony died on St. Just. What the world suspects, but does not know for certain, is that he killed himself. For years I...we have blamed Sasha Calvert for driving my brother into taking his own life."

"What rubbish! She was only fourteen years old at the time!"

"I know that now. I had always believed her to be much older. But Alanna said . . . No, I will not repeat it."

"Do you really believe that Serena was responsible for Tony's death, James? Knowing her, as you knew her in Surrey? Having observed her behaviour since she has been in London? Is there no alternative?"

There was a silence. Then James got up and said, "That is what I am going to the West Indies to find out. It's what I should have done years ago." He gave a wry smile. "Serena believes I am going there to gloat over my new acquisition."

"Have you tried to explain?"

"She would not listen. She dislikes me too much. I think I must go, Lady Ambourne. I have much to do before tomorrow night." He said with feeling, "I wish I did not have to leave England at this moment! Serena needs someone to help her! But I must. My journey to St. Just cannot be delayed. I will be easier in my mind if I know she has someone she can rely on. I thought of writing to Ned, but I know he is anxious about Perdita. Oh, forgive me again—I am so wrapped up in my own concerns that I forget my manners! How is Perdita?"

"We have been quite worried about her, but things are better now. I think I can call on Edward if I need him, James. Meanwhile I wish you *bonne chance* and *bon voyage*. I will watch Serena's interests, never fear."

"You believe in her, don't you, Lady Ambourne?"

"I have never doubted her for a minute."

AT HODDESDON James soon got the landlord's measure, and with a judicious mixture of threats and promises of remuneration even persuaded him to talk of the night in question. Mr. Cartwright had, it appeared, been asked—against suitable payment, of course—to provide a particular room at the head of the first flight of stairs. "Best room in the house, that is." He had agreed to be blind when a certain chaise drove up, to allow the passengers to see themselves to the room, to keep his mouth shut if the lady asked any questions in the morning, and to provide a chaise for her return to London. Everything had been paid for with shining, golden guineas by a man called the Captain. In answer to further questions he said that Sir Harry Birtles had stayed at the Black Lion more than once, always with the same lady, but he didn't know the lady's name. He thought it might be Aurelia, or Amelia—something like that. The Taplows—ah, they were a different sort, they were. Real aristocrats. They stayed regular as clockwork every six weeks when they visited their daughter in Huntingdon. Everyone knew that.

"Who arranged the matter of the rooms and so on?"

"The Captain. He came once beforehand to book the room and have a chat, like." To discuss terms, thought James.

"Did he ask about Sir Harry and the rest? Or any other guests? To find out when they would be staying here?"

"I don't remember that he did. Not then. And apart from the night he came with the lady that's the only time I've seen him, before or since." The landlord hesitated. "One o' the maids— she got the impression the Captain knew Sir Harry's lady. But that don't mean nothing. Sir Harry's lady is the sort who'd know a lot o' gentlemen, if you know what I mean, sir."

He gave James a vague description of the Captain and Sir Harry's lady-friend, but more he would not, or could not, say. James rather thought it was the latter. He paid Mr. Cartwright what he had promised and asked to see the girl. Apart from giggles all he could elicit from her was that Sir Harry had called the lady "Amelia" and that the "Captain" had winked at Amelia in the corridor, and then said something to her. She too gave some sort of description of Amelia and the Captain. James was about to leave when she sidled up to him and whispered that she had something to sell him. She showed him a much handled scrap of paper.

"It were in the bedroom, sir. The one at the top o' the stairs. The lady left it behind. It were all she left, too," she added resentfully. "That and a funny little glass with nothin' in it. I threw it away."

With growing distaste James read the note which Serena had found by the bed when she had woken up that morning.

My love,
You know I have to go, much as I hate to leave you. I'll arrange another meeting as soon as I can get away. Last night was even better than on St. Just. All my love—A.

As he rode back to London James was debating whether the note could be genuine. Who could tell? It was all so uncertain! Some of what the landlord had told him could support Serena's story. On the other hand, much of it could be explained by the very natural desire of a couple sharing an illicit bed to keep themselves anonymous. But—this was perhaps the biggest point in her favour—Serena hadn't been kept anonymous. The presence of Harry Birtles at the inn had made it certain that the whole of London now knew of her "affair." Harry . . . Harry had been with Amelia Banagher, he was sure. It might be worth finding out which of them had set up that assignation. He would call on Amelia when he got back to town. He went over the note again. Who was "A"? If it wasn't genuine it was quite cleverly phrased. Not too much—merely the suggestion that Serena had known the writer on St. Just. Well, he would be there in a few short weeks and would learn a lot more about Sasha Calvert and her family.

AMELIA BANAGHER was resting in her boudoir, a pretty little room of satin, lace and roses, when James came in. She received him with little cries of joy, and fussed over him for several minutes. But she had a fright when he said he had been to Hoddesdon that morning.

"I believe you spent the night there recently. With Harry Birtles."

She started to be coy, but he cut through her protestations and said directly, "Amelia, you and I have usually managed to be open with each other. I will pay your outstanding bills if you will tell me how it happened that you and Harry were at the Black Lion on that particular night."

"I'm not sure why you wish to know, James. And at the moment I have no outstanding bills!"

His eyes narrowed. "Now that I find most interesting. Indeed, it is quite extraordinary. No outstanding bills, eh? I think no further proof is needed, Amelia. Who bribed you?"

She was really frightened. Wintersett was not a man to play with. But nor was Fergus O'Keefe, and it wouldn't surprise her if what she and Fergus had done to Serena Calvert was criminal. Amelia decided to risk losing any influence she had ever had with Lord Wintersett in the interest of saving her skin.

"James, I have to confess I was angry with you for the way you and that woman treated me about the necklace," she said, improvising rapidly. "I wanted to pay you both back. I could see you were interested in her, and . . . and I wanted you to see how she was deceiving you." Amelia got up and fetched a handkerchief. "Would you like some wine, James? I'll send for some, shall I?"

"Thank you, but no, Amelia. Please continue with your story."

"Well . . . I decided to arrange that Harry should witness her meeting with her gentleman friend at the Black Lion. Nothing more. I knew Harry would spread it round. He's from the West Indies, isn't he? Her friend, I mean."

"You knew him?"

"Oh, no!"

"He appeared to know you. One of the maids saw you both."

Amelia felt her cheeks grow pale again. Then she pulled herself together and murmured, "A lot of gentlemen would like to know me, James. Many even exchange a word or two with me. It doesn't mean I know them."

Amelia could see that James was not entirely convinced, but she was confident that her story would be difficult to disprove. Then he asked, "What was he like—this gentleman from the West Indies?"

What should she say? If she described Fergus too well, James might track him down. "I didn't notice him particularly. Fair, I think. Not too tall."

After a while James left, and Amelia sank back with a sigh of relief.

THE NEXT DAY James returned to Rotherfield House. The
Countess was surprised but pleased to see him again. Once
more he found her in the garden room, with a letter in her
hand.

"Come in, James. Come in and sit down. I've had some
pleasing news of Perdita. Edward says she is much better. Quite
her old self again."

James expressed pleasure and the Countess sent for some
wine. Then she sat back in her chair and said, "But now you
shall tell me what you are here for. I thought we had said our
farewells? Have you been to Hoddesdon? What did you find?"

James related to the Countess the result of his visit to Hoddesdon, and his interview with Lady Banagher. She grew grave
immediately.

"A devilish conspiracy—I am not using the word lightly, either."

"I think Amelia Banagher was lying. Her description of the
man does not match what the people at the inn told me in any
respect—they said he was tall and very dark. I am sure she
knows him. Before I leave London I must engage a reliable man
to investigate further."

"James, Rambridge was here today to enquire after Perdita. He said that Serena had already engaged someone—a very
good man, he said. Would you like me to pass your information to him?"

This was quickly decided on, and James promised to let Lady
Ambourne have what he had learned in writing. "But that is
not really why I came, Lady Ambourne. It occurred to me after I left you yesterday that the Warnhams might well be reconsidering their approval of the match between their son and
Miss Lucy Calvert. That would be most unfortunate."

The Countess looked at him pityingly. "And you think I have
not thought of that? James, let me set your mind at rest by
telling you what I plan to do. I shall persuade Serena, if I can,
that she should retire to the country for a while—until we have
time to establish the truth. I shall also suggest that I move into
the house in Dover Street—everyone knows that I detest this
place when I am alone—and that I sponsor Miss Lucy myself.
I think the standing of the Dowager Countess of Ambourne is
enough to silence any possible criticism of Lucy Calvert, do you
not agree?"

James smiled for the first time. "Lady Ambourne, you are, as always, completely right!"

JAMES HAD ONE LAST interview before he left. It was with Serena, and was not planned. But he was irresistibly drawn to Dover Street on his way to the Gloucester coffee house, where he would pick up the coach for Falmouth. She would not receive him at first, but he eventually persuaded John to admit him. She was alone except for a large negress.

"Shall I stay, Mis' Sasha?"

"No, it's all right, Sheba. Lord Wintersett will not be here long." The woman left, giving him a baleful stare as she went.

"I'm leaving tonight, Serena. Have you ... have you any messages for the Pendomers?"

She smiled bitterly. "What could I possibly tell them? That I no longer own Anse Chatelet? That I am disgraced and shunned by most of London society? That Lucy's marriage is no longer so certain?"

"No. Though I think Miss Lucy's happiness is not in danger. But I understand. Then I will bid you goodbye."

"You could not bid me anything more welcome! Goodbye, Lord Wintersett. Enjoy your stay at Anse Chatelet. I hope you are prepared to explain to our—I beg your pardon, *your* people, why the Calverts have finally abandoned them."

"Serena, what will I find when I get there? Was Tony's death an accident, after all? Is there another explanation?"

There was silence while a variety of expressions passed over her mobile features. A flash of temper, a desire to speak, hesitation, doubt and finally sadness. "I cannot tell you," was all she said. "You must judge for yourself." But her voice was gentle.

He moved closer. "Will you be here when I return?"

"I don't know. I hope to see Lucy married but I am not sure when that will be at the moment. After that ... I don't know."

He drew her to him. She looked at him with troubled eyes, but made no effort to resist when he kissed her, a long, sweet kiss. The kiss grew deeper, more passionate until they were closely twined in each other's arms, murmuring to each other and kissing again and again. Serena broke free, but he pulled her back to him, holding her tight, pressing her head to his chest. He said into her hair, "This business at Hoddesdon—do you really think me so despicable? That I would go to such lengths to ruin you, Serena? After the time on the hill in Surrey—William, Trask and Douce, and all those hours when we seemed to share so much?''

"I don't know!" she cried, pulling away from him again. "I'm so confused. I've been told you were there at the inn yesterday, giving money to the landlord. But when you hold me as you did I cannot remember that. One minute I think you're a devil, a monster, and the next you hold me in your arms and I cannot imagine wishing to be anywhere else! If you think we shared so much why did you treat me so badly? Oh, go to St. Just and leave me alone, Lord W... Wintersett!''

"I thought you had mastered that stammer, Serena.''

"It is a weakness I despise, I assure you! It appeared after that first night in London. When you turned into someone I no longer knew... For a while I couldn't even say your name at all.''

"Then don't say it! Say James, instead! After all, I call you Serena—in private.''

"Serena and James—no, Lord W... my lord.''

"Never?''

"Perhaps. After your visit to St. Just you may not wish to see me ever again.''

His face clouded. "Will I hear of the Captain there? The man whose name begins with 'A'?''

She looked blank. "What are you talking about?'' In silence James handed her the note he had bought from the maid. She glanced at it, then with a look of revulsion she threw it from her. She said in a strangled voice, "For a moment I thought I had misjudged you, Lord W...Wintersett. I was even dolt enough to feel sorrow on your behalf! How glad I am that you have reminded me before you go of your true nature.'' Serena's voice grew clearer. She said contemptuously, "Did you enjoy kissing me so tenderly, arousing feelings I thought I had forgotten, while you knew all the while that this... this piece of filth was in your pocket, waiting to be produced? I acquit you of plotting to ruin me, Lord W... W... The devil take it! I will say it! Lord Wintersett! You were purchasing this note from the landlord in order to accuse me, not paying your bribe. But you are despicable, all the same. I have had enough of your tricks and postures. I never, never wish to see you again! And I wish you joy of your discoveries on St. Just!''

She stormed out of the room, calling to John to see to Lord Wintersett.

THE NEXT DAY Serena and Lucy were sitting in the drawing-room of the house in Dover Street. It was a large, airy room furnished in shades of pale yellow and white, and the two ladies in their delicate muslins completed a very pretty picture. But it was evident that all was not well with them, for they were both pale and heavy-eyed. Serena had not slept at all. She had found it impossible to dismiss from her mind the vision of James Stannard travelling south-west to Falmouth. There was a long, tedious voyage ahead of him, and though he would find Anse Chatelet a worthy prize there would be little joy in it for him.

She had been haunted, too, by the events of the previous evening and the curious effect James Stannard had on her. She had told him that she never wanted to see him again, and she still meant it, yet the thought filled her with passionate regret. With a wry smile she recalled her conversation with Lady Pendomer before she had set out for England all those months ago.

"I wouldn't give up control of Anse Chatelet," she had said. "Not after all these years, unless I could find a husband I could trust to manage it better than I can myself..."

In Surrey, she had thought she had found such a man in Lord Wintersett, and the prospect had filled her with incredulous and humble delight. It was bitterly ironical that he should now be the man who had taken Anse Chatelet from her.

He would return, knowing how unjust he had been all these years. But it was too late. For all the feeling he had aroused in her the night before, it was too late. In London Lord Wintersett had been the cold-hearted manipulator everyone had talked of. The man on the hill had gone forever.

With a sigh Serena dismissed Lord Wintersett from her thoughts and turned them instead to Lucy. She was worried about the girl. It was so rare for her niece to be listless and silent—and these should be the happiest days of Lucy's life! But the shadow of society's reaction to her aunt was casting a shade over Lucy, too. Michael had been a constant caller, and the house was filled with his flowers, but even he had failed to lift Lucy's spirits. It was a relief when Lady Ambourne was announced and Serena got up to meet her, smiling in genuine welcome.

"Serena! How do you go on, my dear? And Lucy, too? I have come with all sorts of good news, a basket of fruit and fresh vegetables from Ambourne, and a suggestion."

Serena sent for tea and they were soon comfortably settled.

"First, the good news. You must have seen how preoccupied I have been recently—so much that I fear I have neglected you. But, after worrying us all for a while, Perdita is now quite fit again. I had thought I should go down to Ambourne to be with her, but that is no longer necessary. I will remain in London a little longer."

The two Calvert ladies both expressed their pleasure at this. The Countess continued, "The fruit and vegetables I have given to John to take to Mrs. Starkey..."

"And the suggestion?" smiled Serena.

"Ah, if I may, I should like first to discuss the suggestion with you alone, Serena. Perhaps Lucy could leave us for a while?" As Lucy jumped up to go Lady Ambourne said, "Don't go far away, child. This concerns you, too."

When Lucy had gone the Countess explained her plan to Serena. "What do you think, Serena? Perdita would be pleased to welcome you to Ambourne."

Serena hesitated. "Thank you, Lady Ambourne, but I do not wish to give society the impression that I concede defeat. I have done nothing to earn their censure. And I have hopes that Mr. Barnet will come up with something soon..."

"And if he does not? Oh, I know that James gave him a great deal more to work with—"

"Lord W... Wintersett?"

"Did he not tell you?" asked the Countess, opening her eyes wide in the full knowledge that James would certainly not have told Serena anything. "He learned quite a lot in Hoddesdon. He is almost certain that the woman with Sir Harry was that wretch Amelia Banagher. Mr. Barnet now has her under surveillance. He is hoping that she will lead him to this Captain fellow."

"I see..."

"Do you, Serena? Do you really see?"

"What do you mean?"

"Why should James go to all this trouble to help you? Going to Hoddesdon, undertaking this long journey to St. Just—"

"Oh, no! He's going to St. Just to look at his property."

"Did he say so? I think you are wrong. I think he is going to find out what really happened on the island thirteen years ago. It will be a sad day for him when he does. Incidentally, why have you never told him about Richard and Alanna?"

"I wanted to last night when he came to see me, but it was for all the wrong reasons, Lady Ambourne. I was so angry with him that I wanted to hurt him, to tell him that his brother had died because of Alanna and Richard, not me. He might have refused to believe me, of course. He has refused to trust me so often before. But then I realised I couldn't. However heartlessly he has behaved towards me, I could not tell him this in anger, hoping to hurt him. Perhaps if things had been different...if we had still trusted one another, if I could have told him...in confidence and...love, I might have. But, feeling as I did about Anse Chatelet and his efforts to discredit me, how could I just blurt out to him that his brother had been betrayed by his wife, that his nephew, his heir, the only link with Tony left to him was perhaps not a Stannard at all, but part of the hated Calvert clan?"

"Many would have. As you said, to hurt him."

"I could not."

"And I will tell you why, Serena. I think you love him. As he loves you."

"Lord Wintersett is not capable of the sort of love I am seeking, Lady Ambourne. And if he did once love me, in his fashion, then he will be cured of it by the time he gets back. I told him I never wanted to see him again."

The Countess smiled and said briskly, "I think you are mistaken on both counts, Serena. But it is useless to talk about James for the moment. He must speak for himself when he returns. Now, about my plan..."

In the end Serena capitulated. "But you would be doing so much for us, Lady Ambourne. I hardly know..."

The Countess leaned forward. "The favour is not at all one-sided, believe me. Now that Edward and Perdita are settled I sometimes feel a little lonely—certainly in Rotherfield House! And I myself want to remain in London for the moment. Tell me, is Lucy in love with Michael Warnham? Does she wish to marry him?''

"Oh, yes! But—"

"But the Warnhams are worried, are they not? They are good, kindly people, but they have always been a touch over-conventional. You must let me help. Lucy deserves to be happy. She is a very pretty, well-behaved girl, and I guarantee that the Warnhams will accept her again once the world sees that she is sponsored by the Dowager Countess of Ambourne! Society will soon forget the scandal about Miss Calvert if Miss Calvert is not there to remind them of it. You may trust me, Serena. I know my world. And then, when the mystery is cleared up and your enemies are unmasked—as they certainly will be—you may return in triumph."

After very little further persuasion Serena agreed to call Lucy in to see what she thought. She was afraid that Lucy might reject the offer out of hand, but she had underestimated the Countess. Within minutes all was settled, the only change in the plan being that Serena would not go to Ambourne, but back to Lady Spurston. She told the Countess and Lucy that she would not think of imposing on Perdita at this time, and there was enough sense in what she said for them to accept this. What she did not tell them was that, once with Lady Spurston, she fully intended to find her way to Wintersett Court. She had to see young Tony Stannard for herself! Almost the last thing Serena did in London was to arm herself with a map of Surrey from Hatchard's bookshop in Piccadilly.

The parting with Lucy was not easy, but both the Countess and Sheba assured Serena that her niece would be well cared for. Michael was also there to support Lucy, and Serena had every hope that their story would have a happy end. The Countess embraced her warmly and extracted from her a promise that she would visit Ambourne before long. Otherwise Serena left London without regret. Her hopes had been so high, the reality so painful. Lord Wintersett was now on the high seas, and she might never see him again. Perhaps it was as well.

CHAPTER TWELVE

SERENA GAVE Lady Spurston a limited account of her disastrous adventure, but it was enough to rouse all that lady's sympathy, especially when she heard that the Ambournes were championing her. She agreed that Serena's decision to retire to Surrey for a while had been a wise one.

"For you know, Serena, the season is three-quarters over. The world will soon have forgotten your story. And if you have retained the friendship of the Ambournes you will be able to return to London in time for the next season."

"Not," said Serena with determination, "not unless I am vindicated, Aunt Spurston. And perhaps not even then. Tell me, where can I find a new side-saddle?"

After some argument Lady Spurston had agreed that Serena could ride out as much as she liked as long as Tom, the stable lad, went with her. So Serena shook out her riding habit, learned, not without difficulty, to master the side-saddle again, and about a week after her arrival set off to find Wintersett Court.

ALANNA HAD BEEN burdened with a sense of doom ever since Lord Wintersett's lawyer had come down to Surrey and had announced that his client was off on urgent business in the West Indies. In three months—perhaps less if the winds were favourable—she would be unmasked. What was she to do? She was unable to sleep at night or rest during the day. She was irritable with the servants, and lost her temper more than once with her son. Day after day she walked the gardens, worrying over the problem. Should she go away—to her home in Ireland, perhaps? The thought was not a happy one. She did not relish living with her sister, looking after an elderly father.

But soon another worry was added to her burden. Fergus O'Keefe called, ostensibly to claim the last two instalments of his money, but making it clear that this was not to be his final visit.

"It's a fine house you live in, Alanna, my darlin'. I like callin' on you here, I do. I'll come again next week, shall I?"

She stammered, apologised, but gave in weakly when he said with a laugh, "Now, don't be puttin' me off and me an old friend from Ireland. I'll leave you alone when I have me gaming house in Dublin, I promise you. But that costs a mint o'money, Alanna my love, a...mint...of...money. You wouldn't have a bit more put by now, would you? To help out an old friend. You might call it a security. A security! Now there's a thought!" He roared with laughter, but Alanna shivered and promised him another hundred pounds.

She did not delude herself that this visit would be the end of the story. In an effort to escape from the treadmill of her thoughts she walked the gardens till she was exhausted, but the fact was inescapable. In engaging Fergus O'Keefe she had put herself completely in his power.

SERENA RODE UP the drive to Wintersett Court, and when she caught sight of a figure sitting on a bench under some trees she stopped, dismounted and gave the reins to her groom, who took the horse off to the stable yard. She walked over the grass towards the bench.

"Mrs. Stannard?"

Alanna stood up. "I'm afraid I don't..."

"You possibly do not recognise me. I was only fourteen when you last saw me."

Alanna's eyes widened in horror. She jumped to her feet shrieking, "Oh, no! You must go away from here! Get out, get out!"

"Please spare me the histrionics, Alanna!" Serena made no attempt to disguise her scorn. "You must know by now that your brother-in-law is on his way to St. Just, and that he will learn enough there to expose your lies for what they are."

"Yes, but there may be a storm, a shipwreck..." Alanna's voice died away. "Why are you here?" she whispered at last.

"I have come to see the boy. And to ask you why you did it."

"Did what?" asked Alanna warily.

"Why did you tell the Stannards that it was I who seduced Tony, not that it was Richard who seduced you?"

"What else could I have done?" cried Alanna passionately. "The Stannards would never have given me shelter if they had known... Where else could I have gone? I thought it was safe enough—St. Just was the other side of the Atlantic and I knew the Calverts would hush up Richard's part in the affair. The Stannards were desperate to have Tony's son with them. What else could I do?"

"Tell the truth."

"Tell the truth? And what was that? That your precious brother had rejected me, had laughed in my face when I told him I wanted him to marry me. Can you imagine what I felt when he told me he despised me? That he had no intention of marrying a damned tame bedmate, that he could have more thrills with the native girls in the village? That one bastard more or less made no difference to him, he had plenty." Alanna was now hysterical. The successive shocks and lack of rest had been too much for her nerve. Serena tried to persuade her to sit down but she ignored her.

"He said that to me! Alanna Cashel! Not one of his native girls, but a Cashel of Kildone." Alanna was striding up and down in front of the bench like a caged tiger. She had a handkerchief in her hand and was tearing it in shreds. "He'd told a different tale when he'd been trying to get me into his bed. Oh, yes! I was mad for him, but I didn't let him see it. I held off till he swore he'd marry me if Tony were not in the way. So I let him love me... And then I found that the baby was coming..." Alanna sank down on to the grass. She was hardly conscious of an audience, but stared into space, reliving the past. She whispered, "I went to Tony and told him I was going to leave him. He thought I didn't mean it. He refused to even discuss it. So I... so I... shot him." She hid her face in her hands. Her voice was muffled as she sobbed, "I got rid of Tony, but Richard didn't want me after all..."

"*You* shot Tony?"

Alanna was suddenly quiet. "Did I say that? Oh, what does it matter?" she said wearily. "There's no one else to hear and, anyway, no one can prove it now... I'll be gone soon and you're as good a confessor as any. Yes, I killed Tony Stannard. Everyone was so anxious to hush the whole matter up that no one questioned that it was suicide. But I wish I hadn't killed him!" She put her head back in her hands and wept bitterly. Serena gazed at her in horror. This was much worse than she had suspected.

Alanna looked up. "I'm going away," she whispered brokenly. "But I don't know what to do about Anthony. He cannot travel. But how can I leave him behind? What will happen to him?"

"He's Richard's son, you say?" Alanna nodded. "Then he's my nephew and a Calvert, whatever his birth certificate may say. I'll take care of him if the Stannards won't. He'll be safe, Alanna." Serena tried to feel pity for this woman, but it was impossible. So many lives wrecked through her wicked selfishness all those years ago! Alanna looked up and caught the expression of disgust on Serena's face.

"I've tried to atone. All these years I've stayed here, hardly living. I have never been to London, never travelled. All I have done for thirteen years is to act as companion to Lady Wintersett, and to look after my son...." She caught Serena's hands. "You won't tell him, will you? Anthony, I mean. You won't tell him that I... that his mother..."

"No," Serena disengaged herself. "Alanna, you know I cannot agree to keep silent if you stay here, don't you?"

Alanna nodded. "I shall be gone by next week, I promise you." She started to say something, hesitated, then started again. "There's something else I ought to tell you. I was afraid you'd talk to James. So I...I..." She stopped and looked at Serena uncertainly. Then she said, "No, I cannot. You will not help me if I tell you." She ran into the house as if she was being chased by the hounds of hell. Serena stared after her. What had Alanna been going to say?

THE NEXT TIME Fergus O'Keefe called, Alanna was ready for him.

"I have no more money," she said. "But there are jewels—quite a lot. You can have nearly all of them. I'll just keep a few for myself."

Captain O'Keefe's eyes gleamed. "Where are they, Alanna, my soul?"

"They're in a safe place. You'll get them if you take me to Ireland with you. I could help you in your gaming club."

"Now that is a surprise! It's not often that Fergus O'Keefe is taken unawares, but you've done it, my pretty one." His eyes grew hard. "I wonder why you're suddenly so fond of me, Alanna?"

She forced herself to laugh. "I'm tired of living here, and that's the truth, Fergus O'Keefe! It's a bold man you are, and I've taken a fancy to see more of the world before I die—in your company."

He looked at her appraisingly. "Well, you've worn quite well. You might be an asset at that. It must be the good living you've had, but it won't be as easy a life with me, I warn you. What am I saying? Your jewels should make all the difference. A lot, you say?"

"The Wintersetts are rich—and generous. I've quite a few."

"Where did you say they were?"

"I didn't. And I won't."

Fergus paused. Then he smiled and said, "Well I won't say I don't have a fancy for you, Alanna Stannard."

"Alanna Cashel, Fergus. Alanna Cashel. Wait for me at the end of the drive. I'll come in a short while—we can hire a chaise at the next posting station. My box is already there."

With tears in her eyes Alanna went to her son's room. He was asleep. She kissed him, and went to join Fergus O'Keefe without a thought for anyone else or a look back.

As for Fergus O'Keefe, he was happy to wait for a while. He wasn't worried about the jewels—he'd find them all sooner or later. He might even keep Alanna Cashel for a time. She wasn't bad-looking, for her age.

IMPATIENT AS SHE WAS to see Richard's son, Serena delayed her second visit to Wintersett Court until she could be certain that Alanna had gone. For young Tony's sake she was prepared to give Alanna a chance to get away, but she did not wish to see her again. The revelation that Tony's death had been murder, not suicide, had filled her with horror. Nor did she believe that the act had been the impulse of a moment such as Alanna had described, for there must have been a gun. Alanna must have kept a cool head afterwards, too, for no one had ever questioned the cause of death. Serena felt burdened with the knowledge. Though she saw no sense in making it public after all these years, the Stannards ought to know. But what about the boy? She must do her utmost to keep it from him. In the end she decided to wait. The facts of Tony Stannard's death had remained secret for so long that another month or two would not make any difference.

Confirmation that Alanna had disappeared came in the form of an advertisement in the *Gazette* for someone to act as companion to two invalids—a widow of high birth, and a child confined to a wheelchair. The address given was Wintersett Court, Surrey.

Serena went straight to her aunt and showed her the advertisement. "You must help me, Aunt Spurston. I want you to write me a reference for this post."

"A reference, Serena? Whatever for? There is absolutely no reason for you to seek a post of any kind. Have you forgotten who you are?"

"No, Aunt Spurston, but if Anse Chatelet isn't returned to me then I am almost penniless, and shall have to find something to support me. And I wish to go to Wintersett Court."

Lady Spurston was astonished, annoyed and finally angry, but she could not persuade Serena to change her mind. After a while she reluctantly agreed to provide a reference, but was outraged when she was asked to write it for a person called Prudence Trask.

"Now, that I will never do, for that would be deceit. Why can't you go under your own name, Serena?"

"Aunt Spurston, the Stannard family would never allow a Calvert to darken their doors."

"All the more reason for not going there, I should have thought. What are you up to?"

Serena knelt down beside her great-aunt's chair. "There is something I can do at Wintersett Court, I feel it in my bones— I know I can do more for this child than anyone else could. Don't ask me how I know, I just do. But if I go as Serena Calvert I will never get near him. Please help me! You have been more than kind to me here, but I know you secretly long for your peace and quiet again!"

Lady Spurston took a day to think it over, then agreed to write Prudence Trask a suitable reference. "This is all against my better judgement, Serena, but you are clearly set on it. And you have a way with you, there's no question about that. I only hope you can carry it off. But what will you do when Lord Wintersett gets back?"

"I intend to be gone before that, but I can do a lot in three months."

SERENA'S INTERVIEW with Lady Wintersett in the presence of a representative from the family lawyers was a curious affair. Lady Wintersett looked ill, and said nothing. The lawyer fussed and fiddled interminably. Finally he said, "Well, Miss er...Miss Trask, you might have been suitable, but I am disappointed that you appear to have had so little experience. Though your reference is excellent, it is your only one. We have had other, more experienced applicants. So unfortunately...er..."

Lady Wintersett leaned forward and put her hand on the lawyer's arm. She slowly nodded her head.

"You wish me to appoint Miss—er—Trask, Lady Wintersett?"

Lady Wintersett nodded again.

"Very well. Miss Trask, I have decided that your pleasant appearance and personality outweigh the lack of experience. The position is an unusual one in that you will be expected to oversee the running of the house. Mrs. Stannard dealt with all this until she was er...called away. There is a steward, of course, and a housekeeper..." He went into details of salary and conditions of work, but Serena hardly heard him. She was elated at having passed this hurdle, but she was also puzzled. Lady Wintersett had appeared to take no interest in the interview, so why had she interfered? It was clear that before her intercession the lawyer had been about to refuse Serena the post.

The need for someone to take Mrs. Stannard's place was so urgent that Serena was asked to start as soon as she could, and the weekend saw her installed in her own room in Lord Wintersett's country seat. She was occasionally overwhelmed at her temerity, but whenever she had doubts she thought of her nephew—sick and lonely in his darkened room. It had been explained to her that Mrs. Stannard had been devoted to her son, but that she might have to be away for some time. The boy was already missing his mother, and he would need careful handling. Serena could hardly wait to meet him.

On the day of her arrival she was taken to Tony's room. Her heart was beating strangely as she entered, looked towards the bed, and saw the boy lying there. She had eyes for nothing else as she went over to him, and had to bite her lips to keep them from trembling. He was pale and thin, and had none of Richard's earthy robustness, but for all that Richard's eyes looked out at her from Richard's face—he was unmistakably her brother's child. The boy was staring at her. She saw now that he had been crying, and was trying to disguise the fact.

"You've come to take the place of mama," he said. "I don't want you."

"I couldn't do that, Tony! I've just come to keep you company. It must be rather boring lying here on your own."

His head turned, and Serena saw Lady Wintersett was sitting on the other side. She was regarding them closely. Serena got up in confusion and curtsied. "Ma'am ... Lady Wintersett, I'm sorry. I didn't see you there." Lady Wintersett smiled and shook her head. She indicated that Serena should carry on.

"Tony, I knew your parents in the West Indies, so I've brought you some pictures and books about the islands. Would you like to see them?"

By exercising every ounce of self-control and patience during the following days, Serena began slowly, tediously slowly, to win the boy's confidence. He was not a child. He was now nearly thirteen, at a suspicious, temperamental age, but by concentrating on interests outside the boy himself she was gaining ground. Lady Wintersett's own physician, Dr. Galbraith, soon replaced Tony's former doctor and Serena had a long talk with him about Tony's state—the first of many. What he said gave her the courage to throw open the huge windows in Tony's room and let in some sunshine and fresh air. When Tony complained that the draught from the open windows made him cold, Serena was unsympathetic. "That's because you don't move! Come, let me help you into your wheelchair, and you can throw your arms about a little. No, harder than that!"

It was all uphill work, but Serena persevered. She had never in her life shirked a challenge, and this one was perhaps the most important of all. She made sure that Tony did the exercises Dr. Galbraith recommended, rewarding the boy with treats when she saw he was really trying. Lady Wintersett came to see her grandson one day with a small puppy in her arms, and Pandora, so-called "because she was into everything," quickly won his heart. He exerted himself more for the puppy's sake than for anyone else.

"Look at her, Miss Trask! Quick, she's falling into the chest—no, don't bother, I'll get her!" and he would swing his wheelchair over to rescue the inquisitive puppy from whatever predicament she found herself in. He grew stronger with every day that passed, and seemed to miss his mother less as time went on—perhaps because his life was suddenly filled with so much that was new.

Serena told him stories about "my brother Richard," who was always getting into scrapes—falling from trees, getting trapped in caves, doing all the things boys loved to hear, and it became a kind of continuous saga, where truth and fiction were mingled. She wheeled Tony out into the garden and they sat together on a bench under the trees and watched the birds and small animals at their work, while Pandora chased everything in sight, always with more optimism than success. Serena got the servants to seek out the bats and balls from the Stannard boys' childhood, and she improvised games with them on the lawn, games which often ended in laughter when Serena collapsed breathless on to the bench while a triumphant Pandora ran off with the ball or stick. Slowly she and Pandora together roused in the boy a desire to do more. He would stretch out for a ball thrown slightly wide and exclaim in frustration when he missed it, or he would watch Serena wistfully when she played with Pandora or rode one of the horses up to where he sat on the lawn. And all the time Lady Wintersett watched and occasionally, in fact quite often, smiled.

Serena was waiting for the moment when Tony would realise that he could do so much more if he could only walk. She had talked the matter over with Dr. Galbraith, who had said that the child had started walking at the normal age, and had made good progress.

"Then the poor lad was ill—I forget what it was, measles or chicken pox or the like—and there were complications. After that Mrs. Stannard treated him as such an invalid that he lost the will to use his limbs at all. I argued with her, of course, but she dismissed me and engaged another doctor. It is scandalous, Miss Trask, how much damage can be done by an overfond mother, all in the name of love!"

Tony's cheeks were getting quite sunburned. He grew daily more like his father, his tawny hair bleached by the sun, and his eyes, so like Serena's, sparkling with life. Then one day Serena threw the ball too high. Tony stretched up from the bench, realised he was not going to reach it, and stood up to catch it. He remained there looking down at the ball in his hands for a moment. "Miss Trask?" he said uncertainly. Serena wanted to shout, to dance, to sing, but did none of these.

"Yes, Tony?" she said casually.

"I . . . I stood up!" As Tony said this he sat down suddenly on the bench behind him.

"So? What's so extraordinary about that? Some of us do it all the time."

"But I don't!"

"You do! I've just seen you. Try again." Serena's tone may have been casual, but all her being was concentrated on this boy. She watched his face as the desire to stand battled with his fear of failure. She strolled away, turned and threw the ball high a second time. "Catch!"

Without thinking Tony stood again. He missed the ball, for in her excitement Serena had pitched it wide, but he grinned all over his face as he realised what he had done.

"Do you wish to try a step? I'll keep close by you." Serena nodded encouragingly. Stiffly, awkwardly, Tony Stannard moved towards her, one step, two, three, then he almost fell. Swiftly she took his arm and helped him back to the bench. "No more today," she said firmly. "Let's go back to the house. You must rest for a bit, and tomorrow there's something I want you to see." As she put him back in the wheelchair she caught sight of Lady Wintersett in the large window overlooking the garden and impulsively waved to her. She was delighted to see Lady Wintersett lift a hand in response. That night a bottle of champagne appeared on the dinner table, quite without comment. The following morning she wheeled Tony round to the huge yard at the side of the house. Here she took him into a disused stable.

"What are we here for, Miss Trask? I want to go back to the bench! I want to stand again!"

"We shall go on to the lawn afterwards, Tony. I want you to meet someone here first. Parks has two inventions to show you. He's been waiting for you to be ready. Parks, this is Master Tony. Show him your puzzles."

On the floor of the stable were two curious contraptions. One was a kind of wooden frame, a bit like a clothes horse but sturdier, and the other was a clumsy-looking saddle. Tony studied them carefully in silence.

"I think one might be to put on a horse," he said slowly. "But what are the things at the side for, Mr. Parks?"

"To hold you, Master Tony. It's a special saddle to put on a pony." Parks went out again and led in a broad-backed pie-bald pony. "Like this one."

Tony's eyes were wide with excitement. "For me? I can ride? Now? Oh, Miss Trask!"

Serena laughed. "Try the saddle," she said. "And then you can try the pony. If Parks is satisfied that you'll be safe you can ride round the yard. But first look at this." She took the frame, held it in front of her and took some steps. Tony could now see that the frame took the weight of the body while allowing the legs to move. "It's Parks's walking machine," Serena said. "I gave him the idea, and he made the design and constructed it. You must thank him for his trouble, Tony. He's spent a lot of time on it."

Tony thanked Parks somewhat cursorily, for his eyes were on the pony. In a few minutes he was sitting on its back, well supported by the curious saddle. Parks examined it carefully and then led the pony out into the yard and they walked round it once in solemn procession. They did this several times, but when Parks gave Serena a significant look she said they must stop. Tony objected violently.

"I'm not tired, I'm not, I tell you!" But Serena was adamant.

"You'll have to go slowly, Tony. I want you to have some energy left for learning to use the frame. When you can walk properly on your own you'll be able to try riding on your own."

That was the beginning of a time such as Tony had never known. Serena was hard put to it to restrain him from doing himself harm, so eager was he to be on the move all the time. The weeks passed and each day seemed to bring further improvement. The walking frame was used a lot at first but it gradually became unnecessary, and as Tony's muscles strengthened so the extra supports on the pony saddle were discarded. The boy fairly buzzed with happiness, and each evening as Lady Wintersett sat with him before he went to sleep he grew almost incoherent as he told her of his day.

It seemed to Serena that Lady Wintersett was less remote than she had been. She frequently joined them now out in the garden, and though she never said anything she was obviously taking an interest in their activities. Sometimes Serena was worried about the effect it might have on Lady Wintersett's recovery if she ever found out that Tony was not, in fact, her grandchild. She half hoped that it might never be necessary to tell her.

So high summer passed into early autumn. But though the mornings might be chilly the days remained warm and dry, and the gardens of Wintersett Court rang with the sound of boyish shouts and boyish laughter. Tony's tutor returned after the summer break, and it was decided that he should instruct Tony in the morning and late afternoon leaving the boy free to be outside during the main part of the day. Serena rode out with Tony regularly, always accompanied by a groom, but otherwise free to go where she wished. They rode far and wide, but Serena never took Tony up on the ridge. She felt no desire to see it again.

One afternoon in October they returned from their ride rather late. Tony was overdue for his lessons. They cantered into the stable yard, flushed and breathless, and were greeted by the sight of Douce waiting in the yard, ready saddled, with a tall, bronzed gentleman standing next to her.

"I was just about to come in search of you," he said.

"Uncle James!" shouted Tony, scrambling somewhat inelegantly off his horse. "Look! I can ride!"

"So I see. My congratulations! Someone ought to teach you the finer points of the art—such as dismounting."

Tony wasn't listening. He ran somewhat awkwardly to his uncle and said, "I can walk, too!"

"It was worth coming four thousand miles just to hear that, Tony. How are you?" said James, smiling down at him. "Though I think you have no need to tell me. Come inside, and tell me what you've been doing. Parks!"

"Yes, my lord?"

"See to the horses, would you. Come along, Tony! Miss Trask?"

CHAPTER THIRTEEN

ONCE INSIDE the house Serena excused herself and started for the stairs.

"Miss Trask!" She stopped and slowly turned. Lord Wintersett smiled, presumably for the benefit of those around, for the smile did not reach his eyes. "Where are you off to? I had hoped you would join us."

"I . . . I have to change, Lord Wintersett. Lady Wintersett would not like me to appear as I am in the drawing-room."

"Very well. I thought for a moment you might be attempting to avoid me. I shouldn't like that . . . Miss Trask."

Serena put her chin up. "I shall be down as soon as I can, my lord." He nodded and followed his nephew. Serena continued on her way, but as she mounted the stairs her mind was on the scene in the stableyard. She was furious with herself for the sudden feeling of delight she had felt on seeing Lord Wintersett again. She had only just managed to stop herself from running to welcome him back with all her heart. What a fool she would have looked! His attitude towards her had been cool, almost unfriendly, and when she recalled her words to him before he had left for St. Just she could hardly have expected otherwise. He looked well—the sea voyage had obviously suited him—but there were signs of stress and pain in the tanned face. It was no more than she had expected—not only had he been forced to relive the loss of his brother, but he had also discovered that he had been so wrong, so unjust all these years. For a man of his temperament that must have been painful.

Serena pulled herself up short. Why was she feeling so sorry for him? He was nothing to her! She must go away as soon as she could, especially since his presence seemed to have such a devastating effect on her. He had appeared so unexpectedly that she had had no time to escape, not even any time to prepare for this meeting, to remind herself of all the things he had said and done. Then she frowned and stopped where she was. She suddenly realised that though Lord Wintersett had looked coldly on her in the stableyard he had not looked in the slightest degree surprised. But how could he possibly have known she was living at Wintersett Court under the name of Prudence Trask? She shrugged her shoulders and continued on her way.

Upstairs she had time to reflect on her position. Whatever his feelings for Sasha Calvert were now that he had discovered the truth, he must be furious to find her installed in his home under a false name. And what would Lady Wintersett think when "Miss Trask" was unmasked? Serena could not regret her subterfuge, for the time spent with Tony had been such a joy to her and such an obvious benefit to Tony himself. But she had grown to like silent Lady Wintersett, and was sorry that her employer was about to find how her companion had deceived her. Perhaps her son was telling her "Miss Trask's" real name at this very moment? Serena went downstairs again with reluctance, not knowing what she was about to face.

When she entered the drawing-room she found Lord Wintersett talking to Tony while his mother looked on. A tray of tea and other refreshments was on the table by the sofa. It was a comfortable domestic scene, with no overtones of drama or untoward revelations.

"Ah! The worker of miracles herself. Come in, come in!" Lord Wintersett's tone was affable but patently false. Serena braced herself and walked forward, but as she sat down she was surprised to receive a warmly encouraging smile from Lady Wintersett.

"Tony has been describing your activities, Miss Trask," Lord Wintersett began. "I am astounded at his progress. Some of your machines sound most ingenious. Er... you perhaps have a gift for devices?"

Serena said calmly, "You flatter me, my lord. Parks must have most of the credit for the machines."

"But you designed them, Miss Trask!" cried Tony.

"Ah, a designer! That sounds more probable. But whatever you are, Miss Trask, you deserve our thanks." Serena bowed her head. He went on, "Though I could wish that you had taught young Tony here to dismount more gracefully. In the stableyard he reminded me of nothing so much as a sack of potatoes falling off a cart!"

Serena smiled at Tony's downcast face and said, "But it isn't every day that his uncle returns from . . . where was it?"

"But, Miss Trask, you know! I told you Uncle James was in the West Indies. We've been studying the maps, Uncle James. I found St. Just, and showed it to Miss Trask. It isn't very big, is it?"

With a sardonic look at Serena's pink cheeks Lord Wintersett said, "Not big, but beautiful, Tony. And Anse Chatelet is a wonderful heritage. Now, it's time for you to be off. You have still to change, and I promised Mr. Gimble that you wouldn't be too long. We shall have time tomorrow for more talk, but now you should go to your lessons."

Tony objected, of course, but received little sympathy from his uncle. The boy gave Serena a resigned grin and left.

"Now, Miss . . . Trask. The improvement in your charge is incredible, and we owe you a debt of gratitude—" There was still the false note in Lord Wintersett's voice. Serena dared to interrupt.

"But now that you are back, Lord Wintersett, I dare swear you would prefer to choose a companion for your mother yourself. I was only engaged on a temporary basis. Much as I have enjoyed the work with Tony, I feel he hardly needs me any longer, and I shall understand if you wish me to go." Her voice was matter-of-fact but her eyes pleaded with him not to expose her in front of his mother.

"The question is whether you yourself would rather go, Miss Trask—in the circumstances."

"I would prefer Miss Trask to stay, James!"

The voice was Lady Wintersett's. Both Serena and James looked at her in astonishment, and James said, "Wh . . . what was that, Mama?"

"I should like you to persuade Miss Trask to stay." She smiled vaguely, got up, and before either of them had recovered enough to stop her she left the room, closing the door carefully behind her.

"Another miracle! Wintersett is full of them it seems—since you have been with us!" Lord Wintersett turned back to Serena. "But all the same," he said grimly. "All the same, Serena . . ."

"I know what you are going to say, and I agree with every word. It was deceitful, underhand, and a shameful thing to have done. But I am not in the slightest sorry! And now I shall go to pack my things.''

"You heard my mother. Those must be the first words she has spoken for over ten years. She wants you to stay."

"It was very kind of Lady Wintersett to intercede for me, but now you are back I would not be comfortable here. I am glad to have done what I have done for your nephew—"

"*My* nephew? I think not. Or at least, only in name."

Serena grew pale. "You know?"

James got up and walked about the room. "I think I know most of it now. The days I spent on St. Just were very enlightening, though they did little for my self-esteem. For a man who has always prided himself on being fair-minded, I had been singularly blind. I suppose I understand why you couldn't tell me the truth about Alanna. But why didn't you make any attempt to warn me?"

"Would you have listened to me if I had?"

"Perhaps not. Perhaps it was right that I had to find it all out for myself. I should have gone to St. Just years ago, of course. But at the time there was so much else to be done—my father's death, my mother's illness, Alanna and the baby. Disaster on disaster." He sat down beside her, his head bowed, and though Serena knew he neither wanted nor deserved her sympathy she put out her hand and rested it on his arm. He took the hand in his, holding it tightly. "I thought so much about this on the voyage home—how I would try to explain to you . . . And now it seems so inadequate . . ." He got up suddenly and walked away to look out of the window. "It seems idiotic now, of course, but Alanna's story rang so true that we accepted it without question."

"Parts of it *were* true, but the characters were changed."

"She substituted you for Richard and Tony for herself." He turned round and asked, "Did your father tell Richard to leave the island?"

"Yes."

"Alanna was ingenious in her half-truths."

"And desperate," said Serena quietly. "She may have betrayed your brother, but she had been equally badly betrayed by mine."

"It's a sordid story, Serena, and I am ashamed for my part in it. I think I have most of it now. The last piece fell into place when the boy came into the stable yard this afternoon. I could have sworn it was William with you.''

''William?''

''Yes! William the Turbulent, William Blake, William Serena Calvert—call him what you like. The boy is the image of you, except for his hair.''

''Richard's hair was tawny, not dark like mine. My father used to call him his lion.'' Serena drew a deep breath and said, ''Lord Wintersett—''

''You called me James a short while ago.''

''It was a mistake. What do you propose to do about Tony?''

''What the devil *can* I do?''

''There's your family to consider—if you had no sons yourself Richard's son would inherit the Wintersett title! That would be wrong.''

''Oh, there's no risk of that! It may interest you to know, Miss Trask, that I fully intend to have a wife and sons of my own in the near future!''

His arrogance irritated her and she said tartly, ''You can buy a wife, I suppose, with all that money you keep mentioning. But how can you be sure you'll have children, not to mention sons?''

He burst into unwilling laughter. ''You wretch, Serena! That's a possibility that had never occurred to me, I must admit!'' He suddenly grew sober and said abruptly, ''I owe you an apology...much more than an apology. How can I possibly persuade you to forget the terrible things I have said and done to you? You swore the last time I saw you that you never wanted to see me again. I half thought you would run away when you saw me in the stable-yard, and I wouldn't have blamed you if you had.''

''You didn't appear very pleased to see me,'' Serena said involuntarily. ''You didn't say anything except a haughty, '' 'Come Tony—Miss Trask!' ''

''I assure you I was not feeling haughty in the slightest— what a dreadful word, Serena!—I was never more nervous in my life!''

''Nervous! You?''

''Yes, nervous. I was afraid that if I said anything at all out of the way you would disappear. So I was being very careful— both in the stable-yard and afterwards.''

''Why weren't you surprised?''

"Come, Serena! Don't insult my intelligence! Who else could Prudence Trask be? You forget, I knew by then that Tony was probably Richard's son. I guessed you would be with him. I remembered Prudence from a conversation on the hill. And of course I remembered Trask!"

"I am surprised you remembered so much."

"I don't think I have forgotten anything about you from the day we met." Serena tried to turn away, but he took her hands again and added quickly, "But this is beside the point. I was asking you if you could forgive me—and unless you thought me a graceless monster you must have expected me to do so. Have you thought about your answer?"

"I have thought about it all the time you have been away. I saw the heartbreak Richard's actions had caused in your family, and I weighed that against the heartbreak and tribulations in my own. I think the balance is about equal, don't you?"

"But you are the one who has suffered, Serena. And you have been completely innocent throughout."

"I wasn't alone in that. What about your mother? And young Tony? And Tony's...your brother? No, I think it's time to draw a line under the past."

"You are more generous than I deserve." He put her hands to his lips and kissed them. Serena snatched them back and moved away from him. She was very agitated. He got to his feet, grimaced and then said abruptly, "I have had papers drawn up for the return of Anse Chatelet."

"No! I...I don't want it back!"

He looked astonished. "But I cannot keep it, Serena!"

"Anse Chatelet must go to Tony. You should keep it for him."

He frowned. "Are you sure?"

She said, "Quite sure. Richard would have inherited Anse Chatelet if he had lived, and it should go to his child. But it will have to come as a gift from you. His name will always be Stannard, whatever his parentage. You will make sure he uses his inheritance wisely."

"You would trust me to do this?"

"Yes. Yes, I would. You have always been described as a just man. You will do this. And now I must go."

"No! Don't! You must stay! I have only just returned."

"No, I must go, Lord Wintersett! I knew that you would ask me to forgive you. And I do. But I always intended to be gone from here before you returned."

He saw she meant it. He spoke rapidly, jerkily. "Serena, listen to me. I understand your feelings, believe me."

She shook her head, saying, "You cannot possibly understand what I feel! I don't even know myself." She started to walk to the door.

James strode after her and stopped her. "Wait, Serena! Please!" She looked at him coolly, clearly unwilling to linger. James could see that her mind was made up against him. He said rapidly, "Let me try to explain." He led her back into the middle of the room, where they stood facing one another. He took time to find the right words, and at length he said, "At one time, on the hill, I think we were both very near to complete understanding. More complete than I have ever known with anyone else in my life... That friendship was very precious to me, Serena."

"You destroyed it," she said stonily.

"I know, I know! In my blind prejudice against the Calverts I destroyed it. But give me a chance to rebuild it! I could, I think, given time. Say you'll stay!"

She shook her head. "You are not the man I knew on the hill. I could have loved him—no, I did love him. But you forget, I have known you in London. I have heard what they say about you—" He made a gesture of repudiation, but she raised her voice and went on, "And I know it to be true! There is a hardness in you, a lack of pity, which I hate. I could never love such a man. I am ... repelled."

He grew white, and said almost angrily, "There were times when you did not seem to hate me, Serena. Or will you accuse me of conceit for saying so?"

"I admit there's a strong attraction between us. And given the right circumstances such feelings can lead to love. But not with you. I do not trust you enough."

"Serena!"

"Oh, I trust you to be fair with Anse Chatelet and Tony, and all the rest. But not with my heart, not with myself. You see, I too thought I had found my other self on the hill. It seemed like a miracle, an enchantment. More than I had ever dreamed of... And then ... and then ..." She could not continue but walked about the room in agitation. Finally she stopped and said decisively, "No, I will not allow it to happen again. And if I stay here you will confuse me once more. I cannot stay. I will not!"

He saw that she was not to be moved by appeals to her feelings for him and switched his argument. "What about Tony and my mother?"

"Tony will manage now. He needs the companionship of men, boys of his own age… Perhaps he ought to go to school. If Tony is to live on St. Just it is important that he has the discipline that Richard never knew."

"And my mother, Serena? She surely needs you as much as Tony. I think with you she could in time recover completely." He saw that Serena was still unconvinced and went to take her hands in his again. When she stepped back he said desperately, "Serena, I cannot coerce you into doing my bidding as I did on the hill. I know you too well to think of bribing you. I can only appeal to your reason, if nothing else. Without Anse Chatelet you have no real home. Stay here with my mother. I shall remain in London as much as I can. You will not have to see me very often." He was pale under his tan, and his hands were trembling. For the first time Serena started to have doubts. Could she do as he suggested? Could she keep her unruly heart under control if she saw him only rarely? She was strongly tempted to stay, for she had grown fond of Lady Wintersett, and Tony would not be going to school immediately. And though Lady Spurston would give her a home, Serena knew that her great-aunt would really be happier without her. James was speaking again.

"I really will be in London, Serena. There is much to do there. I was so impatient to see Prudence Trask that I left it all."

Serena looked at him without really seeing him. What should she do? How was she to decide?

"Serena?"

"Oh, forgive me! What did you say?"

"I said that I have to return to London soon. I must at least attempt to trace Alanna."

"Is that wise?" Serena regretted this as soon as the words were said, but James clearly understood her.

"What is it that you are not saying—is it about Alanna? Do you believe, as I do, that she was behind the plot against you? Isn't that a good reason for finding her?"

Serena shook her head. "Your sister-in-law couldn't afford to leave me free to tell the truth about St. Just. I had to be discredited."

"As you indeed were! Have you heard anything from Barnet?"

"He has traced the coach and I believe he has spoken to its driver from whom he had a description of the conspirators. But he has so far failed to trace Lady Banagher. I think Barnet is in Ireland at the moment."

"Perhaps Alanna is there, too."

Serena said urgently, "Surely it's better to let her disappear! You cannot wish for the Stannard name to be dragged into this business."

"I shall do my best to keep our name out of it, Serena, but if disgracing Alanna publicly is the only way to clear you then I shall do that, too."

Serena looked at him with troubled eyes. Should she tell him now that Alanna had more to hide than a plot against Serena Calvert? If she did it might make him more determined than ever to find the woman who had killed his brother. And what would happen to her nephew then? She decided to remain silent for the moment. Instead she said, somewhat formally, "I should thank you for your efforts on my behalf. It will mean a great deal to Lucy, too."

"Have you seen her since you have been in Surrey?"

"We . . . we thought it better not. She writes once or twice a week. After Lady Ambourne took Lucy under her wing the Warnhams were willing for the engagement to be announced, but Lucy refused to consider marrying Michael before I . . . until my reputation was cleared." She tried to smile. "So your efforts are very necessary!"

"Not for yourself?"

"London does not seem so important down here. But yes, I should like to be vindicated, certainly."

"Then why not stay? I promise not to weary you with any more attempt to revive our . . . relationship, Serena—and I will be off to London quite soon."

She took a deep breath. "Very well, Lord Wintersett. I shall agree to stay here for the moment. We shall see how we go on."

Once more she was amazed at the transformation of his whole personality as he smiled. He took her face in his hands

and held it while he kissed her gently, saying as he did, "To seal
the bargain, Serena. That's all."

She almost changed her mind there and then. This man was
dangerous to her peace! This was a man who could win her
heart again. It would be as well for her if this Lord Wintersett
kept his distance!

JAMES REMAINED in Surrey for a little longer, but took care not
to take up too much of Serena's time. Lady Wintersett began
to speak more freely, and he spent hours walking, driving and
sitting in the drawing-room with her. He gave Tony more of his
attention than ever before, too. He took the boy out riding, and
Serena found them one afternoon absorbed in the art of loop-
ing the whip. She was sometimes persuaded to go out with
them, and the three of them roamed the countryside in perfect
harmony.

James and Serena met at dinner each evening, but as it was
always in the company of Lady Wintersett Serena was forced
to play her role of Miss Trask. James watched with amusement "Miss Trask's" efforts to stay in character—her struggles to subdue her natural liveliness and to disguise the air of
authority which was as much part of her as her golden eyes.
With each day that passed he grew more enchanted, and had
difficulty in stopping himself from trying to spend every minute in her company. He constantly reminded himself that he still
had a very long way to go before her confidence in him was restored, and that he must exercise caution.

Each day he put off his return to London, though affairs
there were becoming increasingly urgent, including the one
project which was of paramount importance to him—the
clearing of Serena's name. He told himself that it was wiser to
leave Wintersett before Serena realised how far their friendship had progressed. She might well run away from him if she
saw how close they had become again, and he was eager to keep
her at Wintersett Court where he could at least be sure of seeing her from time to time. But still he lingered, unwilling to tear
himself away.

In the end the matter was decided for him, when Barnet sent
a message that, after a long absence, Lady Banagher was back
in London. She had suddenly left Dublin, where she had been
staying with a certain Captain Fergus O'Keefe and his lady, and

had taken the packet boat to Holyhead. Barnet was sure that
her destination was Portland Place. James left Surrey that same
day, promising Serena that he would soon have the truth out of
Amelia Banagher.

SERENA WAS astonished at the dismay she felt when James announced that he was returning to London. She had grown to
depend on his company, and she suddenly became aware how
much her opinion of him had changed. Without forgetting for
one moment how hard he could be, here in his home she had
seen another side to his nature, had marvelled at his patient
gentleness in dealing with his mother and his apparently genuine interest in Tony. They had often sat long over the evening
meals in the evenings, and Serena had found that she was enjoying herself more than she could have imagined. It had
sometimes been hard to remember that she was ostensibly an
employee in the house, and more than once she had caught
Lady Wintersett eyeing her with amused speculation as she listened to the wit and laughter in the conversation between her
son and her companion.

So after James had left for London Serena felt lost and uneasy. The weather had turned wet and she wandered about the
house restlessly, unable to settle to anything. She was gazing
unhappily out of the drawing-room window when Lady Wintersett said quietly, "You are missing my son, Miss Calvert?"

Serena turned round to deny this. "Oh, no, Lady Wintersett! It's just that the rain . . . *What* did you call me?"

Lady Wintersett smiled. "I think it's time we had a talk.
Come and sit down." She patted the sofa next to her and Serena meekly sat down. "James has told me a great deal since he
came back from St. Just. You have been made very unhappy
because of Alanna's lies, and I wish you to know that I am
sorry. I blame myself."

"But why?"

"I should not have accepted what she said so blindly. Indeed, I sensed that there was something wrong with her story,
for though I spent hours with the child, I could never see my
son in him. Then you came, and of course as soon as I saw you
and young Tony together I knew why."

"I suppose you are angry with me for deceiving you for so
long. I . . . I had no wish to distress you, but it was the only way

I could be close to my nephew. Can you forgive me, Lady
Wintersett?''

"Easily, my dear. In any case, you have never deceived me,
for I knew from the first that you were Serena Calvert. You see,
I was walking in the shrubbery the day you spoke to Alanna—
before you ever came here. I overheard your conversation.''

"You ... heard? All of it?'' Serena was suddenly afraid.
"Even ...''

"Even that Alanna Cashel shot my son?'' said Lady Wintersett with a note of bitterness in her voice. "Yes.''

"And you haven't told anyone?''

"I wanted Alanna out of our lives forever, and was afraid of
saying or doing anything which might prevent that. It is better
so, much better, and I only pray that James will fail in his
present attempts to find her.''

Serena looked at her thoughtfully. "You don't wish to make
Alanna pay for her crime?''

"What good would that do? It would not bring back the
dead, and it might hurt the living beyond redress. Over the
years I have grown to love Alanna's child, and I love him still,
even though I now know he was never my true grandson. Indeed, we have come a long way in the last three months, Tony
and I. And that is thanks to you.''

"What do you mean, Lady Wintersett?''

"I mean that you taught Tony that he must have the courage and determination to live a proper life. Watching you both
has made me look at my own life and I have seen how much I
have wasted! When I heard Tony's laughter about this house I
wondered at my own silence. Each night when he tells me of his
day and I see how eagerly he seizes hold of every minute I am
ashamed of my past cowardice. And you have done this—for
him and for me. I owe it all to you.''

"Lady Wintersett, please! Don't thank me. Whatever I have
done has been willingly done out of love for Tony. I do not deserve your thanks. I have tried to deceive you. And I have taken
the last link with your dead son from you.''

Lady Wintersett smiled. "Strangely, I see more of my dead
son's spirit in Tony now—now that I know he is not my son's
child—than I ever could before.'' She fell silent, then after a
minute she went on, "And far from taking my Tony away, you
have given him back to me. I see that that surprises you, yet it
is easily explained. Until you came and uncovered the truth I

could never understand Tony's death. That he would reject his wife, his child and all of us here enough to take his own life was beyond my understanding. I simply couldn't bear the thought that I had failed him so badly, and it seemed easier not to face it, to escape from it into a sort of dream world of my own. Now I know that he didn't take his own life, and for the first time in thirteen years I am at peace. And I owe that to you, too." She paused and then continued, "I suppose some time young Tony will have to learn the truth of his parentage. I hear that he is to have Anse Chatelet?"

Serena said, "It is his more than mine."

Lady Wintersett smiled. "It is as well. You will not need Anse Chatelet, Serena."

Serena was about to ask her what she meant, when a servant came in with a letter for Lord Wintersett from a Mr. Barnet.

"I know his lordship has already left, my lady, but the letter is marked 'Urgent.' It is also addressed to Miss Trask, should Lord Wintersett be absent."

Serena excused herself and opened the letter, which had obviously been written in haste. One paragraph leapt to her eye.

Since writing my last report I have learned more. First, Lady Banagher is no longer in Portland Place. She has accompanied Captain O'Keefe to Horton Wood House near Epsom Common. Second, further information from Ireland leads me to believe that O'Keefe is the man we have been seeking in connection with our case, but that he is also highly dangerous. I must warn you that it would be foolhardy to approach him with anything less than extreme caution. He left Dublin in order to escape being arrested for murder. I shall give more information when I return from Liverpool, where I have arranged to meet someone who knows more about Captain O'Keefe. Meanwhile be very careful, I beg you.

SERENA SPRANG to her feet. "Oh, no! Oh, my God!"

"What is it? What is the matter, Miss Calvert?" cried Lady Wintersett.

"James is in the gravest danger! I must go to him at once!"

"What are you saying? Why?"

"Read this note, Lady Wintersett! Barnet specifically warns us against O'Keefe, and James is almost certainly already on his way to meeting him! He will have failed to find the Banagher woman at Portland Place, and I have no doubt that he will follow her to Epsom. Lady Wintersett, you must forgive me. I must warn him!"

Serena ran upstairs and rummaged at the bottom of her clothes press. Somewhere, carefully wrapped up, were the boy's clothes she had worn so often before, and she secretly thanked the touch of sentiment which had preserved them so that she could use them again now. Without any hesitation she changed into them, sought and found her pistol, and hurried downstairs. Lady Wintersett was so agitated that she ignored Serena's unconventional dress and urged her to waste no time. As Serena reached the door she called, "Do take care, Miss Calvert. From what I hear, you could be in danger, too!"

She gave a shriek as Serena waved her pistol and replied grimly, "Not while I have this, I assure you!" Then Serena hurried to the stables and, after a short consultation with Parks, who knew the area round Epsom well, she set off on Douce with that gentleman in close attendance.

It was a wild night, and heavy showers alternated with periods of brilliant moonlight as the rainclouds swept across the sky. Parks had produced a greatcoat for Serena and she was glad of it, but as they galloped through the night she noticed very little of the wind or rain. Her one thought was to get to the house in Epsom before James.

CHAPTER FOURTEEN

JAMES HAD ARRIVED in London to find the Portland Place house closed and the knocker off the door. Cursing Barnet for his inaccurate information, he set off on a search round the clubs of London for news of Amelia Banagher, and at White's he met with success. Harry Birtles, who was more than a little the worse for wear, was holding forth on the frailty of women.

"Take the fair Amelia," he said aggrieved. "Nothing too good for her—ribbons, furbelows, flowers—even the odd bit of jewer...jewellery. What does she do?" He stared owlishly round.

"What did she do, old fellow?" asked James sympathetically, leading Sir Harry to a nearby table. "Have some more wine."

Sir Harry drowned his sorrows a little more and turned to clutch James's arm. He looked vaguely surprised to see whose arm it was. "Wintersett? It's kind of you to listen, 'pon my word it is! But you know what she's like."

"What has she done now?"

"Gone off! Portland Place shut, no servants, not a word to me! Only got back two days ago, too." He looked cunning. "But I know where she's gone, Winsh...Wintersett. She can't fool me!"

"Where's that?"

"Tyrrell's place at Epsom. God knows why! He's away in France, know f'r a fact." Here Sir Harry almost lost his balance in an effort to whisper in James's ear. "It's my belief she's got someone down there. Why else go to a godforsaken place like Epsom? 'Cept for the Derby, and that's not run in the autumn, is it? She's with someone else, Wintre...Wintersett." He looked melancholy, hiccuped and subsided quietly under the table. James left him there.

James returned to Upper Brook Street, deep in thought. Tyrrell was Amelia's cousin, and it was quite likely she would go to Horton Wood House if she wished to hide. But he had no means of knowing how long she would stay there—she might well decide to move on soon, tomorrow even. So, though it was late, he must attempt to see her that night. He quickly changed his clothes, wrote a note for Barnet, and set off on the old Brighton Road to Epsom.

He made good time in spite of the weather, for the road had a good surface, and he arrived at the door of Horton Wood House soon after seven. He had visited Tyrrell with Amelia in the old days, and the manservant recognised him.

"I wish to see Lady Banagher on a matter of urgency, Parfitt. Please tell her I am here." He was ushered into a small room off the hall and asked to wait. After a few minutes the manservant returned and showed James to a beautifully furnished salon on the upper floor. Lady Banagher was gracefully arranged on a sofa before the fire.

"James! How pleasant—and unexpected—to see you! I do believe you are looking handsomer than ever. Pray sit down. Have you dined?" Amelia looked relaxed, but her voice was pitched a little too high, and the hand holding the fan to shield her face from the fire was clenched.

"Thank you, but I haven't come to exchange civilised pleasantries, Amelia," said James. "I'm here to tell you that I now know all about Alanna's plot to discredit Serena Calvert. It was she who bribed you, was it not? You and Captain O'Keefe."

The slender stick of the fan snapped, and Amelia turned white as she said with studied calm, "I don't know what you're talking about, James. Why do you always think the worst of me?" With an effort she let her voice soften and she said with a pathetic look, "It was not always so."

"You may save your charms, Amelia. I know a great deal more than I did when I last saw you." James paused. "I know where the false Ambourne carriage came from, and the names of your hired accomplices. I even know what role you played— or should I say roles, *Betty*? And unless you do as I suggest all these details will soon be in the hands of the justices."

"But that would ruin me!" she exclaimed, no longer able to hide her fear.

"As you attempted to ruin Miss Calvert. Yes. But I rather think in your case it might also mean prison." Amelia burst into a shrill tirade, but James waited impassively till she paused for breath. "Are you ready to listen to my suggestion?"

"What is it?" she asked sulkily.

"That you write a full confession, completely exonerating Miss Calvert, which will be sent to a number of prominent members of society, including Sir John and Lady Taplow, and Sir Harry Birtles. After they have read it, and you have confirmed it to them in person, I will help you to escape to Ireland or the Continent, whichever you prefer."

"That sounds like a very fair offer, Amelia, me darlin'. But you'll keep my name out of it, if you please. It wouldn't be good for my health—or yours, either—if I was named in that document." A tall, swarthy man came into the room. James regarded him coldly, ignoring Amelia's reply.

"Fergus O'Keefe?"

"So you know who I am already?" The Captain looked thoughtfully at Amelia. She shivered and said desperately,

"It wasn't me, Fergus! He knew before he arrived. I didn't tell him."

O'Keefe turned his attention to James. "I don't like anyone making free with my name, Lord Wintersett."

"Why? Is it such an honourable one?" asked James, his lip curling in contempt. "The name of a 'gentleman' who accepts money to bring false disgrace to a lady? Of a brave soldier who makes war on women? Of a hero who goes to work on a defenceless gentlewoman, with no more than three or four accomplices? I assure you, I have no desire to make free with the name of a coward such as that. Once you have made amends to Miss Calvert I will willingly obliterate your name—and you—from my mind. They both disgust me."

"James! Don't make him angry! Fergus!" said Amelia nervously. O'Keefe ignored her.

"You might regret those remarks, Wintersett," he said softly.

"There isn't anyone here man enough to make me withdraw them, O'Keefe. Certainly not you!"

O'Keefe said slyly, "I wouldn't get so positive about that, my lord! Wasn't I man enough now to persuade Miss Calvert to enjoy me company that night? Has she not told you how she begged for me favours? Didn't Sir John and his lady see her running to welcome me when I came back to her? A fine story that would make in the courts, would it not, now? And whether

I was believed or not, the lady's name would be blemished forever, I'm thinking.''

James smiled grimly, and took a pistol out of his pocket. ''You have just signed your own death warrant, O'Keefe. I'll be damned if I let you tell that story in public. And I'll be damned if I let a cur like you go free!''

From his pocket he drew a second pistol, the twin of the first. O'Keefe eyed them and laughed.

''A duel, is it? Begorrah, it's ironic! A fine gentleman like you stooping to fight a duel with me. I'm honoured!''

''You shouldn't be, O'Keefe. It's the only way I can kill you and keep roughly within the law. Here, catch!''

O'Keefe caught the pistol and examined it. Then he walked a distance away, saying as he did so, ''But I might kill you, Lord Wintersett!''

''By all means try, fellow! Or is it only against women that you pit your strength?''

Just as O'Keefe turned with a snarl at James's last remark a door to the side burst open and a sorry-looking figure with wild hair and a torn gown ran into the room towards James crying, ''James, oh, thank God! James! Help me, please help me!''

But O'Keefe, beside himself with rage, had already fired without waiting for the count. The figure, caught right in the line of fire, staggered, tripped and fell.

''Alanna!'' James ran to kneel down beside her, casting his pistol aside. He ripped off a piece of her petticoat and made a rough pad, placing it on the growing stain of Alanna's gown. ''Help me, Amelia!'' he cried impatiently.

THESE WERE THE WORDS Serena heard as she came softly up the stairs, closely followed by Parks. The desperation in James's voice was unmistakable, and, grasping her pistol more firmly in her hand, she hurried towards the salon. A dreadful tableau greeted her eyes. Alanna Stannard was lying on the floor covered in blood, and James was kneeling beside her making desperate efforts to stem the flow. Amelia Banagher was nowhere to be seen. A movement to Serena's right caught her eye. The man who had abducted her was moving furtively in the direction of a pistol which was lying on the ground near James. He picked it up and sprang away.

"Now, my fine hero!" he said. "Now we'll see who it is who dies, Lord Wintersett!" He raised the gun. James looked up, his face a mask.

"Alanna is dying," he said. "And you have killed her."

O'Keefe spared a glance for the woman on the ground. Then he said brutally. "Amelia's worth two of her." He grinned. "And she'll soon have company."

James's gaze had passed beyond O'Keefe to where Serena was standing in the door, pistol in hand. Without any change of expression he said, "Any company is more welcome than yours, O'Keefe. Even that of a loathsome toad."

O'Keefe's finger tightened, and Serena fired her pistol. A howl of pain filled the air as O'Keefe staggered away down the room, his arm hanging limply at his side and blood dripping from his hand. The dueling pistol lay harmlessly on the ground.

"Take charge of him, Parks, if you please," said Serena briskly, as she picked up the pistol and handed it to her companion. Then she hurried over to kneel down beside James. Alanna looked ghastly. Her breathing was very faint, her pulse almost non-existent.

"James," she whispered. "I have...to tell...you. Confess...I killed...Tony. Shot...him."

"Don't talk, Alanna. We'll get a surgeon to you soon."

"No...time. Want you...to...forgive...me. Please."

James bent his head and kissed Alanna's cheek. "Of course, Alanna."

"A life...for...a life, James." Her voice died away then grew stronger. "Anthony?"

"Will be safe with us, I promise you." Alanna's eyes closed, then she opened them again and looked pleadingly at Serena. She was beyond saying anything.

Serena took her hand. "Anthony will have Anse Chatelet, Alanna. It is his right. You and I, we both love Richard's son. I shall remember that and forget the rest." A little smile passed over Alanna's face, and then there was nothing.

JAMES GOT UP SLOWLY and then helped Serena to her feet. His face was drawn and tired, and in spite of her own exhaustion Serena had a passionate wish to hold him in her arms and comfort him. Instead she stood looking on as he gazed down at Alanna. Finally he spoke.

"'A life for a life', she said. All the questions, all the anguish, answered in one sentence. Poor Alanna, to have lived with that all these years! And in the end she saved my life," he said sombrely. Then his gaze turned to Serena. "And so did you."

Serena felt like weeping, but she rallied herself and said crossly, "I very nearly decided to let him shoot you. Did you have to refer to me as a loathsome toad?"

His face lightened and he smiled slightly. "I thought that would spur you on. O'Keefe had no idea what a defenceless gentlewoman was capable of!" But in reply to Serena's look of puzzlement he only smiled again and then said, "You must leave here straight away. I take it Parfitt let you in? I can deal with him, but it would not do for you to be discovered here by the surgeon, or anyone else. Parks comes from somewhere round here and he will find you a place to stay." She was about to protest but he stopped her. "I cannot come with you now, much as I would wish—I must deal with poor Alanna and the rest. What happened to O'Keefe?"

"Parks took him downstairs. I don't think I wounded him seriously, but perhaps I should go to see?"

"On no account! You must stay in the background. I shall find out how he is and let you know. Meanwhile come with me."

They went slowly downstairs, and James saw Serena safely hidden in the room off the hall. He came back a few minutes later to tell her that Parfitt had brought in some of the stable lads to guard O'Keefe, though he hardly appeared to need it. He had lost a fair quantity of blood, and was half sitting, half lying on a settle in the kitchen with his eyes closed. One of the lads had bound his arm enough to halt the bleeding, and O'Keefe was now waiting for the surgeon and the parish constable, muttering about a boy in the doorway. Everyone was so shocked at Alanna's death that little attention was being paid to him. Amelia had disappeared, and some of the men had gone in search of her.

"I have told Parks to come here in a few minutes. He already knows where he will take you. You'll be safe with him, Serena."

"What about you?"

"I shall do my best to clear up the mess here to my own satisfaction. With a slight blurring of detail I think I can satisfy the

authorities, too. Thank God you're dressed in your boy's garb!
Outside Parks and ourselves no one has the slightest idea who
you are, so even if O'Keefe's mutterings do receive any attention the boy will never be found. Parks will take you back to
Wintersett tomorrow, and I'll join you as soon as I can. You'll
wait for me there?'' He looked so anxious and so worn that
once again she felt an urge to comfort him, and this time she did
not resist it. She reached up and drew his head down to hers.

"I promise," she said softly, and kissed him. He pulled her
into his arms and returned the kiss, passionately and deeply,
greedily even, as if he was trying to obliterate the memory of
that scene in the salon. She made no attempt to resist, though
he was holding her so tightly that it hurt. He was the first to pull
away.

"I'm sorry," he said. "I'm sorry, Serena. Please, please
forgive me. I don't know what came over me. Oh, God, I've
said that before, haven't I? But it wasn't the same, I swear. Did
I hurt you?''

"No," she lied. "And I do understand, James." She smiled
and caressed his cheek, and with a groan he drew her back into
his arms, this time simply holding her and drawing comfort
from the contact. Parks found them like this and cleared his
throat. Reluctantly they moved apart.

"Sorry, my lord. But if anyone saw you they might get a bit
of a shock—seeing as how Miss Calvert is still in her boy's
clothes. Er...the surgeon is coming up the drive, my lord. He'll
be here any minute.''

Recalled to his duties, James kissed Serena's hand and ad-
jured Parks to take good care of her. Then he went out, and
after a few minutes of waiting while the surgeon arrived and
was taken upstairs Serena and Parks slipped away.

IT WAS NEARLY A MONTH before James managed to return to
Wintersett for more than a night, though he sent daily messages to his mother and to Serena. The formalities of Alanna's
death had to be completed, and after that James decided that
she should be buried near her family home in Ireland. Her
husband's grave was in the West Indies, and no one felt that
there was a place for her in the Wintersett vault. James came
down to collect Tony, and they made the melancholy journey
to Ireland together. Serena visited Lucy and the Countess quite

often during this period of waiting, but always returned to Wintersett after a few days. She heard from Lucy that Amelia Banagher had been caught and, though Amelia steadfastly denied having been present at Alanna Stannard's death, she had publicly confessed to helping in the plot against Miss Calvert. Perhaps to save her own skin, she swore that Fergus O'Keefe had in fact spent the night with her, only appearing in the early morning to play his role before Sir John and the others. Sir Harry rather shamefacedly agreed that he had fallen asleep early the night before, and had known nothing till the next morning. The news of Fergus O'Keefe's villainy had spread throughout a shocked London, and Serena's reputation was completely saved. Indeed, society eagerly welcomed her back, and the Warnhams were anxious to discuss plans for Lucy's wedding. But Serena had promised to be at Wintersett when James returned, and she would keep that promise—they must all be patient just a little longer. What kept her awake at night was the question of what she would do after that. James Stannard was gradually becoming too important to her once again. She had decided some time ago that she could not live with him. But could she live without him? She took the coward's way out and told herself that such questions would have to be shelved until Lucy's future was finally settled.

Eventually James and Tony came back to Wintersett on a brilliantly cold day in November when an early fall of snow covered the ground. Serena had been for a walk, and they all arrived at the house together. There was much exclaiming and embracing, during which it seemed quite natural that James should kiss Serena. Confused and laughing, Serena broke away and said, "Look at the view, all of you! To you it may be commonplace, but to me it is incredible—I have never, ever seen anything more beautiful!"

"Have you not?" asked James, studying her flushed face with glowing eyes. "I believe I have, Serena."

Lady Wintersett smiled and took Tony's arm. "And I believe Tony has grown as tall as I. Come, Tony! I have so much to tell you, and I dare swear that Pandora would like to indicate how much she has missed you, too." Her voice died away and Serena was left alone with James.

"You are recovered from your experience at Epsom? Unnecessary to ask—I can see you have." James's voice was studiously light as he led Serena into the drawing-room. Here they walked to the window and gazed out at the dazzling scene. "Serena—"

"James—"

They spoke together and apologised together, and both laughed. Serena said in a more natural tone, "What were you about to say?"

"That I believe it is now truly over, Serena. The whole sad, ugly story. Alanna and my brother are both at rest—"

"And Richard."

"And Richard, too. Young Tony Stannard will have his Calvert inheritance—perhaps if and when he learns the truth he might even wish to change his name, and Anse Chatelet would then have Calverts in charge again."

"The name is not very important, James. I don't believe the Calverts deserve any special consideration."

"There's one Calvert at least who deserves mine, Serena."

Serena flushed again and said hurriedly, "What else were you going to say? You hadn't finished, I think."

James had been smiling at her confusion, but his face grew sober as he said, "Fergus O'Keefe has been taken to Ireland, too. He's to be hanged for a murder he committed there."

Serena shuddered, and James put an arm round her shoulders. "It's no more than he deserves. I would have killed him if I had had the chance, you know that. Don't think of him, Serena. He's a villain. He would have tried to drag you down with him if he had come to trial in this country. As it is, Amelia has made a full confession and you have been completely vindicated. Did you know?"

"Yes, Lucy told me." Serena moved away. "And that brings me to what I want to say to you."

"I can imagine what the substance of it is. But say it."

"The Warnhams wish Michael's marriage to Lucy to take place quite soon now, and I must go back to Dover Street, James. There are so many things to discuss, so many arrangements to be made. I must go." Serena's voice held a challenge, and James smiled.

"Pax! Pax, Serena! I have too much respect for my skin to fight you!" He grew serious again. "I have had time to think recently. There is nothing like a funeral for concentrating the mind on what is important. I know now what I want, indeed I am not sure that I can live without it. But it will take time, and keeping you here against your better judgement will not help

me to achieve it. It is no part of my plan to attempt to persuade you to neglect your other loyalties—they are more important than any I can claim at the moment, and you must feel
able to go whenever you wish.''

Serena studied him. She hesitated, and then her cheeks grew
slightly pink as she said, ''Not more important, James. More
urgent.'' He drew in his breath, but listened patiently as she
went on, ''I cannot decide anything before Lucy is married.
That is what I came to England to do, and I must do it.''

James smiled suddenly, that wonderfully warm, all-
encompassing smile. ''Then you shall do it with my good will,
and any help I can render. Come, Serena! We have work to
do!''

WITHIN A WEEK Serena was re-installed in Dover Street. London was less full than it had been during the season, but there
were enough members of that small world known as London
society in town to show Miss Calvert their delight at her return. Invitations were showered on her, and no concert or reception seemed to be complete without Miss Calvert's presence.
Serena smiled, talked, listened, and inwardly laughed at the
difference. Lucy and Michael had their own celebrations but
were also carried along in Serena's wake and the Countess
stayed a little longer in London too. The whole world suddenly seemed to be gloriously amusing to all of them. Though
James took care to be discreet in public, he was often to be
found at Dover Street, visiting the Countess it was said. Serena found herself relying heavily on his advice on matters connected with marriage settlements and the like. In fact she found
herself relying on him for more than just advice—he was becoming far too necessary to her altogether.

On the night of the reception held by the Warnhams two days
before the wedding the discerning would have seen that Lord
Wintersett was not himself. Because the Countess had been
called to Ambourne and had been away for nearly a week, the
frequency of James's visits to Dover Street had been severely
curtailed. He had not seen Serena in private for several days,
and he found that he missed her company unbearably. Up till
now he had managed to maintain in public an air of cool indifference towards her, limiting himself to the two dances permitted by convention and never arousing comment from the

curious by paying her any undue attention. This had been far from easy for, to his annoyance, he suffered quite unreasonable pangs of jealousy. If the perfectly harmless gentlemen who gathered round Serena whenever she appeared—Mr. Yardley, General Fanstock and the like—could have read James's mind, they would have retired to their country estates immediately, glad to escape unscathed. But though James counted every dance they dared to dance with Serena, though he knew to a hair how many seconds they spent in her company, he had remained calm.

But tonight was different. He suddenly found he could no longer tolerate their monopoly of Serena's time, and just as she was on the point of accepting Mr. Yardley as her partner for the waltz, James cut in ruthlessly and whirled her away towards the other end of the room before Mr. Yardley had collected himself sufficiently to protest.

"That was quite shamelessly rude, Lord Wintersett!" exclaimed Serena.

"Miss Calvert," said James through his teeth, "I have watched you charm the heads off enough sheep-shanked dolts and idiots in the last few weeks to last me a lifetime. I intend to suffer no more." With a flourish and a neat turn he guided Serena into a small conservatory off the Warnhams' ballroom.

"Oh, no!" Serena said with determination. "I have been in a winter garden with you once before, Lord Wintersett, and I do not intend to repeat the exercise. You will kindly lead me back to the ballroom immediately!"

"Just a few moments of your company, Serena! I promise to behave with the utmost circumspection."

"You will call me 'Miss Calvert' in public, if you please. And forcing me into a private room, even to talk to me, is far from behaving with the 'utmost circumspection'!" Serena was already moving back towards the ballroom, and James placed himself in front of her.

"A winter garden is not a private room, Ser—Miss Calvert."

"Let me pass!" Serena was incensed, and tried to push him away. James laughed as he gathered her effortlessly into his arms, looked down at her flashing golden eyes and then kissed her. For a moment she resisted, then suddenly melted against him and for a moment he exulted in the feeling that once again flared up between them. But then she pulled away, exclaimed angrily, "Utmost circumspection, indeed! I will not let you do this to me!" and slapped his face. The memory of what had happened once before on a similar occasion occurred to them both simultaneously. Serena's eyes widened and she stepped back. "I didn't mean that, Lord W...Wintersett. Please—I didn't mean it!"

But the present situation was very different from the first, and James was amused rather than angry at the sudden change in Serena's manner. How could a man ever know what Serena Calvert would do next? Did she know herself? He started to laugh, and as she looked at him in amazement he laughed even more. Serena was offended and stalked out of the conservatory, head held high.

The Warnhams' guests were intrigued with the sight of Miss Calvert emerging flushed and angry from the winter garden closely followed by Lord Wintersett—whose appeals to her sense of humour were hampered by his inability to stop laughing. With real heroism, for Lord Wintersett's skills were famous, Mr. Yardley hastened to offer Serena his protection.

"Don't tangle with her, Yardley! She doesn't need your help. Pistols or fists, she'd outclass you every time I assure you!" said James.

Since Mr. Yardley took great exception to Lord Wintersett's levity, it was as well that Serena regained her temper in time to intervene.

"Thank you, Mr. Yardley. But it would be better to ignore Lord Wintersett's poor attempt at humour. I cannot imagine what he means by it!" She looked coldly at James, daring him to explain.

James, recalled to himself, apologised with all the solemnity he could muster—an apology which was graciously accepted. Later that evening, when a set of country dances brought them face to face, James said with a glint in his eyes, "All the same— Miss Calvert...you have given me a challenge tonight which I will not forget."

"Pooh!" said Serena, secure in the knowledge that James would hardly demand satisfaction in public, and that there would be little opportunity for them to be private for some time. It took a great deal of determination on her part to stop herself from wondering how that might be arranged.

THE COUNTESS arrived back in Dover Street the following day in time for the last-minute preparations for the wedding. It had been agreed that the ceremony should be held in London, and that the celebrations afterwards should take place in Mrs. Galveston's Portman Square mansion. All the Ambournes had naturally been invited, but the recent birth of the youngest Ambourne of all made it impossible for her parents to be present, though they had sent the kindest of messages and gifts.

The Countess spent a busy day but made time towards the end of it for a quiet, and private, talk with Serena. After rhapsodising over the new baby and talking very affectionately of Lucy the Countess suddenly said, "And when are you and James announcing your engagement?"

Serena almost dropped her cup of chocolate in astonishment. "I . . . I beg your pardon, Lady Ambourne?"

"It should not long be delayed, Serena. From what I have heard all London is speculating on what happened in the Warnhams' winter garden. They are saying, not without satisfaction I may tell you, that James has met his match at last."

"But James—Lord Wintersett—has never mentioned marriage to me! And if he did I should probably refuse him."

The Countess, who had been looking mischievous, grew serious at this. "You cannot mean it? You and James are made for each other."

"I doubt it. Lord Wintersett can be charming enough when he chooses, and I will even admit that a surprisingly strong attraction exists between us. But there is a want of humanity in him which I could not live with. I have told him so."

"So he has broached the subject!"

"Only indirectly," said Serena flushing uncomfortably.

"Serena, I have heard about your exploits in Epsom. They seem to have gone far beyond what anyone would expect, even of a friend. I wish you to look at me and tell me that you do not love James."

Serena lifted her head defiantly and started to speak, but found she could not finish. In the end she was silent.

"You see? For better or worse you do love this monster. Now I want you to forget his past crimes and listen to what I have to tell you of James Stannard." The Countess spoke impressively, and Serena's attention was caught, almost against her will.

"James is not an easy man, I know. He has little patience with self-seekers, rogues or fools, and he doesn't bother to hide his contempt for them. This has made him unpopular in London, where there are many such people. I know what they say, and so do you."

"I have experienced some of his contempt myself, Lady Ambourne. Am I to believe that I am such a person?"

"Serena, you are prevaricating. You know perfectly well that the circumstances of your acquaintance with James have been quite exceptional. And in fact James's violent reaction to you and your family arose from the deepest, most vulnerable part of his character—his love for his own family. For, in spite of the fact that James was a lonely, unloved little boy, in spite of the fact that his father treated him as a milksop and a coward if he showed a mite of affection or fear, in spite of being courted and flattered by half of London solely for his wealth, James has remained as true to those he loves as it is possible to be. It isn't easy to know him—he is very wary of others—but once he accepts you as a friend there is nothing he will not do for you. And if he ever allowed himself to fall in love—as I believe he finally has—then he would be as anxious to please, and as vulnerable to hurt, as anyone else. More so. Do not, I beg you, Serena, reject such a man lightly. You would be throwing away a chance of great happiness. Now that is enough," Lady Ambourne added with a sudden change of tone. "Tell me, where will Lucy live after she is married?"

They talked a little longer, but Serena was impatient to be gone. She knew she still had to see Lucy, and she wanted time to think.

Because of all the fuss of the wedding preparations, Serena had had little opportunity to have any real talk with her beloved niece. Though she knew it was unnecessary, she wanted a last reassurance that Lucy was happy with the thought of sharing her life with Michael Warnham and living in England. She need not have worried. Lucy had no doubts, was serenely certain that this was what she wanted.

"Everyone I love most will be here in England. How could I not be happy to live here?"

"Everyone?"

"Oh, Sasha, you need not pretend with me! I am young, but not stupid. Lord Wintersett may have returned Anse Chatelet to you, but you will never live there again."

Serena wanted to say that Anse Chatelet was no longer hers, but for the moment that was Tony's secret, so she just asked, "What makes you think so?"

"Sasha! You will be at Wintersett Court—everyone knows that! And, do you know, I like Lord Wintersett. He has been very kind to Michael and me."

Serena tried in vain to disabuse Lucy's mind of the notion that Lord Wintersett meant anything to her.

"I know you, Sasha, and it has become clear to me during the past weeks that you are in love with Lord Wintersett. You cannot hide it from me, but don't worry, I won't say anything to anyone else—except perhaps Michael. It is plain for all the world to see that he is nutty about you."

"Nutty!"

"Oh, forgive me—I meant to say that Lord Wintersett is more than a little enamoured of you. Oh, Sasha, I shall miss you! I shall be happy with Michael, I know, but I shall miss our fun together. Thank you, my dearest of aunts, for all the years we have had together. And I hope…no, I am sure that you will one day be as happy as I am. I cannot wait for tomorrow."

They kissed each other and Serena left Lucy to her dreams. She herself had a more wakeful night. Everyone, it seemed, was conspiring to persuade her to look with favour on James Stannard. In the eyes of those closest to them they were apparently the perfect match. Serena wished she could believe they were right. Or that she could be sure they were wrong!

CHAPTER FIFTEEN

LUCY'S WEDDING was the most joyous of occasions. The weather was cold but brilliantly sunny, the guests were cheerful, and the young couple radiant. The marriage of the Warnham heir would always have been an important event, but the Warnhams clearly loved Lucy for her own sake, and the pleasure they took in welcoming her into the family circle gave Serena every reassurance she might have needed. Long after the happy couple had left for a bridal tour to the Continent the celebrations in Portman Square continued. Lady Warnham, who was a great deal cleverer than her loving mama imagined, had suggested that Lady Spurston might be persuaded to come to London if Mrs. Galveston invited her. As a result of Lady Warnham's forethought, the two old ladies spent a most pleasurable time before and after the ceremony indulging in an orgy of gossip and reminiscence and the rest of the party were left to enjoy the feast and the music of the military band provided by their hostesses.

Lady Ambourne was one of the first guests to leave. She had come to Lucy's wedding, but was anxious to return to Ambourne and her family. However, she took time to have a word with Serena before she left.

"Lucy looked a dream in her bridal clothes, Serena. She is destined to be happy, that one!" adding with a roguish look, "I shall look forward to seeing you in yours! Oh, forgive me, my dear. I am an interfering busybody—Perdita could tell you more of that. But I find it impossible not to interfere when I see people turning aside from happiness. Be kind to James. You will not regret it. And come to Ambourne soon!"

Serena started to look for her aunt. They were leaving London the following day to return to Surrey and she wanted to be sure that the old lady was not too tired. But Lady Spurston was having a nap in Mrs. Galveston's private parlour, and Serena had not the heart to disturb her. Instead she wandered down to the library, glad to escape from the revellers and find a quiet place to rest herself. Her head was aching—and her heart.

James finally found her there. He came in, closing the doors carefully behind him, then stood watching her where she sat on the sofa.

"You look tired, Serena. Or sad. Are you thinking of Lucy?"

"Why should that make me sad?"

"I'm not suggesting for one moment that you have any doubts for her—no one who has seen her with Michael Warnham possibly could. But you two have been so close—it would be natural for you to feel a sense of loss."

Serena's eyes filled with tears. Through all the preparations and fuss no one else had thought of this, not even Lucy herself. She looked down to hide her distress. James came over, cursing himself for a tactless fool, and sat down beside her. He took her hands in his. "Serena, don't!" He swore as a teardrop fell on his hand, and pulled out his handkerchief. "You've no idea what it does to me to see you cry—I didn't think you could. Here, let me wipe your cheeks. We can't have the legend of the indomitable Miss Calvert ruined."

She looked up and smiled through her tears at this, but the sight of his face looking down at her so anxiously entirely overset her, and the tears fell faster than ever. He took her into his arms and cradled her, uttering words of comfort, till the sobs gradually faded and Serena regained her composure. She smiled apologetically and gently removed herself from his arms.

"Thank you," she murmured. "Forgive me."

"For what?" he asked with a wry smile. "For sharing your unhappiness with me? I count it a privilege. And it gives me hope you might agree one day to share more, much more than that. Oh, God, Serena, if only you knew how I regret the past! You say you have forgiven me, but the past lies between us like a serpent. If it were not for that I could now make you forget the loss of Lucy, and every other unhappiness. I know I could persuade your body to love me—you tell me that every time we kiss, so how could I not know it? But I want much more than that! I want your mind, your spirit, call it what you will. I once knew the enchantment of that communion, and I shall never forget it, nor cease to desire it." His voice dropped as he said this, and Serena had to strain to hear. She turned towards him.

"James..." she said tentatively. "James, it isn't the past which divides us. I've told you before, it's your lack of..." She stared at the man before her, and could not continue.

His face dissolved, as numbers of images flashed through her mind—James giving an unknown boy a ride to console him on his birthday, James in the park with no reason to trust or like Sasha Calvert, yet sensing her loneliness and taking her for a drive, James comforting the woman who had killed his brother, looking on her with such sorrow as she lay dying, James taking trouble to get to know Alanna's son. The images increased—James teasing, James laughing, James with his mother, James looking so worried just minutes before—until finally all the images melted and refocused into one, beloved, familiar face. She gazed at him in wonder, then she smiled and her wonderful eyes glowed as she started to speak again. "James—"

The doors of the library opened and Mrs. Galveston came in with a flourish. "Ah, Lord Wintersett," she began, "There you are! Oh, forgive me, Serena, I didn't see you at first. We are just about to set up a whist table for the gentlemen. Would you like to play, Lord Wintersett? And if you'll forgive me for saying so, Serena, it isn't at all the thing for you to be in here alone with Wintersett. This may be a wedding party, but—"

"I'd be delighted to join you, Mrs. Galveston," said James swiftly. "Miss Calvert was saying she had the headache, so I am sure she will be glad to be left in peace. I will take my leave of you, Miss Calvert. Shall I see you again before you return to Surrey?"

Under Mrs. Galveston's watchful eye what could Serena do but murmur regretfully that she was setting off the next day? But as he reached the door she asked idly, "Are you intending to stay in London long, Lord Wintersett?"

"I think not. I have been away from home rather a lot recently and my mother will soon start complaining that she never sees me."

Serena hesitated and said, "My young friend William—I believe you know him?—has been asking after you. You might see him when you return to Surrey."

THE MAN STANDING BY the graceful bay mare gazed over the countryside below. The brown and grey landscape was silvered with frost, but the afternoon sun was warm. He turned swiftly as he heard hoofbeats coming up the hill, and his heart leapt as he saw a woman with a laughing, glowing face riding to meet him. She came to a halt beside him and he held up his arms to help her dismount. But when she was on the ground his arms still encircled her.

"I half expected to see you dressed as a boy."

"I was tempted, but I decided it was too dangerous. People might be shocked if they saw me as I am, but if I were dressed as William they would be infinitely more shocked. Besides, my groom is just below, at the bottom of the hill."

"Very nearly respectability itself. But I thought it was William who wanted to speak to me?"

"No, James. I came as Serena, Sasha and William. All three of us have something to say to you, here on the hill where we first met."

"What is it, my love, my torment and my very dearest friend?"

"We . . ." Serena hesitated, then she threw back her head proudly and said, "I love you, James, and I trust you, completely, finally, for always."

He gave a great shout of joy, and lifted her high in the air. The horses moved restlessly, and Serena said, laughing, "Douce and Trask are shocked! Put me down, James, before they abandon such a disgraceful pair."

James set her down and, still holding her hands in his, he said, "Then I shall make us both honest again. Will you marry me, Serena? Will you give me, in William's words—the other William, of course, " 'Th'exchange of thy love's faithful vow for mine?' "

Serena smiled as she replied,

" 'I gave thee mine before thou didst request it.' "

James took her hands to his lips and kissing them he said slowly, "I think Juliet had the best words after all.

My bounty is as boundless as the sea,
My love as deep; the more I give to thee,
The more I have, for both are infinite.

Serena's eyes filled with happy tears as he added, "If you will marry me, Serena, I swear I will love you and cherish you for the rest of our lives."

"Yes! Oh, yes, James, please!" He kissed her again and again, muttering incoherently as he did, and Serena laughed and eagerly responded. After a while he took her to the edge of the hill and they stood looking down on the patchwork of fields below.

Serena said dreamily, "It seems an age since we first met here on the hill. The first words you spoke to me were a quotation. It is fitting that we are quoting again now, though Romeo and Juliet were a sad pair of lovers in the end."

"Quite. I can think of a much more appropriate play."

"Which is that?"

"*The Taming of the Shrew*, of course."

"James!" Serena turned in his arms in mock anger.

He quickly imprisoned her again, and when she protested he said, "I have to protect myself against those fists of yours, Serena! But now that you are here..." James bent his head to her again.

Finally she murmured, "There's one other thing..."

"What is it, my love?"

"If I promise to be a model wife the rest of the time would you, just once a year, take me for a week or so to some remote spot where I might be William again? To dress and ride like William?"

"You may have a fortnight," said James largely. "As long as you promise to become Serena again at nightfall?"

"Done! Now I should go back to tell Aunt Spurston of our engagement. Will you come with me? She will be delighted, I think."

"I thought she disapproved of me?"

"And you so *enormously* wealthy, James?" said Serena opening her eyes wide.

"Devil! But that reminds me, my enchanting, loathsome toad—you gave me a challenge a short while ago in London. Are you prepared to answer it now?"

"What challenge was that, my darling viper?" asked Serena laughing.

"Just this." And, taking her gently into his arms, James proceeded to demonstrate how calm, how breathlessly exciting, how comfortable, and how dangerous a kiss in reply to a challenge could be.

To THE SURPRISE of no one, but to the delight of all who were close to them, Miss Calvert and Lord Wintersett were married very soon after. When Lucy returned to London she was often heard to complain that she saw a lot less of them than she might have expected, for they spent much of their time at Wintersett Court, and took their nephew several times to St. Just—until the arrival of young Edward Anthony Stannard made that difficult. And once a year they disappeared for a fortnight. No one ever found out where.

About the Author

Gail Mallin has a passion for travel. She studied at the University of Wales, where she obtained an honours degree and met her husband, then an officer in the merchant navy. They spent the next three years sailing the world, before settling in Cheshire. Writing soon became another means of exploring, opening up new worlds. A career move took Gail and her husband south, and they now live with their young family in St. Albans.

Books by Gail Mallin

Harlequin Regency Romance

60—A Most Unsuitable Duchess

The Eccentric Miss Delaney (in *Regency Quartet*)

Debt of Honour

Gail Mallin

CHAPTER ONE

THE EXOTIC FIGURE standing outside the handsome-fronted shop caught Kirk Thorburn's attention as he strode down the Highgate. Wintry sunlight burnished the gilded feathers on the Turk's turban and danced down his red jacket and baggy green trousers to catch the upturned tips of his crystal-encrusted slippers. A long clay pipe was held to his lips and in his other hand he clasped a large plug of tobacco.

Kirk halted, his gaze going to the name painted above the wide bow-window. "Fleming and Sons, Snuff-Merchants". It seemed he had found the place he sought. Kendal had been a major centre for the tobacco trade for over a hundred years now, but Flemings was reputed to be the best. Perhaps he would find an answer to his questions here?

Involuntarily, his long fingers tightened around the leather pouch in his coat pocket, but as he made to cross the narrow street to reach his goal a tall young woman stopped outside the shop. She had her back to him, but he spotted the friendly pat she bestowed on the exotic statue before entering.

A brief flicker of amusement lightened Kirk's expression. There had been something decidedly proprietorial about that little gesture! For an instant he wished he had caught a glimpse of the girl's face. Then his curiosity died. He was not here to dangle after any petticoat, pretty or not.

Ten minutes passed.

"Damn the wench!"

His feet were growing numb and Kirk had the feeling that he might become frozen to the spot if he didn't move soon. Caroline had laughingly informed him this morning that his blood must have grown thin during his long absence from his native soil, and Kirk was beginning to think she might have a point. Certainly, he could do with a little of that fierce Bahamian sun right now!

Kirk stirred restlessly. He had hoped for privacy in which to conduct his business, but he had travelled over three thousand, five hundred miles to try and find an answer to a mystery, and his patience, never abundant at the best of times, was all but exhausted.

What the devil could she be doing in there, anyway?

"WHY, MISS SOPHIE, what brings you here on such a cold afternoon?"

Sophie Fleming smiled at the thin, stooped figure behind the polished counter. "I thought I might persuade my uncle to accompany me home, Mr. Hoggarth."

Behind his steel-rimmed spectacles Mr. Hoggarth's faded grey eyes assumed an apologetic sympathy. "I fear you have already missed him. He left a quarter of an hour ago, saying he had an engagement to meet Master Strickland at his warehouse to discuss that new shipment of port."

"In that case there is no point in waiting," Sophie announced ruefully, knowing that such a business might turn out to be protracted.

It had been something of a wasted afternoon. Against Nancy's advice, she had donned her warmest cloak and boots and ventured out in search of ribbons to trim her new gown for tonight's soirée, but the shade she had wanted proved elusive.

"Is Mrs. Nelson waiting for you in the carriage, Miss Sophie? Only it won't do to keep horses standing in this weather," Mr. Hoggarth reminded her gently.

"Oh, I walked," Sophie replied airily, "and left Nancy at home to toast her toes by the fire, since she viewed the prospect of any exercise with such repugnance."

Mr. Hoggarth looked scandalised. "Then I hope you'll let me procure a chair to take you home, Miss Sophie. 'Tis blowing fit to bring the chimney-pots down! You shouldn't ought to be out in this weather, let alone walking."

"It is very kind of you, but there is no need. Truly!" Sophie strove to keep her annoyance out of her tone.

It seemed no one could forget the childhood accident which had almost killed her. The fall from her pony while learning to ride had left her with a weak ankle, but she was not delicate!

"Then won't you at least take a glass of something to warm you before you leave?"

Becoming aware that her uncle's oldest and most trusted employee was regarding her with anxiety, Sophie curbed her impatience and nodded. Mr. Hoggarth had known her ever since she was a baby and, like her uncle, he found it difficult to accept she was a grown woman of one-and-twenty.

When she was settled with a glass of sherry in the most comfortable chair that the shop could boast Mr. Hoggarth enquired how she had enjoyed the recent round of New Year festivities.

"Very well, thank you, sir. Though Nancy swears she is tired of mending all the petticoat frills I have torn while dancing." Sophie laughed. "She is convinced I must have two left feet!"

Mr. Hoggarth chuckled. "You are teasing me, Miss Sophie. You are too light on your feet to be a poor dancer." A beam of fond pride lit his wrinkled face. "I am sure even an elegant London gentleman like Sir Pelham Stanton could not wish for a more graceful partner."

Sophie merely smiled. There was a note of curiosity in the old man's voice, but she had no intention of satisfying it.

Disappointed, Mr. Hoggarth sipped his wine. Everyone in Kendal was agog to see if Sir Pelham's whirlwind courtship would come to anything, but he knew that he would get no hint from Miss Sophie. She was completely lacking in the girlish fluttering he felt appropriate in such momentous circumstances.

Rising to her feet, Sophie set down her empty glass.

"Thank you for the wine," she began, but her speech of farewell ground to a halt as the door flew open with a noisy bang.

Turning automatically, she beheld a tall figure framed for an instant against the doorway, his dark cloak swirling in the icy wind. Then he turned to close the door behind him and the picture dissolved.

Sophie let out the breath she hadn't realised she had been holding as he advanced into the centre of the room. Politely he raised his high-crowned hat in her direction, revealing a head of hair that gleamed like a golden guinea.

"May I enquire if your business is concluded, ma'am?"

His voice was attractive, a deep, rich baritone, but with a curiously heightened sense of awareness Sophie caught the hint of sarcasm behind his question.

Colour flared into her pale cheeks. She was not used to being spoken to in such a fashion.

"No, it is not," she snapped and, turning to the surprised Mr. Hoggarth, she demanded to see a selection of smoking pipes. When a rack was brought for her inspection she viewed them with a show of concentration, but every now and then she allowed her gaze to flick triumphantly to the tall man impatiently waiting next to her.

Kirk restrained the impulse to curse. Unless he missed his guess, the baggage was being deliberately provoking. When she asked to see yet another rack of clay pipes Kirk was sure of it.

Sophie was aware of Mr. Hoggarth's unspoken disapproval but her irritating behaviour owed its origin to more than her hasty temper. Something about this man had caught her on the raw! Only look at the way he was standing there, glowering at her. Over six feet tall if he was an inch, with broad shoulders to match, he reminded her of nothing so much as an angry giant out of a child's fairy-tale.

Sternly Sophie quelled the thought that without the frown he would have been devastatingly handsome.

"Ahem, while the lady makes up her mind, perhaps I could help you, sir?"

Mr. Hoggarth could not fathom what Miss Sophie was up to, but it was against his principles to risk losing custom.

Kirk hesitated fractionally and then nodded.

"I'm obliged to you, sir," he said. Delving into the deep pocket of his coat, he produced a leather pouch. "I have here a snuff-box. Observe the motif on the lid, if you would be so good."

Surreptitiously, Sophie glanced up at the object he handed over.

"Mmm, Odysseus blinding the one-eyed Cyclops, executed in *quarte-couleur* gold." Mr. Hoggarth studied the snuff-box. "A very beautiful item, sir. Did you wish to sell it?"

Kirk laughed, and Sophie thought she had never heard a sound so devoid of mirth.

"Nay, it's not for sale. My purpose in bringing it here was to discover if you have ever seen it before. I have reason to suspect it may have been purchased in Kendal, but none of the other snuff-mills I've tried stock such fine goods."

"It is indeed French workmanship of the highest order," Mr. Hoggarth murmured, turning the box in his hand and surveying it intently. "We do stock such quality pieces on occasion, but I cannot recall one like this."

"Are you sure you don't recognise it? It was bought some time ago. Think, man, think!"

The urgency in his tone caused Sophie to abandon her pretence of indifference. Staring at him in frank amazement, she wondered at the reason for the look of strain which marred his classically cut features. Hot-tempered herself, she sensed that something more than mere impatience lay behind his words.

"I'm sorry, but I cannot help you, sir. I would have remembered such a fine snuff-box had I seen it before, I do assure you."

From the coolness of his reply, Sophie realised that Mr. Hoggarth was somewhat ruffled. He took pride in running the shop like well-oiled clockwork and he plainly resented any implication to the contrary.

The stranger did not seem to notice he had given offence, but let out a low mutter, which sounded suspiciously like an imprecation.

Mr. Hoggarth's disapproval deepened. He coughed and threw a warning glance in Sophie's direction.

"Will that be all, sir? Or did you want it filling?"

He flipped open the snuff box lid in one easy movement and sniffed cautiously at the interior. "Kendal Brown. A popular choice, sir, but we can offer you a large selection of other blends or prepare one to your particular requirements if you would prefer something a little more unusual."

"Thank you. Kendal Brown will suffice."

Sophie received the distinct impression that snuff was the last thing on the stranger's mind, but his casual assent brought a smile to Mr. Hoggarth's face. He was clearly relieved to have matters back on a normal business footing again.

A grin curled Sophie's wide mouth. Plainly he did not share her curiosity; Nancy was forever complaining that it was her besetting sin! But, in truth, she had to admit she was intrigued by this man. It was hard to tear her eyes away from his tall, well-proportioned figure. There was an air of purpose and a sense of energy about him that was exciting, and somehow almost dangerous. With a little shiver, Sophie suddenly decided he would make a ruthless enemy.

Who was he and why was he here in Kendal? His face was deeply tanned, but she did not think he was a foreigner. What was more, his black caped cloak and well-polished leather boots were obviously of the finest quality. No doubt a dandy like Sir Pelham Stanton would decry his lack of fashionable accessories—he carried no Malacca cane and his cravat was plain—but he was undoubtedly a gentleman.

Mr. Hoggarth had reached down one of the many glazed earthenware jars that lined the shelves of the shop and begun weighing out the correct amount of snuff on to his scales. His expression became creased with annoyance when he realised that he was a fraction short of the necessary amount.

"Your pardon, sir. I shall have to fetch a new supply from the store-room. It will only take a moment," he announced, going red with embarrassment. Flustered by this unusual mishap, he hurried out.

The snuff-box lay on the counter where Mr. Hoggarth had placed it, and out of the corner of her eye Sophie could see that the upraised lid was decorated on the inside with an intricate design.

What an odd sort of place to put such an elaborately embossed initial, she thought to herself. That beautifully gilded letter would be constantly splattered with snuff and difficult to clean.

Was it an S? Unconsciously, Sophie moved nearer for a better look.

"You admire my trinket, ma'am?"

The cold voice made Sophie jump and then flush until she felt sure her face must be as red as her hateful fiery hair.

"I...I...that is..." Aware of her appalling lack of manners, Sophie could hardly bring herself to meet his gaze.

Viking eyes he had, as blue as the reflection off a sunlit sea. Her heart began to thump in the strangest way and to her intense annoyance she found she was tongue-tied, something that had not happened to her in years.

If only he would not stare at her in that sardonic way! The more she struggled for composure, the more those azure depths filled with a cool amusement that mocked her efforts.

"Sir, I...I hardly know what to say," she stammered, ending the silence at last.

"You could always try apologising."

The impudence of this remark restored Sophie's wits. Granted, she had behaved in a shameless fashion, but if he possessed any decency at all he would have pretended to ignore her eavesdropping!

"You go too far, sir," she retorted with a haughty frown. "I am sorry if I have given offence, but it is not your place to rebuke me."

"No, that task belongs to your legal guardian," he agreed smoothly. "But obviously he has been shirking his duty."

Sophie's big brown eyes widened as she digested his meaning. "You are insulting, sir! No true gentleman would think of speaking to a lady in such a fashion."

A short bark of laughter answered her. "Then it seems we are quits, my girl, for no real lady would dream of trying to pry into matters that were none of her damned business!"

Sophie sucked in her breath, but before she could deliver a blistering reply Mr. Hoggarth returned and she had to hastily school her expression into serenity. He would be horrified to discover she was quarrelling like a fishwife, and with a man she hadn't even been formally introduced to!

Deciding that the only dignified escape lay in retreat, Sophie smiled sweetly and bade the elderly shopkeeper farewell.

However, before Mr. Hoggarth could extricate himself from behind the counter, the tall stranger said, "Allow me," and swiftly moved to open the door for her.

Gritting her teeth, Sophie inclined her head in a gracious gesture. "Thank you."

"My pleasure, ma'am."

Nettled, Sophie glared at him. He was grinning at her, malicious amusement dancing in his blue eyes.

Quelling the absurd tug of attraction his smile provoked, Sophie swept past him with her chin held high.

A faint chuckle followed her out into the street.

"LORD SAVE US, Miss Sophie, where have you been? Your uncle came home long ago."

Sophie had hoped that the lengthy, roundabout walk she had taken would have restored her temper, but she had reached the Flemings' handsome Queen Anne residence in the Stramongate without being able to dismiss that hateful man from her mind.

Flinging off her fur-lined cloak, she dropped into her favourite armchair by the fire and held her chilled hands to the blaze. "I am frozen to the bone, Nancy."

"Well, you would go out," the older woman scolded, rescuing the abandoned cloak and folding it carefully.

"So I would," Sophie laughed, the tension draining out of her as she watched Nancy's plump figure bustle about, restoring order. There was something very soothing about the familiarity of her companion's action, she decided as she stretched out her long legs, revelling in the warmth and comfort of her boudoir.

It was a very pretty apartment adjoining her bedroom, beautifully decorated and large enough to hold all the expensive presents her uncle had showered upon her over the years, like the elegant rosewood writing-desk that sat before the silk-curtained window. Sophie knew she was very lucky to have been taken in by so kind a man as Thomas Fleming after her parents had been killed in a tragic accident when she was only a baby.

"Your uncle wants to talk to you when you are dressed, but shall I order some tea first? It might restore you. You look as if something more than the cold has upset you." Nancy came to stand before her, her arms folded in a manner that Sophie recognised as a sign of anxiety.

"What nonsense, Nancy," Sophie replied lightly, not wishing to confess the reason for her ill temper. "I think I had best forgo tea if my uncle is already waiting for me. Do you know what he wants to talk to me about?"

Nancy shook her greying head. "He was pleased about something, though," she volunteered.

"Oh, well, I'll find out soon enough, I suppose." Sophie shrugged, moving into the bedroom. She surveyed the daffodil-yellow gown Nancy had already laid out for her. "I have changed my mind. I will wear my blue brocade."

"But the matching petticoat needs pressing."

"Then be a dear and press it for me, Nancy, darling." Sophie smiled coaxingly. "I couldn't find those yellow ribbons I wanted."

Nancy rolled her eyes, but did not argue. The gown was well enough as it was, but stubborn as an ox Miss Sophie could be when she had set her mind on something! She took the sapphire flowered brocade with its sky-blue petticoat from the clothes-press and left her young mistress to her ablutions.

The copper can of hot water Nancy had placed earlier by the fire had kept warm, and as Sophie poured it into the rose-patterned china basin on her wash-stand her mind returned to the man she had encountered at the snuff-mill. Perhaps he was visiting friends in Kendal. She had lived all her life in the old grey town and knew everyone of note. Surely they would be bound to meet again if he was staying for any length of time?

A thread of excitement flickered through her slim frame at the thought. Provoking though he had been, she longed to know his name, and her heart skipped a beat at the prospect of meeting him in more favourable circumstances.

"What a fool you are!"

Sophie pressed her hands to her hot, damp cheeks. She whirled away from the wash-stand, scrubbing furiously at her skin with a towel, and caught a glimpse of her reflection in the ornate mirror above the mantelpiece. A hectic sparkle showed in her dark eyes.

"Perhaps I am coming down with a fever," she murmured ruefully.

Forcing herself to sit down, she tried to be calm. If it wasn't a fever turning her brain, then it must be madness possessing her, for she could not rid herself of the image of a man she had barely spoken to!

A tiny laugh escaped her compressed lips. Perhaps it was his unusual height that had struck a chord. It had made her feel femininely petite, a deliciously novel sensation, since she was taller than most of her friends. Indeed, she towered over her uncle and even her most ardent admirer was only a scant inch or two taller than herself.

The thought of Sir Pelham brought a slight sense of comfort to her self-esteem. At least he would never address her in such a rude manner, unlike that provoking great oaf!

THOMAS FLEMING was comfortably ensconced in the parlour, reading the latest copy of *The Times*, a newssheet brought up from London by mailcoach. The White Hart, where the stage stopped, boasted the best coffee-house in Kendal, and as he was a member of their reading-club the landlord was happy to order a copy for his private use. The news it contained, of the inevitable prospect of war with Revolutionary France and the unhappy position of the imprisoned King Louis, made his expression serious, but his plump face brightened as his niece entered the room.

"You look lovely, lass," he said, surveying her with approval.

Sophie smiled faintly. Her doting relative held partisan views! Still, she had to admit the dazzling creation of flowered brocade suited her, and her rebellious curls had been tamed for once. They fell in artistic disarray to her shoulders and she had used Spanish wool paper and pearl powder to draw attention to her clear complexion. Her long, slender neck was another asset and she wore an ornate necklace of opals and diamonds, a recent Christmas gift from her uncle, to emphasise it.

"Nancy said you had something to tell me," Sophie remarked.

He nodded, his eyes shining with pleasure. "Sir Pelham has asked permission to pay his addresses to you."

Sophie's mouth fell open in sudden dismay.

Her uncle viewed her reaction with surprise.

"I thought you would be pleased. Don't you like the idea of marrying him, m'dear?" he asked, motioning her to sit down and resuming his own seat.

Sophie did not immediately answer and he waited for her reply with growing concern. "Come now, am I such an ogre that you cannot tell me the truth?"

A faint smile touched Sophie's mouth. Anyone less like an ogre would be hard to find. From the top of his silver head to his small feet, Thomas Fleming did not possess a mean bone in his short, rotund body. His generosity was matched only by his girth, and everyone who knew him admired the way he balanced his adroit business skills with a genuine compassion for those less fortunate than himself.

No, it was not fear that tied her tongue in knots, but a desire to avoid hurting her uncle's feelings. He was bursting with pride and plainly longing to boast of her conquest to all his friends. But I cannot pretend about something so important, Sophie decided, summoning all her courage.

"When Sir Pelham began to call on us last autumn I thought his interest in me would not last," she began obliquely. "I told myself it was just a harmless flirtation to while away a sojourn in the country."

"Aye, I thought as much myself." Uncle Thomas nodded.

"Then when he returned from London for Christmas there seemed to be a change in him," Sophie continued slowly.

"I dare say he'd discovered that he had missed you, lass," Thomas chuckled jovially. "I'll own I am a little surprised he has asked for your hand so soon, but we should have known what was in the wind. A man don't dangle after a girl the way he has been doing unless he is serious."

"But why, Uncle?" Sophie flung out her hands in a gesture of bewilderment. "Why should he want to marry me?"

Thomas looked at her in astonishment. "What a question, lass!" he exclaimed. "Why should he not wish to marry you, eh? You are a considerable heiress and a fine, healthy girl into the bargain. He could do a lot worse!"

Sophie shook her head in laughing protest at his indignation. "Thank you, dear Uncle, for your championship, but we both know I am no beauty. I am too tall and I lack fashionable curves, to say nothing of my abominable hair!"

Thomas snorted. "You judge yourself too harshly, m'dear. Not everyone dislikes red hair and you have omitted to mention that you have the loveliest eyes in Kendal! Not that it signifies. A man must consider more than looks when he weds."

"Indeed." Sophie acknowledged the truth of this statement with a little inclination of her head. "But I must confess myself still puzzled. The baronet is wealthy. He has a fine house in London as well as estates in Cumberland. He does not need my dowry."

"A gentleman always has more need of money." An unusual note of cynicism entered Thomas Fleming's voice. "Aristocrats never wed paupers, lass."

"Nor do they usually marry into trade," Sophie countered.

"True, but don't forget that Stanton's grandfather was nothing more than a blacksmith. He isn't one of your fancy noblemen with a pedigree as long as your arm. Perhaps he can see the sense in marrying a healthy lass rather than some over-bred ninny who won't be able to bear him sons for all her blue blood."

Sophie coloured. Plain speaking did not offend her in the normal way, but the thought of sharing such intimacies with the baronet made her feel strangely uneasy.

"Now, Sophie, don't start being missish! It ain't like you." Her uncle wagged a plump finger at her. "You are a sensible puss and you've been brought up to understand the realities of life. I'll own that I've been glad to keep you here at home with me, but girls have to marry some time. You are twenty-one. It's high time you wed like all the rest of your friends. Or do you want to stay a spinster all your life?"

"Of course not!" Sophie shuddered at this dismal prospect.

"Well, then, Stanton can keep you in style and you'll be able to taste fashionable life in London too."

"He's seventeen years older than me."

"Is that what all this fuss is about? Are you wishing he was some romantic young fellow to sweep you off your feet?" Uncle Thomas shook his head in disbelief. "I would have thought better of you, Sophie, than to let yourself get carried away by all that nonsense. Love belongs in those novels you read, m'dear, not the real world. Remember, marriage is a business affair."

At her suddenly downcast expression, his tone softened.

"Eeh, lass, he's had his pick in London, but it's you he wants to wed."

"You think his regard for me may be genuine?" she asked hopefully.

"I'm certain of it. You are a good catch, but, if he's the man he seems, then that wouldn't have weighed with him unless he had a fancy to you."

Sophie shrugged helplessly. It was hard to discern what the baronet was thinking, for his manner was always formally polite, but perhaps the world in which he moved regarded passion as vulgarly undignified.

To tell the truth, Sophie had never met anyone like Sir Pelham Stanton before, and she hardly knew what to make of him.

As she emerged from Holy Trinity Church after morning service one crisp Sunday last October a gust of wind had blown the frivolously beribboned hat from her head. Sir Pelham retrieved it and returned it to her with an elegant bow. Once introduced, he had become a frequent caller to the house in the Stramongate, showering Sophie with small, thoughtful gifts. His urbane charm and witty conversation brought a thrilling whiff of the great metropolis into their quiet life and Sophie had never stopped to question his motives in singling her out.

Until now!

"Do you dislike him?" Doubt edged Thomas's tone.

"Oh, no, I find his company quite agreeable for the most part."

"They say that love comes only after marriage and, although I can be no judge of that, I do know that this would be a good match."

Sophie bit her lip. What her uncle said sounded reasonable, but a little voice murmured in her head that her feelings would not grow warmer in time and that she should trust her instincts and refuse this suitor now.

Desperately, she strove to ignore it and consider the many advantages of marrying such a man. Wealth and influence would indeed be hers, but, to her horror, she found she couldn't bring a single feature of the baronet's to mind. Another face, a devastatingly handsome face alight with a mocking pair of Viking eyes, kept intruding.

"I promise I won't push you into marrying him if that's what's worrying you, m'dear," her uncle announced, seeing her hesitation. "I think it is in your best interests and you'll never get a better opportunity to make a brilliant match, but I will leave the final decision up to you."

Recovering her self-control, Sophie attempted to banish her foolish doubts. Her uncle was right. Marriage was about money, status and the need for children to carry on one's name. It was idiotic to confuse reality with her romantic hopes of falling in love with a man who would love her in return for just herself and not her dowry.

But most of my friends are married already and they are younger than I am; I might end up on the shelf waiting to find such a paragon, she thought ruefully. Perhaps it is better to settle for a man who seems fond of me and can offer me a life of security and comfort than to hang on to my foolish dreams and end up a lonely and embittered spinster.

Thomas heaved his bulk up from the armchair and came to pat her slender shoulder. "I want only your happiness, lass," he said gruffly. "Agree to hear his suit and I swear that, if you should decide you can't stomach the fellow after all, then there'll be no more said."

Sophie laid her own slender hand over his veined one and gave it a grateful little squeeze. "Thank you, Uncle," she murmured.

"Then you'll do as I ask?" he enquired hopefully.

Sophie nodded. She owed her uncle that much at least, and if she could not have love she would at least have the satisfaction of knowing that she had made an old man very proud and happy.

AN HOUR LATER they encountered the baronet as they descended from the carriage at Abbott Hall.

"I have been waiting for you to arrive and, believe me, it was well worth the wait, Miss Fleming," Sir Pelham cried. "You look ravishing."

"You are too kind, sir." Sophie laughed coquettishly.

She did not altogether believe his compliments—she wasn't that vain—but it was pleasant to be admired, even when one's beauty belonged to artifice!

Their host, Sir Alan Chambre, greeted them warmly as they went inside.

"You know Sir Pelham, don't you, Alan?" Thomas Fleming enquired.

The eminent jurist nodded at his old friend. "We have been introduced." He smiled pleasantly at the baronet. "Any friend of the Flemings is welcome in my house, sir."

"Your servant, sir." An elegant bow added distinction to Sir Pelham's greeting. "It was kind of you to have invited me at such short notice."

Sir Alan grinned at Sophie. "Anything to oblige my favourite redhead."

His teasing brought a militant sparkle to Sophie's eyes, but she knew him too well to rise to his bait.

In any event, it would have been foolish to protest. She was well aware of the ripples of interest her arrival on the baronet's arm had created in the crowded candlelit room. She could see the matrons already whispering behind their fans and knew they were busy speculating on how serious his courtship might be.

Wait until they hear the latest news, she thought, excitement bubbling up inside her as she began to realise what a stir such a betrothal would make. Plain Sophie Fleming, so sadly lacking in feminine accomplishments, had made a catch that would turn them all green with envy!

Stealing a look at her future betrothed from beneath her long lashes, Sophie experienced a flicker of pride.

Frequently described as handsome, a slight exaggeration pardonable in view of his fortune, Sir Pelham certainly cut an impressive figure. His height was only average and the trim proportions of his youth had thickened slightly, but he stood out in this provincial gathering by his fastidious elegance. Alone of all the men present, he wore neither wig nor powder, and his light brown hair had been cut short into the new, fashionable Brutus crop. It was a striking departure and one or two old-fashioned folk looked at him askance, but no one could fail to admire the deep blue satin coat he was wearing, Sophie reflected. It managed both to enhance the breadth of his shoulders and to proclaim him the most sumptuously dressed man in the room.

"You are looking a little flushed, Miss Fleming. May I procure you a glass of iced lemonade?"

Blushing faintly at her own thoughts, Sophie became aware that the baronet was gazing at her with an expression of concern.

She nodded hastily. "That would be lovely. It is so hot in here!"

He led her over to a sofa near to the door, where it was cooler, and saw her seated. "I shall only be a moment," he promised with an ardent smile.

Sophie watched him thread his way through the crowd and sank back against the velvet cushions with a tiny sigh of relief. Since he hadn't asked her to marry him yet it was hardly modest to reveal the fact that she was thinking of saying yes! Nancy had always scolded her for her lack of discretion, but she hadn't a circumspect bone in her body. Worse, her face was much too expressive of her wayward thoughts!

The entrance of a latecomer in the doorway deflected Sophie from her musings.

Her dark brows rose in surprise as she took in the new arrival's outfit. Trust that woman to be the first in their circle to wear the new skimpy fashions that had left Uncle Thomas gasping when Sophie had shown them to him recently in a copy of the *Lady's Magazine*!

The high-waisted dress was made of a flimsy pale rose silk, which flattered Caroline Birkett's porcelain complexion and light blue eyes. Like Sophie, she was tall, but her figure was lushly curved and the low neckline revealed her magnificent bosom. A spray of ostrich feathers decorated her flaxen curls and she looked altogether so fashionable that Sophie's heart was quite wrung with envy.

I wonder if I could persuade Uncle Thomas to let me try something so daring? A tiny smile curved her lips. No doubt he would remind her that Caroline had the reputation of being fast, due to the fact that she appeared to spare no thought for her husband, often absent at sea, but gadded about accompanied by a variety of male escorts to every entertainment on offer.

For an instant, Caroline stood quite still, and Sophie suspected that she was deliberately holding her pose so everyone could get a good look at her, but then she turned her blonde head to address someone behind her, apparently oblivious to the stir she had created.

An instant later her escort stepped forward into Sophie's vision: a tall man clad in dark evening clothes; his unpowdered head gleamed gold in the candlelight.

A tiny gasp escaped Sophie. It was her arrogant stranger, but what was he doing here with Caroline Birkett hanging with smug satisfaction on to his arm?

CHAPTER TWO

"WHY DID I LET YOU persuade me into coming here tonight?" Kirk Thorburn demanded quietly as Caroline laid a possessive hand upon his arm to draw him forward into the crowded room.

"Because it's time you stopped being a recluse, my dear friend," she murmured in reply.

For an instant there was a flash of grief in his amazingly blue eyes, and Caroline sighed softly. "Forgive me, I don't mean to criticise, but moping alone at Haraldsgarth will not bring Ingram back."

"Nothing can bring my brother back," he answered flatly.

Her fingers tightened sympathetically on his arm and she felt the tension in the rock-hard muscles beneath his plain black coat. "Don't punish yourself, Kirk. There was nothing you could have done to prevent his death, even if you had been in England when it happened."

"Perhaps not, but I intend to see that he is avenged."

There was a quiet finality about his statement which curtailed further argument, and, dropping the subject, Caroline forced a lighter note into her voice.

"But for tonight, won't you try to enjoy yourself? Please? It will be good for you to meet some new faces and James will be furious with me if he discovers that I had failed to keep you entertained in his absence."

The sombre expression on Kirk's face vanished. "It is very sweet of you to persevere with me, Caroline. I don't deserve such kindness."

"Nonsense, what are friends for?" she returned lightly, but she could not help the *frisson* of pleasure that shot through her at his smile. It is as well I am happily married, no matter what the gossips might think to the contrary, she reflected silently.

Kirk Thorburn was much too handsome for any woman's good. That smile of his could charm the devil himself!

"Look, here comes Sir Alan," she exclaimed in some relief. "He is a genial old busybody, but I'm sure you will like him."

"Caroline, my dear, you look stunning." Sir Alan bowed over her hand. "I'll wager that pretty outfit cost James a goodly part of his fortune. He will need to make several more voyages to recoup it, eh?"

There was nothing malicious in his chuckles, and Caroline took it in good part.

"I knew I should be teased for introducing the latest fashions to Kendal," she lamented, but her eyes twinkled.

"Damme, but I'll rejoice if all the lasses start wearing such gowns," retorted Sir Alan with jovial honesty. Then, deciding that perhaps it was not quite *comme il faut* to harp on about such a delicate topic, he continued hastily, "But where is James? Don't tell me he has set sail again."

"I'm afraid so. A cargo came up that he could not resist." Caroline made a small moue of resignation. "However, as you can see, I am well provided for tonight. Please allow me to introduce my escort, an old friend of ours recently returned from the Bahama Islands."

The two men exchanged civilities for a moment or two and then the inquisitive jurist said, "Did you meet Captain Birkett on New Providence, Mr. Thorburn?"

"We became acquainted when he purchased a cargo of cotton from the plantation I helped my godfather to found. In spite of my finding him a hard man to beat down when it came to negotiating the contract, we became good friends," Kirk explained. He smiled at Caroline. "I met Mrs. Birkett when she accompanied her husband on his next voyage."

"My one and only trip to sea," Caroline shuddered delicately. "I am no sailor, I fear."

The two men smiled and Caroline continued in the same light vein until she could let it slip that Kirk, having become the sole owner on his godfather's death three years ago, was in the process of selling the plantation.

"It should fetch a very handsome profit to add to the fortune Kirk inherited from his father," she continued artlessly.

Sir Alan looked impressed. "Do you intend to settle in England, sir?"

Kirk nodded, but did not elaborate.

Fortunately for Sir Alan's curiosity, this taciturn reply was ameliorated by Caroline swiftly interrupting with the information that Kirk intended to return to farming family property in Cumberland.

"Why on earth did you try to impress him by pretending I was some nabob?" Kirk demanded wrathfully when Sir Alan drifted away to converse with his other guests.

"Because it was the quickest way to establish your credibility, dear friend." Caroline grinned at him unrepentantly. "Don't worry, no one will question my claims."

He frowned at her. "I dislike deceit."

"Oh, pooh, merely a little harmless exaggeration!" she exclaimed with a giggle. "Alan was fascinated and I'll wager he won't waste any time in relating your excellent status to everyone who counts in Kendal."

Kirk snorted, and she shook her head reprovingly at him.

"You may not care a toss for such things, but, believe me, it matters if you wish to be taken seriously. In a small place like this, appearances are very important, Kirk."

"You think my present wealth might offset any rumours about my wicked youth?" he enquired ironically.

"Hush, don't talk about that, you provoking man!" Caroline tried to sound stern. "I doubt if anyone here knows that you fled to join your godfather to avoid scandal. Watendlath is remote enough, heaven knows, and it was ten years ago."

Kirk's grin faded. "Perhaps you are right. It will not help my cause if I set people's backs up. I need them to talk to me freely if I am to discover the real truth about that cheating bastard."

"I know you suspect the baronet, Kirk, but tread carefully." Caroline's smooth brow furrowed at his strong words. "He is very well thought of and you will achieve nothing if you lose your temper and accuse him without proof. For your own sake, don't quarrel with him if he is here tonight."

Aware of the sense in what she said, Kirk did not dispute this advice. "I shall endeavour to control myself if we meet," he promised with a touch of irony, knowing that his hasty temper would make it a difficult task.

"Good. Now come, let me introduce you to a few people." Caroline threaded her arm through his.

They began to circulate slowly around the elegantly furnished room, exchanging greetings and polite civilities as they went.

"Heavens, what a shocking squeeze," Caroline remarked, but, receiving no reply, she glanced up at her companion and saw that his gaze was riveted on the other side of the room, where a log fire blazed in the handsome marble fireplace.

"That girl, the one over there in blue, standing next to the old gentleman, who is she?"

Caroline's brows rose. "That is Miss Sophie Fleming. She is the niece of Thomas Fleming, the snuff-merchant. Do you really desire an introduction?"

At his abrupt nod, she shrugged her shapely white shoulders. What an odd choice he had made when there were several pretty girls discreetly ogling him behind their fans!

"Very well, but I must warn you that she is something of a hoyden. Her uncle dotes on her and popular opinion has it that his lack of discipline has encouraged her independence. She quite jumped down poor James's throat once when he was trying to explain how a new life as a slave in America might actually benefit some of the poor benighted heathens he has seen on his travels round Africa."

"Is that why you dislike her, Caroline?"

"Oh, dear, I suppose I did sound rather spiteful!" Caroline pulled an apologetic little grimace. "Admittedly, I do not care for her, but there is another reason why you would do better to set your sights elsewhere."

He quirked an eyebrow at her hesitant tone.

"She is on the point of becoming betrothed, or so rumour has it, to Sir Pelham Stanton."

"To Stanton?" Kirk echoed incredulously.

"Of course there has been no official announcement," Caroline added quickly. "The old gentleman would have trumpeted it from the rooftops if there had, but Stanton has been very persistent."

"I suppose she is an heiress?"

A little startled by his shrewdness, Caroline nodded. "She is an orphan. Both her parents were drowned one night in the Kent when their coach was swept from the town's main bridge during a storm. Sophie will inherit the old man's entire fortune." She shrugged. "And he is not in the best of health."

"How convenient for Stanton," Kirk murmured.

His gaze returned to the ill-matched pair across the room. It was definitely the same girl. Next to the portly little uncle, she looked taller than ever, but far more attractive than he remembered, thanks to the sparkling smile which animated her irregular features.

"You know, when we met this morning my impression was that she was deuced plain," he said absently and then, seeing his companion's puzzlement, quickly outlined what had happened.

"I told you she was an oddity." Caroline was relieved that there was such a simple explanation for his interest.

"Perhaps." He paused and then continued thoughtfully, "But I think it might repay me to strike up an acquaintance with Miss Fleming."

"Kirk, what are you planning?" Caroline exclaimed uneasily, her relief turning to apprehension at the devilish expression on his handsome face. "Stanton won't take it kindly, if you start flirting with her!"

"I know." He smiled.

DEAR HEAVENS, they are coming over here!

Sophie had been watching them for the last half-hour.

To her chagrin, the man she had not been able to get out of her mind had not even noticed her. He had been much too busy talking to that shameless hussy!

Sophie suspected that she wasn't the only one to be aware of the stranger in their midst. His distinctive height and broad shoulders were causing several maiden hearts to flutter. He was clad in a simple set of evening clothes, consisting of a black coat superbly cut in broadcloth, a pale lemon waistcoat and white silk knee breeches, and somehow their very plainness was more eye-catching than the most sumptuous of satins. When allied to his deeply tanned skin and his short, unpowdered hair, gleaming like new-minted gold in the candlelight, they gave him an intriguing appeal no female was likely to ignore.

Disappointed he had not sought her out, Sophie had tried to follow his progress while attempting to respond to Sir Pelham. Fortunately the baronet, who was in full conversational flow, had not appeared to notice the newcomers and at length had returned her to her uncle before seeking entertainment in the card-room.

How offended he would be if he knew I'd scarcely heard a word he'd said, Sophie mused, free at last to think her own thoughts. A twinge of guilt assailed her, yet she could not pre-

vent her gaze from seeking out that tall, distinctive figure once
more. It was as if she were bewitched!

A momentary panic swept over Sophie as she watched the
couple draw nearer. She was about to get her wish, but suddenly she felt nervous, as if this were her very first party!

He reminds me of nothing so much as some great lazy jun-
gle cat, effortlessly graceful and somehow just as lethal, she
thought, gulping hard.

Quelling a crazy desire to flee, she forced her gaze back to her
uncle, but every other sense tingled. She was acutely aware of
the way her heart was thumping and her palms had gone damp,
but she didn't know what to do about it. She had never felt so
unsure of herself in her life!

The introductions were being performed and Sophie strove
to smile politely.

"Miss Fleming."

In a daze she felt him take her hand in a cool, firm clasp, and
then to her utter consternation he raised it to his lips. It was the
briefest of polite salutes, but Sophie jumped as if she had been
stung.

Blushing furiously at her own folly, she sought to cover her
gaucheness by saying brightly, "So we meet again, Mr. Thorburn. I trust you enjoyed the snuff."

"Eeh, what's this? Do you two know each other, then?"
Thomas Fleming spoke up, eyeing his niece's unexpected
blushes with anxious surprise before turning warily to survey
the tall young man who appeared to be their cause.

About thirty, I reckon, and a handsome, well-built lad, for
all his skimpy coat and short hair. He must be respectable, I
suppose, if he is a friend of James Birkett, but my Sophie is all
but spoken for and I don't want her head turned. Damn it,
Stanton should be here to pay court to her, not playing cards!

Kirk gave a discreetly edited version of how they had met.
"Your niece was kind enough to admire my snuff-box," he
added wickedly.

Sophie's cheeks vied to match her hair.

Wretched man, he was deliberately teasing her! Sophie fluttered her fan, trying to conceal her agitation. "It was a very
beautiful piece. You would have liked it, Uncle," she murmured hastily.

Her remark distracted Thomas Fleming's attention as she
had hoped it would and he beamed on Kirk, who obliged with

a description of the snuff-box, though Sophie noted that he was careful to leave out any mention of the curiously wrought initial on the inner lid.

"*Quatre-couleur* gold, eh?" Thomas remarked and launched into an animated monologue on the techniques employed by the great French smiths to achieve varying shades of gold by alloying it with other metals.

Freed from the necessity of conversation, Kirk was able to study Sophie more closely. Her quick-witted response to deflect her uncle's curiosity and her determination to ignore his provocation aroused his admiration. Whatever else the wench was, she possessed both brains and courage!

Until this moment Kirk had been too preoccupied to take much notice of Sophie as a person in her own right. This morning she had first annoyed and then amused him, and just now Caroline had unwittingly given him an idea how he could use her as an instrument for forwarding his plans, but suddenly he was ashamed of his selfish attitude.

She had done nothing to deserve his enmity! What was more, he would lay odds that her air of sophistication was a mere front. That elaborate gown and those fancy jewels could not conceal her nervousness. Was she as shy as this with all men? Kirk wondered if the old man knew what he was doing, throwing such an innocent at a wolf like Stanton.

From what he remembered of the baronet and from all he'd heard since, Stanton was not the type to find Sophie Fleming's slim, boyish figure appealing. Nor did her irregular features make for beauty. Only her long-lashed dark eyes could claim to be anything out of the ordinary. They gave her thin face a piquant charm, but he'd turn Turk if it was anything other than the girl's dowry that Stanton was after.

"Let me tell you how Mr. Thorburn and I first came to be acquainted, Mr. Fleming. I'm sure you'll find it a most interesting story." Caroline, who had seen Thomas's wary glance, seized the opportunity to establish Kirk's worthy antecedents the instant the old man's discourse on French goldsmiths rambled to an end.

She took a cushioned seat to one side of the fireplace and patted the matching open-armed chair next to it. "Come, we shall be very comfortable here," she said brightly with an inviting smile that left Thomas no choice but to obey her summons.

"I fear we will have to entertain ourselves, Miss Fleming," Kirk remarked lightly. "Would you care to sit down?"

"I prefer to stand," Sophie said stiffly.

"As you wish." He smiled at her politely.

Sophie swallowed hard. He was close enough for her to see the fine network of lines that crinkled the tanned skin around his blue eyes. He must laugh often, she thought dizzily.

His nearness seemed to be affecting her in the most peculiar way. Her pulse was racing and her throat was so tight that she could hardly breathe, let alone talk, but, aware that her silence appeared ill bred, Sophie searched her mind for something to say.

"You're very brown. Are you a sailor, too, like Captain Birkett, Mr. Thorburn?" she blurted desperately.

He shook his gleaming head. "No. I owe my tanned skin to the hot sun of New Providence."

"That is an island in the Bahamas, is it not?" Sophie enquired. "But you are a native of these parts, surely? Your name has a northern ring to it." She frowned thoughtfully. "And I can detect a faint trace of our local accent in your voice."

Kirk hid a grin. Her artless conversation was far from the insipid remarks he expected from young ladies of her station. "You are very shrewd, ma'am. I thought ten years away from Watendlath would have changed my speech beyond recognition."

"What a very long time to be away from home!" Sophie exclaimed. "How old were you when you left?"

"Almost nineteen," he replied, amused by her shameless curiosity.

Sophie's expressive face revealed that she was doing mental arithmetic.

"I shall be thirty next August," Kirk added helpfully.

"Oh, yes, indeed," gasped Sophie, suddenly becoming aware that her curiosity had led her perilously close to discourtesy. She peeped up at him through her thick lashes and to her relief saw he was smiling. Thank heavens, she didn't seem to have offended him!

"I'm sorry, I didn't mean to cross-question you. You must think me very rude, especially after this morning. I should not have behaved the way I did, but you made me angry by glaring at me so impatiently."

This frank apology disarmed Kirk. "I must confess to being at fault there. I was in a hurry and patience is not one of my virtues. Dare I hope we can forget the incident and begin again?"

There was a sincerity in his deep voice that Sophie found compelling. "I should like that." She smiled at him, a dazzling warmth curling up the corners of her wide mouth. "It would be nice if we could be friends," she added shyly.

Kirk stared down into her heart-shaped face. It was amazing how that lovely smile transformed her plain features. She really was a most unusual girl!

His silence made Sophie hold her breath, hoping she had said the right thing. It was suddenly very important that he thought well of her.

I want him to like me! Sophie shivered at the intensity of her emotions. She barely knew him and yet somehow it didn't matter. He was the most attractive man she had ever met. Of course, he was very handsome, but there was more to it than that. Perhaps it was his air of casual confidence that drew her. He had all the assurance of a man accustomed to command, with none of the formal stiffness that marked Sir Pelham's behaviour. Whatever it was, Sophie sensed that he was a man of determination, whose steely strength could be relied upon.

"I should be honoured by your friendship, Miss Fleming," Kirk murmured at last and, taking her hand to his, he bent his head to press an impulsive kiss against the soft skin of her inner wrist.

A wild excitement raced through Sophie's veins, making the pulse at the base of her throat beat rapidly. He lifted his golden head, but did not release her, and she made no move to withdraw her hand from his clasp.

To Kirk's astonishment, he could not drag his eyes away from the pulse he could see fluttering in the white column of her throat. A fierce desire to lay his lips against it possessed him, along with the certain knowledge that she would feel deliciously fragile in his arms!

Firmly he mastered the impulse and released the slender fingers which still lay imprisoned within his. He must be mad! The unfinished business of his brother's death was his priority. He had to find Ingram's murderer. It was a debt of honour and there could be no foolish involvements to distract him.

Disappointment flooded over Sophie. For one breathless instant she had imagined that he wanted to kiss her! Oh, she knew it was impossible that he should actually do such a shocking thing—the scandal would have raised the roof—but it alarmed her to discover how much she wanted him to throw convention to the winds!

"May I call upon you tomorrow afternoon? There is something I have to tell your uncle that I think you have the right to hear."

It was a deliberate change of subject, and as his quiet request broke in on her turbulent thoughts Sophie played with the ivory sticks of her fan for an instant while she tried to regain her composure.

"I have an engagement with friends," she murmured regretfully. "We plan to take advantage of this weather to go skating. One of the meadows down by the river was flooded in the last thaw and now it has completely frozen over."

He grinned. "I had forgotten how cold winters here can be. You don't see much ice in New Providence. Imagine a palm-tree covered in snow!"

Sophie giggled at the incongruity he painted and somehow their shared laughter dissolved the lingering tension, and Kirk knew his decision was right. He had not planned to show his hand so soon, but if his suspicions about Stanton were right then the Flemings deserved to know the truth.

If I wait to gather enough evidence it might be too late to save her from that rogue, he thought, suddenly appalled by the idea that Sophie might become entangled in Stanton's web.

"Tell me more about the Bahamas," Sophie begged, and, suppressing his anxiety, Kirk obliged.

His tales of blue skies, coral reefs and strange plants and birds of every hue made her eyes widen. "How wonderful it sounds," she murmured, enchanted by his description of a beach close to his plantation where the silver sand was lapped by clear turquoise water.

"May I ask you why you chose to settle there?"

"It was my godfather's idea. He had emigrated to Virginia to grow tobacco when I was very young. When the trouble out there began he supported the King's cause. Eventually, the rebels confiscated his property and he sought asylum in East Florida, which had not joined the other colonies in revolt, and he hoped to make a fresh start there."

"But didn't the Treaty of Versailles give Florida to the Spanish when the war ended?"

"Indeed it did, Miss Fleming."

His voice revealed his surprise and Sophie added shyly, "My uncle often discusses politics with me. We have no other close family and in some ways he is in the habit of treating me as if I were a son."

"Then perhaps you know that the same treaty restored the Bahamas to British rule. Many thousands of American loyalists decided to try their luck in the Bahamas. At the time I was keen to travel, and when my godfather wrote asking if I would like to join him in his new endeavour I accepted."

For an instant there was a bleak expression in his eyes, but it vanished so swiftly that Sophie was sure she must have imagined it.

"Did you grow tobacco in New Providence?" Sophie asked with interest. "It sounds a suitable climate for that crop."

"We grew a little, but cotton was the main crop my godfather decided upon. It was very profitable and enabled us to make a success of the plantation, although in the last few years I began planting pineapples as an alternative. Cotton is subject to too many pests to be relied upon."

"Pineapples! How exotic that sounds," Sophie exclaimed with a grin. "England must seem strangely grey and dull after living in such a bountiful place."

"It wasn't all paradise, I assure you." Kirk laughed. "We had to contend with many difficulties, including hurricanes."

Sophie's eyes widened. "I have read about those winds. Are they as terrible as they sound?"

He smiled down into her interested little face. Her questions had revealed a keen intelligence, and it suddenly occurred to him that he had rarely enjoyed a conversation with a woman more. Most of them, even the clever ones like Caroline, were simply not interested in anything beyond their narrow domestic sphere.

A few moments later a loud cough from Thomas Fleming signaled the end of their tête-à-tête.

"It's almost suppertime," he announced as he and Caroline rejoined them. "Come, m'dear, Sir Pelham will be waiting for us."

In the midst of her disappointment at the interruption, Sophie was aware that Kirk had stiffened.

Looking up at him, she saw that his smile had vanished, and she had the sudden conviction that even if her uncle invited him to join them, as she felt sure he was about to do, Kirk Thorburn would refuse.

And she knows there is something wrong too, Sophie concluded, catching a glimpse of the anxiety in Caroline's eyes.

"Kirk, would you be awfully disappointed if we missed supper? I'm afraid I've developed the most devastating headache and I'd like to go home." Caroline laid an urgent hand on his arm.

"Pon 'rep, I'm sorry to hear you are indisposed, ma'am. I should have enjoyed talking to you and Mr. Thorburn over supper," Thomas exclaimed regretfully as Kirk nodded acquiescence.

Thomas's earlier doubts had been allayed. Caroline had taken care to make her escort's position as a family friend very clear; he was no cicisbeo. Nor was there any danger of his turning out to be a fortune-hunter after Sophie's money. Although she had been discreet, Caroline had given him to understand that the lad was wealthy and his background eminently respectable.

"Indeed, sir, it is a pity. I am loath to leave, but . . ." Caroline managed a convincing sigh. "Will you convey our apologies to Sir Alan?"

While her uncle, whose opinion of the flighty Mrs. Birkett had risen considerably in the last half-hour, reassured her, Sophie stared thoughtfully at Caroline, whose rosy, flushed cheeks seemed to belie her headache.

I don't believe she is ill; she just wants to take Kirk away and have him to herself! Sophie's mouth compressed into a thin line. It isn't fair, she thought angrily; she is a married woman!

And what about you? Are you any better than she is to moon over a pair of Viking eyes when you are on the point of becoming betrothed to another man?

The annoyingly honest voice of her conscience delivered a swift warning blow, dissipating Sophie's anger in a rush of guilt.

"I hope we meet again soon, Miss Fleming." Kirk bowed low over her hand.

Sophie dipped a polite curtsy, but said nothing. She was feeling too confused by the riot of conflicting emotions fighting for supremacy within her breast. What was the matter with her tonight?

Kirk controlled his swift stab of disappointment at her lack of response and was immediately rewarded by an invitation from the snuff-merchant to call upon them in the Stramongate if ever he should be passing that way.

"He seems a nice lad. I hope he calls. I should enjoy discussing the merits of Bahamian tobacco with him," Mr. Fleming said a moment later as he led his niece towards the dining-room, where an informal supper was being served.

Sophie managed to find a reply, but before she'd had time to recover her composure the baronet materialised at her side. His flowery apologies for the length of his absence increased her guilty sense of unease.

How could I have felt jealous of that woman? she thought in silent dismay. Good God, I had better sense than that when I was only just out! Now she did not even have the excuse of being a green seventeen-year-old for letting a handsome face turn her head!

"We have just been talking to a neighbour of yours," Thomas announced jovially, interrupting the baronet, much to Sophie's relief. She was too angrily out of patience with her own folly to respond to Sir Pelham's elegant flirtation in the manner he expected.

"I was not aware that any fellow Cumbrians were present tonight," the baronet replied, smiling, transferring his gaze to the elderly merchant.

"Aye, his family hail from Watendlath," Mr. Fleming said.

In the bustle of taking their places only Sophie noticed how the baronet paled at this information. Curiosity roused her from dismal thoughts about her foolish behaviour. Staring at him closely, she saw how a muscle twitched by the corner of his thin mouth as her uncle related their meeting with Kirk Thorburn.

"Really? What a coincidence," drawled Sir Pelham, but his hand was shaking slightly as he reached for his glass of wine.

He took a gulp of the fine burgundy and then said, "Fancy that fellow having the gall to turn up again in decent society. Still, he always was an impudent rogue."

"What do you mean? Are you acquainted with Mr. Thorburn?" The words came out more sharply than Sophie had intended, and she flushed when Sir Pelham raised his eyebrows.

"Unfortunately I do know him, my dear Miss Fleming, but nothing to his good, I'm afraid." The baronet appeared to have recovered his habitual calm.

"The area around Derwent Water is not well populated with good families, but since the Thorburns have owned land there for generations and we were neighbours of a sort, I was allowed to visit Haraldsgarth during the school vacations," he said. "Although he was several years our junior, Kirk sometimes joined his elder brother Ingram and me on our youthful expeditions."

A small shrug disturbed the perfection of Sir Pelham's coat. "Naturally, as I grew older, my association with them ceased. My father was old-fashioned and had—er—rather traditional views on the subject of mingling with one's social inferiors."

A charming, rueful smile accompanied this remark, as if to take away the sting of his words, but Sophie sensed that beneath his careful consideration not to offend their feelings the baronet shared his sire's haughty view. Glancing at her uncle, she saw from his slight frown that he too had noticed the unconscious disdain in Sir Pelham's tone.

True, her family were merchants and not aristocrats, but they had been wealthy and important citizens in Kendal for several generations, and Sophie had been brought up to be a lady. Until this moment it hadn't occurred to her that the baronet, who could boast no distinguished ancestors, might be snobbish enough genuinely to consider her beneath him.

It was a disturbing revelation, but she was too curious to feel angry. "Why do you describe Mr. Thorburn as a rogue?"

Sir Pelham idly fingered the gold lace decorating his cuff. "Really, it is not a story for your delicate ears, my dear young lady."

Sophie's brows drew together in determination.

"You cannot be so cruel as to fob me off thus shabbily, sir," she exclaimed forcefully.

Sir Pelham glanced towards Mr. Fleming.

"My niece is not a child. I do not think you need to shelter her from the truth. And I must own you have whetted my curiosity," the elderly merchant admitted. "Furthermore, since I have issued an open invitation to visit us to that young man, I think it is as well if you enlighten our ignorance before any harm is done."

"I bow to your wish, sir." The baronet shrugged lightly and embarked upon his story. "Kirk Thorburn may have done well for himself in the Bahamas, but some ten years ago he quit these shores under a cloud of disgrace. He had to leave because he had seduced a girl of gentle birth and good character. She was the daughter of the local parson and only sixteen, but when it was discovered she was with child he refused to marry her."

"He denied that he was responsible?" Sophie asked faintly.

"Indeed he did, but he was not believed. He was known to be courting the girl, and although only eighteen himself, he already had the reputation of being a womaniser and a bad lot. She was a pretty young thing if my memory serves me correctly, but he preferred to run away, leaving her to bear the shame alone."

"You know this story for a fact?" Thomas asked shrewdly.

"A lot of my information is based on hearsay—I was in London, you understand, when the scandal broke—but I believe the essentials to be accurate. There was the most dreadful gossip, of course, not helped by the subsequent disappearance of the girl." The baronet heaved a dramatic sigh. "No one ever learnt what had become of her, and her distracted parents were convinced that she might have been driven to commit suicide."

Sophie shuddered.

"I'm sorry, m'dear, I had no wish to cause you distress." Sir Pelham's voice was gentle, but for an instant Sophie was certain she detected a puzzling satisfaction in his tone.

"Humph, I don't hold with gossip in general," snorted Mr. Fleming. "But in this case it sounds as if you have every right to dislike the fellow, Sir Pelham. I wouldn't trust a man who could behave in such a callous fashion."

Sir Alan's servants, hovering discreetly to offer tempting dishes, put an end to their conversation for a while, but when they moved away, the baronet murmured piously, "It was a long time ago. Perhaps Kirk has changed for the better. We must hope so, I suppose, if he intends to sojourn among us for any length of time."

It was a remark uttered with a damning lack of conviction.

"Once a rogue, always a rogue!"

Her uncle's testy answer was so unlike his usual self that Sophie knew that Sir Pelham's revelations had put him out of sorts.

He liked Kirk and now he's disappointed, she thought sadly.

Generous to a fault, her uncle was often inclined to give the benefit of the doubt in his dealings with other people. A firm friend, he hated to be proved wrong in his estimation of anyone, but he could be implacable if he discovered his trust had been abused. Sophie knew she shared the same traits. Once her love or loyalty had been given, it was given for life.

Which was why she simply could not understand how Kirk could have so heartlessly betrayed his young woman. He must have cared something for her if he was courting her, she thought wildly, ignoring the plate of delicacies placed before her.

"You are not eating, Miss Fleming. Do try the game pie. It is very good."

"I'm not hungry, sir."

She glared at the baronet with something akin to loathing. How dare he sit there consuming his meal with every appearance of enjoyment when his sordid story had sickened her to the soul?

Sophie's flicker of rage died as she realised how unreasonable she was being. It wasn't Sir Pelham's fault that she felt so unhappy, but her own for being such a silly fool.

I ought to have known better, she scolded herself roundly. Just because I found him physically attractive, it was no reason to suppose his character was sound!

Sophie shivered. She had been in grave danger of throwing her cap over the windmill for a caressing voice and warm smile! Perhaps it was a good thing her fanciful daydreams had come crashing down around her ears before she'd had time to make an utter idiot of herself.

Her uncle was right. Falling in love was no way to go about choosing a partner to share one's life with. Such volatile emotions made one blind! Kirk Thorburn was a heartless womaniser, and from this moment on she would not let herself forget it.

CHAPTER THREE

OUTSIDE THE TOWN the River Kent had spilled over its banks to form a small, frozen lake. The shining swath of ice glittered temptingly in the pale afternoon sunshine, beckoning to the laughing party of young girls and their escorts.

"Come on, Sophie, I'll race you to that willow tree," shouted a pretty brunette optimistically.

Pausing only to check that her new expensive iron skates were securely fastened to her boots, Sophie followed Charlotte Fletcher on to the ice.

It took both girls some time to recover their skill, half forgotten since last winter. After a lot of giggling and staggering tumbles they found their feet at last and soon were swooping about the ice, giving excited cries.

Sophie's spirits rose. Sir Pelham's revelations last night had left her depressed, but now she spun and twirled with enthusiasm, glad to stop thinking for a while and let herself be caught up in the sheer magic of moving at such speed.

"Heavens, but I'm exhausted," Charlotte giggled. "I need someone to lean on." Raising her voice, she shouted to the few remaining members of their party who stood chatting at the edge of the lake. "William, come and join us!"

Her husband shook his head and gestured his reluctance.

"Oh, what a lazy-bones!"

Sophie laughed. "He knows you too well."

Charlotte's eyes sparkled as she dashed off to drag her reluctant spouse on to the ice.

Sophie watched their laughing antics with wistful amusement. Charlotte and William had been married last summer. They didn't have much money and lived in a poky little house, but it didn't seem to matter; their happiness was obvious to everyone.

Deliberately, Sophie turned and looked in the opposite direction. Her mood was too fragile today to bear comparisons with her friend. Self-pity was even more abhorrent than envy and she would not let it spoil her sport!

The scene that met her eyes was colourful enough to ensure her resolve. The lake was thronged with people intent on enjoying themselves, many clad in a peculiar assortment of clothes to combat the freezing cold weather. Shawls, hats, coats and scarves in all the colours of the rainbow muffled bodies already swollen by extra layers of garments until all that could be seen were red-tipped noses and laughing eyes.

Frequent bursts of laughter as someone took a tumble or loud applause for a skilful turn of speed shattered the crystalline silence. One of the spectators had brought along his fiddle, and the cheerful music floated out over the ice, causing several couples to swing into an impromptu jig.

Suddenly Sophie found her hands clasped by a young boy she recognised as an apprentice to the town's foremost tailor.

"Come and dance, Miss Fleming," he begged with an impudent grin, and laughingly she consented, much to his delight.

Sophie was soon as breathless as Charlotte had been and she was glad when the musician finally stopped playing to refresh himself from a hip-flask. Thanking her partner, she began skating back to the spot where her friends were gathered.

"Have a drink, my dear," invited Maria Strickland as she reached the edge of the shallow lake and stepped off on to the frozen grass.

Accepting the welcome hot coffee, Sophie thanked the dark-haired woman who held it out to her.

"Would you like something to eat? I brought along a hamper of food, knowing how you young people would work up an appetite," Maria said.

Her smile was warm, and Sophie reflected how much she liked this kind middle-aged woman, who was wife to one of her uncle's closest friends. Twenty years younger than Josiah Strickland, Maria, with her easy informality, was very popular. Having no children of her own, she took a particular interest in her stepson and his circle of friends.

Frederick Strickland, the only child of Josiah's first marriage, had been one of Sophie's earliest playmates. At one time the two merchants had hoped to make a match of it between their offspring, but they regarded each other like brother and sister. Then Frederick, who worked alongside his father in their wine-importing business, had fallen madly in love with a French girl he had met on his travels abroad and married her.

"I had a letter from Frederick yesterday," Maria announced as Sophie bit into a crisp home-baked pastry. "He is very well, but says that the weather in Bordeaux is atrocious. It has done nothing but rain, apparently."

Frederick and Genevieve were paying an extended visit to her parents, and Sophie listened with interest to Maria's recital of their doings.

"Frederick sends you his regards." Mrs. Strickland paused, a twinkle in her fine grey eyes. "But he wants to know the truth of these rumours he has been hearing about Sir Pelham Stanton."

Sophie choked over the last morsel of her pasty.

"I'd ... I'd rather not talk about it if you don't mind," she murmured in a distracted manner.

Maria regarded her with surprise, having confidently expected her to laugh. It was not like Sophie to be so reticent! Over the years a close relationship had developed between them, and Maria had become accustomed to hearing her girlish confidences.

"Of course, my dear, but, if you do decide to change your mind, remember that I am always here," she replied sympathetically, wondering what was troubling her young friend. It would be an excellent match, but those lovely dark eyes were filled with something suspiciously close to reluctance.

Sophie smiled mechanically. "Thank you."

"Would you like something else to eat?"

The red curls shook in answer, setting aquiver the small plume adorning Sophie's jade velvet bonnet. It was a colour that admirably matched her deeper green coat.

"I think I will have another turn about the ice before it is time to go," Sophie explained. "It gets dark so early that I expect we will be leaving shortly."

Maria nodded and watched Sophie depart with a vague feeling of unease she couldn't put a name to.

Immediately Sophie was hailed by Charlotte and William, who were forming a long chain of skaters with the intention of travelling around the ice as quickly as they could. On the end of this line, Sophie was glad she had recovered her skill, for the tempo soon became hectic. The front leaders snaked into loops and wild turns with whoops of glee and she was swung from side to side with increasing rapidity.

She was on the point of dizziness when her gloved hands slipped from the coat of the person in front of her as the chain swung into a particularly frenzied arc, and she felt herself go spinning as she was flung outwards across the ice. Her balance couldn't sustain the momentum, and just as she felt herself beginning to fall a strong pair of hands grasped her firmly about the waist and hauled her upright.

Raising her gaze to thank her rescuer, Sophie met an amused pair of vivid blue eyes.

"You!"

Her gasp of alarm and the way in which she paled forestalled Kirk Thorburn's greeting. Instead he transferred one arm to support her around the waist before asking tersely, "Can you skate towards the bank? Don't worry, I won't let you fall."

For one weak moment Sophie allowed herself the luxury of permitting him to guide her across the ice. It was surprisingly reassuring to lean back against the broad bulk of his chest. One strong arm still supported her around the waist and she could feel the comforting warmth of his body penetrating her chilled frame. Like a child, she felt safe and protected, with no need to concern herself with what might happen next.

This strange lassitude lasted until they reached the shelter of the far bank and Sophie realised that she was at the opposite end of the ice from all her friends. Worse, there was hardly anyone about by this stretch of lake. The sun was already beginning to sink in a fiery ball, and as she gazed around she saw that the crowds had thinned.

Sophie's giddiness flared into new life as Kirk smiled at her. "Are you feeling better now?"

He was still holding her close, and his nearness was beginning to arouse sensations in her treacherous body that owed nothing to gratitude. She could smell the clean, fresh scent of his skin and feel the warmth from his hands penetrating her garments.

Her pulse racing, she nodded and said abruptly, "Thank you. You may release me."

"Are you sure you won't faint?"

"I am not in the habit of fainting, sir."

The annoyance in her voice seemed to convince him and he let her go, remarking, "I'd hoped you might be here. I wanted a chance to talk to you, but I didn't expect our meeting to be quite so dramatic.''

Sophie hesitated. He might be an unprincipled womaniser, but she could hardly depart without hearing what he had to say when he had just saved her from a nasty fall. That would merely give him the opportunity to criticise her manners again. And yet she didn't want to stay. Listening to his deep, attractive voice sent peculiar quivers down her spine!

"What is it that you wish to say to me, sir? It is growing late and I must rejoin my friends.''

Her bald statement surprised Kirk. He stared down at her and realised that she had meant her answer to sound as unfriendly as her expression. There was no trace of last night's smile in her eyes.

He shrugged his puzzlement aside. He could deal with it later. This chance for a private conversation seemed heaven-sent.

"You'll find it worth a few moments of your time, I fancy,'' Kirk announced wryly. "It concerns Stanton.''

"Sir Pelham?'' Sophie's brows climbed in astonishment.

"Aye. Is it true you are about to become betrothed to him?''

"That is none of your business!'' Angry colour flooded Sophie's cheeks.

"Probably not, but if you are thinking of marrying him I feel compelled to warn you that you are making a mistake.''

Sophie's fingers clenched together. "Putting aside your impertinence, you are still talking in riddles. What could anyone have against a gentleman like Sir Pelham?''

"I'll grant he appears every inch the rich and elegant aristocrat, but I've known him too long to be deceived.'' Kirk's mouth twisted savagely. "He's a liar and a cheat, if not worse!''

A gasp escaped Sophie. "However, he is not malicious, which is more than can be said for you, Mr. Thorburn. How dare you try and blacken his reputation when it is you who are the one with a wicked past!''

Kirk's expression darkened. "I see he has been spreading his lies already. How very clever of him! No doubt he warned you to beware of anything I might say.''

Sophie bit her lip. It was true. On leaving them last night after the soirée, Sir Pelham had whispered in her ear that Kirk might attempt to malign him.

"Eighteen months ago I became involved in a minor dispute with his brother. I will not bore you with the details, my dear, but Ingram Thorburn had the audacity to claim I had not honoured a debt. It would not surprise me if Kirk has inherited his brother's grudge and tries to continue the quarrel." The baronet's lip had curled scornfully. "Men of his stamp rarely have scruples. However, I have no intention of giving in to blackmail."

The heavy silence gave Kirk his answer. It hung uncomfortably between them for an instant, and then Kirk shrugged. Her lack of trust was only to be expected, he supposed, but somehow it was strangely hurtful, and his voice was rough as he continued. "Believe what you wish of me, but don't let it blind you to the truth. Stanton is no fit husband for an innocent like you!"

"I think my uncle is the best judge of that," Sophie snapped.

"Really?" Kirk glared at her. "Has Mr. Fleming actually investigated Stanton's claim to affluence?" His mouth twisted. "Don't let him fool you. He cheated my brother out of a considerable sum of money and when Ingram tried to remonstrate he arranged for—"

"Enough! I will hear no more of your accusations, sir. I did not believe it when Sir Pelham said you would stoop to underhand tactics, but you have condemned yourself out of your own mouth!"

Sophie didn't know whether she was more furious with herself for imagining that Kirk Thorburn was a man whose integrity could be trusted or with him for proving her wrong and shattering the illusions her stubborn heart had clung to. Anguish gripped her as she realised that Sir Pelham had not been mistaken in his low estimation of Kirk Thorburn's character. He was nothing more than a handsome-faced adventurer!

"You silly little fool . . ." Kirk struggled to maintain his own temper. He longed to shake some sense into her.

Sophie stiffened indignantly. She would not stay here to be insulted! "Good day, Mr. Thorburn." Her tone was as arctic as the weather.

She turned to go, but Kirk's hand shot out to prevent her. "Wait. I haven't finished. There is more you must know."

"You have no right to detain me, sir. Pray release me at once!"

In spite of her outrage, Sophie felt a warm glow where he held her by the arm. It spread rapidly outwards, as if he had lit a fire in her veins. Horrified, she realised she liked him holding her. Worse, she actually wanted to fling her arms around his strong neck and melt into his embrace!

In the past, mild flirtations of the sort conducted by her friends, which were all that a properly brought-up young lady might enjoy, of course, had never interested Sophie. None of the young men with whom she was acquainted had stirred her senses, but Kirk Thorburn was different. She had been attracted to him the instant they'd met and now at last her instincts warned her that this disturbing emotion she experienced in his presence was desire.

A surge of wild panic set her heart slamming against her breastbone. How was she to deal with these unknown, frightening sensations? Until this moment it had never even occurred to her that it was possible to yearn so very desperately for a man's mouth on her own!

Their eyes met. To her utter consternation, she recognised the same hungry expression in Kirk's vivid gaze.

The sudden surge of fierce desire which had shot through him when he touched her astounded Kirk. "Sophie?" He murmured her name softly. He wanted to take her into his arms, but did not wish to frighten her.

Blushing furiously, Sophie wanted to reject his unspoken question, but her voice would not obey her. She could not even look away!

Kirk felt a blaze of satisfaction. He had not been mistaken. She felt the spark of attraction too. He began to draw her gently towards him.

"No!" Panic gave Sophie the strength to break desire's thrall and shake off his restraining hold. "Leave me alone! I want nothing to do with you!"

Her cry was shrill. Heads turned in their direction.

"Listen to me... Wait!"

The green plume shook denial and she whirled away across the ice.

Kirk started after her and then halted abruptly.

People were already staring and he did not wish to cause any gossip that might hurt her reputation. Not that it would do him any good to chase after her; a group of skaters were hurrying to meet her and he knew he would get no further chance to be private with her today.

Damn it, he still hadn't told her the full story! She might declare that she wanted nothing further to do with him, but he would not give up so easily. A grim frown marred his brow. Tomorrow morning I shall try again, he vowed.

TO KIRK'S IRRITATION he discovered it was impossible to carry out his vow. He presented himself at the Flemings' residence only to discover that neither Sophie nor her uncle were at home. When questioned, the maidservant, susceptible to his warm smile, told him that Miss Sophie was spending the morning with Mrs. Strickland, helping her write out invitations for her forthcoming birthday celebrations.

Kirk frowned. He had met the Stricklands last night, but was not upon such terms with them that he dared invade their home and demand to see Sophie in private. Such an outrageous act would occasion the kind of gossip he was trying to avoid.

"Please give this to Miss Fleming on her return and tell her that I shall call on her this afternoon." He handed over his card, glad he had followed Caroline's advice after all. When she had first suggested he might have calling cards printed he had laughed and told her he was a plain farmer and not some fashionable fop, until her insistence that they might prove useful during his quest had finally persuaded him.

The maid bobbed an acquiescent curtsy and Kirk strode off.

He was doomed to spend the rest of the morning uselessly trying to discover if any of the smaller snuff-merchants knew the origins of the snuff-box found clutched in Ingram's dead hand, but his thoughts kept constantly returning to the flame-haired little termagant who had spurned his offer of help.

On the other side of town, Sophie's red head was spinning. It had proved impossible to push Kirk Thorburn's dark hints aside. She could scarcely credit that his allegations might be true, but somehow she could not dismiss them. He had seemed too passionately sincere!

"Sophie, would you like to have a rest from this?"

Maria's amused voice broke into her preoccupied thoughts.

"Oh, I'm sorry," she exclaimed guiltily, seeing the mess of blots her careless pen had made. "I wasn't concentrating."

"Never mind, we are almost finished in any case," Maria replied cheerfully. She ripped up the spoiled invitation and tossed it aside. "Let's have some tea."

She rose from her task and went to pull the bell to summon one of the maids to the drawing-room in which they were sitting. It was a pretty room, recently refurbished in the latest style, copied by a local cabinet-maker from Master Sheraton's *Drawing-Book*. The delicate colours and naturalistic floral decorations were to Maria's taste, and her husband, trusting her superior judgement in such matters, was happy to indulge her whims.

"I was wondering whether we should also open up the conservatory for my party," she said, turning back to Sophie. "It would offer our guests somewhere pleasant to stroll if they tired of cards and dancing. What do you think?"

Sophie flexed her ink-stained fingers. "Won't it be difficult to maintain the correct temperature for your rare plants if people are wandering in and out all the evening?"

"I'm not sure. I shall have to consult John. I'm sure he will know a way. He is a marvel!" Maria beamed happily. Her gardener's enthusiasm for the conservatory almost equalled her own.

Sophie grinned. Maria revelled in the amazement and envy her large, glass-walled hothouse created among her visitors! "You love those plants as if they were children," she teased, wiping her pen and setting it aside.

Maria's eyes twinkled. "That was Josh's intention, I suspect!"

The conservatory had been erected to run the full length of the south side of the house soon after Frederick's wedding. Master Strickland's unusual surprise gift had delighted his bereft wife and channelled her considerable energies in a new fulfilling direction. It was an extravagance that had caused tongues to wag, but both the Stricklands thought it money well spent.

The maid arrived, and as Maria unlocked the tea caddy and carefully mixed the leaves to her requirements Sophie joined her on the pale straw-coloured sofa.

When the silver kettle had boiled Maria poured the fragrant beverage and handed her a delicate porcelain cup. "And now that we have settled most of the arrangements for my birthday party, are you going to tell me what has been bothering you all morning?''

Sophie choked on the hot liquid. "What do you mean? There is nothing troubling me," she answered as lightly as she could.

"Oh, Sophie, when will you learn that you are a terrible liar?" Maria laughed. "Your face always betrays you, my dear. I dare say you heard not one word in twenty of my plans to open up the doors between the drawing-rooms and clear them of furniture so that we could have a little dancing."

A faint guilty colour rose in Sophie's cheeks. "I haven't been much help, have I?" she murmured ruefully.

"That wasn't my meaning." Maria quickly shook her dark head. "I was merely wondering if you were worried about your uncle's health."

"He did seem tired at breakfast," Sophie admitted. "But that is probably nothing more than a result of all our junketing since Christmas. No, I wasn't thinking of Uncle Thomas."

She fell silent and Maria hesitated to press her. Casting about for a fresh topic of conversation, she said at random, "I never got a chance to ask you yesterday, but what did you think of Caroline Birkett's outfit at Sir Alan's soirée?"

A fierce frown answered her. "It was positively indecent."

"Well, I thought it a trifle bold myself, but it is the coming fashion." Maria smiled pacifically. "Actually, that style would suit you, you know, Sophie. You have the height and slenderness to wear it, unlike me. I am much too short and dumpy to carry off such simple lines."

Sophie snorted, but in her heart she knew Maria was right. She did envy Caroline's daring and wished she had thought of wearing such a striking gown first, but she wasn't going to admit it.

"It's not just her clothes. I dislike her attitude. James Birkett is a lovely man and yet she flaunts herself all over town in the company of the most undesirable types, like...like that Kirk Thorburn!"

"Didn't you like Mr. Thorburn?" Maria questioned in surprise. "I thought him charming, and he is so very handsome!" She laughed naughtily. "One can quite see Caroline's point in his case. Why languish alone at home when one could be escorted by such a virile-looking man?"

Sophie's teeth ground together in an effort to hold in an angry reply. Oh, it was mortifying to feel so jealous of that...that hussy!

"Do you think she will ask him to be her escort to my party? I doubt if James will be home in time."

"I didn't know you had invited her!"

"The Birketts' card must have been one in my pile." Maria stared at her, puzzled by the vehemence in her tone. "After all, I could hardly withhold an invitation. It would be an insult. We have known them for years and James often carries wine for us."

"I suppose so," Sophie muttered begrudgingly, but she couldn't control the hot words that sprang to her lips. "All the same, I detest the woman! It wouldn't surprise me if she was Kirk Thorburn's mistress."

"Sophie!" Maria's eyes widened in shock. "You really mustn't say such things. It is most unbecoming in a girl your age."

"Even if it is true?"

"We do not know that." Maria was distressed by the unsuitable turn their conversation had taken, but her sense of fair play drove her on to defend the absent Mrs. Birkett. "Caroline is a shocking flirt, but I doubt if she lacks all moral sense. She is not someone I regard as a close friend—she is too frivolous—but there is no harm in her. I do not think she would actually go so far as to betray James."

Sophie sniffed, not in the least convinced. Maria always thought the best of everyone! She had seen the way Caroline looked at Kirk when she thought no one was watching!

Noting the stubborn set of her friend's mouth, Maria sighed. "Really, Sophie, it is none of our business anyway. Caroline's reputation is James's affair, not ours. If he sees no harm in his wife associating with a man like Mr. Thorburn, then neither should we."

"Are you implying that there is something shady about Kirk Thorburn?" Sophie pounced.

Maria blinked. Heavens, what an odd mood the child was in! "To be frank, my dear, I have heard rumours to that effect in the latest letter from my sister. Emma mentioned an old scandal which is circulating once again in Cockermouth, revived by Mr. Thorburn's recent reappearance and the mysterious death of his brother."

"Mysterious?" Sophie was momentarily diverted.

"Ingram Thorburn died in a fire at his farm last April. No one else was hurt, but there was a great deal of damage done, so much so that some people believed it must have been started as a deliberate act of malice." Maria sighed. "No one knows, of course, exactly what happened, but talk that it was not an accident persists. According to rumour, Kirk Thorburn believes his brother had an unknown enemy and is searching for proof."

The mention of Kirk's name goaded Sophie's attention back to the main issue at stake. "But Emma wrote that it was Kirk Thorburn himself who was involved in scandal?"

Maria agreed. "However, it happened years ago and it is an unsavoury tale. Can't we discuss something more pleasant, my dear?" she pleaded, hoping that Sophie's fierce curiosity wasn't aroused.

When she found that her young friend would not be put off she reluctantly repeated Emma's story, which, to Sophie's dismay, echoed Sir Pelham's version only too accurately.

"However, Emma added that she thought Mr. Thorburn seemed changed by his time spent abroad. She thinks he may well have reformed, which is why I must ask you not to repeat the story to anyone else, since it would be most unfair to spread such idle gossip," Maria concluded firmly.

Sophie nodded dully, hardly listening. In spite of the fact that he had not bothered to deny it, she realised that she had still been desperately hoping that the tale wasn't true. Now she knew she had been deliberately deceiving herself.

Ten years ago Kirk Thorburn had been a heartless womaniser. Maria's sister thought him a reformed character, but Sir Pelham Stanton believed he had not changed at all.

Oh, I don't know what to think!

Sophie wanted to cry the words out aloud in bewilderment. Logic told her that Kirk was the kind of determined man who if he bore a grudge might well act upon it, but instinct denied that his motives might be underhand or cruel.

Despite all the evidence to the contrary, her foolish heart insisted that he was a man of honour, but Sophie was too afraid of her own feelings to listen.

"WHY, UNCLE, I did not expect you home so early!" Sophie exclaimed in surprise as Thomas Fleming entered the cosy parlour. She had only just returned herself, having declined to dine with her friend. Maria's searching glances had made her feel uncomfortable, but all thoughts of the enigma that was Kirk Thorburn flew out of her head when she saw how grey her uncle looked.

Leaping from her seat, she ushered him towards his favourite armchair by the fire. "Are you warm enough?" she chafed his cold hand. "Have you eaten? Shall I tell Jennie to lay another place?"

"Nay, lass, don't fuss. I'm not hungry, only a little tired."

Sophie bit her lips anxiously. Her uncle possessed a hearty appetite. It was a sure sign that he was feeling ill if he declined his dinner.

Thomas began to ask her how she had spent her morning, but it was obvious that he wasn't really listening to her answers.

Eventually, abandoning this pretence at normality, Sophie declared he must go to bed and rest.

"You are a bully, my lass," Thomas protested, but so half-heartedly that she knew he wanted her to insist.

"If you have a nap now, I'll make you your favourite egg-custard tart for when you wake up," she cajoled.

"What a wicked wench you are to bribe an old man so," her uncle chuckled, but broke off laughing as a spasm of pain made him gasp.

"Shall I send for Dr. Wilson?"

Thomas waved her anxious suggestion aside. "Nay, I'll be as right as rain once I have had a nap," he said and asked her to ring for Ben, his manservant, to assist him to bed.

All through the solitary meal which followed Sophie pondered on whether she ought to ignore her uncle's instruction and send for the doctor. Leaving her dessert unfinished, she went upstairs to seek Nancy's advice.

"Reckon you'd best wait a while, Miss Sophie," Nancy said. "You know how it frets him to be fussed. Happen he will be feeling better when he wakes up."

"Then in that case I will go and make him that tart I promised him," Sophie decided, relieved to have something to do to take her mind off her worries.

"Change your gown first," Nancy shrieked as she headed for the door. "No sense in spoiling that pretty taffeta messing about in the kitchen."

Sophie grinned, but did as she was bid. Nancy did not approve of her penchant for cooking and frequently scolded that it wasn't a ladylike occupation, but it was a hobby Sophie enjoyed.

"I don't know why you can't practice on your pianoforte or sit quietly with some embroidery," Nancy muttered, helping Sophie into the faded blue gown she had chosen. "And this old thing makes you look a fright. It is only fit for the rag-bag!"

A peal of laughter answered her complaints. "But it is comfortable and it doesn't matter if I get stains on it."

Nancy snorted.

Sophie ruthlessly dragged her curls back into a tight knot and confined them. "Now don't scold, Nancy, darling," she said quickly, seeing her nurse's outraged expression. "I know I look terrible, but there's no one to notice except Mrs. Gilpin, and she won't mind."

Nancy's frown eased. "Oh, very well, I suppose you can't have your hair dangling in your face when you are in the kitchen. But for the life of me I can't understand why you enjoy getting all hot and bothered in there."

"It is my one talent," Sophie quipped.

Her answer wasn't strictly true. She had some skill at sketching, but none of the other usual occupations thought suitable for a young lady interested her.

"You could do better if you tried," Nancy retorted darkly.

"But let's face it, I'll never learn to sing in tune." Sophie grinned.

Nancy laughed reluctantly and gave up.

Descending to the kitchens, Sophie greeted their cook and explained what she wanted to do.

Mrs. Gilpin assigned one of the kitchen maids to help her and Sophie donned an apron and became happily absorbed in making pastry.

"The oven is hot enough whenever you are ready, Miss Sophie," Mrs. Gilpin announced, checking on the Robinson patented range Mr. Fleming had installed recently to make their work easier.

"Thank you," Sophie replied absently, trimming the edges of her pie-dish.

Seeing her concentration, Mrs. Gilpin smiled fondly. She had never expected the childish interest Miss Sophie had displayed to blossom into this competence. The little wench had haunted the kitchen, begging to be allowed to roll out scraps of dough. Those happy sessions making cakes for her dolls had developed over the years until Mrs. Gilpin thought the lass could earn her living as a cook.

Not that it would ever come to such a thing, of course. It was easy to forget it in this informal atmosphere, but Miss Fleming was a considerable heiress. The old master had no other close relatives. All the money from the business and the snuff-mill itself would go to her.

The man who marries her will be a lucky fellow, thought the cook. Not only would he control her fortune, but she was an intelligent, sweet girl, not spoilt for all that the old master had indulged her. Oh, she liked getting her own way right enough, and she had a fierce temper, but underneath it she was a kind-hearted lass with a sense of fun and no snobbish airs.

Sophie was just mixing the eggs, milk and sugar for her custard when Jennie appeared with the message that someone wished to see her.

"What, now?" Sophie frowned in annoyance.

"The gentleman did call this morning," the maid explained. "He says it's urgent."

"Damn. I suppose I shall have to come, then," muttered Sophie under her breath.

"I'll see to this for you," Mrs. Gilpin promised, indicating the unfinished tart.

Sophie smiled her thanks and, stripping off her apron, reluctantly left the kitchen.

"You said he was a stranger. Didn't he give his name?" she asked as they hurried across the hall.

Blushing, Jennie confessed he had left his card earlier. "I forgot to give it to you, Miss Sophie."

Sophie shrugged. It was too late to worry now, but as she glanced down at her shabby dress she was glad her visitor was not Sir Pelham. He was always praising her flair for choosing tasteful, well-cut gowns that flattered her tall, thin figure, and she could imagine how his eyebrows would climb if faced with her present dishevelled appearance.

Jennie had shown the caller into the morning-room. It was the most modern room in the house and used almost exclusively for the formal entertainment of visitors. Thomas Fleming preferred to relax in the comfort of the parlour, with its oak panelling and massive old-fashioned furniture, but he had let Sophie have a free hand in re-decorating the morning-room when she was seventeen.

"You'll need somewhere to receive your guests now you are out, lass," he'd told her with a jovial smile. "Pick what you like and hang the expense."

The result of Sophie's efforts was charming. She had chosen a delicate classical-style suite of matching furniture in beech gilt upholstered in pale green satin. This colour was echoed in the window drapes and it combined well with the jonquil wash on the walls and the darker green carpet to give an airy, spring-time effect, which was heightened by the clever use of several landscape paintings.

Unfortunately, the visitor standing gazing out of the window and drumming his long fingers impatiently upon the white-painted sill did not accord well with the graceful harmony of the room. His unusual height and broad shoulders stood out with shocking impact against the feminine delicacy all around him, and there was an air of almost palpable tension about his superbly muscled figure.

"What are you doing here?"

At Sophie's gasp of surprise Kirk whirled round.

"You are not welcome in this house, sir. Please go." Sophie spoke quickly, but her starved senses greedily drank in every detail of his immaculate appearance. He was wearing a coat of navy corduroy with a double-breasted short waistcoat in a paler blue. Light cream pantaloons clung revealingly to his long legs, and Sophie had to drag her fascinated gaze away from the muscles in his strong thighs that this new fashion displayed.

"Not before I've said what I came to say."

Kirk resisted the impulse to tug at the tight folds of his muslin cravat. He had gone to a great deal of trouble for this interview, abandoning his usual casual attire in the hope that his smart appearance would create a favourable impression. Old Mr. Fleming was known to set great store upon respectability.

The thought that he might also wish to impress Miss Fleming was one he decided firmly to ignore.

"Mr. Thorburn, I told you at our last meeting that I did not wish to listen to your accusations. If I had known you would have the audacity to pursue me in this shameless manner I would have given orders that you were not to be admitted. Please leave at once." Sophie's tone was cold, but her fingers unconsciously pleated together in a manner that betrayed her nervousness.

Kirk laughed mockingly. "How very prim and proper you sound, not in the least like the girl I know."

Sophie reddened. He had the knack of throwing her off balance. "You do not know me at all," she retorted angrily, but even as she snapped the words at him she knew it wasn't true. In some strange way, it was as if they had known each other for years, as though instinct had taken over to reveal the hidden depths of feeling normally kept concealed.

Stepping to one side, she threw the door open still wider. "Now please go, or I shall be forced to call for assistance!"

To her alarm, he strode across the room and banged the door shut. "Will you stop this damned silly play-acting and listen?" he demanded, his patience wearing thin.

Sophie made a snatch for the handle, but he was too quick, and, planting his wide shoulders against the white-painted panels, he growled, "I've had enough of this nonsense. Sit down!"

Sophie glared at him indignantly, but the angry look on his handsome face dictated prudence, so she decided to do as she was bid. "Well?" she said curtly.

"I'm sorry. I realise that I'm behaving badly, but it is vital you hear what I have to say." He gave her a rueful smile. "If I promise not to shout at you again, may I continue?"

Kirk's quiet apology surprised Sophie. She gazed at him uncertainly and then gave a little confused nod of assent. "Please sit down," she murmured.

Kirk swiftly left his post to join her on the elegant sofa. "I know you will find this painful, but please hear me out. The person to whom you are contemplating becoming betrothed is not what he seems. It would be a dreadful mistake. He is a dangerous man."

About to contradict him, Sophie paused, trying to consider his statement fairly. "It is true I have known the baronet for only a few months, but I cannot think him capable of dishonourable behaviour. He is too much of a gentleman."

"Appearances are deceptive. My brother committed the same error of trusting Stanton, and it led to his death."

Staring at Kirk's grim expression, Sophie suddenly understood his meaning. "You cannot think the baronet killed your brother!"

Her dismayed exclamation made him start. "You have heard about the fire?"

"A little," Sophie admitted and reluctantly explained.

"Then you will see I must discover the truth. It is a debt of honour. I have to bring Ingram's murderer to justice, and I believe Stanton was responsible, because—"

"You must be mad!" Sophie interrupted. In other circumstances she would have been tempted to laugh. "How can you imagine that Sir Pelham could lose his cool self-possession long enough to commit an act of such violence? The whole idea is ridiculous!"

"I do not think he was the one to actually strike Ingram down. He would not care to soil his hands," Kirk replied roughly. "But I'd stake my life he arranged it and the fire which almost destroyed Haraldsgarth."

Sophie shook her head in bewilderment. He seemed so convinced, so sincere! "Do you have proof of what you say?" she asked.

"I have one clue I am following, but nothing that would convince a jury as yet. However, the circumstances fit damningly."

He gave her a searching look, wondering how much he dared reveal. Could he trust her not to go running to Stanton?

"Please, if you expect me to believe you, I must know more."

Her anxiety convinced him and he nodded curtly.

"It began almost a year ago when I received a letter from Ingram saying that he had been cheated out of a considerable amount of money. Stanton had tricked him into selling some shares our family had held for many years in a Borrowdale wad mine. My brother was not a worldly man. He didn't realise how their value had soared due to the recent increase in demand and he let Stanton have them for a pittance."

Sophie digested this information. She knew that this pure form of graphite was highly prized. Uncle Thomas had told her that it was used for medicinal purposes and in the manufacture of cannon balls as well as being an important material for artists. A single pack-load could fetch up to eight hundred pounds, and blood-curdling stories abounded of how it was

stolen and smuggled out to the coast at Whitehaven and Rav-
englass.

"When Ingram discovered he had been gulled he tried to get
Stanton to pay him the proper value of the shares, but Stanton
refused," Kirk continued in a grim tone. "Ingram persisted,
and I think it was in order to silence him that Stanton had him
murdered."

"I'm sorry, I still cannot believe you." Sophie shook her
head slowly. "Even allowing that the baronet would ever behave in such a dreadful way, it simply doesn't make sense. Why
on earth should he gull your brother? The scandal had he been
found out would have been ruinous! Only someone who was
desperate for money would take such a risk, but Sir Pelham is
rich."

"You misunderstand. Stanton has run through his fortune
and is heavily in debt."

"In debt?" Sophie ejaculated in lively astonishment.

"He is a gamester. He has been careful here in Kendal, but
money flows through his hands like water. His creditors in
London forced him into seeking refuge in the country last autumn, but time is growing short for him. Unless he finds a rich
wife to rescue him, they will very soon catch up with him."

Kirk paused. Her lovely eyes were dilated with shock, and he
felt a brute, forcing her to hear such unpalatable facts. "Without money his position is vulnerable. He knows I am on his trail
and he dare not risk a scandal when he needs all the influence
he can muster. He must marry soon or he will be disgraced."

"Are you saying that he only wishes to wed me for my
money?" Sophie felt the blood drain from her face.

There was a fleeting sympathy in his face which convinced
her that she had hit the nail on the head. Was she so unattractive, then? So plain and unladylike that she couldn't catch a
suitor except with her dowry?

"You insolent knave!" Sophie's hands flew up in swift, un-
thinking reaction. It hurt unbearably to hear her secret fears
voiced by the one man whose admiration she craved.

The blow left a red mark on his cheek and for an instant an
answering anger flared in the vivid blue eyes, making Sophie
regret her impulsive slap. It took a considerable effort not to
shrink away from him, but she managed to keep her composure and continued to glare at him, her chin proudly tilted.
"How dare you suggest such a thing?"

However, Kirk made no attempt to retaliate in kind, but merely shrugged.

"I meant no insult." Surely she couldn't be so foolish as to imagine *he* thought her unattractive? "Stanton simply cannot afford a poor bride. He would not marry the Goddess Venus unless she came decked in garlands of gold!"

"Or, to put it more bluntly, I could be as plain as a pikestaff and he would still marry me. Is that what you mean?" Sophie enquired with awful sarcasm.

"Damn it, woman, why must you harp on about your looks? It doesn't matter a whit whether you are a beauty or no. It is Stanton's perfidy which concerns me and should concern you." Anxiety for her made Kirk's voice rough. "If you haven't the sense to see that, then perhaps I'd best speak to your uncle without further ado."

Humiliatingly conscious of her shabby appearance, Sophie felt her self-confidence ooze away. He sounded so indifferent! Why had she been so foolish as to imagine he might desire her?

A sickening sense of disappointment swept over her. Suddenly, even his wild accusations seemed irrelevant, set against the discovery that Kirk Thorburn was only interested in her because Sir Pelham sought to make her his bride.

"My uncle is unwell. You cannot see him."

Abruptly, Sophie got to her feet to indicate the interview was over.

Kirk rose. "You will pass on my message?"

Sophie raised her eyebrows. "I shall think about what you have said."

Kirk's mouth thinned at her dismissive tone. "Take care that you do, Miss Fleming."

She shrugged, and with a curt bow he strode from the room.

CHAPTER FOUR

"AND NOW LET US KNEEL and give thanks for the many blessings the Lord has bestowed upon us..."

The sonorous voice of the parson echoed throughout the old church of Holy Trinity, but it barely penetrated the shell of Sophie's troubled thoughts as she sat in the Fleming family pew.

A light touch on her arm reminded her of her surroundings.

"Thank you, Sir Pelham," she whispered hastily, glad that she had accepted his escort. He had been kindness itself the last few days and his discreet attentiveness was soothing to her stretched nerves.

Throughout the rest of the service she marshalled her wits to concentrate on what was being said, but as the congregation began to file out her anxiety returned.

They encountered the Stricklands outside the church in the usual Sunday morning press of people exchanging greetings with their neighbours.

"Please try not to worry. I'm sure your uncle's illness is just a temporary setback." Maria smiled at her encouragingly. "I'm convinced he will be better in time for you to attend my party on Wednesday."

Sophie nodded, but her manner was strained.

Several other acquaintances drifted up to ask after her uncle's health, and Sophie tried her best to respond cheerfully, but she was relieved when the baronet smoothly intervened by announcing it was time he took her home.

Wearily, she let her head sink back against the velvet squabs of his comfortable carriage.

"Perhaps Dr. Wilson could prescribe a sleeping draught for you, my dear, to ensure you get a proper rest."

Sophie's eyes snapped open. "Forgive me," she murmured in some embarrassment, realising that the rocking motion of the vehicle had almost lulled her to sleep. "I never take such things; I dislike the idea of interfering with nature," she added in a firmer tone.

"There are times when drugs may be useful." The baronet looked amused by her disapproval.

Sophie shrugged. "Perhaps."

Accepting her dismissal of the subject, the baronet turned to lighter matters, but although she pretended to listen to him Sophie was thinking about her uncle, whose heart was not strong. The chill he had taken a week ago had turned feverish, and she sensed that Dr. Wilson was more concerned than he admitted.

In the last few days she had scarcely left the sick-room, but this morning Nancy had insisted that she needed a breath of fresh air when Sir Pelham called to see if she wished to attend divine service. It wasn't until they were seated in the ancient church that Sophie had begun to worry in case Nancy had packed her off because the crisis in Uncle Thomas's illness was approaching.

I'll never forgive myself if anything happened to him while I wasn't there, she thought in anguish, realising afresh how much she loved the old man who had made her the pivot of his life.

Hurrying indoors, Sophie was alarmed to find Nancy awaiting them in the hall, but a quick glance at her smiling face told a different story from the one Sophie feared.

"His fever has broken at last, Miss Sophie," Nancy announced joyfully. "I sent for Dr. Wilson and he says that it's just a matter of rest and good nursing now."

Relief exploded in Sophie's chest, easing the tension that had gripped her ever since her uncle had been confined to his bed.

"Nancy, ask Jennie to bring up a bottle of the best claret to toast his recovery," she cried in jubilation. Turning to her escort, she added hastily, "Pray excuse me. I must see how my uncle does." And she rushed up the oaken staircase without a backward glance.

Ten minutes later she came dancing into the mourning-room, her face aglow. "He is sleeping peacefully."

"So you are at last convinced that the good doctor spoke the truth," the baronet remarked with a little burst of laughter that rang distinctly hollow.

"I'm sorry, I shouldn't have deserted you in such a rag-mannered way." Sophie suddenly realised that he was offended.

A spurt of irritation clouded her happiness. Devil take the man; need he always be so touchy? Surely he didn't think she had intended any insult? Or was he such a dry stick that he couldn't see she had acted solely on impulse?

The baronet had already helped himself to the claret, so Sophie poured herself a glass and forced herself to sit down without giving vent to the irritation she felt. To be fair, in his eyes she supposed she had behaved discourteously, but it was her nature to act without thinking first.

Surely he must know that by now, she thought rebelliously. Impetuosity might not be considered ladylike, but if he was so hell-bent on marrying someone prim and proper why was he dancing attendance on her?

"To Master Fleming." Sir Pelham raised his glass. "It is good news about his health."

"I'm glad you think so," Sophie replied somewhat tartly, immediately forgetting her resolution to curb her unruly tongue.

"My dear, I hope you speak in jest! I would be wounded to discover that you doubted my sincerity." The baronet's tone was earnest. "Naturally, I esteem your uncle most highly, but it has been even more disturbing for me to see you so anxious on his account."

Sophie avoided his gaze. She tried to cover her confusion by smoothing the green and white striped skirts of her Italian taffeta gown, but his words startled her.

"You do not doubt I am most fond of you, I hope, Miss Fleming?"

Sophie blushed. She couldn't help remembering his frequent attempts to please her. "Sir, you are too kind," she muttered, feeling miserably uncharitable, because only a moment ago she had inwardly cavilled at his punctiliousness.

The baronet's expression grew warmer. "Indeed, I am happier than you can imagine at Mr. Fleming's recovery, for it gives me the opportunity to speak at last."

Sophie stiffened warily.

"It did not seem appropriate to ask you in such difficult circumstances, but now I do not think I can contain my impatience any longer." His reserved smile flickered, but his manner remained so dignified that for an instant Sophie wondered if her vivid imagination was leading her astray, until he drew out a small velvet ring-box from the pocket of his extravagantly tailed morning coat.

Opening it, he held it out towards her.

"My dear Miss Fleming—or dare I call you Sophie?—will you do me the honour of becoming my wife and accepting this bauble as a token of our betrothal?"

The magnificent diamond glittered in the light, and Sophie's eyes widened.

"Sir . . . I was not expecting a declaration," she faltered.

"Your modesty is most becoming, my dear. I quite understand, but surely my proposal does not come as a complete shock? We have known each other for only a short time, but, unless I am mistaken, your uncle has spoken to you on my intentions." The baronet's tone was indulgent, but Sophie sensed his eager impatience as he waited for an answer.

"My uncle did mention the matter before he became ill," she admitted reluctantly. "But to be frank with you, sir, there has been no time of late to think on how I must answer you."

"Then can you give the matter some thought now?" Sir Pelham laughed with unaccustomed joviality.

Sophie responded with a strained smile and a little shrug. "I shall do my best," she murmured, knowing how much her uncle wanted the match.

Clearly the baronet had been expecting a different answer. For an instant a frown creased his brow, but it disappeared so swiftly that Sophie could not gauge if he was annoyed or not.

"You do not have anyone else in mind, I hope?"

The unexpected sharp question made Sophie jump. "No, indeed."

"Only I did hear a little rumour that you had been seen with Mr. Kirk Thorburn." The baronet's voice was once more smooth. He smiled at her deprecatingly. "I am aware he has a great charm for unwary ladies, but I should not like to think of you becoming embroiled in his unsavoury net."

Sophie's brows rose indignantly. "I trust that remark was not meant to be taken seriously! I encountered Mr. Thorburn while skating, and our meeting was as brief as it was accidental." She glared at him. How dared he spy on her?

"That is reassuring news." The baronet's smile became sympathetic. "Believe me, my dear, I did not intend to question your conduct, but I must confess myself anxious. That man regards me as an enemy and he is unscrupulous enough to use any means to injure me. Everyone in Kendal must know how I feel about you. It is no secret.''

"You think he is spiteful enough to try and engage my affections merely to hit back at you?'' Sophie gasped.

"Sadly, I would not put such a false, despicable trick beyond him,'' the baronet sighed.

Sophie tasted blood as she bit her lip in a fierce effort to contain the instinctive denial that rose in Kirk's defence. He couldn't—wouldn't—behave in such a shabby way...could he? But what if the baronet was right? A flood of pain washed over her as she realised how little she knew of the real man behind that handsome Viking face.

"I can see I have inadvertently distressed you, my dear, so perhaps we should put aside such unpleasant speculations,'' Sir Pelham continued smoothly.

Sophie nodded hastily. The whole idea was abhorrent!

"Then, to return to our original conversation, dare I hope for an answer today?''

Sophie shrugged helplessly. "I think not, sir.'' Her mind seemed bogged down and all her usual decisiveness was left floundering in confusion.

"Ah, well. I must bow to your wishes, but I cannot pretend I am not disappointed.'' Stretching out his hand, Sir Pelham deposited the ring-box on a giltwood side-table. "However, let this small token of the deep respect and affection I feel for you remain here to remind you of me in my absence.''

"Oh, please, take it home with you! It is too valuable! I should be in dread of something happening to it.''

"Nonsense,'' the baronet chuckled. "I'm sure you will take the greatest care of it, my dear.'' He brushed an imaginary speck of dust from his breeches. "Yet you are right, of course, in thinking that it cost a pretty penny. It actually belonged to a Queen!''

Her look of enquiry made him preen. "Ah, I knew you would be impressed, my dear! What woman could resist such a gem, eh? Well, I shall not tease you any longer. It is one of the stones that made up Marie-Antoinette's celebrated necklace. I saw it in Jeffrey's—the famous jeweller's in Piccadilly, you know—on my last visit to town and decided to buy it for you. Nothing is too good for the next Lady Stanton!''

Sophie wondered at his lapse of taste. To be sure, it was a very beautiful ring, but it seemed vulgar to talk of money in the circumstances, and, what was more, its history struck her as decidedly unlucky. That infamous diamond necklace had helped contribute to the present imprisonment of the lovely, foolish Queen of France, hardly an omen to boast of!

This view had obviously not occurred to the baronet, for he was smiling, almost as if he considered matters satisfactorily settled.

"I must take my leave, my dear." Sir Pelham rose to his feet and Sophie closed her mouth on the further protests which burned her lips. Plainly they would do no good, and she did not wish to provoke an argument. She owed him something in recompense for her dilatoriness!

"Due to the press of business affairs, I will not be able to wait upon you as usual, but I hope I will see you at Mrs. Strickland's birthday celebrations."

Sophie's red curls nodded in agreement. Maria had been insistent that she should take a respite from the sick-room, and now that her uncle was recovering there was no need to disappoint her friend.

"Excellent," murmured the baronet, bending low over her hand. He straightened. "I know it is the fashion for young ladies to tantalise, but I shall hope you will be kind enough to give me your answer then, my dear Sophie."

Feeling trapped, Sophie forced herself to smile. "Of course."

"I'M SORRY, SIR, you cannot see the master. Them's Miss Sophie's orders, I durst not admit you."

Kirk stared in frustration at the maid's apologetic face.

"Yet I've heard that Master Fleming is recovering."

"Aye, sir." Jennie's expression brightened. "But Dr. Wilson says he needs peace and quiet lest he has a relapse."

Kirk nodded abruptly. He felt tempted to ignore convention and push his way into the house but he had no desire to be the cause of any setback to the old man's health. Caroline had already mentioned that Tomes Fleming had suffered a heart attack the previous year, and Kirk did not doubt the wisdom of the doctor's advice.

"Then may I speak with Miss Fleming?"

Jennie coloured unhappily. She had taken a shine to this handsome, well-spoken gentleman who had called several times in the last few days, but Miss Sophie's orders had been very clear. "I'm afraid not, sir. She's not at home."

A frown darkened Kirk's eyes. He was convinced the girl was lying.

Taking his leave, he realised any optimistic hope that he might encounter Sophie Fleming by chance was also doomed to failure. The wench was avoiding him!

In desperation he decided to consult Caroline.

"I applaud your generosity in wanting to warn Mr. Fleming, Kirk, but do you think it is wise to continue to involve yourself?"

Caroline had risen from partaking of her customary breakfast in bed to accommodate his precipitate arrival and sat facing him in her pretty little parlour. "After all, you have already informed Sophie of your suspicions," she continued.

"I suppose I should wait until I have firm proof about Stanton's perfidy, but I hardly think that signifies in the circumstances," Kirk muttered irritably. "Once she becomes betrothed to him it will be too late to break things off without a great deal of unpleasant gossip."

Refusing the offer of refreshment, Kirk began to pace about the room in a way that threatened to give Caroline a headache.

"What a restless fellow you are," she sighed, faintly piqued that he had no eyes for the charming picture she made reclining upon a scroll-backed *chaise-longue* in a state of fashionable dishabille worn especially to impress him.

"I'm sorry." Kirk came to a halt. "I'm behaving like a fool, and at this hour too! It was good of you to agree to see me, Caroline." He smiled at her with a warmth that melted her irritation. "Particularly when all I do is contradict your excellent advice."

"Nonsense!" Caroline coloured a little and, making the effort to control her wayward thoughts, she begged him to sit down while she considered the matter further.

"Perhaps I could invite her here. I should be happy to act as a chaperon."

"I do not think she would accept," he replied wryly.

"Whyever not?"

Kirk tugged at his neckcloth in a manner which suggested it had suddenly grown too tight. "We . . . we parted with angry words and I think she has taken me in dislike," he muttered, unwilling to say more.

Caroline's eyes widened. He had said nothing earlier of a quarrel! "Hmm, that does make things difficult," she murmured.

There was another short silence.

"I have it!" Kirk exclaimed. "You must go and see her, Caroline. She might listen to you."

Caroline's mouth formed a little circle of astonishment. "But, Kirk, I hardly know the girl!"

"That hardly signifies." He shrugged this objection aside impatiently. "In fact, it might work to our advantage. You have no axe to grind. She is more likely to heed your warning than mine."

Personally Caroline thought this hope was a trifle sanguine. "But she knows that I am your friend and she might think my advice prejudiced."

"It's a risk we will have to take." He leant forward in his chair. "Please, Caroline. I know it is a lot to ask of you, but I cannot bear the idea of sitting idly by and letting her commit the folly of marrying that brute."

Caroline blinked. She knew him for a kind-hearted man in spite of his impatient temper, but this zeal for Sophie Fleming's welfare seemed a little excessive. He had only just met the girl, after all! "That is very commendable of you, my dear," she said rather tartly. "Yet I could have sworn you had it in mind at Sir Alan Chambre's soirée to make use of her in some way to trap Stanton."

"It did occur to me that I might be able to provoke him into a duel by arousing his jealousy," he admitted, somewhat shamefaced.

"Well, I'm glad you changed your mind." Caroline shuddered. "I know you are an excellent shot, but I detest duels. They are nasty, dangerous affairs!"

He smiled at her in amusement. "Men hold a different view of such things, my dear."

"Oh, affairs of honour!" Caroline sniffed. It was never possible to talk to any man sensibly on the subject of honour, and Kirk was more stubborn than most. "All the same, Kirk, although it might afford you great personal satisfaction to do so, I cannot see how blowing a hole in the baronet would solve the problem of showing him to blame for Ingram's death.

Everyone would still continue to think the fire just a tragic accident.''

Kirk nodded. "It was precisely for that reason that I changed my mind about using Miss Fleming. Leaving aside the impropriety of causing her distress, I cannot risk losing my temper with that man. If I do, I play straight into his hands.''

Caroline thoughtfully pleated a fold into her wrapper. "Indeed, he would simply claim you were unhinged by grief and had a grudge against him because he had benefitted by Ingram's unwise sale.''

Waiting for proof was the advice she had already prescribed, but she knew how it galled his impetuous nature to bide his time when he longed to take direct action. "Have you managed to learn anything further about the snuff-box?''

"Nothing.'' He shook his fair head impatiently. "No one here in Kendal recognises it.''

"He must have purchased it in London.''

"No doubt.'' Kirk's large, well-kept hands clenched into tight fists. "It is a poor lead, but it is the only proof I have, other than the letter which Ingram wrote to me last February. But Stanton was at Haraldsgarth the day of the fire, I know it!''

The baronet, of course, had denied it and no magistrate would doubt his word without convincing evidence to the contrary.

"I'll have to go to London to see if I can discover anything new there,'' Kirk said.

"What if a betrothal takes place before your return?'' Caroline enquired delicately.

A savage frown appeared on Kirk's handsome face.

"It must be prevented.'' He fixed her with his vivid gaze. "Sophie will not receive me, but you could see her as my emissary, Caroline. Please, there is no time to waste. Won't you try, as a personal favour to me?''

Unable to refuse this appeal, Caroline sighed in resignation. "Oh, very well, my friend, but I dare say I shall regret it!''

"MISS FLEMING.''

Sophie turned at the sound of her name and saw a chaise drawing up. Her grip tightened on the selection of books she had just chosen from Manson's circulating library when she realised who had hailed her.

"May I give you a lift home?"

"No, thank you, Mrs. Birkett. I do not wish to inconvenience you."

"But I am going that way." Caroline beamed. "It is no trouble at all."

Sophie smiled politely. "You are very kind, but I enjoy walking."

"Of course, but actually I wanted a word with you."

Faced with such persistence, Sophie hesitated, and Caroline quickly added, "Look, it is coming on to rain. Please get in, my dear, you don't want to get wet."

Sophie was of the opinion that she would prefer a drenching to Caroline's company, but good manners forced her to climb into the carriage.

"What was it you wished to say to me, Mrs. Birkett?" she enquired after they had exchanged polite inanities for a moment or two.

Caroline forced a smile. "Oh, heavens, it is rather delicate," she murmured with pretty hesitation.

Sophie's dark brows lifted in supercilious silence.

"It has to do with Mr. Thorburn," Caroline began, feeling rather daunted by this lack of encouragement. "I understand that he has made you privy to the circumstances of his brother's death."

Sophie's mouth thinned. "Yes, but I do not see that it is any of your business."

Her bald statement made Caroline wince. What an uncouth, prickly girl she was!

"You may be right, my dear, but the fact remains that Kirk is anxious on your behalf. He feels that you do not truly comprehend the dangers of allying yourself to a man like Stanton."

Sophie could feel her temper beginning to bubble.

"My matrimonial plans are no concern of Mr. Thorburn's!" she snapped. "You may tell him to keep his anxiety to himself, since you appear to be his emissary. I do not believe he is correct in his suspicions concerning the baronet and I do not wish to hear another word on the whole ridiculous subject."

"Have you mentioned the matter to your uncle?"

"Of course not! He is too frail to be worried with such nonsense." Impatience made Sophie's tone sharp.

"He might not think it was nonsense," Caroline countered. "You might not like it, Miss Fleming, but the facts fit. In my opinion Stanton is guilty."

"Really?" Sophie smiled scornfully. "And your—er—close friendship with Mr. Thorburn has nothing to do with how you came to this conclusion, I suppose?"

Caroline flushed angrily. "You do not much care for me, Miss Fleming, and I admit that the feeling is mutual, but there is no need for us to descend to insults. Whatever you may think to the contrary, Kirk is merely a family friend. My relationship with him is perfectly proper."

Sophie stared hard at her gloved fingertips. She was aware she had overstepped the bounds of propriety, but she couldn't force an apology from her tight throat. Every bone in her body was jealously screaming that Caroline was lying. If she wasn't Kirk's mistress, then she wanted to be. Her very tone betrayed her!

"This conversation was intended as a sincere warning," Caroline broke the terse silence. "You think I am interfering, but you are young and inexperienced—"

"But not in need of advice from you!" Sophie flashed back rudely.

Caroline sucked in her breath. "Very well, have it your own way, you stupid girl! I promised Kirk I would try and persuade you to see sense, but if you will not listen then let the results of your obstinacy be on your own head."

"You are just jealous because I am marrying a man of rank and fortune," Sophie declared, but for all her efforts her voice came out uncertainly.

Caroline laughed. "You poor little fool, Stanton will make mincemeat of you! All that interests him is your dowry."

The blood drained from Sophie's face, leaving her deathly white.

"Oh, damn, I should not have said that..." Caroline stretched out a repentant hand, but Sophie shrugged it off and in one swift movement banged hard on the roof to alert the coachman to stop and then wrenched open the door.

Before Caroline could stop her she had jumped down even as the chaise slowed and was hurrying away down the street.

Watching her go, Caroline sighed. She had probably made things worse. "Not that I ever stood a chance of success," she murmured ruefully. For whatever reasons of her own, that stubborn young madam was determined not to listen to anything Kirk Thorburn had to say!

MARIA STRICKLAND'S birthday party was in full flow by the time Kirk arrived with Caroline on his arm. The news of Sophie's rejection of his advice had come as a blow and it had not improved his temper to be kept kicking his heels for over an hour waiting for Caroline to complete her toilette.

"What do you think of my new gown? Is it too daring for Kendal?" Caroline asked with a giggle of excitement as she swept into the parlour.

"You look stunning," Kirk replied, concealing his impatience. How the devil could it take so long to dress in so little? All she was wearing was a wisp of white silk gauze!

"I fear we shall be late," he added, offering her his arm, and in the carriage he reflected, not for the first time, that his ideal woman wouldn't give a damn whether her curls were in place or her rouge perfect.

His thoughts made him suddenly smile cynically. He was asking for the moon!

Maria and her husband were still receiving guests in the entrance hall.

"Mr. Thorburn, how nice of you to come!"

Maria's greeting was filled with warmth. She still felt rather guilty at having betrayed the story of his youthful peccadillo and was determined to do all she could to make him feel welcome in her home.

Kirk was pleasantly surprised by her friendliness and his devastating smile was still in place when he strolled into the salon a few moments later.

It was the first thing Sophie saw.

Automatically she noted that he looked incredibly handsome in formal evening dress. His dark blue coat was set admirably across his broad shoulders and there was scarcely a crease in his satin knee-breeches. A chaste white waistcoat and elegant neckcloth completed his distinguished appearance.

Her heart began to beat faster.

Fortunately, a few minutes earlier the baronet had quit her side to seek entertainment at the faro-table Mr. Strickland had set up in the small salon and there was no one to observe the way her colour fluctuated at Kirk's approach.

"Miss Fleming."

His bow was a model of propriety, but Sophie remained tense. "Where is Mrs. Birkett? I had expected to see her here with you," she murmured after a hesitant pause.

"She is talking to a friend in the drawing-room," he replied.

Some of Sophie's tension ebbed when he did not pursue the subject. She had been half expecting him to launch into a tirade berating her for refusing to listen to Caroline.

"Don't worry, I won't cause a scene," he murmured, reading her thoughts.

Sophie cursed her expressive face. "I should hope not," she muttered. "I'm not in the mood to hear a lecture, thank you."

"Then dance with me instead." He held out a hand towards her.

Sophie's card was full, but her partner for the next dance had not yet appeared. "Very well." Recklessly she nodded. Why not? She might never get another chance after tonight!

They were just in time to join a set forming for the quadrille, and as Kirk led her on to the floor Sophie experienced a rush of excited pleasure.

To her delight she discovered that he was an excellent dancer, moving with elegant precision through the complex steps of the *grande ronde* and the *pas de zephyr*.

She was enjoying herself so much that she was determined to ignore the constant ache in her left ankle, but to her chagrin a particularly sharp twinge of pain made her footsteps falter as the dance drew to its conclusion.

"Take my arm," Kirk urged, alarmed by her sudden pallor.

"I'm perfectly all right," Sophie declared, but she was glad to obey him. "It is only my wretched ankle playing up." She smiled gamely. "I sustained an injury in a fall from my pony when I was a child and suffer for it occasionally."

She had also twisted it slightly jumping down from Caroline's coach, a fact she did not wish to admit in case it reminded him of the disagreement between them she wanted to ignore. "I shall be as fit as a fiddle again if only I can sit somewhere quiet for a moment or two."

"You know this house much better than I do. Where do you suggest?"

"The conservatory might make a suitable spot for recuperation," she answered and was thankful to lean discreetly on his arm as they made their way towards this quiet haven.

"Very impressive," Kirk announced as he gazed admiringly about him.

"Maria would be delighted to hear you say so. She was very disappointed when her gardener advised that the present weather was too cold to leave all the doors open so that her guests could stroll in and out of here as freely as they wished. She said it was the penalty of having a birthday on the twenty-third of January!"

Kirk nodded. Her remarks explained the deserted silence of this enchanting green paradise.

"I'm sorry Mrs. Strickland was disappointed. However, it would be a pity to spoil this peaceful oasis with a chattering throng."

"Does it make you a little homesick for the Bahamas?" Sophie asked impulsively.

"How acute of you, Miss Fleming," he drawled to cover his embarrassment of her unexpected perceptiveness, and then was sorry for his sarcasm when she blushed.

"Forgive me, you are right of course. It does remind me of my plantation," he murmured, gently pressed her fingers, which still rested upon his coat sleeve.

Sophie's pulse quickened. She was suddenly very aware of the fact that, defying convention, they were completely alone.

The warm, perfumed silence wrapped itself around them and she had the craziest notion that they had stepped out of ordinary everyday reality into an enchanted world.

She took a deep breath to dispel this absurd fantasy, but the languid air did nothing to ease the tight knot of tension twisting in her stomach.

"Shall we sit down?" Kirk pointed to one of the charming little rustic benches Maria had scattered about the conservatory for the comfort of those who wished to sit and admire her plants.

Sophie agreed with a nervous smile, but she was in such a state that she forgot to favour her sore ankle. A yelp of pain escaped her as her full weight bore down her left foot.

"Allow me." Kirk swung her up into his arms.

"Please, there is no need. Put me down," Sophie implored as he carried her towards the bench.

"It is no hardship." He grinned. "You are as light as a feather."

Sophie subsided into silence. Of their own volition her arms slid around his neck. I am only steadying myself, she told her uneasy conscience, but she knew she was lying.

Her cheek came to rest against his shoulder and she let out a sigh of voluptuous content. She could smell the clean, fresh scent of the cologne he had used and feel the warmth of his skin. Her eyelids drooped to a languorous close. His arms felt so strong, so safe...so desirable!

Sophie's eyes snapped open in horrified shock. What on earth was she thinking of? She had no right to let her wayward imagination wander off into such improper daydreams!

"Are you comfortable?"

Kirk settled her carefully upon the bench and Sophie hastily nodded her thanks, trying to hide her blushes in a flurry of arranging her amethyst satin skirts.

He sat down next to her. To her relief he did not appear to notice her disordered breathing, but began making remarks about the plants all around them, and after a few moments she felt composed enough to lift her gaze again.

"That's better," Kirk murmured.

Sophie laughed nervously. "Whatever do you mean, sir?"

"Your eyes are much too beautiful to hide, my sweet."

The gentle teasing note in his voice made Sophie's heart skip a beat. "I...I don't know what you mean," she whispered.

"Don't you, Sophie? You have the loveliest eyes in Kendal—eyes any man must admire."

She could only stare at him silently, her tongue paralysed by shyness.

"What, no blistering retort to put me firmly in my place? You surprise me, Miss Fleming." Kirk smiled at her with a faintly mocking amusement, but beneath his banter lurked a note of passion. "I wonder if I dare hope your acquiescence will stretch a little further?"

Sophie's mouth began to tremble and his need to kiss her grew intolerable.

"Silence gives consent, so they say," he murmured wickedly, drawing her into his arms with a skilful dexterity that left her breathless. "Do you consent, sweetheart?"

"Yes...no! I mean, let me go! This is madness!" she gasped.

"Is it?" he enquired. "Then tell me you feel nothing when I do this . . . and this . . ."

The touch of his lips was as gentle as the caress of a butterfly, brushing against the exposed curve of her white shoulder, exploring a path of exquisite sensation into the secret hollow of her throat.

Sophie jumped as if she had been stung.

"Please . . . you mustn't," she muttered feebly.

"Why not?" he demanded in a hoarse whisper. "Are you going to pretend that you don't feel the same way I do?"

"We hardly know one another," she wailed.

"What has that got to do with it?" He laughed a little wildly, his arms tightening. "Oh, Sophie!"

His golden head dipped and as he captured her mouth Sophie's feeble opposition dissolved completely. She couldn't control the wild excitement that flooded her suddenly shaking limbs, but clung to him as tightly as she could, eager for the wonderful sensations he was arousing in her untutored body to continue.

"Sweetheart!" Her uninhibited response brought a growl of surprised delight to Kirk's throat. He deepened the kiss, parting her lips until their breath mingled.

At the intimate touch of his tongue, all rational thought fled. Nothing mattered any more but the incredible pleasure pulsating through her entire body. Her eyes were tight shut, but for the first time in her life she felt she could see. At last she understood the emotion she had scorned in her friends!

Dazzling flashes of colour exploded behind her lids. It was like being engulfed in a hot, vibrant sunburst, she thought in a daze, a sunburst of desire, and she was no longer blind to its devastating power! This was the passion poets raved over, and it was sweeter than she had dreamt possible!

"God, but you are desirable!"

Kirk tore his mouth away from hers for an instant and looked down at her flushed face. "I ought to return you to your chaperon," he muttered feverishly.

Sophie moaned in protest. Wordlessly, she buried her fingers in the thick curls that clustered at the back of his neck and pulled his head down to hers.

Kirk groaned as her tongue teased his, darting into the warmth of his mouth with an instinctive wantonness. He hadn't bargained for this! In some dim corner of his mind, he was aware that she had no idea of the dangerously powerful urges she was releasing in him, but her passionate abandonment was rapidly making restraint impossible.

His hand slid across the amethyst bodice to cup her left breast. She quivered with shock, her eyes snapping open. He released her mouth, giving her the chance to withdraw, but instead she smiled at him slowly with an unconscious seductiveness.

"I like it when you hold me," she whispered.

"I like it too," he replied with a hoarse chuckle.

Very gently he began to caress her. Through the thin satin he felt her nipple harden, and the last vestiges of sanity were lost.

The waves of desire sweeping over her made Sophie's head spin. When she felt him push the low *décolletage* of her gown aside to stroke her naked flesh she had to bite down hard on her lower lip to prevent an exclamation of pleasure.

His long brown fingers were so skilful! Sensuously, she pressed herself against him. Their bodies were so close! She wanted to rip aside his waistcoat and immaculate linen shirt to feel the nakedness of his skin beneath her own hands...

"Oh!"

Still breathing hard, Kirk forced himself to let her go. Moving away, he grinned at her ruefully. "I'm sorry, sweetheart, but that's what happens when you drive a man almost to distraction."

Her cheek stained crimson, Sophie dropped her eyes in confusion. Cursing her lack of sophistication, she realised that she didn't have the faintest idea how to handle the embarrassing situation her folly had led them into.

Realising that she had been genuinely shocked by his body's arousal, Kirk forced aside his own frustration. She looked so ashamed as she fumbled to set her gown to rights that he couldn't be angry in spite of his aching loins.

"Let me help you," he murmured.

With a kind of numb resignation Sophie abandoned her attempt, and within a few moments he had restored even her tumbled curls to order.

The uncomfortable silence continued.

"Sophie, you mustn't be upset..." Kirk began awkwardly, but a fiery glance from her dark eyes made him pause.

"My behaviour has been disgraceful." Sophie forced her chin high, but her voice shook. "Please accept my apologies, sir."

"Your apologies . . . ?" Kirk was dumbfounded.

"Yes! I had no business kissing you!"

Her anger puzzled him. "Apologies be damned! I enjoyed it!"

"Oh, don't!" Sophie gazed at him beseechingly. "Please don't say such a thing. We are little more than strangers. There can be no possibility of intimacy between us."

"If you believe that nonsense you'll believe anything," Kirk declared roundly, putting his arms around her again. "Time and the conventions of society have got nothing to do with it. The kind of attraction we felt for one another just now obeys no polite rules."

"It is wicked to give in to carnal impulses," Sophie whispered.

"And yet God fashioned desire to bring men and women together." His vivid gaze was lit by tender amusement when she shook her head violently. "Sweetheart, you'd feel better if you admitted the truth. You wanted me as much as I wanted you!"

"I can't!" Despairingly Sophie struggled to pull free from his embrace. "Oh, don't you see? I cannot, dare not feel anything for you, Kirk Thorburn. I am already promised to another man!"

CHAPTER FIVE

"STANTON?" Kirk snarled the name. "Good God, you haven't consented to marry him, have you?"

Miserable, Sophie nodded.

"You little idiot!" Kirk was appalled. "Of all the damned stupid things to do!"

"There is no need for you to be so rude," Sophie retorted, her drooping spirits beginning to revive.

"I beg to differ there, my girl. I suppose you thought you owed it to your uncle, but—"

"I do not need to justify my actions to you," she interrupted angrily, his abrasive tone restoring her self-possession as if by magic.

Kirk bit back a savage answer and took a deep breath. "Your uncle is old and ill and I dare say he is fretting to see you and his business suitably settled, but—"

"And what is wrong with that, pray?" Sophie demanded.

"Nothing, but—"

"My uncle has a right to be concerned for the future. He is my guardian," Sophie interrupted once more. "I owe him everything and it is my duty to repay his kindness."

"Will you let me finish?" He glared at her. "I don't doubt that your motives were honourable, but you must have taken leave of your senses. Do you really think sacrificing yourself in marriage to that murdering cheat will serve your uncle's interests?"

"It is merely your prejudice that paints Sir Pelham in such a villainous light. Everyone else thinks he is the best catch in Kendal!"

Her heated reply brought a look of scorn to his handsome face. "So, now we come to the truth. You have a fancy to be my Lady Stanton and play the fine aristocrat. Flaunting a title is of more interest to you than the truth."

"Oh, don't talk such fustian rubbish! You sound like one of those wretched sansculottes," Sophie exploded. "Of course I wish to see justice done. If your brother was murdered, then the person who did it deserves to be punished, but I am sure you are mistaken in assuming Sir Pelham to be the man responsible."

She let out a sigh and impatiently pushed aside one of the curls that had fallen on to her hot forehead. "Oh, Kirk, there is no point in going over this same ground again! I don't wish to quarrel with you. I want us to be friends."

"Then tell Stanton you have changed your mind."

"I cannot. I have given him my word."

Restlessly, she twisted a fold of her gown in her fingers. "You are right in thinking that I agreed to the match to please my uncle," she continued in a low, rapid voice. "He was delighted by the news. In fact, when Sir Pelham suggested it, he gave his permission for the betrothal to be announced immediately."

Kirk grimaced. The baronet was wasting no time.

"When is this announcement to take place?"

"Tonight. At supper. The Stricklands already know."

Sophie glanced down nervously at her shoes. "It must be almost that time now. I had better go." She did not have to add that she dreaded the baronet coming to look for her and finding her alone with Kirk, for her expressive face revealed her thoughts only too clearly.

"Sophie, I can't let you go ahead with it." Kirk grasped her by the shoulders as she made to rise.

She lifted startled eyes to meet his intent gaze.

"Kirk?" Excitement made her voice emerge as a husky whisper. "Oh, Kirk, what do you mean?"

Too late Kirk perceived the full enormity of his behaviour. A gentleman did not seek his pleasure with respectable young virgins! His only excuse was that he had imagined she would respond in kind with a flirtatious kiss or two, but her passionate abandonment had aroused an answering flame in him which had consumed all sense. In the circumstances he could hardly blame her for thinking he intended marriage!

A searing guilt assailed him. He was in no position to look for a bride. His duty was to avenge his brother's death, and his own personal life had to take second place to this debt of honour.

Sophie touched her dry lips with the tip of her tongue. Could she have possibly misunderstood him? Surely not! Unless all her senses were lying, she couldn't believe he had merely been leading her on for his own amusement. He must care something for her! Oh, why didn't he speak? She would have preferred one of his fearsome outbursts of rage to this dreadful silence.

Kirk swallowed hard. Her great dark eyes were watching him anxiously, and he angrily cursed his own folly. How the devil was he to explain without hurting her?

"It would be a great pity to waste yourself upon a scoundrel like Stanton. If I were the marrying kind, I could look no higher for my bride. I am not in that fortunate position, but there must be a dozen more worthy suitors you could choose from in Kendal alone," he said lightly, masking his true feelings.

The last remnant of joy was wiped instantly from Sophie's expression. What a fool she was! He hadn't been about to propose at all!

Kirk felt a complete blackguard. "Believe me, you are too good for Stanton. You deserve a better life than he could give you," he continued gruffly.

Her feelings were in such turmoil of humiliation that Sophie scarcely heard him. How idiotic she'd been to think he was serious! His scandalous behaviour was nothing more than the automatic reaction of a confirmed womaniser who finds himself alone with any woman who wasn't a positive hag.

Her cheeks burned with embarrassment. Bitterly, she reflected that she ought to have learnt by now that her main attraction was her dowry. Men didn't admire her skinny body or her independent tongue.

"Thank you for your concern, sir," she said coldly, getting to her feet in an angry rustle of skirts. "But you must forgive me if I decline to take your advice. You see, somehow I have come to doubt the wisdom of listening to a single word you say!"

Kirk rose, pride warring with his innate honesty. "Sophie, I know I have not behaved as I ought, but I swear to God I didn't mean to hurt you." The words were wrenched from him.

"Hurt?" Sophie forced a light trill of laughter, ignoring the conciliatory hand he stretched out to her. "Do not flatter yourself, Mr. Thorburn. I must confess myself a little shocked at my own folly, but then I am not used to the society of gentlemen like yourself who find it amusing to occupy their idle moments by taking advantage of unwary girls. Or do you deny that you are a rake, sir?''

A muscle flickered at the corner of Kirk's well-cut mouth, but he did not attempt to defend himself. He deserved her scorn. He should never have succumbed to the temptation to kiss her. If anyone had walked in and seen them her reputation would have been hopelessly compromised and it would have been his fault.

Sophie waited for a second, silently praying that he would deny her accusation.

Still he remained silent.

"I hope we never meet again, Kirk Thorburn," she said in accents of frozen despair and walked from the room, the ache in her ankle nothing compared to the pain he had inflicted on her heart.

"AH, HERE COMES JOSH now. They must have hitched up the new team," Maria Strickland announced. "If you have finished your coffee, my dear, I think we should be leaving, or it will be dark before we reach Stanton Hall."

"Of course," Sophie obediently swallowed the last hot mouthful and reached for her gloves.

An errant beam of sunshine lancing in through the window of the coffee-room caught her left hand, bathing the ring she wore. Instantly, the huge diamond flashed with scintillating fire.

Like a beautiful rainbow, Sophie thought with a touch of bitterness.

She could take no pleasure in her betrothal ring. It acted as a constant reminder of a night she wanted to forget. Sir Pelham had placed it on her finger only moments after she had fled from Kirk Thorburn, and not all the congratulations of her friends had been able to wash away her feelings of despair.

Almost six weeks had passed since that night, but the memory of her humiliation had not lessened. She still writhed inwardly whenever she thought of her shameless behaviour.

In a way, she was glad of the whirlwind of activity that had followed on the announcement of her betrothal. They were fêted everywhere as everyone vied to entertain the happy couple, and having to present a joyful face to the world had kept her from dwelling on her stupidity, except in the privacy of her bedroom.

Her deception had been aided by the shocking news from France. The execution of King Louis was the talk of the town, and whenever she felt unable to respond in the manner befitting a bride Sophie rapidly turned the conversation into a discussion about the dreadful events going on across the Channel.

Nancy, of course, guessed something was wrong, but Sophie was able to brush her anxious questions aside, and, fortunately, her uncle entertained no such suspicions. His delight was only marred by the fact that his ill health made it impossible for him to accept Sir Pelham's invitation to visit Stanton Hall.

"I should have liked to meet this aunt of his and see where you will be living once you are wed," he had said rather wistfully one chilly afternoon towards the end of February when Sophie sat by his bedside, busy penning a list of things she wanted to take with her.

Sophie immediately abandoned her task and announced that she would not go if it displeased him.

"Nay, lass, it ain't fair to disappoint the man," Thomas protested. "We've already agreed to the scheme and you know he's mighty keen to show off his home. I'm just being selfish. You'll have Nancy to take care of you and I know that Josh and Maria will make sure you don't come to any harm on the journey."

Sophie nodded, agreeing that it was providential that the Stricklands intended to visit Maria's sister in Cockermouth at the end of the month and were therefore able to offer her their protection. A journey north so early in the year was beset with hazards, and Thomas felt easier in his mind entrusting Sophie to his old friends rather than to any hired bodyguards. The baronet himself would not be accompanying his fiancée but going on ahead to attend to urgent business matters and make sure all was in a readiness for his guests.

"I mustn't begrudge him your company, lass. You'll soon be home again, and then once you are back from your honeymoon I'll be able to visit you at Stanton Hall," Thomas continued in a voice of determined cheer.

Sophie nodded. They were to be married in the first week of May, and Pelham had suggested a bridal trip to Portugal.

"Normally I would have taken you to Italy, my dear," the baronet had informed her with one of his gracious smiles. "But travelling across France, the way things are at the present...!" He had shuddered delicately.

"No." He had bobbed his head decisively. "Portugal shall do us very well. I have friends in Oporto. It will be pleasant to visit them and no doubt you will enjoy the sea voyage."

Sophie had agreed. She had never been abroad before and she had always longed to travel.

It was the only thing she was looking forward to.

Sophie stifled a sigh. She had made her decision and it was the right one, but the prospect of being Lady Stanton did not enthrall her. Her future was assured, but her feelings for the baronet had not altered one whit, in spite of all the pretty speeches he had made her since she had agreed to marry him.

Thank God he did not deem it necessary to show his devotion in a more physical way!

Apart from an occasional dry salute pressed upon her cheek he had not sought to kiss her. His restraint came as a relief, since she was already dreading the intimacy which would follow upon the wedding ceremony. The thought of permitting him the kind of embrace she had offered so freely to Kirk Thorburn kept her awake at nights. Her only consolation was the conviction that he would not expect her to enjoy the sexual act.

His fashionable world did not consider such behaviour necessary in a wife, she reflected, but decreed that aristocrats took mistresses instead for their pleasure.

Pelham would not think it odd if she did not respond to him, but deep in her heart Sophie knew that she was not cold. Her response to Kirk's touch had taught her that there could be a wild delight in the joining of a man and woman, but her instincts warned that such pleasure only came with love.

And I do not love Pelham and I doubt I ever will!

"Sophie, don't forget your muff, my dear. It is so cold out here."

Maria's voice broke in on Sophie's troubled thoughts, and, picking up the sealskin muff, she followed her friend out into the innyard, where Nancy had already resumed her place in the Stricklands' travelling berlin.

It was a well-sprung conveyance and Maria had taken care to furnish plenty of rugs and foot-warmers to combat the severe weather, but they had been travelling since first light, and they were all weary of the gruelling journey by the time Derwent Water came into sight an hour later.

"Thank heavens we are nearly there!" Maria exclaimed. "I declare I am shaken almost to pieces. These roads are nothing but pot-holes!"

"It's the recent icy spell that has made them worse than usual," Josh said with a placatory smile. "We should be grateful that they are at least clear of snowdrifts, my love."

Maria laughed. "I might have known you would take the most optimistic view, dearest husband." She glanced at Sophie, who was sitting next to her, expecting to see an answering gleam of amusement on her friend's face at this male perversity, but the younger woman was lost in the brown study that seemed to envelop her whenever she thought no one was looking.

Looking away again, Maria encountered Nancy's gaze, and recognised the same anxiety that troubled her. There was definitely something wrong!

As the berlin laboured over the last few miles along the lakeside Maria had no eyes for the view, but sat racking her brains. Absurd though it seemed, she was beginning to wonder if Sophie's depression could have some connection with Kirk Thorburn. That handsome young man had disappeared the day after her birthday party and Maria had heard that he had gone haring off to London.

Thinking back, she remembered how he had abruptly quit her party. He hadn't even taken his leave of them, and, unless she was mistaken, his departure had come as a surprise to Caroline Birkett too, which also indicated it was a snap decision.

But what could have compelled him to behave in such an unconventional way? The only unusual event that evening was the announcement of Sophie's betrothal, but why should that have affected Kirk Thorburn? Even if Kirk disliked the baronet, and from Caroline's conversation she had gathered that there was no love lost between them, it seemed very uncivil to walk out just for that reason alone.

Unless... Maria bit her lip. No, she was being foolish! There was no reason to suspect he cared a straw for Sophie or she for him!

And yet...why was Sophie so lacking her usual sparkle? Where was the joyful anticipation of a prospective bride on a

visit to view her future home? About to be reunited with her
betrothed after a week's absence, she looked more like one of
those unfortunate French *aristos* condemned to the scaffold!

Suddenly Sophie's reticence on the subject of her betrothal
assumed a disturbing aspect. Could it be that she never spoke
of the baronet because her heart had been engaged by another
man? If so, it did not bode well for this marriage!

Maria sighed. Probably she was being over-imaginative, but
all the same she decided that she must have a long talk with
Sophie before they left for Cockermouth. Sir Pelham's aunt
was to assume the task of chaperonage, but their departure
would leave Sophie without an equal to confide in.

"Here's the gatehouse," her husband's voice cut into her
musings, and Maria joined the others in craning her neck to see
more of their surroundings.

"Why, 'tis a palace!"

Nancy's exclamation was full of awe and, in spite of her determination to appear cool, Sophie also found herself gog-
gling at the magnificent house which came into view as they
swept round the final curve of the long drive.

Sir Pelham had told her that it was a modern house, having
been designed for his father by the well-known architect John
Plaw only fifteen years ago. Set in a formally landscaped park,
it was a Palladian masterpiece, framed by views of snow-topped
mountains.

"What a marvellous situation," Maria remarked, fluttering
her fan to conceal her surprise.

Sophie hadn't been expecting anything so grand and she
glanced uneasily at Master Strickland when he pithily observed that such an enormous place must devour money.

"It's as well Sir Pelham is a rich man, eh, Sophie lass," he
laughed. "Otherwise all your dowry would be spent in a twinkling."

Fortunately the slowing of the coach saved Sophie from
having to find a suitable reply.

The baronet appeared at the top of the imposing flight of
entrance steps as they emerged, stretching their cramped limbs
and breathing deeply of the cold fresh air after being so long
confined in the stuffy interior of the berlin.

A haughty-looking butler accompanied his master and
Nancy effaced herself, ready to follow in this dignitary's footsteps. He would show her the way to the servants' quarters,

where hopefully she would be able to thaw out with a hot drink before starting to unpack her mistress's belongings.

"Welcome to Stanton Hall," Sir Pelham greeted his guests, and ushered them inside.

The vast entrance hall was decorated with Italian marble columns and scantily draped statues set into recessed niches around the walls. An enormous fire roared from a hearth big enough to roast an ox in, but her first glimpse of her new home struck a chill of dismay into Sophie. She stared down at what seemed an acre of black and white marble lozenges stretching out before her and tried to imagine herself mistress of all this imposing grandeur.

"Come, you must be frozen to the bone. I have ordered tea to be served in the gold drawing-room," the baronet announced, so plainly cock-a-hoop that Sophie knew he was enjoying their stunned amazement.

A wide marble staircase, heavily embellished with ornate carving, curved up to the first floor, where the baronet led them into an apartment as grand as its name implied. The heavy velvet curtains, the luxuriously thick carpet and every stick of furniture in the massive room, all were coloured gold or decorated in gold-leaf. Even the walls had been hung in a rich yellow silk, and Sophie blinked as her dazzled eyes tried to take in such overwhelming opulence.

"What a delightful room," Maria said weakly, breaking the silence. "And such a glorious fire, so inviting on a day like this one!"

Sir Pelham ushered both ladies towards it, making a fuss of finding them the most comfortable chairs.

Sophie smiled at him stiffly. She knew she ought to speak, but the expected compliments would not come to her lips. Her new surroundings appalled her!

Luckily the baronet mistook her silence for awe and, over tea, served in a magnificent set of Sèvres porcelain, he expounded lengthily upon the precious *objets d'art* that littered every available surface of the room.

"I hope you will share my love of collecting beautiful things, my dear Sophie," he concluded at last.

"I'm afraid I know little of art," Sophie admitted.

"It will be my pleasure to teach you." He smiled at her with such patronising smugness that Sophie almost ground her teeth.

He would do better to learn a little restraint himself first, she thought rebelliously. The pieces he treasured were undoubtedly handsome, taken on an individual basis, but they were so tightly crammed together that the beholder had difficulty in distinguishing between them. The whole effect reminded her of nothing so much as a gaudy painting she had once seen of an Arab bazaar!

She would never had dreamt that the baronet could be capable of such vulgarity. In personal dress he showed good taste, his obvious liking for expensive fabrics balanced by a certain modesty in style, but now she began to wonder if that restraint was due to the influence of his tailor.

"My housekeeper shall show you to your rooms." Sir Pelham rang the bell after they had finished their refreshments. "We dine at seven. I prefer to keep town hours, you understand, even in the depths of this wilderness."

He spread his hands in a gesture of apology. "Unfortunately my aunt will not be joining us. She has a nasty head cold and has asked me to present her apologies."

He chuckled. "However, my chef has been instructed to produce something special in honour of your arrival."

Sophie stifled a groan. She felt so weary that all she really wanted was an early, light supper, preferably served on a tray in her room.

A hot bath eased her aching muscles and revived her a little. Nancy had laid out her clothes, and she was almost finished dressing when a light tap at her door announced Maria's arrival.

"I've come to see if you are ready, my love."

"Very nearly. You look extremely grand." Sophie said, half turning from the dressing-table, where Nancy was arranging her hair.

"I thought I had better make an effort, since the baronet seems to set such store by fine appearances." Maria laughed. Her formal gown was of purple shot-silk and she gave the matching beplumed turban she wore a little pat to ensure it was in place.

Sophie grinned. "Well, I cannot hope to hold a candle to such elegance. The most I can wish for is that the dining-room is warm. This outfit was not designed for icy draughts."

"What nonsense you do talk, Sophie! You look enchanting. I knew that the new fashions would become you," Maria scolded.

Sophie had indulged in several new dresses for this trip, all of them in the latest high waisted style. Tonight was the first time she had worn any of them and it felt very strange to wear something so flimsy after the stiff, embroidered dresses she was used to.

"You'll catch your death," sniffed Nancy, twisting the last bright red curl into place. "Immodest, that's what these new gowns are."

Sophie chuckled. Nancy was cross because she'd had her waist-long hair cut to a new, fashionable shorter length and, even worse, had abandoned her stays. They were no longer practical, and all she wore beneath the delicate, semi-transparent ivory muslin was a single petticoat and a pair of white silk tights. For the first time in her life there was an advantage of being slender!

Nancy brought her the matching pair of heel-less ivory silk slippers, and Sophie was thrilled to see what an improvement they wrought. She didn't tower over Maria, who was wearing a pair of ordinary high-heeled shoes, half as much as usual!

"Where is Josh? Has he gone down already?" Sophie asked, accepting the silk shawl Nancy handed her and draping it prettily over her arms.

"I left him sleeping," Maria confessed.

Sophie nodded. It was easy to forget that Josh was almost her uncle's age. He had the upright figure of a much younger man, but she wasn't surprised that he was tired after their early start and bone-shaking journey.

"I shall wake him before we go downstairs," Maria yawned and hastily tried to cover it.

"It would have been more considerate of Pelham to postpone his elaborate plans until we had all recovered," Sophie muttered irritably, picking up her fan.

"Perhaps, but I am sure he meant well," Maria soothed.

"Like giving me this room?"

Sophie's wry enquiry forced a reluctant chuckle from the older woman. "But it is pretty," she murmured.

"Only if you like pink," Sophie retorted. It was a colour she never wore, since it clashed with her hair. "What's more, I'm scared to sit down. I feel like an elephant trespassing in a rose garden.''

Maria hid a grin. She could see exactly what Sophie meant. All the furnishings were frivolously gilded rococo, so flamboyantly carved and spindly-legged that they lacked any comfort. Worse, after a while the pink and white décor felt distinctly stifling. Its cloying sweetness was more suited to a porcelain figurine, a dainty Dresden shepherdess perhaps, rather than the needs of a real woman like her tall, red-headed friend.

When they entered the dining-room a short while later Sophie's growing conviction that the baronet had let pride get the better of his common sense was finally sealed.

This is worse than all the rest, she thought, subduing a desire to giggle.

Everything was in shades of red: glowing scarlet, deep crimson and a vibrant poppy that assaulted the senses. Even the massive table, groaning under a plethora of silverware and crystal, was a rich mahogany. How could anyone eat in such overpowering surroundings? Sophie was sure it would defeat a heartier appetite than hers.

"Never mind, my dear," Maria whispered under the cover of seeking their places. "Josh was just the same. No eye for colour at all! You will be able to reform Pelham's taste once you are wed."

The meal was as elaborate as Sophie feared.

"Are you not hungry, my dear?"

"I'm afraid the journey destroyed my appetite, Pelham," Sophie said quickly. "This is delicious, but . . ." With a polite smile she laid down her fork, abandoning her struggle with the rich chicken à l'Orleans. "I simply cannot manage another mouthful."

"No matter." The baronet smiled back at her, but Sophie sensed that he was annoyed.

They repaired to the drawing-room, where the baronet insisted that they play cards until the tea-tray was brought in.

Guilt warred with resentment in Sophie's breast as the long evening dragged on. She felt exhausted by the time they were finally able to escape to bed, where she tossed and turned in the soft embrace of her goose-down mattress.

Perhaps it is unfair of me to be so critical when Pelham went to such efforts to entertain us, Sophie thought, but she couldn't

prevent a suspicion forming that pride and vanity lay behind his
welcome, rather than any real desire for their comfort. Either
that or he was completely lacking in sensitivity!

Could he really be so self-centred, so careless of the feelings
of others?

Sophie bit her lip, her uneasiness deepening. How little she
knew of the real Pelham! Today had revealed completely unexpected facets to his character, unwelcome traits she had never
suspected he possessed.

I scorned Kirk when he told me that there was a hidden side
to Pelham's nature, she mused unhappily, and then pulled
herself up sharply as she realised where her thoughts were
leading.

She was not going to think of that man! She had shed her last
tears over Kirk Thorburn. No matter how vain Pelham was, at
least he had always behaved honourably towards her. No, she
had made her decision and now she must abide by it. It was too
late for foolish regrets!

THAT FIRST EVENING set a pattern for the next few days. Sir
Pelham entertained them lavishly, but his attitude was patronising. He seems to expect us to fall in with his every whim, Sophie thought indignantly, when her mild protest that she did not
wish to play cards every evening was brushed aside with the
dismissive comment that everyone of quality indulged in gaming.

Maria and Josh were too polite to complain of his conde-
scension, but Sophie hated being treated like a half-witted child.
Her resentment bubbled over on the evening that the baronet
invited the neighbouring gentry to the Hall to meet his future
bride.

"I cannot understand it! When he was courting me in Kendal he professed to admire my independence, so why does he
now dislike me saying what I think?" she demanded angrily of
Maria after the dinner party was over. "It seems he wants me
to be nothing more than his echo. I am beginning to believe all
he requires is a passive doll!"

"Many men hold such narrow views concerning their wives,
I'm afraid, my dear," Maria murmured in a placatory tone,
hiding her own misgivings. She wouldn't have dreamt of say-

ing so to Sophie, but to her it had seemed almost as if the baronet was ashamed of his betrothed.

It was understandable perhaps that he had made no mention of Sophie's connections with the tobacco trade, but why had he deliberately fostered a false impression that she was of aristocratic birth? It was all very worrying, and Maria wished that tomorrow was not their last day at Stanton Hall.

They had been kept so busy that she hadn't found the right opportunity to speak privately to Sophie about Kirk Thorburn, but she could see that this was not the moment to do so. Her young friend was in no mood to share confidences.

"I think it wisest to try to get some sleep, my dear," she advised. "It is very late and you are tired. Things will seem better in the morning."

Sophie snorted disbelievingly, but when she awoke the next day to bright sunshine she began to feel more optimistic. The air was noticeably warmer and the thought that spring was on its way at last was cheering. Perhaps Pelham, who professed to dislike winters in the country, would also be in a better mood.

It was a Sunday and they were to accompany the baronet to the morning service at the little sixteenth-century church of Saint Kentigern in the parish of Crosthwaite, a tiny hamlet close to Keswick. The servants' humbler waggon followed the baronet's opulent carriage, and Sophie enjoyed the drive.

"How charming," she remarked, enchanted by her first glimpse of the tiny church.

Sir Pelham raised his brows. "I find it cramped and inconvenient. If it were not for the fact that I come here to exchange greetings with my acquaintance I would open up the chapel at Stanton Hall."

Sophie bit back a rejoinder. So much for her hopes that his difficult mood might have improved!

I wonder if his ill temper has anything to do with Conrad, she mused as they slowed to a halt.

Sir Pelham's private secretary, a tall, fleshy young man in his late twenties named Simon Conrad, had arrived at the Hall last night. Sophie had been introduced to him at breakfast, but he had soon excused himself, disappearing into Sir Pelham's study, where he had remained closeted with his employer until it was time for the baronet to leave for church.

There had been little time for Sophie to form an opinion of Conrad—he had not accompanied them—but his arrival certainly seemed to have brought Pelham no pleasure.

"Is something wrong, sir? Did your secretary bring bad news?" she enquired in a low voice as the baronet handed her down from the carriage.

"What? No, no, my dear. Pray don't trouble your pretty head with such gloomy thoughts!"

His joviality seemed forced to Sophie, but she obediently fell silent, curbing a sigh of regret.

The service was excellent, but Sophie found her mind wandering. How she wished Pelham would treat her as an adult! She had always hoped to marry someone who believed marriage was an equal partnership, but it was going to be very difficult if Pelham persisted in acting as if she were an irresponsible idiot, incapable of offering him friendship or support.

On the way home Maria remarked, "That was an excellent sermon. It is a pity your aunt had to miss the service."

"Indeed, Mrs. Strickland, she was very disappointed," the baronet answered smoothly, not missing the edge to Maria's tone. "Her illness has been most unfortunate. I know she regrets not having made your acquaintance sooner, but she has expressed the desire that you will take tea with her this afternoon so that she can at least meet you before you leave. You intend to make a very early start tomorrow, do you not?"

Maria nodded, mollified by this promise. It would have been a dereliction of the duty she owed to Thomas Fleming to leave Sophie in the care of a woman she hadn't laid eyes on, although Sophie herself had met the old lady.

The baronet had accompanied Sophie to Mrs. Stanton's overheated boudoir the previous day. Sophie's first impression was of a tiny, stooped figure bundled in shawls, huddling over an enormous fire.

Reporting back to the anxious Maria, Sophie had played down the extent of Mrs. Stanton's obvious ill health, not wishing to alarm her friend, but she had been shocked by the old lady's air of fragility. She had barely said a word during the brief meeting, and Sophie knew that her uncle Thomas would be furious if he found out how the baronet had misled him.

Thank God Pelham's behaviour is not ardent enough to make it necessary to require a real chaperon, she thought with a silent giggle as the carriage swept up the long drive to the Hall. Otherwise Maria might insist on staying, and I know she is looking forward to seeing her sister.

Sophie had wondered if Pelham would become more lover-like in the privacy of his own home, but his manner had remained coolly dignified, even on the rare occasions Maria had tactfully left them alone for a few moments. Although she was relieved by his restraint, a tiny part of Sophie felt rather insulted. Was she so unattractive?

Perhaps I would feel better if he did show some signs of desiring me. Sophie tried to picture the baronet sweeping her into a wild embrace and almost burst out laughing at the incongruous image. He was much too distant and self-contained ever to behave as Kirk Thorburn had done . . .

For an instant she was back in Maria's conservatory . . . She could feel Kirk's strong hands at her waist, smell the intoxicating scent of his skin, taste his lips on hers . . .

The longing to be back in his arms was as sharp as a knife!

Sophie abruptly shook her head to clear it. She was a fool to remember that kiss, just as Kirk was a fool to imagine that the baronet could ever lose his icy self-possession long enough to commit murder!

Such self-delusion was dangerous. Too much thinking led only to useless regret. It was best to concentrate on the reality of here and now!

There are plenty of good things in my life, she thought determinedly. I will never go hungry or barefoot and soon I shall have the rank and status my friends envied.

And love, what about love?

I shall love my children, she told herself defiantly, ignoring the scream of protest that rang in her head.

Determined to look on the bright side, Sophie pinned a smile to her lips as she bade her friends farewell early the next morning.

"If you need me, send a message at once," Maria whispered, leaning out of the carriage window. "I'm not sure I trust Mrs. Stanton to look after you as I would wish."

Sophie shook her glowing curls in laughing protest, but Maria's expression remained anxious.

Pelham's aunt had been much livelier when they had taken tea with her yesterday, but it was plain that Maria wasn't entirely convinced that someone so frail was a suitable chaperon.

"Perhaps I should stay."

"You haven't seen Emma in months," Sophie said in a coaxing tone. "I wouldn't dream of spoiling your visit."

She giggled and added naughtily, "Anyway, Pelham isn't likely to try and ravish me, you know!"

"Sophie!" Maria couldn't help laughing, and the awkward moment passed.

When the berlin could no longer be seen Sophie stopped waving and turned to her betrothed. Sir Pelham, who had courteously stood back to allow her a few moments of privacy, came to claim her arm to escort her inside.

"Dare I ask you to excuse me this morning, my dear? I'm afraid Conrad brought a mountain of papers for me to examine."

Sophie shrugged lightly. "I'm sure I can entertain myself, Pelham. I'm not entirely helpless."

"Of course not."

His jovial smile did not reach his eyes, she noticed.

The morning dragged slowly. Annoyed that she should miss Maria so much, Sophie tried to settle to some embroidery in the drawing-room, but found she couldn't concentrate.

What am I doing here? she thought, in a sudden panic.

Her luxurious surroundings seemed to close in on her and Sophie felt like a bird in a cage. The claustrophobic sensation was suddenly so intense that she cast aside her tambour-frame and fled outside to the wide marble terrace which overlooked the gardens.

The cold, crisp air was like wine to her gasping throat. Gradually her heart ceased to thud and her flushed cheeks cooled, but it took several moments before her panic had ebbed sufficiently for Sophie to take any notice of the magnificent landscape laid out before her.

It was marvellously executed, but somehow the very formality of the French *allées* radiating between the *bosquets* of evergreen trees, cool green lawns, fountains and marble statues suddenly struck her as unbearably false in contrast to the wild natural scenery beyond the gates.

Sophie's head was whirling. Was her betrothed like this elegant sham? Would his gentlemanly façade crumble and revert to rough nature once the wedding was over?

Stop it! Stop letting your vivid imagination run away with you because you are feeling lonely and homesick, she scolded herself silently.

She drew a deep breath. Very well, she *was* disappointed with the way things had turned out, but dissatisfaction with her betrothed was no reason to think him a monster!

"What you need, my girl, is some exercise to blow away these cobwebs from your brain," she muttered, moving indoors again and going swiftly up to her room.

Knowing Nancy was bound to exclaim over her pallor, Sophie did not ring for her. She did not need assistance to exchange her delicate morning gown for a warmer walking dress in blue merino. A thick pelisse, her stoutest boots, a neat little bonnet, and she was ready.

At the door she checked.

Her enormous betrothal diamond winked back at her as she stared down at the hand holding the doorknob, and after the briefest of hesitations she stripped the ring from her finger and laid it away in her jewellery box.

It feels a little loose in this cold weather, she told herself, but even as she tried to rationalise her decision Sophie knew she was prevaricating. It wasn't fear of losing the diamond that prompted her, but a growing dislike for all that it symbolised!

"Should the baronet request my presence, please inform him that I have gone for a walk and may not return in time for luncheon," Sophie instructed the footman who opened the front door for her.

Once beyond the elaborately wrought gates an indescribable feeling of freedom lightened her steps. Not caring where she went, she turned southwards, following a path alongside the lake.

An hour passed and Sophie paused to rest, perching upon a handy boulder. She hadn't been hurrying, but the going was rough and muddy and now her weak ankle was aching. She was also beginning to feel hungry.

"I should have brought some provisions with me," she told an inquisitive sparrow watching her from a nearby bush.

She grinned at the notion of demanding bread and cheese from Sir Pelham's haughty butler.

"Perhaps I could scoop up some water in my hands," she added, eyeing the pebbly shoreline doubtfully. Thirsty as she was, she didn't relish the idea of accidentally slipping and falling into the lake. "It looks shallow here, so I dare say I wouldn't drown, but I'll warrant it's cold."

"As cold as Pelham Stanton's heart," a deep voice behind her affirmed.

and into the tent. A faint afterglow shows us a chimney? a window? direct... but the evening is cool... under your folded blankets...

CHAPTER SIX

SOPHIE'S HEAD jerked round so abruptly at the familiar sound of his voice that she felt the muscles in her neck protest.

"What are you doing here?" she demanded, scrambling from her perch with more haste than dignity.

"I live in the next valley."

This answer was so unexpected that Sophie could think of no reply.

Kirk Thorburn gazed at her with a hunger he could not conceal. God, how he had missed her!

Sophie's cheeks flamed.

"I... I must be going," she murmured, quelling the longing to cross the narrow stretch of earth that separated them.

"Wait!" Kirk moved a step nearer. "Our meeting like this isn't entirely coincidental. I'd heard you had arrived at the Hall and I've been keeping a watch in the hope that I might get the chance to speak to you." He paused significantly. "In private."

"Then I must regret that I did not bring along my maid," Sophie retorted, cursing her independence. "For I have nothing to say to you, sir."

"Sophie, surely you have realised by now what a mistake this betrothal is—"

"Please!" Sophie flung up her hand to cut him off, scared he might give voice to her own doubts. "Pray do not seek to interfere, I beg of you!"

Pride dictated that she defend her decision. Tilting her chin at him defiantly, she added haughtily, "I am perfectly content with my betrothal."

The sharpness of her answer was belied by the shadows in her eyes, and Kirk frowned.

"I don't believe you," he stated flatly.

Sophie bristled. "You have no manners, Kirk Thorburn!" She glared at him. "Why don't you just go away and leave me alone?"

"I can't."

The intensity of his gaze pierced the defences Sophie had striven to raise against her own unruly emotions. She shivered helplessly as he continued in the same gruff tone, "I have tried, God knows, but I cannot bear the thought of you in that scoundrel's clutches. He will make you dreadfully unhappy, sweetheart."

"Don't call me that!" Sophie's voice quivered.

This would never do! In another moment she would be in tears and he would guess she still cared for him, no matter how hard she tried not to.

"You must think me a fool to believe you have any real interest in my happiness after what happened last time we met," she snapped.

Kirk's tanned skin assumed an unaccustomed tinge of colour. "I know I behaved badly," he muttered. He cleared his throat. "But that doesn't alter matters."

Sophie shrugged pettishly and Kirk's beautifully shaped mouth twisted. Was she rejecting his advice from mere pique?

"Are you so spoilt that you would cut off your nose to be revenged on your face?"

Sophie gasped. How dared he say she was spoilt? "You have no right to criticise me, sir. Why should I believe your wild accusations? For all I know, your motive might be envy."

Kirk let out a bitter laugh. Envy? Well, perhaps, but how could he admit he would give anything to stand in Stanton's wedding shoes? She would never believe him; he could hardly credit it himself!

In the past Kirk had been careful not to let any woman come too close. He enjoyed their company, when he could spare time from his exacting duties on the plantation, but that disastrous business with Rebecca Hurst when he was only eighteen had taught him to be wary of giving his heart.

The blow Becky's treachery had dealt him had destroyed his youthful faith in women. It might have turned him bitter if his nature had been less resilient. Fortunately a passionate affair with a French widow on New Providence soon afterwards had restored his confidence and helped him to see things in perspective.

Several pretty girls had succeeded Louise as his mistress, but he had never felt anything more than a mild affection for any of them. His heart had remained untouched ... until now.

"I find nothing amusing in this situation, sir." Sophie glowered at him. Why was he looking at her with that rueful smile? She did not understand him!

Deeply disturbed, she knew she had to get away. "Pelham says you are nothing but a trouble maker. I will not listen to you."

"Then, by God, I shall make you listen, you stubborn minx!" Kirk exploded, seizing her as she turned to go.

"Put me down!" Sophie shrieked in alarm as he swung her up over his shoulder.

Ignoring her, Kirk strode over to where his horse stood waiting with well-trained patience and, before Sophie had time to grasp his intention, flung her over the bow of his saddle.

Leaping up behind her, he spurred the bay into motion, and they wheeled off at a speed that drove the little remaining breath from Sophie's lungs.

Bounced against the stallion's side, Sophie could do nothing but try to shield her face from being bruised. The ground seemed terrifyingly close and she was petrified by the thought of falling beneath those flashing hoofs.

She had no idea of where they were going. Her field of vision was limited to the shiny, sweat-stained coat of the great beast beneath her and the strong smell of hot horseflesh filled her nostrils.

The journey seemed to last forever, but at last the stallion slowed and came to a halt.

"Down you come."

Strong hands plucked her from her uncomfortable perch, but as her feet touched the ground Sophie's knees buckled.

Kirk expected her to hurl a torrent of abuse at his head, but she surprised him.

"I think I am going to be sick," she gasped weakly as he hauled her upright.

"Oh, no, you're not, my girl." Kirk crushed a pang of remorse as he observed her greenish pallor. "All you need is to get your breath back." Propelling her towards a fallen tree trunk, he pushed her down on to it. "Sit here quietly for a moment while I stable Sultan. I won't be long."

Glowering after his departing back, Sophie subsided on to her rough seat. After a few moments her stomach stopped performing somersaults, and as her head cleared she was able to take in her surroundings.

"What on earth . . . ?"

Mystified, she stared at the ruin before her. Once upon a time it must have been a handsome dwelling, for enough remained to show that it had been a substantial building.

Sophie's indignation gave way to curiosity. To judge by its construction, it had probably been a farmhouse. Indeed, there were outbuildings scattered close by, but, unlike the house, they were in good repair. Kirk had presumably disappeared into one of them, but there was no sound of any animals...nor any other sign of life!

The silence was faintly eerie and Sophie could not repress a little quiver of relief when she spotted Kirk emerging from the stables. Getting to her feet as he approached, she said without preamble, "Why have you brought me here?"

"To view your betrothed's handiwork."

This sardonic reply made Sophie gasp. Her shocked gaze flew back to the ruined farmhouse. "*This* was your brother's property?"

"Aye. Those smoke-blackened walls are all that is left of Haraldsgarth," he said grimly.

Sophie touched her dry lips with her tongue. Such wholesale destruction made her own problems seem insignificant. No wonder Kirk was so angry! "Perhaps it can be repaired," she murmured rather helplessly.

"Oh, I shall restore it! My family have farmed in this valley since Viking times and I have no intention of letting Stanton's miserable conniving force us out."

There was a fierce ruthlessness in his words that made Sophie shiver. He would let nothing stand in his way.

"I hope you do manage to restore your home, Kirk," she said with quiet sincerity.

He raised his brows at her and then nodded in curt acknowledgement.

"But now I have seen it, I would like to go home," Sophie continued with all the firmness she could muster.

"No."

This bald reply infuriated Sophie. "Oh, for heaven's sake!" she snapped. "I am prepared to overlook your disgraceful behaviour in dragging me up here, but you go too far, Kirk Thorburn! I insist on returning to Stanton Hall at once!"

"Very well then, off you go," Kirk replied with a grim dark humour.

Sophie flinched involuntarily. "You expect me to ride down there unescorted?"

"Oh, no," he said sweetly. "I'm not loaning you my horse. You will have to walk. It isn't far. Not much more than five miles."

To her annoyance Sophie heard her voice emerge as a squeak as she protested, "Five miles? But I don't even know the way!"

"Then you'll have to wait until I'm ready to take you, won't you?" he remarked, smiling at her pleasantly.

Sophie glared at him. "And when will that be?"

"When I'm convinced you finally understand what I have been trying to tell you," he said, dropping his flippant manner.

"You have no right to detain me!"

"Maybe not, but you are staying here until you see sense."

"If by that you mean until I agree to give up my betrothal, then hell will freeze over first!"

Kirk laughed harshly. "I wonder, Miss Fleming. Perhaps you will see things differently after spending the night in the barn."

Sophie blanched. Surely he couldn't intend to keep her here overnight?

"You cannot . . . you simply cannot treat me this way!" she spluttered indignantly. "It's barbaric. I *must* return to the Hall before they start to worry."

"The solution is in your own hands." Kirk shrugged. "When you are ready to listen, I'll be in the barn." And he strode off, leaving Sophie to glare after him in furious frustration.

THREE HOURS LATER the sun had been obscured by thick cloud. Sophie looked up at the ominous black sky with resentment. Rain was all she needed to complete her misery! She hadn't had anything to eat or drink since breakfast and she was chilled to the bone.

After Kirk had disappeared she had made an attempt to find her way out of this God-forsaken valley, only to discover that she had no idea which way to turn once she finally came in sight of the lake. The wide expanse of Derwent Water had shimmered before her anxious gaze. If only she had managed at least to catch a glimpse of the direction Kirk Thorburn had taken!

To add to her frustration, there wasn't a dwelling in sight nor a soul to ask. Hating to admit defeat, Sophie hesitated, but after several long moments common sense prevailed. If she took the wrong track she would soon be hopelessly lost, and already the brief day was dwindling. In a few hours it would be dark and the temperature would drop even lower.

Much as she was loath to admit it, her only chance of safety lay back at the derelict farm. Surely Kirk would stop playing this silly game once he realised that she did not intend to give in to his bullying?

This hope had buoyed Sophie's weary footsteps as she trudged back up the narrow track to Haraldsgarth, but to her disappointment Kirk had not emerged when she resumed her seat on the fallen log.

Now an icy wind sprung up and with each passing minute the sky was growing darker. No matter how often she swung her arms and legs in a brisk circling movement, she couldn't get warm.

I shall have to ask him for shelter soon before I turn into a frozen statue, she decided bitterly, but even as the thought occurred to her her pride rebelled.

Damn it, I won't beg! It isn't fair! I won't meekly humble myself like some penitent when I have done nothing to deserve such Turkish treatment, she raged silently.

How long this wave of fresh fury would have lasted Sophie was never afterwards sure, for just at that instant the heavens opened and a deluge of rain descended upon her unprotected head.

In a few moments she was soaked until, gasping and spluttering, she rose slowly to her feet. Fighting her reluctance, she began to move towards the barn . . .

"You stubborn little fool!"

Blinking the rain out of her eyes, Sophie saw Kirk appear, looming up out of the dense curtain of water like some avenging Norse god.

He swept her up into his arms.

"Let me go!"

Kirk ignored her shriek of protest and ran for the barn, where once safely inside he set her down.

"Thank you!"

Sophie's tone was heavy with sarcasm, but Kirk didn't seem to notice as he busied himself with closing the heavy wooden doors, cutting off the noise of the lashing rain and icy wind.

"Come over here to the fire."

Her eyes growing accustomed to the gloom, Sophie saw that an iron brazier glowed in the centre of the barn, shedding light and heat. Further illumination was provided by a lantern hanging up on a post, and the first thing she noticed was an artist's easel placed beneath it to catch the light.

This oddity puzzled her, but she didn't stop to wonder at it once she spotted the only other contents of the barn: a straw pallet and a few items more usually found in a kitchen.

Her dark brows rose.

Kirk stretched out an encouraging hand. "Don't worry. There are no rats and the floor is clean. I swept it myself only yesterday."

So it was true. He was *living* here!

Her nose wrinkled disdainfully. "How cosy," she murmured, and had the satisfaction of seeing a muscle twitch by his well-cut mouth.

Kirk let his hand fall back to his side. He should have expected it, but her scorn was painful.

"I am here because it is the best place for me to concentrate on drawing up plans for a new Haraldsgarth," he said curtly.

Sophie's cheeks vied with her hair. "How was I to know you were an architect?" she muttered sulkily.

Kirk shrugged. "I learnt the rudiments of the trade when I helped raise several houses on New Providence. Once the weather improves, the builders I've hired can begin." He paused and added sweetly, "I will supervise their work, but I won't join in their labours, you understand."

A quiver of annoyance ran through Sophie, but she stayed silent, unhappily aware that she deserved his sarcasm, having behaved with a snobbishness almost equal to Pelham's.

"Occasionally, when I tire of my own company, I stay with some friends who live further up the valley," Kirk continued in a more conciliatory tone. "But they are farmers who work hard for their living, and I don't like to impose on their kindness too often."

Sophie stamped her foot. "I don't care if they are Emperors of China," she shouted, losing her precarious hold on her patience. "All I am interested in is going home!"

To her mortification, Sophie felt angry tears prick at her
eyelids, and she tried to blink them away.

Kirk saw them, and the blistering retort died on his lips.

"You are cold and wet and no doubt hungry too. Why don't
we postpone this discussion until you feel more comfortable?"

Sniffing hard to combat the tears which still threatened, Sophie wondered if he was trying to apologise.

Kirk crossed to the straw pallet and snatched up a blanket.

"Here, get out of that wet dress and wrap yourself in this.
You'll soon warm up if you sit by the fire."

Sophie stared at him in consternation.

"Don't worry. I'll make myself scarce while you change. It's
time I checked on Sultan anyway. He doesn't like rain-storms."

He smiled at her. "Will five minutes suffice? Then I'll make
you some hot soup."

Sophie nodded, trying to tell herself it was the promise of
food that suddenly made her feel more cheerful and not the
effect of his engaging smile.

Once he had gone she stripped off her sodden clothes down
to her lace-trimmed chemise. Modesty demanded she cover her
bare arms and shoulders, but, having done so, she quickly discovered that the least movement dislodged the blanket from its
place.

"I'll never be able to eat huddled up like this," she muttered impatiently.

Yanking it off, she tried again, this time twisting the rectan-
gle of grey wool around her so that it came taut across her
breasts, where she secured it by tucking in the loose end. It
probably looked inelegant, Sophie reflected, wishing she had a
mirror, but it was no more revealing than a ball-gown, and at
least she now had her hands free.

Next she removed the pins from her hair and shook it loose
to dry off. Thank goodness she'd had it cut! Bestowing the hair-
pins in the pocket of her pelisse, she caught sight of her boots
peeping out from beneath the uneven hem. Deciding they
looked ridiculous, she pulled them off, exposing her pretty silk
stockings, before draping her wet garments over a large cart-
wheel propped up against one wall.

Sophie moved towards the brazier. She couldn't see any
chairs or even a stool, and she was wondering if Kirk's claim

that the floor was clean was true when the door swung open to admit him.

"Let me pull the pallet up for you," he offered, striding forward to arrange it.

His manner was so briskly impersonal that Sophie's faint shyness concerning her costume faded.

"Come, won't you sit down?"

Sophie considered refusing. It seemed most improper to sit on his bed, such as it was, but then this whole situation was unconventional, she decided, watching him strip off his wet coat.

His waistcoat and neckcloth followed, and Sophie swallowed hard when she caught a glimpse of his sun-bronzed throat.

Don't be such a ninny, she told herself sternly. You have seen men in their shirt-sleeves before now!

"Why are you smiling?" Kirk asked, throwing another blanket over the pallet to make it more comfortable.

"I was just wondering what Nancy would say if she could see me now," Sophie admitted with a chuckle, amusement vanquishing her embarrassment.

"Your Mrs. Nelson strikes me as a practical soul who would tell you to make the best of things."

Sophie nodded. It seemed silly to refuse the only comfortable seat available, so she sat down on the pallet, keeping a careful hold on her improvised costume.

Kirk began to prepare their meal. Swiftly extracting bread from a knapsack, he laid it on a pewter platter before carefully tipping the contents of a stone jar into a saucepan.

Placing this on top of the glowing coals, he said, "It won't take long to heat up."

After a few moments a savoury aroma arose from the pan, blotting out the faint lingering smell of hay that still permeated the barn.

Sophie's mouth began to water. She hadn't realised how hungry she was until now!

A well bred young lady, Sophie reflected, ought to be more concerned with the indelicacy of her predicament, but all she was aware of was a delicious contentment stealing over her. She was warm and dry at last, and when Kirk handed her an earthenware bowl filled to the brim with thick, hot soup a little sigh of pleasure escaped her.

"This is really good," she murmured, after a few eager spoonfuls.

Kirk grinned. "I'll convey your compliments to the cook when I next see her."

Sophie stiffened involuntarily. "You didn't make it yourself?"

His laughter rang out. "I wish I could cook. It would be useful, but luckily Rose often provides me with supplies."

So her name was Rose. But who was she and why did Kirk speak of her so warmly?

Sophie continued to eat, but her pleasure in the meal was diminished, and when Kirk offered her more of the flat, coarse bread she refused.

"Clap bread is an acquired taste, I suppose."

Sophie's curiosity overcame the pang of jealousy that had assailed her. "Is that what it is called? It doesn't taste like the bread we have at home. Do you know what it is made from?"

"From oatmeal, I believe," Kirk replied absently, watching how her dark eyes sparkled in the mellow light.

She looked a different girl from the fashionably sophisticated creature he had encountered in Kendal. Her hair was drying into a riot of soft curls that fell to her shoulders, framing her piquant little face, and the rain had washed away the powder and paint she usually wore.

Sophie put aside her empty bowl and raised a self-conscious hand to her nose. Was he staring at her loathsome freckles?

"Is my face dirty?" she demanded.

"On the contrary, you look lovely," Kirk said slowly, meaning it. Oh, she would never be a conventional beauty—her features were too irregular for that—but she glowed with vibrant life in a way that was utterly enchanting.

"You are making a mock of me," Sophie declared once she had recovered her breath.

"Well, I must admit your costume wouldn't find its way into the fashion-plates," he agreed so solemnly that Sophie almost giggled. "But otherwise you look charming, Miss Fleming."

Sophie stared at him, a small flame of excitement igniting in her veins.

Something in her expression made Kirk catch his breath. He started to stretch out his hand to her and then came to his senses.

"I'd better clear these away, unless you want some more? I think there is a drop of soup left."

His gruff manner restored Sophie to reality. Sternly she told herself to stop being so foolish. He was a womaniser. He couldn't help flirting with her, but it meant nothing!

When he had removed the debris of their impromptu meal Kirk returned to sit on the end of the pallet, being careful to leave the maximum space possible between them.

"Are you feeling better now?"

Sophie nodded.

"Then may I ask you a question? Are you sure you haven't had any second thoughts about this betrothal?"

"Oh, Kirk, must we talk about it?" A little sigh escaped her, but she knew from his expression that he wouldn't be put off so easily.

"Stanton Hall is not as I expected," she confessed, her fingers playing with a fold of grey wool. "I find it rather overpowering, but I suppose I shall grow used to it in time. Unfortunately Pelham's behaviour has changed to suit his surroundings."

"And that disturbs you? Good. I'm glad you are beginning to see sense."

"I'll admit I'm disappointed," she agreed, "but that doesn't mean I believe he is a murderer." She met his gaze with more calmness than she felt. "Did you find the proof you were looking for? Have you discovered the owner of that snuff-box?"

"Not yet, but I've hired an agent to continue the search." Sophie heard the frustration in his tone as he continued gruffly. "London is too big a place to comb in such a short time."

"Then why did you return so soon?"

Kirk merely shrugged, unwilling to answer.

Everything had gone wrong in London. Bad news about the sale of his plantation had reached him. He hadn't expected it to fetch so little and he wished he had taken more care to refute Caroline's extravagant claims.

Even worse, he hadn't been able to stop thinking about Sophie. His instincts warned him that she was in danger from the baronet, distracting him from what he knew should be his real purpose. Troubled by the thought that he was neglecting his duty, he had redoubled his efforts, but in the end had been unable to resist hiring an ex-Bow Street Runner and returning north.

"Have you met Stanton's aunt yet?" Kirk asked abruptly, trying to ignore his uneasy conscience.

Sophie nodded. "I suppose you were acquainted with her when you were a boy." Something in his expression told her that he knew how frail the old lady was.

"Aye, a kindly woman, but blindly devoted to Pelham," Kirk said, his tone grim. "She used to shield him from any trouble even then."

He took Sophie's hands in his own and pressed them urgently. "Can't you see what a devilish situation you are in, Sophie? Old Mrs. Stanton cannot protect you. She rarely leaves her room, and I doubt if she would gainsay her nephew's wishes, whatever they might be."

Sophie stared at him in troubled silence. In Kendal she would have pooh-poohed the idea that she might have anything to fear from the baronet, but somehow after his incredibly arrogant behaviour it didn't seem so far-fetched any longer.

"But there is no reason for Pelham to harm me," she said at last. "Not that he cares a straw for me," she added, with a little grimace. "I've learnt that much at least. He was merely pretending to admire me in Kendal, but he thinks me beneath him."

"He was always a fool." There was a warmth Kirk could not conceal in his voice.

Sophie was intensely aware of the fact that he was still holding her hands. "Kirk, I cannot break off my betrothal just because I've realised that Pelham is overbearing," she said a little breathlessly. "Many men behave arrogantly and most husbands expect their wives to be meek and obedient. How can I disappoint my uncle for such a trivial reason?"

"Trivial?" He raised his brows at her.

She blushed. "Everyone will condemn me if I jilt Pelham."

"I didn't think you'd care if people gossiped."

Sophie shook her head, setting her curls dancing in exasperation. "Of course I would care! No girl wishes to be left a spinster, you know. It's different for men, but scandal can ruin a woman's reputation."

She halted abruptly, giving him a troubled look, and Kirk guessed what she was thinking.

"In spite of what Stanton may have told you, I was *not* responsible for getting Becky Hurst with child," he said emphatically. "Oh, I don't deny I was in love with her at the time, but we were a pair of young innocents. Nothing more than the exchange of a few kisses passed between us."

Sophie believed him. A weight seemed to drop away from her heart, but she knew that her situation had not changed and she returned to the attack.

"Kirk, I cannot stay here overnight without a chaperon. Surely you can see what a furore it would cause?"

Kirk hadn't given this aspect of the matter a thought. He had been much too concerned with trying to knock some sense into her stubborn head. She had made him so angry that he had acted on impulse, but now his temper had cooled.

"Perhaps I should not have been so hasty," he murmured.

"No, you should not," Sophie said darkly, remembering the indignity of being thrown over his horse like a sack of potatoes. "I shall have bruises for a week!"

"Did you hurt yourself when we rode up here?" Kirk was appalled. "I'm sorry, I never dreamt you might do so."

The shocked dismay on his face touched Sophie's heart.

"It doesn't matter," she said swiftly.

"But it does! I hoped I might persuade you to listen to me, perhaps even induce you into returning to your uncle, but I didn't stop to think things through."

A little smile flickered over Sophie's face for an instant. "I am impetuous myself," she consoled him.

Kirk wasn't listening. "Your poor arms," he murmured, staring at the ominous patches already darkening the soft skin.

He lifted his guinea-gold head. "Forgive me, I wouldn't have had this happen for the world!"

"Oh, Kirk," Sophie breathed, her right hand gliding up to bestow a gentle benediction upon his cheek.

Kirk stiffened at her touch and for an instant they remained frozen in the same position, the silence so tense that it was almost palpable.

Then in the same instant that she swayed towards him he caught her in his arms so fiercely that the breath was almost crushed from her lungs.

"Sophie! Sophie!"

His sun-bronzed face swam before her vision and giddily she closed her eyes. With a long, shivering sigh, she yielded to his kiss.

With exquisite slowness his mouth took possession of hers. Gently, his lips brushed hers in a delicate caress, which gradually deepened as the moments ticked by, until their tongues were entwined in a passionately exciting duel.

The blood drummed wildly in Sophie's veins. Her body was awakening to feelings which made her long for more than just kisses. She clung to Kirk, forgetting her betrothal, Pelham, Uncle Thomas, everything, as the fire his skilful caresses were kindling blazed into a passion beyond reason.

"Kiss me, Kirk, kiss me hard!"

Casting aside all reservation, Sophie sank back into the enveloping softness of his bed, her urgent hands reaching up to pull Kirk down with her. For one brief moment he resisted, and impatiently she transferred her slim fingers to tug at the wrapping of grey wool which covered her, flinging it aside.

Kirk swallowed hard as the blanket fell open, revealing her slender body, clad in her lace-trimmed chemise. It was made of a lawn so fine that it was semitransparent. He stared hypnotised at her firm young breasts rising from the low neckline, the rosy nipples clearly visible through the thin material.

"Don't you like me, Kirk?" Sophie asked in a provocative voice she hardly recognised as her own.

"You little witch, you make it impossible for a man to resist," he replied hoarsely, his control snapping as she held out her arms to him.

He lowered himself to the pallet and Sophie felt her body suffuse with heat as their lips met in another passionate kiss. Her heart was beating so frantically that she felt giddy, but she wanted the moment to go on forever and was desolate when he lifted his mouth away.

"You are utterly intoxicating," Kirk said, his breath rasping in his throat.

His gaze roamed over her body and elation fizzed through Sophie's veins at the desire in his eyes. Knowing she wasn't pretty, she had never thought she would have the confidence to try and tempt a man. Instinct alone had given her the confidence to behave so boldly, but now for the first time in her life she felt truly beautiful!

They kissed again and the desperate desire for him to touch her breasts as he had done once before grew intolerable. She pressed herself even more closely to him and Kirk divined her wish.

"Oh, yes!" A sigh of exquisite relief escaped her as he pushed the flimsy barrier of her chemise aside, his long, skilful fingers moving to cup the softly swelling flesh, stroking and caressing both breasts in turn until Sophie moaned with pleasure.

At his touch her nipples hardened, exciting them both, until Kirk swiftly dipped his head to capture one rosy crest.

His mouth was hot and thrillingly moist against her sensitive skin and Sophie gasped as his tongue circled her nipple, teasing and sucking with an expertise that made her clutch at his shoulders, her senses reeling.

Through the mists of passion wreathing his brain, Kirk was dimly aware that he ought to draw back, but when he reluctantly raised his head to tell her so Sophie let out a little wail of despair.

"Oh, don't stop, don't ever stop!" she implored, eagerly guiding his mouth back to her breast.

A few delicious moments later the urgent desire to feel his naked skin against her own made Sophie tug imperiously at his shirt. "Take it off," she whispered. "I want to touch you too."

Infected by her madness, Kirk's resolve melted. He sat up and pulled the shirt over his head with an unsteady laugh, throwing it aside into the darkness that lapped their small, warm island of enchantment.

Sophie shivered with delight as his virile chest rubbed against her bare breasts. She ran her fingers experimentally over the bronzed skin, feeling the muscles beneath. The light glinted off the short golden hairs as she ruffled them between her exploring fingers. They felt surprisingly soft to the touch, and Sophie was fascinated.

"What are you thinking?" Kirk asked, intrigued by her silent attentions.

She chuckled throatily. "Just how delightfully different your body is from mine. So strong, so brown, so hard . . . Oh!"

Kirk could not help grinning as a crimson blush climbed from her neck to her hairline as she realised what she had said . . . and how entirely appropriate her comment was!

"Darling Sophie, that's the effect you always have on me, I'm afraid," he murmured wickedly.

Sophie's embarrassment faded when she saw the tender warmth in his eyes. "You aren't laughing at me at all, are you?" she exclaimed in relief.

"Not in the least, sweetheart."

"Well, it was an idiotic thing to say!" Sophie coloured faintly even as she giggled.

"You are adorable!" Kirk couldn't restrain his need to kiss her again.

Laughter died as their lips met, and their mutual passion was reborn in a frenzy of caresses, each one a little bolder than the last, until Kirk's hand slid lightly over the silk of Sophie's stocking to discover the equally smooth skin of her inner thigh.

His long brown fingers explored delicately, slowly climbing higher and higher...

Sophie clung to him with her eyes fast shut, her breath coming in short little pants. The feelings he was arousing in her were excitingly new and so vividly intense that she could barely keep still...

"Oh!" She gasped aloud in a sudden flare of ecstasy as his skilful fingers found the core of her being and he began to gently caress her tenderest flesh until she trembled with pleasure.

A liquid heat suffused her, and of their own accord her hips began to writhe against him...

"God help me, but I want you so!"

Kirk's voice was a harsh thread of sound, shattering the silence.

"Sophie, do you understand what I'm saying?" Kirk transferred his hands to her shoulders, gripping them tightly. "If you want me to stop, my darling, it must be *now*, for I don't think I shall be able to if we carry on even for another second!"

Sophie's eyes fluttered open. "What... what did you say?" she asked reluctantly, as his urgency penetrated the pleasure-drugged haze of rapture that enfolded her.

"This is madness!"

Releasing her, he sat up abruptly.

Every fibre of her being screamed in protest. "Kirk?" She tried to put her arms around him, but he shrugged her off.

"Sweetheart, I'm no saint!" he growled.

All at once Sophie was catapulted back into harsh reality. For the first time, she could feel the straw prickling against her back and hear the rain drumming on the roof. An icy draught swirled across her naked bosom and she shivered.

"I'm sorry," she whispered, flushing painfully. "I hope you don't think...I mean...I wasn't deliberately..." She stumbled to a piteous halt.

Kirk took a deep breath, forcing down his frustration. "No, I know," he said tightly. "And, believe me, I am sorry too. More sorry than you'll ever know," he concluded ruefully.

He stood up quickly and retrieved his shirt. "I'll bring your clothes. They ought to be reasonably dry by now."

Totally tongue-tied with embarrassment, Sophie kept her gaze on the floor and nodded silently.

She had hastily adjusted her chemise by the time he returned with her dress.

"It's still damp, I'm afraid."

"It doesn't matter." Sophie took it thankfully.

By the time she had finished dressing she felt a little more composed and was able to tidy her hair with hands that no longer shook.

Kirk had already donned his coat and was inspecting the weather from the door of the barn. When Sophie joined him she saw that it was dark and the rain was still lashing down.

"Heavens, do you know what time it is?"

Kirk shook his head. "I left my watch behind at the Hyndes'," he said. "But I reckon it is about six—maybe seven—o'clock."

Sophie gazed at him in dismay. "I had no idea that it was so late!"

He grinned at her suddenly. "Well, no. We were a trifle preoccupied."

Sophie blushed, but then began to laugh, unable to resist the wicked twinkle in his eyes.

Laughter was a useful antidote to embarrassment, she decided. Her incredible foolishness had led to the brink of disaster. If Kirk had not acted so selflessly she would have thrown away her virginity and counted it well lost!

"I was to blame, Sophie," Kirk said. "If I had not been so stupid and kidnapped you there would have been no opportunity for me to behave so badly."

His uncanny ability to guess her thoughts no longer astonished Sophie. "Thank you," she murmured, accepting the apology, even though the stubbornly honest voice of her conscience knew it was not deserved. *She* had wanted him to make love to her, and they both knew it! Even now she still yearned to put her arms around him and feel his lips on hers.

Stifling this dangerous longing, she said, "Kirk, will you take me back to the Hall now? Nancy will be frantic—"

The rest of her request was drowned out by a clap of thunder.

Kirk glanced at the sky. "I suppose I could borrow a mount for you from the Hyndes'..." He paused, seeing a look of dismay cloud her expressive face. "You *can* ride?"

Sophie swallowed nervously. "Not very well," she admitted.

Kirk shook his head. "Then I don't think I can take you back tonight," he said. "Sultan hates storms. He won't suffer a stranger on his back all the way to Stanton Hall."

"But we can't stay here!" Panic made Sophie's voice rise sharply.

"I agree." Kirk's tone was wry. He was unwilling to trust his self-control a second time. Another moment and he would have taken the gift she offered so freely, plunging into the yielding softness of her delectable body and satisfying the aching need that held them both in thrall.

A cold sweat broke out along his spine. God, what a mull he had made of things!

"There's no help for it. You'll have to come up to the farm with me and spend the night there."

Sophie opened her mouth to protest at this abrupt pronouncement, but closed it again as she realised he was right. But how on earth was she going to explain to Pelham? He was bound to ask what she had been doing, wandering so far away from the Hall.

"The Hyndes are perfectly respectable. No one will question your reputation once they know you stayed with them, and I'll arrange your return first thing in the morning," Kirk reassured her.

She nodded and tried to smile.

"Good girl." Kirk touched her shoulder briefly and moved to unhook the lantern. "Come, we had best be leaving."

They ran for the stable and were drenched before they reached its shelter.

"Here, take this and tie it over your head." Kirk finished saddling up his horse and offered her a piece of ragged sacking. "It's fairly clean."

Sophie gazed at it, her lip curling. "No, thank you!" she shuddered.

"You'll lose your bonnet," he warned.

"Oh, very well!" Sophie took it with a grimace and fastened it around her head and shoulders like a muffler.

Kirk opened the stable door and the fierce wind swirled around them, making Sultan snort and back, his burnished hoofs dancing.

"Up with you."

Sophie stared at the great stallion and her mouth dried with fear. "Kirk, I . . ."

She swallowed hard, sensing his impatience. Somehow it didn't seem the right moment to confess she was frightened of horses! So with a silent prayer she allowed him to toss her up into the saddle, where she sat rigid with tension while he led Sultan outside.

"Hold him while I shut the door."

Sophie obeyed, her stomach churning. She had never sat on such a big horse before and the ground seemed very far away.

The wind howled, snatching at Sophie's hair and tugging loose several strands as it drove the rain into her face like an icy lash. Sultan neighed shrilly and began to prance.

"Steady, boy, steady." Kirk's voice was soothing. Quickly completing his task, he vaulted lightly up behind Sophie. "You did splendidly."

Thankfully Sophie relinquished the reins into his care. She could feel the warmth emanating from his tall, strong body and began to relax.

Recognising his master, Sultan settled, and they trotted sedately out of the yard.

"Lean against me if you wish."

Sophie was glad to avail herself of this invitation, but away from the farm Sultan's stride lengthened. Seized by panic, she jerked bolt upright, burying her fingers deeply into the dark mane.

"Don't worry, I've got you." Kirk adjusted his grip on the reins to hold her securely within the circle of his arms, but even his deep voice did not carry easily above the shrieking wind.

The narrow track became rougher still as the valley contracted. Her vision blurred by rain, Sophie could hardly make out the dark looming shapes that surrounded them, but she knew that they must be the mountains so close that they seemed about to fall on them.

From somewhere near by a crashing noise that must surely be a waterfall thundered above the storm, and she had to fight the impulse to clap her hands over her stunned ears.

"Not far now."

Sophie nodded to show she had heard. It was impossible to attempt conversation, but she could see that they were close to a river. The rushing waters tumbled past, an occasional flash of white spray shining eerily in the dark as they began to climb once more.

Sultan was nervous. If Kirk wasn't such a superb rider he would throw us both, Sophie thought, as the stallion bucked and reared. Every tooth in her head felt as if it was being loosened, and she had almost begun to think that her ordeal would never end when she beheld a light ahead.

Kirk swung himself down with an ease she could only envy as she allowed herself to tumble stiffly into his waiting arms.

"Oh, thank God," she groaned with relief.

Kirk chuckled. "Never mind, sweetheart. You'll feel better once we are inside."

Sophie hadn't the energy to contradict him. The short but hellish ride had left her exhausted and caked in mud; even her face was bespattered with it. A hot bath, a soothing tisane and the tender ministrations of Nancy *might* restore her, but she doubted it!

Stop wishing for the moon, Sophie Fleming, she told herself sternly.

Squaring her shoulders, she followed Kirk down a muddy path, which led to the long, low farmhouse. It was pitch-black inside the low porch, but Kirk's hand did not falter. He turned an iron handle and the heavy wooden door swung smoothly open.

"Watch out—"

Kirk's warning came too late and Sophie let out a squeak of surprise as her shin came into painful contact with an iron

horseshoe fastened to the centre of a broad oak beam let into
the floor of the doorway.

"A charm against witches," Kirk informed her apologetically.

Sophie gritted her teeth, resisting the impulse to make sar-
castic comments about the foolishness of his friends' primitive
beliefs.

It was almost as dark inside the house as it had been outside. Sophie peered around her, trying to judge her surroundings by the faint crack of light showing from under a door at the
other end of the rough-walled passage they were standing in. It
was quite long and about four feet wide, she decided, and she
could just make out a shelf at shoulder-height running along its
length.

"Keep to the middle and follow me," said Kirk.

Sophie moved cautiously after him. Beneath her feet was a
pebble floor, and her skirts brushed against lumpy shapes,
which she imagined must be sacks lining the walls.

Kirk opened the far door with a shout of greeting and then
they were in what Sophie at first took to be another, narrower,
passage, but it turned out to be just a short corridor which
opened out abruptly into what she guessed was the main living-room. It was a small, squarish chamber, dimly lit and
dominated by a massive hearth, which took up most of one wall
and was slightly raised above the slate-flagged floor.

But the room was empty.

CHAPTER SEVEN

"WHERE THE DEVIL can they be?"

Sophie scarcely heard the anxiety in Kirk's exclamation. An enormous funnel-shaped plaster chimney canopy rose above the hearth. It jutted out into the room at a height higher than Kirk's head before it narrowed and disappeared into the smoky darkness of the rafters, and her attention was riveted to the blazing fire it sheltered.

"Do you think your friends will mind if I warm myself?" she asked, her teeth chattering.

Kirk recovered his composure. "Of course they won't," he said briskly.

They both moved forward under the canopy and Sophie let out a sigh. "Oh, that's better!" She closed her eyes blissfully. "I could toast myself all night!"

Kirk grinned involuntarily. She looked a complete urchin, but he suspected that for once she was oblivious to her appearance.

The area in which they were standing was brighter than the rest of the room, thanks to the firelight and a pair of candles glowing in their tin candlesticks. Noticing them, Kirk experienced profound relief. His will power was not about to be tested to breaking-point, thank God!

"Will cannot have gone far," he announced. "He is too thrifty to waste good candles. He would have snuffed them out if he intended to stay away for more than a few minutes."

Such notions of economy had never played any part in Sophie's life, and she blinked in surprise. "I thought your friends would be rich," she blurted without thinking.

Kirk laughed somewhat harshly. "No one who farms for their living hereabouts is rich, sweetheart. It is the fancy landlords like your betrothed who wring the easy money out of these dales."

Sophie's cheeks coloured. She wished he had not brought Pelham's name up! "I did not mean to imply your friends were not gentlemen," she said stiffly, trying to suppress the wish that he had brought her to less stark surroundings.

"Gentlemen? I doubt if Will or his son Ned would care to describe themselves as such." Kirk's tone warned her that he knew what she was thinking. "I'm sorry if you are disappointed, but my friends are simple statesmen . . ."

He checked at her puzzled look. "You would describe them as small freeholders, but, don't worry, you needn't fear for the sheets. We dalesmen are quite civilised, you know."

Sophie gasped indignantly. She was too exhausted to realise that the strain of the last few hours was also beginning to tell on Kirk, and heard only the sharpness in his tone.

"You are being very unfair, Kirk Thorburn," she said angrily. "If it weren't for you, I would not be in the awkward position of having to ask strangers for help. Or have you forgotten why we have to seek shelter? It is your fault—"

The sound of the front door banging made her pause. Footsteps followed, and she hastily composed her expression to serenity.

An elderly little gnome of a man dressed in brown fustian advanced into the room, followed by another man, similarly dressed, but much younger and broadly built.

The older man's weather-beaten face broke into a smile as he caught sight of them. "Why, Kirk. Welcome, lad. I'm sorry we weren't here to greet ye, but we were checking on the flock."

"Will." Kirk shook the older man's hand. "I've come to ask you a favour. Do you think you could shelter a friend of mine tonight?" He drew Sophie forward. "We were caught out by the storm."

Suppressing her annoyance, Sophie exerted herself to exchange polite greetings with her host and his son.

"Aye, both of ye must stay the night." Will nodded his balding head vigorously. "Ye can have my chamber, Miss Fleming. I'll sleep up in the loft with the others."

Sophie flushed. "I have no wish to inconvenience you, sir," she murmured.

It hadn't occurred to her that there would only be one bedchamber.

"Ain't no bother, lass." He turned to his son. "Ned, go and see to Sultan," he ordered.

With a silent nod the tall young man left the room.

"Now, will ye take a bite of supper?"

Sophie was so tired that her appetite had deserted her, but she sensed that the old man would be disappointed if she refused, so she accepted his hospitality with a pretty show of thanks that won her a smile of approval from Kirk.

Pointedly Sophie ignored him. The impudence of the man! Did he think she had no manners?

"Mebbe ye would like to wash your hands first?" Will asked her hesitantly.

"Please!" Sophie suddenly realised what a fright she must look.

"Come with me, lass."

Sophie followed her host to a door at the opposite end of the room. It opened on to a small bedchamber, and when Will had lit the solitary candle that stood on the plain wooden wash-stand he said, "I'll fetch ye some hot water and a clean towel."

It was too dark to see much of her surroundings, but Sophie noticed a rocking-chair under the window and a carved kist at the foot of the half-tester bed, which took up most of the remaining space. Although uncurtained, it had a handsomely carved bedhead of fruit and flowers entwined in an intricate design.

Experimentally, she pressed the mattress with the flat of her hand. It felt hard, but mercifully free of lumps.

Sophie longed to stretch out her weary limbs, but she resisted the temptation. Her gown was muddy and she didn't want to spoil the coverlet.

A knock at the door heralded her host's arrival. "Here ye are." He set down a jug and sliver of soap on the wash-stand. "I wish I could offer ye some dry clothes, but perhaps this will do ye later as a nightgown. Kirk thought ye might like it. It's one of his. He keeps a change of clothes here, ye see. It'll be too big, of course, but it's good linen and clean."

"Thank you." Sophie took the shirt he held out to her. The material was fine and soft and she could smell a hint of lavender lingering in the folds.

I wonder who took such trouble to launder it so nicely? Was it the mysterious Rose?

The thought popped unbidden into her mind, but she dismissed it firmly. She had enough to worry about without indulging in such useless speculations.

The bedchamber was unheated, and Sophie shivered as she completed her hasty ablutions. Once she was comparatively clean she turned her attention to her hair. Most of the pins had fallen out and her ringlets were in painful confusion. Lacking a comb, she could only attempt to smooth them with her fingers.

There was no dressing-table, but a glance in the little mirror hung up on the white-washed wall revealed what a dismal failure her efforts had been.

"You look terrible," she told her reflection.

Her re-entry into the living-room brought the three men seated at the massive oak dining-table to their feet. Feeling somewhat self-conscious, Sophie allowed Will to usher her to a chair next to Kirk's, and a plate loaded with a generous helping of rabbit pie was placed before her.

"Will ye try some ale, Miss Fleming?"

"Do you have any tea?" Sophie responded without thinking.

"Nay, we don't drink tea, 'cepting on rare occasions. 'Tis too dear," Will informed her rather apologetically.

"Oh, I see." Sophie coloured, cursing her tactlessness. "Then I'll take some ale, if I may," she said, avoiding Kirk's gaze as she accepted the pewter tankard he handed her.

He had changed out of his muddy clothes and was wearing a suit of dark green corduroy. It was plainly cut, but, watching him covertly under the pretence of eating her meal, she decided that no one would ever mistake him for a simple farmer. He had the unmistakable air of a man accustomed to authority, his manner a blend of assurance and self-confidence that had no need to resort to arrogance.

He is the true gentleman, not Pelham, Sophie thought in a sudden blinding flash of understanding. He is easy in his own skin; he doesn't need to shore himself up with fancy clothes and possessions to prove his worth.

If Pelham were here now he would be trying to lord it over everyone. Annoyed though she was with him, Sophie knew that Kirk would never stoop to such tactics.

He is different. He has no need to impress anyone. That's why Will and Ned like him. They sense his friendship is genuine.

And it is one of the reasons why you love him, the same little voice in her head said so matter-of-factly that it took Sophie a moment to register its import.

She sat very still.

Could it be true? Had she really fallen for a man everyone else believed to be a womaniser? Oh, she knew she was attracted to him in a physical way! That had never been in any doubt, but love was more than just desire. There had to be liking too, and respect. She had never been in love before, but she was sure of that. Just as she was sure that she enjoyed Kirk's company more than anyone else's. He might drive her distracted at times, but she was never bored when he was around.

I care about him, she thought dreamily; that's why I can't stop thinking about him. I wasn't really sure of my feelings until today, but as soon as I met him again I knew it wasn't infatuation. He is very good-looking, but there is more to it than that. I admire him. He has more determination and energy than any man I've met, and I want to spend the rest of my life making him happy.

Sophie took a deep breath. She had answered her own question.

SOPHIE AWOKE to a hard grey light pouring in from the uncurtained window. Momentarily disorientated, she lay quite still, her brain whirling.

Of course! She was at the Hyndes' farm in Watendlath. Kirk had brought her here last night after they had been trapped by a rain-storm.

Kirk. A rosy glow of warmth enveloped her as she thought of him and the tender way he had bidden her goodnight.

When supper had ended Will Hynde was all for a sociable discussion of what had brought Sophie to the shores of Derwent Water, but Kirk had intervened.

"I think Miss Fleming is tired, Will," he had said gently, curbing the old man's chatter.

"Aye, mebbe it would be best if ye retired, lass. Ye look right pale." Will had smiled sympathetically. "I'll lay fresh sheets on the bed and put in a hot brick to help warm ye."

He had bustled off, firmly refusing Sophie's tentative offer of assistance with a chuckling comment that he'd been a widower for many years and was well able to manage domestic chores.

"I'll away and fix Dad up a pallet in the loft," Ned had said, getting to his feet. "There's one ready for ye, Kirk, if ye've a mind to stay."

"I think I must." Kirk had smiled ruefully. "From the sound of it, that rain hasn't abated yet."

Even the thick stone walls of the farmhouse could not disguise the noise of the storm, and Ned nodded.

"Shall I check on Sultan for ye afore I go up?"

"No, thank you, Ned. I'll see to him myself in a minute."

The room seemed very quiet when Ned was gone, and Sophie desperately wanted to say something to break the silence, but it was as if the knowledge of her true feelings lay like a lead weight on her tongue.

"Sophie..." Kirk started to speak and then stopped.

She stared at him as he abruptly pushed back his chair and began pacing the flagstones.

"I...I... Blister it, but I don't know how to say this to you!" Kirk ran a hand through his thick hair in a distracted gesture.

Sophie rose to her feet in alarm. "Kirk?"

He turned back to face her, his expression rueful.

"I'd be a liar if I pretended remorse for what happened earlier at Haraldsgarth, but I don't want you to go to bed thinking I am a complete boor. You are a well-bred young lady. I shouldn't have treated you that way and I'm sorry if my lack of control upset you."

Sophie echoed blankly. "Upset me?"

A tinge of red showed in his sun-bronzed face and realisation dawned. "Oh, I see," she murmured.

He looked so uncomfortable that she was tempted to tease him, but she shook her head and said firmly, "There's no need to apologise for treating me as a flesh-and-blood woman! I'm not some mindless porcelain figurine, Kirk. I was as much to blame as you." She lifted her chin defiantly. "It was very wrong of me, but I wanted you to kiss me."

Kirk stared at her with dawning respect. "By God, but you are honest, Sophie Fleming!" he exclaimed.

Every other woman he had ever known would have pretended a simpering coyness, happy to enjoy the pleasure of their misdemeanours while laying the blame upon his shoulders.

Sophie shrugged. "I know. It is very inconvenient!" She grinned at him suddenly. "I wish I were not so outspoken. You can have no notion of the trouble my unruly tongue gets me into."

He crossed to her side in a couple of swift strides and, clasping her hands in his, smiled down at her.

"Don't ever change, Sophie," he said softly. "You are unique." And he raised her hands to his lips and kissed them both in turn before releasing her.

"Sleep well and try not to worry. You will be back with Nancy in the morning."

Sophie had drifted off to bed on a cloud of happiness, where, contrary to her expectations, she had fallen asleep as soon as her head touched the pillow.

Her dreams had been sweet.

Sophie smiled. Not even the uncomfortable thought that she still had to face Sir Pelham could disturb her this morning.

She stretched luxuriously, inhaling the faint smell of lavender that arose from her unconventional nightgown. She snuggled its generous folds around her. It had given her a secret pleasure to wear something that belonged to Kirk.

I wonder if he is awake yet, she thought, wishing she knew what time it was.

Then, just as she was debating on whether or not it was too early to rise, she heard voices.

The sound was surprisingly loud, and as she glanced up she saw to her astonishment that the inner wall of the bedchamber did not reach the ceiling. Last night it had been too dark to notice, but it wasn't a solid wall at all, but merely a wooden partition, dividing the chamber from the living-room.

"Damn it, are you sure, Will?"

Sophie detected Kirk's deep tones.

"I hope I'm wrong, lad, but Ned seemed certain, and ye know how good he is with nags."

"Yes, of course. Well, I'd better go and see for myself."

Kirk's voice sounded fainter, as if he was moving away.

On the point of leaping out bed to go and find out what was wrong, Sophie was startled by a brisk knock at the door.

"Come in."

A brown-haired young woman in her late twenties entered. She had a pretty face, but Sophie saw how her figure was heavily swollen by pregnancy.

"Good morning to ye. I'm Rose, Will's daughter," she announced with a cheerful smile.

"*You* are Rose!"

The girl nodded, plainly puzzled. "Aye. I'm married to Sam Braithewaite. He lives close by. Did Dad not mention it?"

"Er—no." Sophie fell back against her pillows, stifling the urge to giggle. So much for her wild imaginings! Let that be a lesson to you, Sophie Fleming, she admonished herself, not to be so hasty in future.

Rose smiled at her placidly. "I'm glad to see you have recovered, miss. Dad came over early to tell us how you had got caught in the storm, and I've brung ye something to wear."

"How very kind of you!" Sophie sat up and beamed at her. "I'll get up."

"Nay. 'Tis a bitter morning. Bide where ye are 'til I've fetched you some washing water and then I'll help you get dressed."

Amused by Rose's brisk manner, Sophie nodded meekly and stayed under the covers until the older girl returned.

"You were right. It is a lot colder today," Sophie observed with a shiver when she emerged from her warm nest.

The chill in the air encouraged her to wash quickly, in spite of feeling rather stiff and sore from yesterday. Her undergarments had dried overnight, and she put them on as Rose unwrapped the gown she had brought.

"I hope it will fit you," Rose said doubtfully. "Dad never said you were so tall."

Correctly guessing that the plainly styled brown kerseymere was probably Rose's best, Sophie smiled polite thanks, but her heart sank. Those wide skirts were years behind the fashion and brown was not her colour; it drained her pale skin of life.

As she had feared, the gown did nothing to enhance her looks. The bodice, cut for Rose's ample curves, hung loose on her in an unflattering manner and the skirt was several inches too short, revealing a scandalous amount of slim leg.

"Eeh, it won't do! I am sorry!" Rose shook her dark head. "Mebbe you'd best wear your own dress after all."

Sophie picked up the stained merino. She had hung it over the back of the rocking-chair to dry, but it was still very damp.

"Perhaps I could try sponging it clean for ye. 'Tis still windy. It ought to dry quite quick," Rose suggested doubtfully.

"I think it is beyond help," Sophie replied with a faint grin, dropping it carelessly on to the floor. "And anyway, there isn't time. So I think I shall have to wear your gown if you don't mind lending it me for a day or two, Rose. You see, I must go home this morning, but I will send it back to you."

Sitting down on the edge of the bed to draw on her high boots, Sophie missed the expression that crossed Rose's plump face.

"Well, at least these should ensure no one's modesty is offended."

Rose smiled faintly.

Sophie moved to the mirror and fluffed out her untidy hair. "I don't think I know where to start," she muttered ruefully.

"I've brung my comb. Shall I give ye a hand?"

"Would you? Oh, thank you." Sophie hurried to sit down. "Nancy—that's my maid—always says I haven't the least notion of how to dress hair!" Sophie grinned. "She's right, too. All I do is make my eyes water!"

"Such pretty hair," Rose murmured, deftly drawing the wooden comb through the tangled mass of curls.

Sophie twisted round to gape at her. "You cannot think so! It is a dreadful colour!"

"Well, it is very red, to be sure, but I wish my hair was so thick and shiny. I'd swap my mouse-tails with ye any day," Rose chuckled, pulling a brown strand free from the mob-cap she wore.

This compliment left Sophie speechless.

"There, I'm done." Rose stood back and gave her handiwork a critical look. "Aye. Ye'll do." She nodded decisively. "Now will ye come and break your fast? I made some poddish earlier for the men and it should be still hot."

Sophie obediently followed her into the living-room. "Have the others breakfasted already?"

"Aye." Rose sounded surprised. "'Tis gone seven. But I let you sleep on. Kirk said not to disturb ye too early."

Sophie blinked. At home she never rose before eight.

"I'll put on some elding to brighten the fire," Rose announced, pausing by the wooden bench which stood fixed to the wall by the hearth.

Seeing Sophie's slightly puzzled expression, she laughed. "That's what we call fuel hereabouts. We have lots of special names for things in the dales." She waved a hand to the bench.

"This is called a scone and the corridor behind it is known as the mell. It acts as a screen to cut out draughts, you see."

Sophie nodded, trying to look interested. What she really wanted to know was where Kirk could have got to, but she didn't like to interrupt her new friend, who was now in full flow.

"The big passageway ye entered by is called the hallan. It separates what we use as living quarters from the down-house, which is the service area. I'll show it to ye later if ye like, but first ye had best have your breakfast," Rose concluded briskly, pulling out several bricks of peat from beneath the scone and arranging them carefully on the glowing embers.

"Ye'll find a bowl and spoon in that cupboard," Rose said, pointing it out to Sophie.

While Sophie found these items Rose drew on the adjustable chain hung from a beam set across the chimney-breast and swung the iron pot it held off the fire. It was full of porridge, and Rose filled Sophie's bowl with a generous helping.

When Sophie declined the offer of ale to drink with it Rose asked if she would prefer some milk, and when she nodded said, "I'll get a jug for ye from the buttery, then."

She moved past the massive dining-table to a door Sophie hadn't noticed in last night's gloom. Out of curiosity Sophie followed her and saw that the buttery was a tiny room, lit by a large window let into the thick stone wall.

"It is very cold in here," she murmured.

Rose grinned. "It's north-facing to help stop the milk turning."

Sophie surveyed the great cheese press standing in one corner alongside a large butter churn and a long wooden bench tidily set with assorted crocks and butterhands. Several empty milk pails stood underneath, while on the shelf above varioussized cheeses were maturing.

"It were churning-day last week, so there is plenty of butter, and cream too if ye like it on your poddish," Rose commented, picking up a jug of milk from the bench.

Sophie refused, anxious to get back to the fire, but to her disappointment Rose would not stay to keep her company while she ate but announced that she had to leave.

"I'd like to chat for a while, but Sam is minding the little ones," she explained almost apologetically.

"You have other children?" Sophie exclaimed with an involuntary glance at Rose's swelling figure.

"I've four at home." Rose nodded proudly. "Three boys and one girl, little imps all."

"They must keep you very busy," Sophie murmured half enviously.

She liked children and suddenly it occurred to her that she would enjoy having a baby of her own. Kirk's baby. A bonny little boy, perhaps with hair as golden as a guinea . . .

Sophie blushed furiously at her thoughts.

"Ye must come to our cottage and meet them. If ye get time, of course," Rose added hastily.

Something about her tone made Sophie glance at her sharply, but before she could frame a question Kirk walked into the room.

"I'll be off, then," Rose announced with what sounded suspiciously like relief, and she whisked out of the room with a speed that belied her condition.

"Good morning. I hope you slept well."

Kirk smiled at her and Sophie forgot her suspicions in the sheer pleasure of gazing at him.

"Like a babe." Her wide mouth curled up at the corners as she replied.

"I see Rose brought you a dress. I was sure she would want to help."

"Yes, she was very kind." Ruefully Sophie reflected that yet again he was seeing her unflatteringly garbed.

"Have you eaten?"

Sophie indicted her bowl of porridge. "I've almost finished."

"Don't hurry." Kirk sat down opposite her.

Sophie spooned up the last mouthful and swallowed it hastily. "But we have to leave soon," she pointed out.

A shadow passed over Kirk's clear-cut features.

"Actually, there is a slight problem," he murmured.

"I knew it!" Sophie's expression hardened. "I could tell Rose was concealing something."

"Hang on, sweetheart," Kirk said, half laughing. "Damme, if I ever knew a girl so hot to hand!"

Sophie flushed. "I'm sorry." She shrugged awkwardly. "I know I am too impetuous, but there is something wrong, isn't there?"

"I'm afraid so. Sultan's left hock has developed a slight strain. I've put a poultice on it, but he won't be fit to ride for a couple of days."

"Oh, no!"

"What's worse, Ned left early to pick up some supplies in Keswick."

"Don't they have more horses to spare?" Sophie asked hopefully.

Kirk shook his head, frowning. "It's partly my fault. I should have asked Will last night if I could borrow a mount, but we got talking of other matters and I assumed there would be plenty of time to sort something out this morning." He gave her a rueful grin. "But then I overslept."

Sophie was about to remonstrate when it occurred to her that he had still got up long before she had done, so instead she asked him if he knew when Ned would be back.

"Probably not until late afternoon. Will said he was planning to eat his dinner at the Queen's Head inn."

"Damn!" Sophie was betrayed into an unladylike exclamation. "Nancy will be worried sick by now."

Kirk saw how her great dark eyes clouded and said abruptly, "We could always walk."

Sophie stared at him, open-mouthed. Then, realising it was hardly flattering, she snapped her lips shut as he continued, "It isn't so very far. We could probably do it in less than three hours."

"You would come with me?" Sophie couldn't keep a note of gladness out of her voice.

He grinned at her. "I was planning to ask Ned to escort you, since I didn't think I would be a very welcome visitor, but in the circumstances..." He shrugged. "It's the least I can do."

Sophie immediately decided that she would persuade him to leave her once they got in sight of the gatehouse.

It will only cause more trouble if Pelham thinks I have been with Kirk, she thought. She bit her lip. Last night sleep had claimed her before she'd had time to review the impossible situation she now found herself in with regard to the baronet, but she couldn't keep postponing a decision.

What am I going to do? It was difficult enough, heaven knows, to reconcile myself to marrying him when I wasn't certain of the depths of my feelings for Kirk! Now I know I love

Kirk I don't think I can go through with it, not even to please Uncle Thomas.

Sophie winced. The scandal was going to be immense.

Kirk's deep voice broke into her troubled thoughts.

"You'll need to wrap up warmly. It has turned very cold and that pelisse of yours isn't going to keep the wind out."

"It wasn't designed for walking on these fells," Sophie retorted tartly.

Kirk grinned at her. "Come on. Let's have a look in the down-house. Will keeps all sorts of spare garments in there. We might find something to fit you."

Relinquishing all hope of ever looking presentable, Sophie agreed to this plan and followed him out across the wide passageway Rose had called the hallan and into a large chamber open to the rafters.

It was full of interesting-looking objects whose use Sophie hadn't the faintest idea of, but then she spotted something she did recognise.

A spinning-wheel stood against one rough wall, and she reached out a hand to touch it. "I've always wanted to try one of these," she murmured.

Kirk looked up from sorting through a rack of cloaks hung up near the door. "That used to belong to Will's wife," he informed her. "But you should ask Rose to give you lessons if you are interested. She makes fine cloth."

He turned his attention back to his search and Sophie wondered wistfully if she would ever get the chance. In spite of the differences in their station she had liked Rose, and instinct told her that they could be friends if only they had the chance to spend any time together.

But would she ever come to Watendlath again? Her future seemed so uncertain!

Yesterday Kirk had said he wanted her, but he had not spoken of love. Coming to terms with her own feelings had been a marvellous release, making her feel happier than she had done in weeks, but now that her first euphoria was over Sophie suddenly realised with a sense of shock that nothing else had changed.

How could she have been so blind? Happiness had dazzled her into thinking that all might be well if only she could withdraw from her unwanted betrothal, but how did Kirk feel? He desired her, but was that all?

He cares about me; he doesn't want me to become entangled with Pelham, she told herself stoutly.

But he is a kind man. His concern might stem purely from chivalrous motives, answered the obstinately honest voice in her head.

He likes me. I know he does!

Yes, but does he like you enough to give up his carefree bachelor existence? Because that's what you want, isn't it, Sophie Fleming? You want to marry him and nothing less will do!

Sophie shivered.

"I'm sorry, I know it's cold in here," Kirk apologised. "Anyway, I think I've found something which will help." And he held out a stout hodden cloak to her.

Sophie took it with a silent nod.

She was very quiet as they completed their preparations, and Kirk began to feel slightly worried. Was she so nervous about having to explain her absence to Stanton? I won't let her face him alone, Kirk vowed to himself.

Aloud, he said, "I'll write a quick note for Will in case we don't see him on our way and then we'll be off."

Kirk lifted down a ponderous family bible from the recessed shelf above the small window which gave light to the hearth. Beneath it lay a supply of writing-paper, which somehow didn't surprise Sophie. The Hyndes were not the simple, illiterate farmers one might expect to find in such a remote spot.

She sat down to wait on a stool by the fire. Staring into the flames, she remembered that Kirk had said that they did not claim to be gentlemen, but Will's conversation at supper last night had shown he had a sound grasp of what was going on in the wider world beyond Watendlath.

"Education is much prized here in the dales, though not, I must admit, for women," Kirk remarked, looking up from where he was sitting at the dining-table and guessing at her thoughts with the perception she found so uncanny.

He laid down his pen. "It goes hand in hand with their fierce sense of independence. You won't find statesmen like Will showing any deference due to rank or position. They judge a man by his actions, and birth or wealth alone will not win their respect."

"You really despise Pelham, don't you?" Sophie exclaimed impulsively.

Kirk shrugged. "I won't deny that I was thinking of him," he admitted. He gave her an intent look. "How much do you know of Stanton's background?"

Startled by the unexpected question, Sophie spread her hands wide in an uncertain gesture. "Not very much."

"They aren't a local family, you know. His grandfather was a Derbyshire blacksmith who made good and brought his family here when he retired. His wife hailed from Cockermouth and apparently enjoyed the idea of returning north as a lady, but she filled her son's head with such grandiose notions that he ended up building that absurd house."

Kirk's well-cut mouth curled derisively. "He also decided to send his son away to school to become a proper gentleman. I dare say Pelham went through hell, but when he came back he'd lost his accent and was more inclined to despise the rest of us than ever."

Sophie winced at the memory he evoked of Sir Alan's soirée. That was the first time she had begun to realise how snobbishly arrogant her suitor was, but foolishly she had ignored her misgivings.

"Unfortunately for him, even after his father died and there was no evidence left to remind them of his lowly origins, the local gentry still regarded him as an upstart and wouldn't accept him as their equal. That's when he removed to live more or less permanently in London. From what I can gather, he was able to play the fine lord there to his heart's content, but he became addicted to the gaming-tables."

He gave Sophie a level stare. "And that's why he's hanging out for a rich wife."

She bit her lip. "I'm beginning to believe you."

Kirk's heart gave a joyful leap. "Then you'll reconsider your decision to continue with this betrothal?"

Sophie hesitated. "I think I must," she muttered in a low voice, fidgeting with a fold of brown kerseymere and avoiding his gaze.

She longed for the courage to tell him the real reason why she doubted if she could go through with the marriage, but pride forbade her to make the first move. She would not shame herself by appearing eager for his kisses! It was bad enough having to admit that she'd been wrong.

"I'm glad." Kirk carefully refrained from saying more. One wrong word and he might undo all the good he had achieved.

He stood up and placed the note where Will was sure to find it. "It's time we were leaving."

Sophie nodded, but she got to her feet with a strange reluctance. Now that the moment had come, she found herself wanting to stay. For a few brief hours she had been happy here!

OUTSIDE the cold struck Sophie like a blow.

"No one would think it was March," she gasped.

"Take my arm." Kirk moved so that he was sheltering her from the icy wind.

Sophie smiled at him gratefully. "Thank you. I think I've caught my breath now."

The wind got worse as they left the shelter of the porch, and, even huddled within the thick hodden cloak, Sophie shivered.

"Oh, Kirk, how beautiful!"

Last night it had been too dark to catch a glimpse of her surroundings, but now the magnificence of the scenery made her forget the temperature for the moment.

Ahead lay a narrow, ancient stone bridge, its graceful arch spanning a turbulent stream. Beyond it, Sophie could see a swirling waterfall, descending in a ladder of pools from a small round lake whose rippling waters reflected back the pewter-dark sky.

In the distance hills arose, and on their greening lower slopes she spotted a flock of greyish-fleeced sheep.

"Those are Will's Herdwicks," Kirk informed her. "Tough little devils they are too."

"I should think they need to be," Sophie replied, noticing how the hilltops were still smothered in winter snow.

She turned to watch the stream, which she knew was often called a beck, tumble away down the valley.

"Is that the way we rode up here?" she asked, marveling at the narrow chasm.

Kirk grinned. "Aye. Quite a sight, eh?"

Sophie nodded wordlessly. The whole valley seemed to hang like a jewel in its cup of hills, isolated from the rest of the world.

But it wasn't completely cut off, she realised, spotting a narrow trail up the fell away to the east. "Where does that lead to?"

"It's the pack-horse route over the Armboth," Kirk said. "There's another out to Rosthwaite too," he added, pointing out a track Sophie had missed. "But neither of them is of any use to us. I'm afraid we have to go back the way we came."

Sophie had been afraid he would say that. Suddenly the scenery lost its power to charm away the vicious cold, and she sighed.

But as they began walking she started to warm up and strode out more vigorously, trying to match Kirk's long stride. The journey didn't seem quite so daunting now that they were on their way.

"At this rate we'll be at the Hall before noon," she said cheerfully.

Kirk glanced up at the grey sky. "Providing it doesn't snow."

Sophie's expressive face fell. "Snow," she echoed in disbelief. "But it's spring. It can't snow!"

"I'm afraid it can," Kirk retorted grimly. "And, if it does, there'll be the devil to pay with this wind. We'll just have to hope it holds off long enough for us to reach our destination."

He smiled down into her suddenly anxious face.

"Don't look so concerned, sweetheart. I wouldn't have started out if I thought we couldn't make it in time. Only fools take risks on these fells."

"But how will you get back if there's a blizzard?" Sophie demanded, ignoring his attempt to comfort her. "I know you wouldn't accept Pelham's hospitality, even if he were to offer it!"

Kirk looked amused. "No, I wouldn't," he agreed with a slight shrug of his broad shoulders.

Sophie would have argued, but he forestalled her. "There's no guarantee it will snow. But if it does, let me worry about it."

Sophie could see he had made his mind up, and since he was probably even more obstinate than she was herself she knew she wouldn't get any sense out of him on the subject, so she merely sniffed eloquently.

When the going got rough soon afterwards she was glad she had saved her breath. She wasn't used to walking in such conditions and her boots weren't strong enough. Every sharp stone on the rutted path seemed to cut into her and her weak ankle was beginning to ache abominably.

I shall have blisters, she thought ruefully, her pace slowing as they reached a particularly rough patch.

Kirk turned to offer her a helping hand, but she waved him on.

"I think I shall do better on my own for a minute," she said rather breathlessly, not wishing to admit she was finding it hard to keep up.

Guessing what was going through her mind, Kirk did not insist, but tactfully walked on as slowly as possible.

I wish I could tell her how I admire her spirit, he thought. Most women would have been complaining long since! She hadn't even moaned about wearing a dress he knew she hated.

Kirk grinned briefly to himself. Once he'd thought it impossible to find a woman who was prepared to ignore her looks when necessary, but he hadn't known Sophie well then.

But it would be foolish to pay her compliments, his conscience warned. Already you have become far more involved than is wise. Your duty is to Ingram's memory, and she is a distraction you can do without.

Wrapped up in his thoughts, Kirk failed to register that someone was coming up the valley.

"Kirk? Kirk! Kirk Thorburn!"

The shouts echoed from the rocks, startling Sophie, who ran forward, her sore feet forgotten. She clasped Kirk's arm, staring in alarm at the heavily swathed and bundled-up figure staggering wildly up the track towards them.

"Who is it?" she gasped. "Do you know who it is?"

Kirk stiffened.

The figure came nearer, becoming recognisably female.

"Kirk! Oh, God, it *is* you!"

"Do you know her?" Sophie demanded, but, to her dismay, instead of answering Kirk shook off the restraint of her anxious hand on his arm.

He walked slowly forward like a man in a dream.

The woman stopped, dropping the small valise she carried. Then, as she waited for him to reach her, she threw back her enveloping hood to reveal a face of surpassing loveliness.

Watching in thunderstruck amazement, Sophie saw her throw her arms around Kirk's neck.

"Oh, darling, how I have missed you!" she cried, reaching up to kiss him.

CHAPTER EIGHT

AFTER WHAT SEEMED an eternity, Kirk disengaged the girl's arms from around his neck and stood back.

"That's enough," he said gruffly.

A trill of silvery laughter answered him.

"Dear me! Haven't you forgiven me yet, my love?"

There was a mocking note in the husky contralto voice, and the frown on Kirk's handsome face deepened.

Recovering from her astonishment, Sophie moved forward to join them.

The girl's violet-blue eyes scanned her up and down with rapid calculation and then her pink rosebud mouth curled dismissively.

Sophie gritted her teeth. "Won't you introduce us, Kirk?"

"Miss Sophie Fleming. Miss Rebecca Hurst," he said as though the words choked him.

"How formal you have grown, Kirk! It used to be Becky, remember." The husky voice was caressing and she tapped him meaningfully on the arm.

"That was a long time ago."

The curtness of this reply was not lost on Sophie, and the anguish gripping her heart eased. He doesn't care for her, she decided with relief.

The beautiful stranger didn't seem put out by Kirk's coolness.

"A lifetime," she agreed, "but some things don't change." She smiled sweetly. "You are just the same."

"Don't count on it, Becky."

Now where have I heard that name before? Sophie thought anxiously. Her brain wouldn't oblige. It was too blasted cold to think, yet she was sure it was important if only she could remember.

"Why have you come back?" Kirk's tone remained as unpromising as the weather. "Your family moved away years ago."

Sophie thought she detected a look of remorse flash over the blonde's perfect features, but it vanished so quickly that she couldn't be sure she hadn't imagined it.

"I'm here to see Rose."

Kirk stared at her hard. "Does she know you are coming?"

A petulant shrug answered him. "As a matter of fact, I didn't have time to write to her, but I know she will be more welcoming than you!" The violet eyes turned defiant. "She was always a good friend of mine."

Sophie's curiosity deepened. There were undercurrents here she didn't understand.

"Rose has always been too tender-hearted," Kirk said. "But this time you've made a mistake, Becky. She can't pander to your whims. She's with child and the babe is expected soon."

Becky paled as the implications of his remark sank in.

"But I *need* a place to stay," she whispered, almost seeming to shrink in on herself.

After a moment of tense silence she straightened, her slight figure becoming rigid. "Kirk, don't try to stop me," she said tightly, the flippancy draining from her manner. "I want to come home!"

"You made your choice ten years ago." Sophie had never imagined that Kirk's attractive voice could sound so harsh. "It's too late to change your mind now. Go back to London and your inamorato."

Bitter laughter answered him.

"You fool, why do you think I'm here? He has thrown me out. I've nowhere else to go."

In spite of her initial dislike, Sophie felt a stirring of sympathy for the older girl as tears began to stream down Becky's face.

"Do you really expect me to feel sorry for you?" Kirk demanded with a fury that made Sophie wince.

She had never seen him look so angry and she wasn't in the least bit surprised when Becky began to cry in earnest.

"You are cruel, Kirk Thorburn!" she sobbed wildly. "Cruel to hold a grudge after all this time! But I won't let you stop me." Her face turned even more pale. "Don't you understand? I can't go back, I can't!'' she screamed on a rising note of hysteria.

"Kirk." Sophie laid an urgent hand on his arm. "I don't know what this is all about, but I do know she is badly over-wrought. Please don't provoke her further, I beg you."

His mouth tightened. "She always threw fits of temper whenever she couldn't get her own way," he said savagely. "It is all affectation. She can cry at will."

Sophie tugged at his sleeve. "Please."

He jerked his head in reluctant assent, but it was already too late.

With one last hysterical sob Becky collapsed into a deep faint, and only Kirk's swift reactions enabled him to catch her as she fell.

"Damn!" Kirk said with feeling. "What the devil do we do now?" He glared down at the fragile burden he held in his arms. There were deep shadows beneath the closed eyelids and he could feel an unhealthy heat emanating from the waxen skin. "I think she might be genuinely ill."

Sophie hesitated for a fraction, but even as she struggled to reconcile her obvious Christian duty with her desperate desire to return to Stanton Hall a featherlight snowflake drifted down from the leaden sky to brush her cheek.

"We'll have to turn back," she answered wryly, picking up the abandoned valise. "There is nothing else we can do."

"COME AWAY IN." Will Hynde wasted no time in asking questions when they appeared on his doorstep, but took the valise from Sophie's weary hand and bustled ahead to build up the fire.

"Lay her down there, lad," he said, turning to point at the scone-bench as they followed him into the room. "I'll fetch a blanket . . ."

Sophie saw his expression change.

"Good God, Parson Hurst's daughter!" Will's gaze flew to Kirk's face. "What's she doing here?"

Kirk said laconically, "You'll have to ask her."

"I'll not have that strumpet in my house!"

Sophie blinked in surprise.

"Come, Will, can't you see she's ill?" Kirk laid the uncon-scious girl down and straightened to face his friend.

Strumpet? Becky?

Sophie's brain worked furiously and the elusive memory clicked into place.

"She's the one, isn't she? The girl who was the cause of your leaving home?"

Her outburst interrupted their heated discussion.

Kirk answered her anxious gaze with a tiny shrug, but Will said bluntly, "Aye. She blamed Kirk for her condition, the little trouble-maker—"

"Leave it, Will," Kirk said sharply. "It's water long since under the bridge."

"Nay, I'll not be silent this time, lad." Will ignored the interruption. "I kept my mouth shut to please ye once before, but I'll not see that slut blacken the Thorburn name again. Your father was my good friend and I owe his memory that much at least!"

Becky began to stir, and Will glared at her. "Ye should have denied her insinuations at the time. Because ye did not wish folk to think her a whore, everyone assumed she was telling the truth. When ye left in such a hurry it only confirmed their belief that ye were responsible."

"I thought I was acting for the best." Kirk's expression hardened. "It turned sour at the end, but she meant a lot to me once, Will, and I won't see her insulted. If you intend to turn her out, I must warn you that I'll leave too."

Sophie winced at Kirk's implacable tone. He hadn't seemed pleased to see Becky, but now he was defending her. Perhaps his love for her hadn't faded as much as he claimed.

Will snorted. "Ye are a fool, lad!" He shook his balding head. "Oh, very well, she may stay here until she recovers, but don't expect me to wait on her."

"Thank you." Kirk smiled at him.

"Mind, once she is on her feet again I won't house her," Will added sternly. "She's nothing but trouble, and ye'd do well to remember it, lad."

This warning delivered, Will stomped out of the room, his slight figure stiff with indignation.

Sophie let out the breath she didn't realise she had been holding and Kirk flashed her a rueful smile before moving to check on Becky, who seemed to have slipped into a restless sleep.

"She is hot. I think she would do better out of this damp cloak," he said, feeling Becky's forehead.

"Oh, let me do it!" Sophie exclaimed, watching him struggle to remove Becky's thick outer garments.

When she had performed this task with a neat dexterity that made Kirk stare Sophie said, "I'll fetch some pillows and a blanket from Will's room."

Returning swiftly, she covered the older girl up, noting with a faint envy how beautifully Becky's expensive silk gown clung to her voluptuous curves.

"There. At least she won't catch a chill." Sophie stared thoughtfully at the sleeping girl. "I wonder what is wrong with her. Still, her fever isn't very high and she doesn't show any other signs of illness that I recognise, so I don't think it can be very serious."

"If she's been travelling in this bad weather she's probably more exhausted than anything else," Kirk commented. He surveyed Sophie and added tersely, "And so will you be if you don't sit down, my girl."

Sophie grinned, but obediently sat by the fire.

"Here, drink this."

Sophie took one of the tankards of mulled ale he had prepared while she had been out of the room.

"Thank you." She sipped it gratefully, relishing the glow it spread through her weary limbs.

"It is I who should thank you," Kirk replied with engaging frankness. "Becky looks much more comfortable now. You are very efficient. Where did you learn the knack of nursing people so well?"

"My uncle has been poorly on several occasions these last few years," Sophie said, cupping her long, slim fingers around her tankard. "Nothing serious. I wouldn't claim to be able to deal with any real illness, but I do know enough to make myself useful in the sick-room."

Kirk nodded thoughtfully.

There was a short silence and then Kirk said abruptly, "You must wish the lot of us at the devil. You would be safely back with Nancy by now if we hadn't met Becky."

"It can't be helped," Sophie muttered gruffly, inordinately pleased by the fact that he was thinking of her in the midst of his own problems.

"None the less, I am sorry. It wasn't my intention to embroil you in my affairs, Sophie."

"Oh, don't apologise yet," Sophie retorted with a tartness that concealed her true feelings. "You might as well save your breath until I have agreed to help you nurse her."

"Ah." Kirk let out a low whistle. "How did you guess what I intended to ask of you?"

"I'm not entirely stupid, you know," Sophie declared with an impatient toss of her head. "She can hardly stay up in the loft with the rest of you, but there is a truckle-bed in Will's chamber. I'll sleep on that and she can have the big bed."

"You won't mind sharing the room with her?"

Sophie shrugged. If she were honest, she would have to admit that she hated the idea. She didn't want anything at all to do with Kirk's former love, but common humanity bade her answer, "Someone will have to see to her if she requires nursing in the night."

"I could ask Rose." Kirk proffered the suggestion.

"Don't be absurd." Sophie glared at him. "Rose's cottage must be full to bursting with all those children. Becky wouldn't get the peace and quiet she needs, and besides, it would be too much for Rose."

She shook her red curls. "It will have to be me."

"I'll help as much as I can."

Sophie's mouth twisted. "Not at night, though, Kirk. It wouldn't be proper for you to share Will's bedchamber with me."

"Of course not," Kirk agreed meekly, but there was a sudden bright gleam in his Viking eyes that made Sophie swiftly lift her tankard to hide her face in case he suspected how much she would have liked to spend the night in the same room with him in other circumstances.

"I wish there were somewhere else available, but you are right about the loft being impossible," Kirk said, putting down his own empty tankard. "It is open to the rafters, and although the cracks between the roof-slates have been mossed in they are liable to start dripping once the snow settles."

"It would be too cold anyway," Sophie murmured absently, her wayward thoughts still occupied by the enticing vision of a night in Kirk's arms.

Kirk stood up. "I think I'd better go and make my peace with Will. He could probably do with some help in getting the flock to safety."

"Do you suppose this snow will last long?" Sophie forgot her fantasies, her mind jumping anxiously ahead.

"I doubt it." He gave her a reassuring smile as he pulled on his damp cloak "Try not to fret, sweetheart. You'll only wear yourself out by worrying needlessly over something you cannot change."

It was on the tip of Sophie's tongue to retort that *he* was a fine one to hand out such advice when he could not let the matter of his brother's death drop, but the look in his eyes stopped her.

"Go on, go and help Will," she said quietly, touched by this fresh evidence of his concern. "I'll look after Becky."

"Good girl." Kirk put out his hand and let it linger in a brief caress against her cheek.

He very much wanted to draw her into his arms and chase away the shadows that clouded her dark eyes, but he knew it would be folly, so he quickly withdrew his hand and with a silent nod of farewell strode from the room.

Sophie watched him go, feeling oddly desolate. It was all she could do to curb the desire to call him back. She felt bereft and lost without his comforting presence.

"Idiot!" She muttered the word in contemptuous self-castigation and resolutely turned away to see how her patient did.

BY SUPPER TIME Sophie was regretting her decision.

Becky had awoken shortly after Kirk's departure and her mood had been sullen. She complained continually, and nothing Sophie did for her was right.

"Do you expect me to eat this rubbish?" she had demanded angrily when Sophie had set bread and cheese before her a little after noon.

"The men did not complain, and they'd been out working in bad weather," Sophie retorted.

Becky sniffed disdainfully. "Will Hynde is a peasant," she declared. "He wouldn't know good food if he saw it."

Gritting her teeth, Sophie removed the tray she had prepared. "As you wish, but there isn't anything else," she warned.

"Why not? Do you intend to starve me?"

Sophie let this gibe pass, refusing to let the petulance in Becky's tone upset her. "Will didn't have time to cook dinner."

"What happened to Mally?" Becky saw her look of incomprehension and added impatiently, "She used to be the servant here."

Sophie remembered Will apologising for not being able to offer her a maid to assist her. "I think she left to get married. Will mentioned that he had tried a couple of others, but nowadays he prefers to manage on his own. Rose told me that she helps out in the dairy and with the laundry and—"

"Oh, never mind all that!" Becky interrupted rudely. "If Will was busy, why didn't you cook the meal?"

Sophie resisted the temptation to point out that she had been kept busy sorting linen and organising the necessary changes to Will's bedchamber. Any explanation would doubtless be interpreted as an excuse.

"And you've let the fire die down! I shall freeze to death."

The room was still warm, but Sophie decided to humour her, and placed more elding on the fire.

"Thank you." Becky's tone was wreathed in sarcasm.

"Would you like something to drink?" Sophie ignored this provocation.

Becky nodded grudgingly and Sophie brought her a cup of cool milk.

She drained it and then burst out abruptly, "Who are you anyway and what are you doing here? I've never heard of any Flemings living in Watendlath."

"My home is in Kendal," Sophie answered with more composure than she felt. "I came up here to visit . . . a friend—"

"You came to visit Kirk?" Becky demanded, seizing on Sophie's slight hesitation.

"No!" Sophie moderated her tone. "No. I encountered him by accident and when the storm broke he suggested taking shelter here."

"Really? How very convenient!"

Becky's pansy eyes rolled disbelievingly and Sophie experienced a flicker of alarm. Was Becky a naturally suspicious person or was it that her story sounded weak? If a stranger did not believe her, then what chance was there that Pelham would accept it as true?

Fortunately for Sophie's nerves, Becky soon lost interest in her and returned to her own affairs.

"I don't understand why Kirk couldn't take me to Rose's cottage," she announced petulantly.

"He told you why." Sophie strove for patience. "Rose must not be bothered with guests in her present condition."

"He knows Will dislikes me." Becky ignored Sophie's answer, a sulky pout disfiguring her perfect rosebud mouth. "I don't want to stay here."

"There's nowhere else." Sophie tactfully forbore to mention Will's reaction.

"Oh, how I wish Haraldsgarth was still as it used to be!" Becky let out a plaintive sigh.

"You know about the fire?" Sophie enquired sharply. "I thought you were living in London."

Becky's lovely face assumed a secretive expression. "I was." She paused for a moment and then continued airily, "I saw the ruins on my way up the dale."

This explanation rang false to Sophie, but before she could say another word Becky snuggled down into her blanket and announced she was tired.

"I want to sleep," she declared imperiously. "Go away."

Seething, Sophie removed the dirty cup and withdrew, seeking refuge in the down-house.

If she speaks to me like that again, I'll ... I'll ...

The angry voice in her head stuttered to a halt.

What could she do? She had promised Kirk she would help him, and, in any case, she was trapped here until the snow stopped.

Even then, I'll probably not be able to leave until it melts, she thought to herself gloomily. *My ankle won't stand that rough walk in the snow.*

All she could hope for was that the weather would improve before Nancy was driven frantic. As for Pelham, well, she doubted if he would really care whether she was lost on the fells or not.

She swallowed a painful lump in her throat. Kirk had been right. Pelham only wanted her for her money. All those compliments were just a ploy to turn her up sweet.

A little sigh escaped her. If she was honest with herself, she had known the truth almost from the start, but she had let his flattery lull her into thinking that she could make a success of their marriage.

Perhaps if she were as beautiful as Becky things might have been different . . .

Stop it, Sophie Fleming, stop this deplorable self-pity at once, her conscience said firmly. Don't forget that Pelham thinks you beneath him and his pride is such that a face like Helen of Troy's would not change his views. Anyway, do you really want him to be in love with you?

No, I don't, I don't even like the man, she realised with a start of surprise. His mouth is thin and hard and his eyes are like chips of hazel ice. Why did I never realise it before?

Because you were too dazzled by his sophistication, she answered herself, shivering slightly. She wanted to push the painful revelation away, but an innate honesty warned her not to ignore the truth.

I wouldn't be in this mess now if I had trusted my instincts, she thought ruefully. I ought to have told Uncle Thomas no at the beginning.

Instead, she had taken the easy way out, only to find herself trapped.

Sophie shuddered. What was she going to do?

"Sophie? Sophie, why are you in here? It's cold enough to freeze your marrow."

"Rose! You shouldn't have come out in this weather!"

Rose shook her head. "'Tis only a step from my cottage," she said stoutly. "Kirk called to tell me that Becky was here and taken bad."

"Yes, but she's sleeping now," Sophie explained.

"Then we'd best try to be quiet, since we can't stop out here," Rose said practically.

She turned to lead the way back to the living-room, and Sophie followed obediently. To her relief, Becky didn't stir at the sound made by Rose's clogs on the flagged floor.

"She don't seem too bad. Just a touch of low fever, I reckon," Rose stated, removing her shawl and draping it over a stool by the hearth to dry.

"That's my thought too." Sophie was glad to have her diagnosis confirmed.

"Dad don't keep much in the way of remedies," Rose continued quietly, searching in the wicker basket she carried on one arm. "So I've brung ye a few things ye might need." She held up a stubby brown bottle. "This is sorrel-leaf tea, 'tis champion for cooling a fever. Ye can give her some when she wakes."

Delving into the basket again, she produced a stone jar. "Beef jelly," she said. "Sounds as if she needs building up."

Her thick eyebrows drew together. "Ye look as if ye could do with some an' all, Sophie, lass. Has she been playing her tricks off on ye?"

Sophie gave a shaky little laugh. "You are very perceptive, Rose," she answered, careful to keep her voice low.

"I don't know about that, but I know Becky used to enjoy causing a stir." Rose shook her head disapprovingly. "Don't let her aggravate ye."

"Was she always so petulant, Rose?" Sophie asked impetuously.

Rose hesitated and Sophie added quickly, "Forgive me, you are her friend. I shouldn't have said anything."

"It's true enough we were friends in the old days, but even then I don't think I was blind to Becky's faults," Rose announced with a faintly rueful smile. "Aye, she was often rude and ungrateful, but she could be very charming when she wanted and, well ... somehow ye ended up forgiving her bad moods."

Rose's smile deepened.

"She was so very pretty, ye see. Like something out of a picture-book."

"Weren't you jealous?"

Rose chuckled. "More times than I can count! Mind, there were compensations. Becky was an only child and her parents spoilt her. Parson might rant about self-denial in the pulpit, but he never refused her anything. Oh, the cakes and sweetmeats she used to share with us when we were children!"

Rose shook her head with a little chuckle at the memory.

"Was Kirk interested in her then?" Sophie asked, trying desperately to sound casual.

Rose gave her a sharp look, but answered readily enough. "Nay. Like most lads, he thought us girls nothing but a plaguy nuisance. It wasn't until after he came home, when he'd finished at the grammar school in Cockermouth, that his attitude changed. While he'd been away Becky had grown up."

An expressive shrug shook Rose's plump shoulders.

"They began courting soon afterwards and everyone thought they would make a match of it. Kirk was mad for her! She led him a merry dance, but he put up with her whims. I just hope he's learnt more sense than to fall for her again, or else he'll rue the day, if I know Becky."

Sophie nodded, striving to suppress the irrational jealousy which tore through her. Was Kirk really as immune to Becky's charms as he claimed?

"Ye know what happened next? About the babe, I mean?"

This demand forced Sophie to pay attention. "Kirk says he was not the father."

"Not many folk believed him, I can tell ye," Rose retorted. "Dad did and so did me and Ned, 'cos we knew Kirk. He's no liar, but we couldn't understand it. There'd never been any hint that Becky was seeing anyone else."

"Do you think Kirk knew who it was?" Sophie fiddled with the bottle of sorrel-leaf tea that Rose had handed to her.

"I'm not sure. Sometimes I think he did guess, but wild horses couldn't drag a word out of him on the subject." Rose sighed. "Gossip is a nasty business. 'Tis a thousand pities that his return home has been tarred with the same brush."

"Do you believe Sir Pelham Stanton had Ingram murdered?"

Rose's eyes widened. "That's a blunt question, lass."

"I have a particular reason for asking," Sophie strove to keep her voice level. "A private matter, you understand."

Rose gave her a curious look. "Well, for your sake, I hope it ain't that Stanton is a friend of yours, Sophie, for he's not well thought of in these parts. He's a hard landlord and most folk hereabouts dislike that crowd of off-comers he's imported from London to serve him. They're a bad lot, and aye, I reckon Kirk might be right. I wouldn't put it past one of them to carry out Stanton's dirty work for him."

"I see," said Sophie in a rather breathless voice.

Anxious to avoid Rose's searching gaze, she moved towards the fire.

"I'll warm this tisane for Becky," she murmured over her shoulder.

"Aye. Well, I'd best be going or else they'll be wondering what has become of me," Rose replied. She picked up her shawl and wound it tightly around her and Sophie prepared to escort her to the door.

"Nay, carry on with what ye are doing. I'll see myself out." Rose took a few steps and then paused. "You'll send word if ye need any help?" she said.

"Of course."

Rose nodded briskly and was gone.

After her departure, Sophie was uncannily aware of the silence, broken only by the spluttering of the fire.

Rose meant more by that offer of help than it sounded, she decided, sure that Rose had somehow guessed she was deeply involved with the master of Stanton Hall. If only she'd had the courage to explain . . .

But Rose's fierce condemnation of the baronet had shaken Sophie. It was further proof, if any were needed, of the truth of Kirk's claims and the foolishness of her own behaviour in accepting the suit of a man she hardly knew.

Sophie sighed. What a dreadful tangle it all was!

Becky groaned, and the sound immediately roused Sophie from her contemplations. She hurried over to the bench, but Becky was still asleep, although restless.

Realising that her patient would soon be awake, Sophie finishing warming the sorrel-leaf tea and poured it into a cup. Once it was ready she decided she might as well prepare the strengthening broth Rose had brought too. Becky hadn't eaten anything earlier, but perhaps she could be tempted to try this.

It didn't take long to empty the contents of the jar into a saucepan and suspend it over the fire, but Becky continued to sleep on, so Sophie sat down again.

Staring into the flames, she found her thoughts kept returning to what Rose had said, and in an effort to banish them she leapt to her feet. Casting about for some task to keep her occupied, she began to light the candles, for it was growing gloomy.

The winter dark made it seem later than the actual hour, but, even so, if Will didn't appear soon it would be another cold meal.

Perhaps I should prepare supper.

The idea, sparked by Becky's demand, planted itself in Sophie's head. Surely Will wouldn't mind if she helped? And it would give her something to do.

After checking once more on Becky, Sophie set to work.

She found root vegetables stored in the down-house and enough ham to create savoury stew. Peeling the vegetables and slicing them was a routine that soothed her strained nerves, but she couldn't help wishing for the sophisticated kitchen range she was used to in the Stramongate once her preparations were complete.

"Oh, well, if it burns, it burns," she muttered, filling the kail-pot with her concoction. On its three short legs it could be positioned to stand neatly over the fire, but Sophie suspected that its contents would need frequent stirring to prevent a disaster.

She had just finished when Becky woke and demanded a drink.

"What is this disgusting stuff?" she snapped, thrusting the half-full cup back into Sophie's hands.

"Sorrel-leaf tea. Rose brought it over for you. She says it is good for combating fever."

Becky squirmed. "It's horrid." To Sophie's surprise she evinced no further interest in the news that Rose had visited but said impatiently, "Bring me something else, for God's sake."

Realising that it would probably do more harm than good to insist, Sophie acquiesced and offered warm broth instead.

Becky drank it greedily and then lay back against the pillows Sophie had propped behind her.

"I want to go to bed," she said pettishly. "My neck aches and I cannot get comfortable lying here."

Sophie hesitated. Will's chamber was cold.

"Oh, don't fuss," Becky cried irritably when she said so. "Surely there are enough blankets, and you can warm the bed for me with a hot brick, or are you too stupid to see how easily the thing can be done if only you will make shift?"

Sophie compressed her lips, swallowing down her anger.

"You could try asking more politely if you want people to help you," she said tightly.

"Oh, indeed! I must remember that in future in case I should meet anyone worthy of my regard."

The big pansy eyes mocked, and Sophie was on the point of losing her temper when she heard the sound of approaching footsteps that had been previously drowned out by Becky's taunting voice.

"Kirk! Oh, Kirk, come and tell this fool to do as I say!"

Sophie spun round to meet Kirk's startled gaze.

"She won't let me go to bed, and I am so tired!"

Becky stretched out her arms to him in a pretty gesture of appeal, and Sophie experienced a flicker of jealousy as Kirk's expression softened.

He moved closer to the bench and took one of Becky's trembling hands. "Don't upset yourself," he said in a far gentler voice than any he had used previously to her.

Sophie suppressed a sniff of indignation. Surely he wasn't going to be fooled by this piece of nonsense? Granted, Becky looked the picture of distressed frailty, but Sophie was rapidly coming to the conclusion that there was nothing much wrong with her other than an over-developed taste for dramatics!

"It is cold in the chamber—" she began, but Kirk interrupted her.

"I'll fetch a brazier to warm it once you've got the bed ready," he said without turning his head.

Sophie stared at his broad back, experiencing a most unladylike desire to hammer her clenched fists against it. Oh, why couldn't he see sense?

Her stomach plummeted.

Was history about to repeat itself? Rose had said that he could never resist Becky's wiles, and Kirk's ridiculous behaviour seemed proof that she was right, in spite of his assertions that the lovely blonde no longer meant anything to him.

Over Kirk's shoulder Becky flashed her a smile that reminded Sophie of nothing so much as a cat who'd got at the cream-bowl. "Well, go on, then," she said sweetly.

Sophie spun on her heel and marched out of the room.

"YOU NEEDN'T BOTHER trying to finish. I know it is inedible!"

Sophie thrust an errant lock of hair behind her ear and glared at Kirk Thorburn.

They were alone in the living-room. Will and Ned had retired early to bed, Will worn out by his exertions in getting the Herdwicks to safety and Ned by the struggle to return to the dale in thickening snow.

He had brought a copy of the *Cumberland Pacquet* with him, along with sundry provisions, and over supper the two Hyndes had discussed a lurid report which claimed that the imprisoned Queen of France had gone mad with grief, locked away from the world in her bleak tower in the temple gardens, but even this shocking news failed to pierce Sophie's gloomy abstraction.

Earlier in the evening Kirk had closeted himself with Becky, emerging only when supper was ready. Then, to Sophie's chagrin, he had excused himself to attend to Sultan.

"Well, I suppose we'd best sit down and eat like the lad said," Will announced in a cheerful tone, breaking the moment of awkward silence after Kirk's departure. "There's no sense in waiting when it smells so good."

Sophie finished ladling the stew into bowls and handed them round, but she did not immediately sit down. "Please don't let it grow cold on my account. I'll be back as soon as I've seen whether Becky wants any."

Will's smile faded as he acknowledged her remark with a curt nod.

It didn't surprise Sophie that Becky spurned the simple fare on offer. Instead she asked for a cup of milk and drank it thirstily.

"Will you try some more of Rose's sorrel-leaf remedy?"

"No!" Becky pulled a face.

"Then I'll leave you."

Becky's mouth fell open and Sophie experienced a spurt of satisfaction as she turned away.

Let that be a lesson to you, she thought savagely. If the older girl was determined to be rude and hostile, then two could play at that game. She would do her duty, but no more!

She could feel Becky's eyes boring into her back, but her relief at quitting the chamber was short-lived.

"Oh, heavens, it's much too salty!" she exclaimed after taking one mouthful of the meal she had so laboriously prepared.

"Is it?" Will enquired. "Tastes all right to me."

Sophie shot him a suspicious glance.

"Aye, I like a bit of a bite to my stew," Ned said, a rare grin tempering his usual laconic brevity.

Sophie blinked away a sudden tear as she watched them manfully ploughing their way through to the bottom of their bowls.

They were trying to be kind to her, and Sophie responded by doing her best to reply sensibly to any questions put to her during the discussion that followed, but she found it hard to concentrate. She was too achingly aware of Kirk's continuing absence.

Was he trying to avoid her?

She pushed aside her unwanted stew, her appetite destroyed. Even if it had turned out as well as she had hoped, it would have choked her.

The Hyndes had almost finished by the time Kirk came in, and although he apologised for taking so long Sophie sensed his mind was far away.

Will took a last pull at his ale and rose, yawning, to his feet. "If ye'll excuse me, I'm away to bed. It's been a hard day."

Ned nodded and also stood up. "I'll come with ye, Dad."

When they had gone Sophie filled a bowl and banged it down on the table.

"Your supper is ready if you want it," she said coldly.

Kirk sat down promptly and smiled at her. "Thank you."

Sophie meant to turn away, but she couldn't prevent herself from watching as he raised the spoon to his mouth.

Kirk half choked. "It's a little . . . hot."

"Hot! You lying hypocrite, it's damned well burnt, and no wonder!" Sophie planted her balled fists on her hips and glared at him.

"If it is, then it's my own fault," Kirk answered mildly.

His unexpected meekness was the last straw.

Sophie exploded.

"Have you quite finished?"

Temporarily out of breath, Sophie nodded truculently.

Kirk laid down his spoon.

"You're right. It is too salty, but I hadn't intended to say so."

His frankness took the wind out of Sophie's sails, and, seeing that she was beginning to calm down, Kirk continued in the same level voice. "You see, I knew you had gone to a great deal of trouble to cook something for everyone when you were already busy looking after Becky."

Sophie blinked. She didn't think he'd noticed!

"I'm sorry if you found my prevarication offensive. That's the last thing I wanted. I owe you too much already."

Kirk regarded her steadily, and Sophie began to blush.

"I forgot to allow for the fact that the ham would be salty," she muttered, sheepishly regarding the tips of her boots.

"Damn the stew!" Kirk sprang to his feet and came to put his arms around her. "It doesn't matter a toss. All I care about is that you shouldn't be upset."

Summoning all her will-power, Sophie placed her hands flat against the broad plain of his chest and held him off.

"Oh, really? In that case, why have you been avoiding me, Kirk Thorburn?"

"Avoiding you? What maggot has got into your brain now, you little shrew?" Kirk demanded, looking so stunned by this accusation that Sophie quite overlooked his unflattering appellation.

"You spent half the evening in there," she cried, waving an agitated arm in the direction of Will's chamber, "and then you disappear into the stables! Is it any wonder I should think you were avoiding me?"

Kirk tightened his grip on her narrow waist.

"I think this cold weather has turned your wits, my girl," he declared.

"Oh...oh, you..." Sophie squirmed in his hold.

She opened her mouth to continue the argument, but Kirk swiftly put a stop to her protests by the simple expedient of kissing her.

At the touch of his lips, Sophie's anger melted. The tension went out of her taut limbs and she allowed herself to relax into his embrace, accepting the comfort of being held in his strong arms.

She clung to him, relishing the warmth of lips against her own, but to her disappointment Kirk did not seek to deepen the kiss, but released her after an all too brief moment.

"I'm sorry I flew into a temper," she whispered, gazing into his vivid eyes.

He was still standing very close, and Sophie saw a muscle flicker at the corner of his mouth, but there was no trace of amusement in his voice when he answered her.

"There's no need to apologise. I should have had more sense and waited until after supper to attend to Sultan, but I wanted to be sure of a moment alone with you. You see, I have an idea to suggest to you."

Sophie gazed at him anxiously. "Is it about Becky?" she blurted.

"Becky?" Kirk's expression was puzzled. "What has she got to do with it?"

"You don't deny that you spent a long time with her this evening?" Recovering herself, Sophie tilted her chin. "Or that you took her part this afternoon?"

"Did that rankle?"

"You practically ordered me out of the room!"

Kirk coughed ruefully. "I never meant to treat you like a servant, sweetheart. I just thought it would be easier on everyone if Becky was safely tucked up in bed before supper."

He grinned suddenly. "But if I tried to suggest it, Becky would have been determined to remain on that bench all night! That's why I wanted to hurry, before she changed her mind."

Sophie nodded. His explanation made sense, but somehow she didn't feel reassured. You are turning into a jealous woman, Sophie Fleming, she thought to herself with rueful dismay.

"Surely you didn't imagine there was anything more to it than that?" Kirk stared at her hard.

"No, of course not," Sophie lied quickly.

"Good." Kirk heaved a sigh of relief.

Sophie thought it prudent to change the subject.

"Would you like something else to eat? I can easily—"

"Thank you, but no. I'm not hungry," Kirk interrupted with one of his charming smiles, and then, putting his arm around Sophie, he steered her towards the settle.

"Let's sit down," he said.

"What was it that you wanted to tell me?" Sophie asked once they were comfortable.

"I've asked Ned if I can borrow his horse in the morning, and he's agreed, so I intend to try and get a message through to your Nancy."

"But Kirk, it's too dangerous!" Sophie paled and laid an urgent hand on his arm. "Ned said he'd had a terrible journey home."

"He probably did." Kirk did not appear unduly concerned.

"I don't want you to run any risks!" Sophie's fingers tightened and Kirk gently removed them from his arm.

Holding both her hands lightly in his own clasp, he said, "I don't intend to, sweetheart, but we both know Nancy will be desperately worried by now, and I feel it is my responsibility to let her know you are safe."

"But even if you make it to Stanton House Pelham won't receive you!" Sophie pulled her hands free, waving them in wild agitation. "He might refuse to let you see Nancy."

"Perhaps. But I shall find a way all the same." He smiled at her, his confidence unimpaired. "There is no point in trying to dissuade me. My mind's made up."

Sophie glared at him. "You are a very stubborn man, Kirk Thorburn."

"I know," he replied tranquilly.

CHAPTER NINE

SOPHIE CREPT noiselessly to drape a thick shawl over the window. The pale light of dawn was instantly cut off and gloom descended once more upon the stuffy bedchamber.

It had been a very long night.

Becky had woken up just as Sophie slipped wearily between the sheets of the little truckle-bed, and at first Sophie had been inclined to think that she was exaggerating her aches and pains in a bid for attention. However, it was soon clear that Becky's fever had taken a turn for the worse.

She had tossed and turned all night, keeping Sophie busy bathing her forehead with cool water and trying to get her to take a few sips of medicine, before finally falling into a deeper sleep only moments ago.

Sophie stretched her weary limbs. Her eyes felt gritty from lack of sleep and she longed to snatch away the shawl and throw the window wide open so that she could feel the sunlight on her face and breathe in some fresh air.

Not that she would ever do such a foolish thing, of course!

The sound of movement coming from the adjoining room informed her that someone else was astir, and with a last look at her patient Sophie slipped from the chamber.

"Good morning. Did you know that the snow has stopped at last—"

Kirk's cheerful greeting came to an abrupt halt when he saw the dark shadows beneath eyes which lacked their usual sparkle.

"God, you look awful!" he exclaimed.

"Thank you!" Sophie bridled for an instant, but her indignation changed to amusement as a look of horrified dismay swept over Kirk's face.

"And I thought *I* was the tactless one!" she chuckled.

Relieved to be so easily forgiven, Kirk grinned. "Let me make amends by offering you a cup of tea."

"Tea?" Sophie shot him a glance of puzzled enquiry.

"I asked Ned to get some yesterday when he was in Keswick, but he forgot to unpack it last night. I reminded him just now."

Kirk held out the little lead-foil wrapper to her, but Sophie hesitated.

"Oh, don't worry, I gave Ned enough money to pay for it."

"Then I am in your debt, sir."

Kirk's grin broadened. "I dare say I shall think of a way for you to repay me."

There was a devilish glint in his Viking eyes as their fingers touched, warning Sophie exactly what he was thinking, and she coloured in confusion, snatching her hand away.

"But first things first, eh? I don't know about you, sweetheart, but I'm not at my best in the mornings until I've had my breakfast," Kirk added wickedly, admiring the way her blushes heightened the fine texture of her pale skin.

Relenting, he continued in a less provocative tone, "I asked Ned to make sure that the grocer blended the tea while he waited, just in case the fellow tried to eke it out with some cheaper rubbish."

Realising that he'd been teasing her, Sophie recovered her composure.

"You have a most suspicious mind, Mr. Thorburn," she said with a gravity belied by the dancing merriment in her eyes.

"Very probably."

There was an unexpected curtness in his voice which baffled Sophie for a moment, and then it suddenly occurred to her that he might think she was baiting him about Pelham.

"Kirk, I . . . I didn't mean to sound as if I were criticising you," she said quickly.

Kirk's handsome face lost its frown.

"I know you didn't," he answered softly. "It's my curst hot temper. Sometimes I say things I don't mean, but I'm not fool enough to deliberately quarrel with you. I value your friendship too much to want to antagonise you, Sophie."

Sophie's smile lit up her irregular features.

And I don't want any more arguments to spoil things between us either, she reflected, her fatigue vanishing as she basked in the warmth his unexpected compliment had generated.

Kirk put the kettle on to boil while Sophie found the little-used china tea-set and washed everything carefully.

"I shall make a whole pot," Sophie announced gaily, spooning expensive Chinese leaves with a liberal hand.

"Ned and Will have already gone out," Kirk warned.

Sophie turned a surprised gaze on him. "I thought they were still abed," she murmured.

Kirk shook his head. "They went to check on the animals, but they'll be back in time for breakfast." He paused slightly. "However, Becky would probably enjoy a cup."

"She is sleeping." Sophie's tone lost its animation.

"How is she?"

"She was feverish in the night, but she's well enough now." Sophie shrugged, hating the pang of jealousy that shot through her at the concern underlying his deep voice.

"In that case, we'd better not disturb her." Kirk spoke easily, but he wondered why Sophie's mouth had suddenly tightened.

They sat down to drink their tea, and Sophie stifled a yawn. "Oh, excuse me," she murmured.

Kirk's puzzlement lifted. Of course! The poor girl was exhausted after nursing Becky all night. No wonder she had seemed out of spirits a moment ago.

"Why don't you step outside for a breath of air while I cook breakfast?" he suggested.

Sophie laid aside her empty cup. "I'm not sure if I should," she murmured.

"Don't you trust my cooking?" Kirk challenged.

A rueful grin curled Sophie's wide mouth. "You couldn't make a worse botch than I did last night."

Her failure to impress him with her skill was upsetting, but she'd had plenty of time during the long, silent hours of the night to realise that it didn't really matter. With any luck, she would do better next time, and anyway, she doubted if Kirk was the sort of man to care about such things. He was more interested in what people *were* than what they *did*.

I want him to like me for myself and not because I can cook or paint or dance, she thought. He's the only man I've ever met who showed more interest in *me* than my dowry. His good opinion counts because I know he will tell me the truth and not seek to flatter me.

"It is refreshing to find a woman with a sense of humour," Kirk answered slowly. His engaging smile dawned, unsettling Sophie's pulse. "Go on, enjoy a stroll while I endeavour to produce a meal worthy of your regard."

Sophie collected her stout hodden cloak and muffler from the down-house and ventured outside.

Taking a deep gulp of air, she revelled in its cold, crisp sweetness as she walked down the path towards the tarn.

The whole world was swathed in white and the valley looked like a page out of a child's book of fairy-tales. The hills had become dazzling sentinels guarding the treasure of the shining diamond lake, while the branches of every tree and bush seemed sprinkled with glittering crystals.

The last remnants of the stale fatigue which had enveloped her earlier dropped away, and Sophie lingered for a moment to admire the scene before taking the track that led to where Rose lived.

It was a small white-washed cottage with no feature to distinguish it, except for a wooden spinning-gallery under the eaves. Smoke emerging from its little chimney indicated that the occupants were already astir, so Sophie was emboldened to knock.

Rose herself answered the door.

"Why, Sophie. Come in and thaw yeself out by the fire."

What seemed a dozen curious pairs of eyes turned in her direction as Sophie entered and a deep silence fell on the little room.

"Sam's out on the fell," Rose explained, thrusting a poker into the heart of the fire as she spoke.

After a moment the children's shyness evaporated and Sophie found herself deluged with noisy questions, which she did her best to answer.

"Away into the bedroom." Rose shooed her noisy brood out of the kitchen and pressed a mug of mulled ale into Sophie's hands.

Sophie thanked her. "They are lovely children," she added with a sincerity that made Rose beam with pride.

"Is there something I can do for ye, Sophie?" Rose asked after they had chatted for a while.

"Do you have any more of that sorrel-leaf tea?" Sophie was glad that Rose had guessed this was not just a social call. "I don't want to be a nuisance, but Becky was very feverish in the night and it is all finished."

"'Tis no bother. There's plenty to spare." Rose's expression grew solemn. "How is the lass this morning?"

"She was sleeping when I left." Sophie paused and then exclaimed impulsively, "I wish I knew whether she means to stay in Watendlath!"

"Have ye asked her?"

"She refuses to talk to me," Sophie replied with a faint smile. "I am too lowly to merit her attention. Kirk is the only one she favours with her confidences."

"And ye are worried that he'll fall under her spell again," Rose said with a shrewdness that made Sophie gasp.

"I...I..." Sophie fiddled frantically with a loose strand of hair, but couldn't find the right words to refute this claim. After a moment she gave up the struggle. "You are right, of course. How did you guess?"

"Your face gives ye away, lass."

"Oh, dear, are my feelings for him so very obvious?" Sophie let out a squeak of dismay.

"No more than his." Rose began to chuckle. "Eeh, a blind man on a galloping horse could see that the pair of ye are smitten! Ye were made for each other, even if that great looby ain't realised it yet."

Sophie couldn't help laughing. "Oh, Rose!"

Her wry amusement quickly faded. "I wish it were so simple, but there are ... complications."

"Ye mean Stanton, I expect."

Sophie stared at her in amazement.

"Kirk mentioned that ye were betrothed to him," Rose explained.

"I see."

"Nay, don't take offence, lass. Kirk knew Sam would be busy yesterday on account of the snow, so he called to see if I needed a hand with anything, and I asked him how matters stood with his search for Ingram's murderer. He happened to let slip how ye had agreed to marry Stanton to please your uncle, but once he'd realised what he'd said he swore me to silence, so ye needn't think he's been going around telling your private business to all and sundry."

Sophie relaxed. "I would have told you myself, but it was . . . well . . . awkward."

"I wouldn't have wrapped my opinion about that rogue in clean linen even if I'd known about your betrothal," Rose declared with characteristic bluntness. "Ye'd be a fool to marry him, Sophie."

"I know, but it's not as easy you might imagine to withdraw from such a contract," Sophie sighed.

She might have said more, but just then a yell rose in protest from the bedroom, followed in swift succession by several further cries and the sound of scuffling.

"I must be going." Sophie got to her feet even as Rose moved to quell the riot.

"I'll fetch that medicine over later." Rose nodded.

Thanking her, Sophie flung her cloak over her shoulders and hurried back to the farm.

A delicious smell of frying bacon greeted her.

"Come and join us, lass," Will hailed her from his position at the head of the table.

Unconsciously, Sophie had been hoping that she would find Kirk still alone, but she stifled her disappointment and sat down to partake of the excellent breakfast set before her.

"Aye, we rear good pigs here," Will said, casting a complacent glance at the sides of meat hanging up to dry in the dim, smoky recesses of the canopy when she complimented him on the bacon.

"And Kirk's cooking has improved," Ned chimed in unexpectedly. "He used to burn everything when he first got home."

Sophie glanced mischievously at Kirk, who exclaimed, "Ned, you traitor!"

"Did I say something wrong?" Ned's broad, honest face wore a bewildered expression.

To the astonishment of the Hyndes, both their guests burst out laughing.

"A private jest," Kirk explained when he had recovered his breath.

"Aye, well, we'd best be getting back to work," Will announced, a sudden suspicion forming in his mind as he watched his young friend smile across the table at the lively redhead he'd brought to the dale.

Will chivvied Ned to his feet, ignoring his son's protests.

"Ye bide here and keep Miss Fleming company. We can manage," he insisted when Kirk offered his services.

Kirk yielded with a smile and Will went off, pleased to see him in such good spirits. The lad had been right moped since his return; not that anyone could blame him. Ingram's death had been a shocking business, but the lad was too young to wrap himself up in nothing but gloom and fury. If that attractive lass had given Kirk's thoughts a new direction, then he for one approved!

"I'd like to stay and talk, Sophie, but I think it's time I set out if I'm to get back from Stanton Hall before it grows dark," Kirk said, once the door had closed behind the Hyndes.

Sophie had blithely forgotten all about his intention to go and see Nancy, and she gazed at him in consternation.

"Do you really think it is wise?" she said desperately. "The snow has stopped. Surely we could both go tomorrow?"

"I hope so, but in the meantime your disappearance will be causing anxiety." Kirk shrugged. "I dare say Stanton will try and have me thrown out, but I reckon it's worth the risk." He was tempted to add that almost anything would be worth it to lessen the anxiety he could read in her lovely eyes. Even when she was laughing, as she had done a moment ago, that shadow remained.

Damn it, but he hated to see her unhappy!

"I must go," he said, rising to his feet. "Call it a quirk of my nature if you like, but I should feel I have failed if I did not try."

"Then at least promise me that you will not attempt to see Pelham," Sophie implored. "You can leave a message at the gatehouse."

Kirk hesitated.

"Please, Kirk. Pelham is suspicious of you and it will not help my position if he learns that I have been in your company before I get the chance to explain matters."

"Then you still intend to marry him?"

The words exploded from his throat, but Kirk cursed his impatience when Sophie paled and dropped her gaze. He had promised himself that he would not harry her for a decision!

"Forget I asked," he said gruffly. "Very well, then, I'll do as you suggest, but only if you will write a note for your maid. That way we won't have to rely on the gatekeeper's memory."

"Of course!" Sophie flew to find pen and paper.

"You won't give your name, will you?" she said anxiously, handing him the hastily scrawled missive.

It went against the grain, but Kirk consented to this stipulation.

His preparations for the journey were soon complete.

"I'll be back before dusk," he announced with such cheerful confidence that Sophie took heart and managed to wave him off with a creditable attempt at a smile.

Indoors again, she checked on her patient and, finding Becky still asleep, she set to work on the household chores. The novelty of sweeping floors and washing dishes quickly wore off, but she persisted until every task was eventually accomplished, though not without some unladylike mutterings.

"Perhaps I ought to attend to you too," she said aloud, eyeing a pile of shirts awaiting mending.

Sewing was not a task Sophie enjoyed, but she knew herself well enough to know that her imagination would run riot if she did not find something to keep her occupied.

"What a pity Will's taste in reading doesn't include novels," she sighed, settling herself under the canopy and picking up the first shirt.

"Damn!"

A splatter of black sooty liquid dropping from the open chimney some minutes later made Sophie jump in alarm.

"No wonder Will jokes about needing to keep his hat on!" she groaned, surveying the dirty mark the *hallandrop* had left. "Now this needs washing, and I had only just finished repairing it!"

Her lukewarm interest in the job completely destroyed, Sophie put the rest of the mending away, but before she could start to launder the spoilt shirt a cry from the bedchamber alerted her to the fact that Becky was awake.

"Here, sip this. Slowly, now."

Sophie held the cup to Becky's cracked lips and patiently helped the older girl drink a little water.

"That tastes so good. Thank you."

The animosity which had formerly marked the husky contralto voice was missing, Sophie noticed.

"Could you manage to eat something?"

"Later, perhaps." Becky shook her blonde head.

"Very well." Sophie gently lowered her back against the pillows and after a moment's hesitation enquired if Becky would like to wash her hands and face. "It might make you feel a little more the thing."

This offer was eagerly accepted, and when Sophie had helped her to complete her toilette Becky let out a sigh of relief. "I was beginning to feel filthy," she said with a slight chuckle.

It was the first time Sophie had seen her smile, except for that hateful superior smirk!

"I'm glad you are feeling better," she said and meant it.

Becky heard the sincerity in her voice, and a faint blush stained her wan cheeks. "Thank you for nursing me," she muttered. "If things had been the other way around I would have probably thrown that sorrel-leaf tea over you, not looked after you with such unstinting care and patience!"

Sophie grinned. "I must admit I was tempted!"

The lines of strain around Becky's taut mouth eased and she gazed at Sophie with a winning frankness.

"I'm sorry, I didn't mean to behave so abominably. It's just that feeling ill on top of all my other problems was the last straw, and I took my wretchedness out on you." A charming smile lit up her perfect features. "Please say that you forgive me. I promise I will conduct myself with more decorum from now on."

Sophie wondered how sincere this volte-face was, but said pleasantly, "I'm willing to start afresh if you are."

"Wonderful! I'm sure we are going to be great friends," Becky exclaimed brightly.

There was something almost childlike in the appeal of those big eyes and that dimpling smile. It made it difficult to resist her charm, Sophie thought. Moreover, a truce would certainly help while they had to remain cooped up here, but she strongly suspected that Becky's mood might just as easily turn hostile once more if it suited her purposes.

"Is there anything else I can get you or would you prefer to rest now?" Sophie asked, removing the basin and towel.

"Actually there is something." Becky waved her towards the rocking-chair. "Have you time to listen? I would welcome the advice of another woman."

Don't trust her, Sophie warned herself as she sat down. Remember what Rose said! No matter how charming she may seem, she is a determined manipulator, willing to use other people to gain her own ends.

"You are a stranger and somehow I feel more comfortable talking to you about my problem than someone I know," Becky began slowly.

"Perhaps it's because you hope I may be able to offer you an unprejudiced view," Sophie answered, understanding exactly what the older girl meant.

"Well, I certainly stand in need of advice! If I lie here worrying any longer I swear I shall end in Bedlam!"

Sophie nodded. She had spent too much time pondering her own situation lately not to feel a kindred sympathy.

"You see, I am virtually penniless, but yesterday I received an unexpected offer from Kirk."

Sophie stiffened.

"Oh, I don't mean that kind of offer!" A trill of laughter escaped Becky, and Sophie blushed, angry that she had betrayed herself. "Once upon a time... Ah, but that's another story, as they say!" Becky shook her head in a pretty gesture. "No, he has offered me money, not marriage."

"Why?"

The bluntness of this question didn't disturb Becky.

"I don't know. Such kindness is the last thing I expected." She gave Sophie a direct look, devoid of her usual coquettishness. "Don't you find it strange?"

"Have you asked Kirk his reasons?"

"He says it is to help me get settled in a new life."

"Perhaps he is fond of you." Sophie managed to force the words out, although they nearly choked her.

"After the way I treated him?" Becky laughed, but it was an unpleasant sound.

After a moment she continued, "I take it you have heard the story of my wanton past."

Sophie nodded, hardly knowing how to answer.

"I thought as much. Puritans like Will Hynde won't ever let me forget!" The petulant note was back in Becky's voice, and Sophie studied her fingernails in embarrassment.

"Not that his opinion matters. He never liked me anyway." Becky shrugged. "But I don't understand why Kirk has changed his attitude. When we met the other day I was hoping he might have forgiven me, but he was still angry, almost as angry as the last time we met."

A wry grimace twisted Becky's rosebud mouth.

"We quarrelled bitterly. He wanted me to tell my parents about the baby, but I refused. Papa was indulgent. He would have overlooked most misdemeanours, but how could he condone such a sin? To have shown mercy would have made him the laughing-stock of the district!"

A little sigh escaped her. "I meant to leave Watendlath before my condition became obvious, but unfortunately my mother guessed the truth. She became hysterical and Papa came rushing in to see what was wrong. In the recriminations that followed I blurted Kirk's name."

"You could have retracted it later and told your parents who the real father was."

"I dared not!" Becky shuddered. "I knew he would deny it. He had no wish to marry someone like me."

Sophie stared at her in astonishment.

"Not all men are as honourable as Kirk Thorburn, you know," Becky snapped. "My lover was rich and I found his world exciting, but even then, green though I was, I knew he would never accept responsibility for my predicament. In fact he had already warned me that if I breathed a word of our affair he would make sure that my name became a byword! I had no choice but to blame Kirk!"

Sensing that argument would only increase Becky's distress, Sophie remained silent, and after a short pause Becky resumed her story.

"I didn't want to harm Kirk. I was fond of him—who could not be?—but I knew if I didn't pretend he was responsible my parents would give me no peace, and I needed time until my lover could help me get away."

"Was that when you went to London?"

Becky nodded. "It was wildly exciting. He installed me as his mistress in a grand house where I lived like a queen! I had fine clothes, jewels—"

"But what about the baby?" Sophie couldn't contain her curiosity.

"Oh, I miscarried and lost it," Becky replied with an airy unconcern that took Sophie's breath away.

"Didn't you mind?" she gasped.

Becky tossed her head. "I didn't want it, you know! Perhaps if Sir...I mean my lover...had been pleased about my condition I would have felt differently. In fact he made no secret of his relief, so I could see no point in staying at home moping and pretending to grieve when he wanted me to accompany him to parties..." She halted, catching the look of disgust that flashed across Sophie's expressive face.

"No doubt you think me very unprincipled to abandon all the beliefs that my parents had taught me, but life in London was different! It was all so sophisticated and new and I was fascinated by..." She paused, a little uncertainty entering her manner. "I have never spoken his name to anyone in Watendlath."

Sophie stifled her curiosity and said briskly, "It doesn't matter. I wouldn't know him anyway."

"No, of course." Becky let out a faint sigh of relief. "I know my secret departure hurt my parents, as well as causing a great deal of bother for Kirk, but I didn't regret my decision. I was in love! The man I had chosen could be very reserved and haughty, but I was happy with him, even when the passion between us eventually faded and I knew he was no longer entirely faithful to me. By that time I had my own circle of friends, and fidelity didn't seem to matter. He continued to keep me in great style and I still enjoyed all the pleasures London had to offer."

"Then why did you decide to come back?" Caught up in the older girl's story, Sophie had forgotten the cry of despair Becky had hurled at Kirk at their first meeting.

The pansy eyes darkened.

"He swore to me that he would never cast me off. I knew that one day he must marry to provide himself with an heir, but I thought that need not change our relationship—in fashionable circles no one blinks at a man keeping a mistress—but then a few months ago his manner towards me began to change. Nothing I did pleased him! He was tense and sullen, refusing to buy me trinkets if I asked."

Becky pouted.

"Finally, just before Christmas he declared that he would no longer pay my bills, and when I asked him how I was to keep up the house and servants he coolly informed me that he meant to let the lease run out!

"At first I thought he was joking, but he answered my protests with a curt shake of his head, saying that he intended to marry and that he could no longer afford to keep me. I knew he had money troubles—what fine gentleman does not?—but I hadn't realised things were so bad."

Becky let out a bitter laugh. "Do you know I actually offered to move to a smaller house and practise economy? But he laughed in my face and told me he was tired of me. 'Any man is entitled to a change after ten years,' that's what he said. Is it any wonder that I began to hate him?"

Sophie gulped and wondered what she could say. "Now that your feelings for him have altered, perhaps it is better that you should seek a new life," she ventured at last.

"I'd be glad to, if I had the money. Do you know I had barely enough in my purse to cover the stage fare? He made me return every piece of jewellery, every trinket of value! He even ordered my maid to parcel up my clothes for sale before he dismissed her. I was left with nothing but the garments I stood up in!"

Becky shook her head in angry disbelief.

"I knew he was secretive and could be cold, but to do such a callous thing after all the years we had been together...! When the lease on my house finally ran out a few weeks ago I would have been reduced to sleeping on the streets if a friend had not helped me!"

She shuddered dramatically.

"The whole business made me feel so sick that all I wanted to do was to lie down and die! I longed to get away from him and away from London, where everyone knew of my humiliation."

A sigh escaped her. "Watendlath suddenly seemed very desirable."

"Only now you are having second thoughts?" Sophie queried perceptively.

"It was folly coming back." The big violet eyes turned to her with a miserable expression in their depths. "I simply can't settle to living a quiet country life, even if the people around here would accept me back into the fold. Lord, I should have realised it before I set foot in the coach! After all, it was the main reason I rejected Kirk in the first place. He is the sort of man any girl might want to marry, but he would hate to live in a city. He wanted to stay at Haraldsgarth. I wanted excitement, gaiety! Now that I have tasted that kind of life I don't think I can give it up. It's in my blood."

"Then you had better take his money and go back to London." To hear Becky casually dismiss Kirk's love when it was all she longed for made Sophie boil, and her voice was so sharp that Becky blinked at her.

"But don't you see? It wouldn't be fair to take advantage of Kirk a second time," she explained. "I know I am selfish, but I am not a complete monster! I can't let Kirk make such a sacrifice for me. Haraldsgarth is ruined. He cannot afford to help me out."

Sophie began to choke with harsh, jerky laughter. "Your sentiments do you credit. But you are sadly misinformed. Kirk acquired considerable wealth in the Bahamas. He is a rich man now."

Becky goggled at her. "I had no idea!" she gasped.

Struggling to control her unseemly mirth, Sophie didn't perceive the significance of Becky's sudden fit of silent abstraction until Becky lifted her downcast gaze and said, "How very interesting! Thank you, Sophie. You have put quite a different complexion on matters."

There was a distinctly acquisitive gleam in the pansy eyes, and Sophie could have kicked herself as she realised her mistake.

Why, oh, why had she opened her big mouth?

By THE TIME the afternoon shadows were drawing in, Sophie's anxiety regarding Becky's intentions was submerged in a greater fear for Kirk's safety.

Providing a noonday meal for everyone had been a distraction, and Rose's promised visit had also helped, but now it was nearly dusk and her imagination kept conjuring up visions of Kirk lying injured and helpless in the snow.

"I think I'll take a turn by the lake before it gets too dark," she announced abruptly.

Ned gazed at her in open-mouthed surprise, but Will merely nodded.

"Aye, you do that, lass. Mind you don't stay out too long, though. I reckon it's going to be another cold night and it'll be like glass underfoot once the sun goes down."

Sophie nodded. During the day the top layer of snow had thawed, but it would freeze again once the temperature dropped.

Out by the tarn Sophie felt her over-stretched nerves beginning to relax. The wind had dropped and the sky was a miracle of golden fire as the sun flamed to its rest in a sunset so spectacular that it was almost enough to make her forget how cold the temperature still was.

Sophie took a deep breath. It was utterly peaceful; only the faint pee-wit cry of a curlew in the distance disturbed the silence. A perfect time and place to dream of love!

She lifted her face to catch the last rays of the sun, and somehow it was no surprise to see a lone horseman riding down the track. It was in keeping with the magic of the hour that Kirk should be returning safely, dissolving her nightmare fears.

Excitement shot through her as she waved to him, and she had to bite back the urge to laugh aloud as he raised an arm in acknowledgment.

"Kirk! I'm so glad you are back!"

Sophie greeted him with a warm smile as he dismounted.

"Sophie." Kirk swept her a courtly bow that hid his dismay. How strained and pale she looked!

"How do you like Watendlath now?" he enquired lightly, waving an arm to encompass the scene around them.

"It's beautiful. I never realised how dirty snow looks in the streets of a town until now."

Kirk laughed, but his attention was diverted when she raised a hand to push back a lock of hair that had strayed from the confines of the muffler she wore.

"Here, take these," he said, stripping off his gloves. "Your hands look frozen."

Sophie glanced down and was horrified to see how waxen her bare hands appeared, apart from the chapped and reddened knuckles. To make matters worse, she had broken two of her long fingernails into the bargain.

Feeling embarrassed, she nevertheless managed a feeble grin. "I'm not used to housework."

Kirk's mouth tightened and, wondering if she'd said the wrong thing yet again, Sophie quickly moved to take the gloves he was still holding out to her.

One of them slipped through her cold fingers and fell to the ground. She stooped hastily to retrieve it and felt herself beginning to slither on the icy path.

The squeak of alarm died in her throat as Kirk caught her in his strong clasp and steadied her.

Her pulse began to hammer and she stood very still, not daring to move.

"This reminds me of the time we were skating in Kendal," Kirk said in a voice that was suddenly hoarse.

Sophie lifted her head, and as he gazed down into her vivid little face Kirk's arms tightened of their own volition.

"I remember. We quarrelled like a pair of shrews," Sophie said shakily.

A slow smile dawned on Kirk's handsome features.

"We have wasted a lot of time arguing. Very foolish of us, don't you agree? We could have found out we were friends so much the sooner."

His words brought a shine of happiness to her dark eyes and the smiling curve of her generous mouth proved so irresistible that he abandoned the last vestiges of common sense and gave in to his urge to kiss her.

The touch of his warm lips made Sophie's senses swim. She clung to him tightly, and Kirk's initial intention faded. Instead of releasing her, he deepened the kiss, and found she answered his growing passion with a matching fervour.

Sophie twined her fingers into the golden mane that curled crisply on to the back of Kirk's strong neck, pressing herself even closer to him. He let out a growl of pleasure, and every single nerve in her body stirred with heady delight as his tongue demanded admission into the intimacy of her mouth.

The taste of him left her giddy with longing. The potent male smell of him was in her nostrils. The animal warmth of his big, strong body lapped around her, banishing the cold weariness frozen into her bones. She was alive for the first time in days . . . and consumed by desire!

"I think we had better go in. You'll freeze to death if we linger."

Kirk reluctantly broke their embrace, trying to mask his emotions with a smile, but his breathing remained ragged.

Sophie laughed a little shakily. How could he think she felt the cold while in his arms?

They moved slowly away from the tarn, Kirk leading his horse by the reins. The treacherous path required close attention, and Sophie had recovered her composure by the time they reached the shelter of the stable, where Kirk unsaddled Ned's roan and rubbed him down.

Once this task was accomplished he said, "I need to take a look at Sultan. Perhaps you ought to go in."

Sophie gazed at him in surprise. She had been expecting him to explain what had happened at Stanton Hall.

"Don't worry. I left your note as we planned," Kirk replied when she ventured to ask how his mission had fared. "Apart from that, there's nothing to tell."

It cost Kirk a great deal to sound offhand when he longed to reassure her, but he had come to the conclusion that it was about time he put a little distance between himself and the delectable Miss Fleming.

Damn it, all he really wanted to do was catch her up in his arms and kiss her again, but the walk back from the tarn had given him time to think.

It was not the act of a gentleman to lead a lady on, and until this business of finding Ingram's murderer was over and he was free to decide his own future he had no right to treat Sophie in such a cavalier way. No matter how he might long to kiss her, it simply wasn't fair when he was in no position to offer marriage until he had fulfilled his duty to his dead brother.

Sophie turned to go and then hesitated. Perhaps she had imagined that coolness in his tone.

"I'd like to stay and watch, if I won't be in the way," she murmured, swallowing her pride.

"Of course." Kirk nodded politely. "Why don't you stand over there where you won't get your skirts dirty?"

Sophie's spirits plunged. This time there was no mistaking the reserve in his deep voice!

Taking up the position he had suggested, she watched him attend to the great bay stallion, her thoughts in a turmoil. Why had he turned cold? Could her ardour have embarrassed him? From conversations with friends like Charlotte Fletcher, she knew many men didn't like a girl to be too forward.

"They like to do the chasing, not the other way round," Charlotte had declared with an authority Sophie saw no reason to doubt.

A hot flush mantled Sophie's cheeks. Did Kirk think she was fast? She pressed a clenched fist to her mouth. Of course he must! After the shameless way she had behaved, it would be a miracle if he thought anything else!

And yet... He had never shown any sign of disliking her fervent response to his caresses before, so perhaps there was something else.

Becky.

She was so beautiful! Had her own attractions paled to nothing beside that glamorous allure?

It was a depressingly logical conclusion.

Desire is not the same thing as love, Sophie reminded herself bitterly. It was perfectly possible that Kirk might want to enjoy Becky's lush body even though he no longer cared for her.

But he kissed *me*, not her, Sophie told herself frantically.

You were there, replied the inexorable voice in her head. Kirk might not be the womaniser you once thought him, but he is a man, not a monk! What did you expect him to do in those circumstances after the way you've been throwing yourself at him ever since you met?

Sophie shivered.

And Becky, how would she react if Kirk offered her a *carte blanche*? She had made no secret of her attraction to him. No doubt she would welcome him as a lover, particularly as he was now rich enough to give her the things she wanted!

Shocked by the meanness of her thoughts, Sophie gasped, and Kirk turned round abruptly.

"Is something wrong?"

"No, no...nothing."

"You're shivering." Kirk wiped his hands clean on a rag. "Come, let's go inside. I've just about finished here anyway."

He offered her his arm, but to his surprise she drew away.

"I think you still have some liniment on you. I don't want to get this cloak dirty," Sophie said hastily.

Kirk's eyebrows rose, but he accepted this feeble excuse without comment.

Sophie's spirits sank even lower, and it was a relief to regain the farmhouse, where her tongue-tied silence might go unnoticed.

"Eeh, but the pair of ye look frozen to the marrow!" Will exclaimed. "Ye could do with warming up, but supper is nowhere near ready."

Kirk repressed a smile. "It doesn't matter in the least, Will. I must go and change out of these damp clothes in any case."

A frown of concentration appeared on Will's wrinkled nut-brown face.

"What do ye say to a bowl of powsowdy while we are waiting?" he declared triumphantly. "I can have it ready in two shakes of a lamb's tail."

Not wishing to offend his friend, Kirk accepted, and Will crossed to the spice cupboard built into the wall by the hearth. Here cinnamon and nutmeg were stored along with the household's block of salt to keep dry, and Sophie watched with interest as Will carefully grated and measured out the amount of spices he required.

"Off ye go, lad, or ye'll be catching a chill," Will admonished, and Kirk left to climb the slate stairs to the loft while Sophie made herself comfortable by the brightly burning fire.

"Would ye mind toasting this, lass, while ye are sitting there?"

Sophie took the toasting fork Will handed her. He had speared a thick slice of bread on to the prongs and she held it close to the flames, glad to have some task on which to fix her attention.

"Mind ye don't burn it, lass," Will directed, busying himself with setting a pan of strong ale to heat.

Sophie grinned. Sometimes Will reminded her of her uncle Thomas!

When everything was ready, Will poured the hot ale into a big basin, and threw in a dash of brandy, followed by the spices and crisp toast.

"That smells good," Kirk remarked, walking back into the room.

He was wearing a pair of tan breeches and a fine linen shirt beneath a dark brown riding coat, and it struck Sophie afresh how informal attire suited him. He looked so handsome that her heart contracted, and she longed to stroke smooth a wayward lock of hair that had escaped his brush.

Will began handing round piggins of his potent brew as Ned emerged from the down-house, a bundle of elding in his arms.

"Powsowdy! What a good idea, Dad!"

Accepting the little wooden barrel-shaped dish and sipping at the hot drink with a spoon as the others did, Sophie soon understood Ned's enthusiasm. It sent an immediate rush of warmth along her veins and she could feel the tension beginning to drain out of her.

"Do you expect the weather to continue to improve, Will?" Kirk spoke up, laying aside his empty piggin.

"I heard a thrush sing afore Candlemas Day, and that's always a bad sign, but I reckon we're over the worst of it." Will grinned and added, "Anyway, for now at least."

"Then I shall escort Miss Fleming home in the morning."

Sophie's bright head jerked up and she dropped her spoon, her nerves tautening once more.

"*Tomorrow* morning?" she said shakily.

"Of course. Sultan's hock is healed and we have imposed upon Will's hospitality for long enough."

There was a cool finality in Kirk's words, and Sophie saw that his expression was determined.

"Ye are more than welcome to stay, both of ye," Will began a little uncertainly, sensing the tension that had suddenly flared between his guests.

"No, thank you, Mr. Hynde." Sophie strove for composure. "Mr. Thorburn is right. It is high time I left."

"Can you be ready to make an early departure?"

Sophie forced herself to meet his vivid gaze.

"As early as you wish. Becky is on the mend. She no longer requires the services of a nurse."

With an effort Kirk kept his face impassive. "That's good news. I'm glad she is better," he murmured.

Hellfire, he had forgotten all about Becky! Perhaps he should tell her that he would be away for a short time. In any case, he ought to find out whether she had decided to accept his offer to stake her or not.

To Kirk's surprise, he found he no longer cared either way. He still wanted Becky gone from the dale, but the fury she had aroused in him had faded. It belonged to the past, like the love he had once borne her.

"That makes two of us glad to hear your news, lass." Will's emphatic declaration interrupted Kirk's thoughts.

"I meant what I said," Will continued grimly, putting down his piggin. "If that hussy is better, then she leaves my house."

Kirk frowned, but before he could speak Sophie intervened. "I don't think she is fit to travel, not for another day or two at least."

Will snorted. "Very well, lass." He nodded grudgingly.

Relief washed over Sophie. Leaving Watendlath would be hard enough, but she didn't think she could bear it if her last moments with Kirk were tainted by Becky's presence!

"Pray excuse me." Kirk rose abruptly to his feet. "Since we are to make an early start, I'll say farewell to Becky now."

Sophie watched him go.

He has forgotten I exist, she thought sadly, longing to call him back, but knowing it was no use.

For a few lovely moments earlier by the tarn she had allowed herself to dream that Kirk Thorburn might come to love her, but for the sake of her own self-respect it was time to stop pretending. She was nothing more than a momentary distraction in his life, and the sooner she accepted it, the sooner her heart might begin to heal!

CHAPTER TEN

SOPHIE STARED in the mirror and let out a sigh. Heavens, what a fright she looked, in spite of her best efforts to refurbish her appearance for the journey ahead.

"What time is it?"

Becky's muttered remark made Sophie spin round. "Did I wake you? I was trying to be quiet," she murmured apologetically.

Becky shrugged sleepily and sat up in bed. Her violet gaze took in the new daylight pouring in through the uncurtained window and she grimaced in distaste.

"What on earth possessed Kirk to want to leave so early? This is an ungodly hour!"

Sophie felt much the same, but she recognised the necessity. "We may get bogged down," she reminded Becky, who shuddered.

"I'm glad I'm not travelling with you," she said frankly. "I shall stay snug in bed. Will Hynde will have to wait on me whether he likes it or not."

Sophie turned back to the mirror before her hasty tongue could produce a sharp retort.

"Would you like to borrow one of my hair ribbons?" Becky asked a moment later, watching Sophie's struggle to tame her riot of brilliant curls.

She rummaged in the reticule she kept by the bed and held out a length of violet silk. "You may keep it if you wish."

This offer was so at odds with Becky's customary lack of interest in any concerns but her own that Sophie stared at her in surprise.

"Oh, I know what you are thinking. I am a selfish beast, but you've been kind to me, Sophie." Becky had the grace to blush. "I just wish I had the means to repay you, but my purse is empty."

"I wouldn't dream of taking your money even if I stood in need of it, which I can assure you I do not!" Sophie exclaimed hotly.

"I'm sorry," Becky apologised, looking so bewildered that Sophie felt forced to clarify her position.

"I didn't realise that you were an heiress." Becky stared at the borrowed brown dress, now sadly stained by Sophie's attempts at housekeeping, and laughed rather shortly. "You certainly don't look it."

"I know," Sophie answered lightly, choosing to ignore the note of envy in the older girl's tone.

"If I had your wealth I should cut a dash! What's the point in being rich if no one knows it?"

"You sound like my betrothed," Sophie chuckled and then regretted this unguarded remark when Becky began to hurl questions at her.

"I didn't mention my betrothal for reasons I prefer to keep private," she replied evasively.

Becky pouted. "Forgive me for asking, I'm sure!"

There was a short silence while Sophie finally managed to bind up her curls with the silk ribbon.

"It clashes with your hair," Becky announced with an air of satisfaction.

Sophie laid her comb down. "It doesn't matter," she said dully, too depressed by the thought that in a few moments she would be leaving Watendlath forever to be upset by Becky's envious spitefulness.

A strange expression, almost of remorse, flickered over Becky's perfect features.

"I'm sorry. I shouldn't pick at you when you are feeling miserable."

Sophie forced a smile. "Nonsense."

"I mean, anyone can see that you are in love with Kirk," Becky persisted. "It must be very galling for you that he doesn't return your affections."

Sophie stared at her in dismay, but Becky continued to rattle on.

"Of course, since you are betrothed elsewhere it is probably best that Kirk thinks of you as merely a friend."

"Did he say so?" Sophie asked through clenched teeth.

Becky's eyes widened innocently.

"Not in quite those words, but his meaning was plain," she replied with a childlike earnestness. "We talked about it last night when he came to say farewell." A delicate blush coloured her cheeks. "We have come to an understanding, you see."

Sophie thought she understood only too well and she shivered, suddenly chilled to the bone.

Pride came to her rescue.

"My congratulations on solving your pecuniary difficulties," she said coolly. "However, you mistake the matter. I am perfectly content with my betrothal." The lie slid smoothly off her tongue and she saw a frown crease Becky's brow.

"I doubt if there will be time to prepare a proper breakfast, but I'm going to make some tea. Would you like a cup?" Sophie took advantage of Becky's puzzlement to make her escape.

Will was already down and had the kettle on to boil.

"*Hoo ista, lass*?" He hailed her with the traditional greeting, and Sophie forced herself to smile and reply in a composed manner, as though her heart was not breaking.

She had been right! Kirk no longer desired her. He had denied that she was anything more than a friend. No doubt he was relieved to be free of the strange tug of attraction that had bound them, the oddest pair of unlikely lovers, together.

Will and Ned had finished their morning ale and were gone before Kirk strode into the room. Sophie was about to make a tart comment on his belated arrival when she noticed the lines of strain carved around his deep blue eyes.

He looks like a man who has had very little sleep, she thought to herself, and the words of censure died in her throat, to be replaced by a concern she could not quell, try as she might.

"Are you ready to leave?"

"Don't you want any breakfast?" Sophie exclaimed in response to this curt greeting.

Kirk shook his head impatiently. "We have wasted enough time already." Seeing her indignant expression, a crooked grin split his clear-cut features. "Sorry, *I* have wasted enough time."

"A delay of a few minutes more will make no odds," Sophie said firmly, pushing a plate of bread and cheese towards him.

Kirk shrugged. "You are an obstinate woman, Sophie Fleming," he muttered, but he accepted the tankard of ale and quickly ate a slice of bread.

"Thank you," he said, wiping his mouth free of crumbs. "No doubt I shall be glad of that later on, since Stanton is hardly likely to offer me any hospitality."

Sophie had been stacking the used dishes together, but she halted abruptly. "What do you mean? I hope you won't even see Pelham, much less have occasion to talk to him."

Kirk returned her worried gaze calmly. "Of course I shall have a word with him, Sophie. You didn't imagine that I would leave you on his doorstep like a parcel, did you?"

Sophie's eyes widened. "But Kirk, you can't!" she protested. "He will be furious if you dare appear at the Hall!"

"My dear, you and I both know he is very likely to be furious anyway," Kirk answered, his tone softening.

Sophie swallowed hard. She could feel the palms of her hands grow clammy and knew he had put her secret fear into words. Not normally a timid person, she found herself oddly apprehensive and unwilling to face Pelham's anger, because at heart she sensed that her betrothed was not the cold fish he pretended.

"Perhaps it would be wiser if you remained here at the farm," Kirk suggested. "I could deliver a message—"

"No!" Every feeling in Sophie was revolted by the idea of running away from her responsibilities. "I owe it to him to return. I will not make him a laughing-stock even if I finally decide not to marry him."

Kirk frowned. In his opinion Stanton didn't deserve such consideration, but he knew that they would only quarrel if he said so.

"Very well, I accept your reasoning, although I think it unwise," he said curtly. "But why not wait for a while until the Stricklands return? Then you could travel home with them as soon as you had spoken to him."

For an instant Sophie was tempted, but she shook her bright head.

"I want to get it over with," she murmured, reluctant to confess that she could not bear to stay and watch him dote on Becky.

"In that case, I insist on accompanying you," Kirk announced with a grim set to his mouth. "My conscience will not permit me to abandon you without first ensuring that all is well. I shall explain that Will found and housed you, but asked me to escort you home, since he could not leave the farm. Stanton won't like it—he hates me—but at least he won't question your story."

Sophie twisted her fingers together in agitation.

"Come, now, sweetheart, there is no need to look so worried. He is hardly likely to shoot me on sight!"

"What if he tries to set his men on you?" Sophie couldn't respond to his teasing grin, and a little quiver shook her voice.

"I doubt he would be so foolish, but . . ." Kirk shrugged his broad shoulders in a telling gesture. "I'm not exactly a novice when it comes to taking part in a mill."

Sophie gasped. "I won't have you fighting over me!" she exclaimed in accents of disgust, her temper flaring under this new strain.

Kirk raised his brows.

"Don't you frown at me, Kirk Thorburn!" Sophie had endured a very trying morning and she was in no mood to mince her words. "I find the idea of grown men fighting utterly abhorrent!"

"It's easy to see you don't have brothers," Kirk replied lightly, trying to defuse her anger, but Sophie's blood was up.

"Nor will I allow you to use me as another bone of contention in your dispute with Pelham," she declared angrily. "I am not a parcel, as you so inelegantly term it, and I will not permit you to entangle yourself in my affairs. I do not want you to speak to Pelham on my behalf. You will only make things worse!"

Kirk could feel his temper beginning to simmer. He had spent a large part of the previous night mulling over the difficulties inherent in returning Sophie to the Hall, and her haughty dismissal of his solution rubbed him raw.

"Do you imagine I want to waste my time smiling politely at that scoundrel? I wouldn't offer to do so unless I thought it necessary, you silly chit! Good God, anyone would think you suspected I had some devious scheme in mind, rather than worrying about you."

"It wouldn't surprise me if you had," Sophie flashed back at him. "I think you would use anything or anyone if it furthered your scheme to obtain revenge for your brother's death." Tears stung at her eyelids, but she ignored them and continued fiercely, "In fact I sometimes wonder whether you didn't decide to worm your way into my affections for that very purpose!" She glared at him. "Did you hope I might spy on Pelham for you?"

"You impudent baggage!" Kirk roared, but, even as he began to deny her slanderous accusation, the inconveniently honest voice of his conscience reminded him he had once thought he might try to see if jealousy would make the baronet grow careless.

"Perhaps I did briefly entertain such foolish notions when we first met at the soirée, but I swear to you they did not last beyond our first conversation," he said gruffly.

Too angry to hear the note of apology in his voice, Sophie failed to realise that the unaccustomed tide of colour flooding his bronzed face stemmed from embarrassment, and took it for a sign of guilt.

"It was all a trick from the start!" She stared at him, her great dark eyes stricken. Pelham had tried to tell her that Kirk might use her as a means of revenge, but she had buried that warning deep in her subconscious. "I should have known you would never care a scrap for a girl like me!"

Oh, how could she have been so foolish? Hadn't she learned the hard way that men did not care for her unfashionable looks or sharp tongue? It was evidence of her own idiocy that she could have believed even for a moment that Kirk Thorburn might have tumbled into love with her in the same crazy way that she had fallen for him.

"What the devil are you talking about?" Kirk demanded hoarsely, his conscience pricking him. "I have done my best for you, but you have thrown all my advice in my face."

"Advice? Damn your good advice!" Sophie could hear her voice turning shrill, but she couldn't stop herself. If she couldn't have his love, then at least she would keep her pride.

"Advice is the last thing I want from you, Kirk Thorburn! Keep out of my life! I shall go back to the Hall and deal with Pelham as I see fit. I do not need your help. You were only pretending to like me anyway—"

"Stop it!" Kirk grabbed her by the shoulders. "You are talking hysterical nonsense. I have admitted that I might have originally sought you out because of Stanton, but surely you *cannot* think all that has passed between us since was some kind of nefarious plot on my part? My God, I know I haven't always behaved as a gentleman ought to, but that doesn't make me a complete monster!''

Sophie gazed up at him rebelliously and he gave her an infuriated shake. ''Well, do you believe me or not, damn you?''

''I don't know! I don't know what to think any more!'' Sophie screamed at him, pulling away so violently that Kirk was startled into releasing her.

Sophie fought for control and managed to quieten her ragged breathing. ''You say one thing, Kirk, but do another,'' she murmured wearily, her temper spent. ''One minute you act as if you desire me, the next you are cold. What *am* I supposed to think?''

''Sophie.'' He brushed her cheek with a repentant finger. ''I told you once before that I did not mean to hurt you. Please believe that, in spite of my ungentlemanly behaviour.''

The tenderness in his Viking gaze penetrated the shell of anger Sophie had been frantically building around her bruised feelings.

''My own behaviour hasn't always been that of a lady,'' she sighed, her sense of fair play returning. ''I encouraged your advances, Kirk.''

''Would you deny me my wicked reputation?'' he asked with a wry grimace.

''Nonsense! You aren't some heartless womaniser, I know that now,'' Sophie asserted. ''But that leaves me with only one conclusion, namely that you care far more for your brother's memory than whatever it is that you feel for me.'' Sophie lifted her gaze to meet his. ''Your duty binds you, Kirk, and it leaves no room in your life for me. Becky will suit you far better.''

''Becky?'' Kirk's expression changed to one of puzzlement, but before he could question her a flush of hot colour stained the skin over Sophie's high cheekbones and her gaze flew in embarrassment to the partition wall dividing the bedchamber from where they stood.

Was Becky awake? Had she overheard them?

Sophie wished the floor would open up and swallow her. ''I am going to go and say goodbye to Rose,'' she gasped, whirling beyond the hand Kirk put out to detain her.

''Kirk, let her go.''

The husky contralto voice carried to Sophie's ears as she fled, and she knew if she turned back she would see Becky gliding seductively towards him, her arms outstretched in welcome.

"I DON'T RIGHTLY KNOW, Miss Fleming," Sam Braithewaite's freckled face wore a frown. "What do ye think, wife?"

Rose took her gaze from Sophie's anxious eyes and nodded briskly. "I think ye should take Sophie into Keswick as she asks. You were saying that we need a few supplies, and there's no time like the present."

Sam's anxious look melted. "Aye. Well, in that case, I'll go and saddle Darkie up." He turned to Sophie and added in a faintly apologetic tone, "Ye won't mind riding pillion, Miss Fleming, will ye?"

"Not in the least," Sophie assured him fervently.

When her husband had gone Rose said, "Are ye sure ye wish to leave in such haste, lass? I shouldn't wish ye to change your mind and regret your decision when it's too late to mend matters. Both of ye have hot tempers, but I doubt if Kirk meant to quarrel with ye."

Sophie shook her head firmly. "I won't change my mind."

The cold air had cleared her head as she walked to Rose's cottage. Before she had completed the short distance she had known what she must do. Kirk had chosen Becky, and for the sake of her own sanity she had to get away.

"I must leave immediately, Rose. Kirk cannot be permitted to confront the baronet. He says he would be able to control his temper, but it would end in bloodshed, I know it would!"

"Aye, I reckon it might at that. They never could abide each other."

Sophie smiled faintly. "Will you thank your father for his hospitality?"

Rose nodded. "Do ye want me to say goodbye to Kirk for ye as well?" she enquired perceptively.

Sophie winced.

Outside, the wind was fresh, and Sophie told herself that it was responsible for the tears stinging her eyes. Stoutly she refused to let them fall and scrambled up behind Sam, striving to control a tremor of fear at the thought of the journey ahead.

"I'm not much of a rider," she murmured apologetically, accepting his help to settle herself on the pony's broad back.

Thankful to hear him describe Darkie as a placid beast, Sophie bent down to clasp his wife's hand in farewell. "I'll return your dress as soon as I can," she informed her. "Good luck with the new baby and thank you for all your help and kindness, Rose."

Rose nodded in acknowledgement. "I hope all goes well for ye too, Sophie."

"It will." Sophie forced a note of optimism into her voice and waved farewell with a bright smile.

"Hey up, Darkie!"

Sam encouraged the pony into a trot and Sophie murmured, "I just hope she can persuade Kirk not to follow me!"

"What's that ye said, Miss Fleming?"

"Oh, nothing, I was merely thinking aloud," Sophie replied quickly, cursing her lack of self-control.

It was time she pulled herself together. She had to stop thinking about Kirk Thorburn. Hadn't the events of this morning proved to her beyond all doubt that their destinies lay with separate paths? Becky was the one he wanted, and it was only his keen sense of honour that had made him offer to escort her into what was for him a lion's den.

Honour and some small fondness, for he did care a little for her happiness. She knew that was what he had been trying to tell her this morning, but mere fondness wasn't enough. She wanted his *love*; nothing less would do.

But Kirk Thorburn wasn't prepared to offer that kind of commitment to her or any other woman.

THE SIGHT OF THE little town of Keswick gladdened Sophie, but she felt too uncomfortable to take much interest in the quaint old courthouse which presided over the market-place or the tiny cottages that clustered in its shadow. The ride had been marginally less frightening than she had feared, but she was frozen and aching in every limb.

Darkie's hoofs clattered against the white cobblestones of the main street and Sophie made a mental resolve to improve her riding skills. The prejudice induced by that fall when she was a child ought to be put behind her!

"Where do ye wish me to set ye down, Miss Fleming?" Sam enquired.

"I don't know exactly," Sophie confessed. "But I want to hire a carriage to convey me to Stanton Hall."

Sam sniffed, but, deciding it wasn't his place to criticise, said, "I think they might have a gig available at the George."

To Sophie's relief the landlord of this establishment was eventually willing to accept her word that he would receive payment when she reached her destination. His thick eyebrows had risen at her request and she had coloured as his gaze had swept over her bedraggled appearance. For one embarrassing moment she had thought he would insist on the money in advance, but Sam had indignantly vouched for her.

"Thank you, Mr. Braithewaite, for all your help," she said as the gig was brought out into the innyard with surprising speed.

Sam ducked his head in embarrassment, muttering that he was glad to oblige.

He assisted her up into the rather shabby vehicle and stood back to wave her off.

Twisting round on the hard seat to return his gesture of farewell, Sophie experienced an odd flicker of desolation. He was her last link with Watendlath!

The gig jolted along over the half-frozen roads, but Sophie was too preoccupied to notice any discomfort. For the past few days she had been putting off making a decision, but now she was rapidly running out of time.

Could she endure to marry the baronet? For if she could not, now was the time to tell him so!

It was impossible to ignore her feelings for Kirk Thorburn, but Sophie tried as she struggled to view the situation dispassionately.

She didn't love Pelham, but then she never had. What had changed was that she had lost the mild liking and respect she'd previously felt for him. Kirk's revelations had begun the rot, but Pelham's own recent behaviour was the main cause of her dissatisfaction.

On the other hand, there was Uncle Thomas to consider, and all the embarrassment of returning in disgrace to Kendal. Every malicious tongue would snigger and say the Flemings had overreached themselves. Even worse, in her heart Sophie was beginning to wonder if the gossips were right. Perhaps she was doomed to remain a spinster, unwanted by anyone except for her enormous dowry.

Stanton Hall loomed up on the horizon and Sophie shivered. What a coward I am, she thought in despair. If only I had some proof that Pelham was the monster that Kirk paints him, then my conscience would be eased!

"Shall I drive on up to the house, miss?"

The question roused Sophie from her wretched thoughts and she nodded, sitting up straighter. It was too late now to do anything other than brace herself to face the storm ahead.

The driver brought the gig to a halt at the foot of the imposing flight of steps that led to the main entrance, and Sophie had barely alighted before the massive double doors were flung open and Sir Pelham appeared, flanked by his butler and two footmen.

Taking a deep breath to steady her nerves, Sophie began to ascend.

"Where the devil have you been?"

The baronet flung this demand at her almost before she had reached the top step.

Sophie returned his angry stare with a calmness she was far from feeling. "I shall answer your questions in a moment, Pelham, but first pray be so good as to pay off the driver so that he may return to Keswick before it gets dark."

"Keswick!" the baronet ejaculated.

For an instant Sophie thought he might argue, but then with a sulky glare he snapped his fingers at his butler and said, "See to it."

He followed Sophie into the house, but she pretended not to notice and walked across the wide marble hall towards the log fire that blazed in the massive hearth.

"Well? What have you to say for yourself, ma'am?" the baronet barked at her. "Seeking refuge with that bunch of peasants! Did you want to humiliate me?"

Sophie continued to rub her hands before the blaze for a moment before she turned to answer him. "I am not deaf, Pelham. There is no need to shout, unless, of course, you wish to air your grievances for every servant in the house to hear."

The baronet goggled at her, utterly disconcerted by her unexpected insouciance. "I had expected you would have the decency to apologise at least," he growled at last. "Don't you realise what a furore your ridiculous behaviour has caused?"

Sophie shrugged nonchalantly. "I cannot think why," she said coolly. "I am sorry if I caused you any anxiety, but, after all, I wrote to tell you that I was safe and would return as soon as the weather permitted."

"You wrote to your maid, you mean!" He glowered at her. "Didn't you consider how distressing I should find it to hear such news at second hand?"

"Did you really?" She lifted her brows delicately. "You surprise me, Pelham."

This interview was not going in the least as the baronet had imagined. He had consoled his frustration over Sophie's disappearance by picturing the agreeable scene in which his distraught betrothed begged his forgiveness in a flood of repentant tears.

"By Hades, Sophie, your absence has not improved your manners!" His fists clenched involuntarily and Sophie experienced a flutter of fear.

He looks as if he would like to hit me, she thought, wondering if her impulse to brazen things out had been the right one. But what other choice had she? If she allowed him the upper hand now, he would ruthlessly exploit her weakness in future.

Sensing her confusion, the baronet pounced. "And what have you been doing to yourself, my dear? Is that absurd garment meant to be a dress or a cleaning rag?"

Sophie couldn't prevent a deep blush from colouring her cheeks. "I'm sorry my appearance displeases you, sir," she snapped. "My own clothes were ruined and I was forced to borrow this one from Mr. Hynde's daughter."

Sir Pelham laughed scornfully. "Couldn't she find you anything better? You were never a beauty, my dear, but now you look like a scarecrow."

Suddenly all Sophie's doubts vanished and her anger boiled over at his deliberate rudeness.

"Since neither my manners nor my appearance pleases you, am I to assume that you wish to curtail our betrothal?"

The hot words sprang of their own volition to her lips. For an instant she was too shocked to feel anything but dismay that she had not waited to seek her uncle's permission to break off the betrothal, but then an upsurge of joy banished her consternation and she was able to meet his astounded stare with a fiercely proud look.

"You mistake my concern for you," the baronet muttered, his complexion turning grey. "Pray forgive me if I have inadvertently offended. I fear I am overwrought. Your absence caused me great anxiety." He essayed a smile. "How can you think I wish to break off our betrothal? I desire it to continue above all things!"

Presented with such a handsome apology, Sophie could do nothing but incline her head in gracious acceptance, but she carefully refrained from reassuring him.

Instead she said, ''Please excuse me, Pelham. I long for a hot bath and a change of clothes.''

''Of course. Will I see you at dinner?''

There was a rare note of hesitancy in his tone, and Sophie experienced a flicker of triumph. Her instinctive decision not to show any weakness had been the correct one! Now all she had to do was to choose the right moment to tell him that she wanted her freedom.

''I think not. I am exceedingly weary,'' she murmured, eager to see how he would react.

''Then you must rest, my dear.'' The baronet smiled at her fulsomely and bowed.

Hiding her satisfaction, Sophie nodded and moved towards the stairs.

Nancy was waiting for her in her room.

''Oh, Miss Sophie, you don't know how glad I am to see you!'' she exclaimed.

Sophie hugged her soundly. ''I missed you too,'' she affirmed.

Nancy searched her with a keen glance. ''You've lost weight,'' she pronounced with a frown. ''And what have you been doing to your hair? I've seen tidier bird's nests.''

''Don't start scolding me the minute I walk in through the door,'' Sophie begged.

Nancy's gaze softened. ''Nay. I've ordered them to bring up a tray of tea and enough hot water for your bath.''

''Bless you! You cannot know how much I long to discard this dress. It was loaned to me by the dearest person, but we do not share the same size or taste!''

Nancy began to help her out of it.

''It's good material and I dare say it was cleaner before you got up to your tricks, Miss Sophie,'' she commented, holding out a loose robe for Sophie to slip into.

''Do you think you could restore it? I could make Rose a present of a new gown, but I don't want to risk offending her. She is very proud and independent, like most of the people I met in Watendlath.''

Nancy's eyebrows climbed. ''Oh, aye?''

Sophie obliged with a somewhat censored version of her adventures while she soaked in a tubful of hot water.

"When will you learn to act like a young lady, Miss Sophie?" Nancy scolded. "Fancy cooking and cleaning like that, as if you were a . . . a kitchen-maid."

"Now don't fuss, Nancy. I could hardly sit there and expect to be waited upon when the Hyndes were being driven distracted by the weather."

Nancy snorted. "I reckon there's more to it than you are letting on, miss!" She gave Sophie a sharp look. "I wish I'd got a look at this Mr. Thorburn of yours when we were in Kendal."

"He isn't my Mr. Thorburn," Sophie replied, adding hastily, "Be a dear and rinse my hair."

The subject was forgotten and a few minutes later Sophie was ensconced before the fire, sipping her tea. "Oh, it's so nice to feel clean!" she sighed luxuriously.

"Shall I lay out your cream silk?" Nancy smiled at her indulgently. "I'll warrant you want to erase the bad impression that brown horror must have had on Sir Pelham."

Sophie hesitated. Much as she loved her maid, she was loath to confide in her. Nancy was inclined to treat her as a child still, and she would be shocked to hear that Sophie proposed to give the baronet his *congé* without consulting her uncle first.

"No, there's no need," she murmured at last. "I intend to dine here in my room this evening. My ankle is aching and I feel a little weary."

As expected, this reply brought a flurry of searching questions concerning the state of Sophie's health before Nancy announced, "You need an early night, my girl."

Sophie agreed with a meekness that might have aroused Nancy's suspicions had her thoughts not been on brewing a posset to revive her beloved nursling.

"You rest now until supper," she admonished, after watching Sophie drink this concoction.

Sophie nodded, but when Nancy had quit the room she rose and crossed to the dressing-table on which resided her jewel-case. Opening it, she took out her betrothal ring and stared at it thoughtfully.

The enormous diamond winked up at her, dazzling in the candlelight. For an instant she was tempted to slide it on to her finger, but then she thrust it back into the case and slammed the lid shut.

"I'm sorry, Uncle Thomas," she murmured softly. "But my mind's made up."

A LONG-CASE CLOCK, its polished brass plate bearing the name of Jonas Barber, the celebrated clockmaker of Winster, decorated the corridor leading to Sir Pelham's study, and Sophie paused to check the time.

It wanted ten minutes to the hour. She was a little early. The baronet had answered her message asking to see him with a note saying that he would be pleased to receive her at ten.

Sophie had dressed with great care for this meeting. Rejecting all of her new diaphanous gowns, she had selected a pale lemon-coloured caraco dress. The longish jacket fell almost to her thighs over the matching petticoat and it was nipped in at the waist by a bright red sash which emphasised her slender waist.

The style was a slightly mannish one, devoid of any feminine frills, and it flattered Sophie's tall, slim figure. It also suited her mood. This morning she wanted to feel brisk and businesslike. I won't let him accuse me of being silly or hysterical, she vowed silently to herself. He will have to take me seriously!

The corridor was richly carpeted, another of the baronet's expensive whims. Sophie smiled grimly to herself. He'll have to find another dowry to squander on such extravagances!

The door to her betrothed's sanctum was ajar and Sophie could hear the murmur of male tones. Annoyance flickered through her as she recognised Simon Conrad's voice. If Pelham was closeted with his secretary, then she would be kept waiting just when she had screwed up her courage!

Damn Conrad, I feel like walking in on them, she thought crossly.

"You fool!"

The baronet's angry shout made Sophie jump in alarm, and she forgot all thoughts of announcing her presence. Instead she cast aside her scruples and crept closer, the thick carpet deadening her footfalls.

"I am sorry, sir, but I have done my best." Simon Conrad sounded harried. "Unless you repay the sum you owe him by the end of the month the Duke insists he will foreclose the mortgage.''

"That's less than three weeks away!"

"He was most insistent, sir."

"I will not lose the Hall!"

Sophie smothered a gasp and pressed her ear to the door to catch Conrad's reply.

"My dear sir, you stand to lose everything! When I arrived I warned you of the Duke's mood and you promised me that you would be careful, but you lost another two hundred at cards to old Mr. Curwen the other night."

"By Hades, are you never satisfied?" Sophie could have sworn she heard the grinding of teeth. "I gave up my mistress to suit your notions of economy and still you lecture me, you insolent puppy!"

"But sir, you said yourself that you were tired of Miss Hurst."

Sophie's heart missed a beat. Had she heard aright?

"Aye, ten years is enough with any woman, and so I told Becky. God knows I need a fresh start! Maybe my luck will change once I'm wed." The baronet laughed unpleasantly.

So *he* was Becky's mysterious lover! Sophie felt the bile rise in her throat. The hypocrite!

The sound of Sir Pelham's voice interrupted her angry reflections.

"There's only one answer if that stupid fool is going to kick up a dust. This accursed wedding will have to be brought forward. Waiting until May is too risky. We can be married here, and once I have my hands on that dowry he'll sing a different tune."

Shock sent all thoughts of Becky out of Sophie's head.

"Will Miss Fleming agree?" Doubt edged Conrad's tone. "I cannot help wondering if she could have somehow got wind of your debts. Why else should she run away like that?"

"Nonsense, she didn't run away. The silly wench got lost." The baronet snorted dismissively. "Don't forget, I kept my nose clean in Kendal. There was no difficulty in cozening her or that old fool Fleming. They think me as rich as Croesus."

Sophie's lips tightened at the insult to her uncle, but she forced down her fury so that she could concentrate on what was being said.

"Would to God that I had been able to convince one of the society mamas in London that my fortune was still intact! I am sick of rustic simplicity. Still, I suppose I shouldn't complain. The wench might be a lanky bag of bones, but she is young and not too ill-favoured."

Sophie's anger was increased by Conrad's answering laugh. Oh, how dared Pelham talk about her like this?

Not trusting her temper a moment longer, she began to back away.

"Never fear, I shall tame Miss Fleming. She will do precisely what she is told." Sir Pelham chuckled and then his amusement abruptly ceased. "Speaking of which, I expect her here in a few minutes. You may go. We will discuss the Duke's terms another time."

"Very well, sir, but . . ."

Sophie didn't linger to listen to the rest of the secretary's reply, but took to her heels. Anger lent her speed, but her stomach turned over with a sickening lurch as she heard the study door creaking behind her.

There was no time to escape from the long corridor, so she ducked behind the long-cased Barber clock, pressing herself flat against the wall.

If Conrad came in this direction instead of heading for the stairs . . . !

Sophie's heart was pounding so loudly that it was several moments before she realised that the danger of discovery had passed. The relief made her feel dizzy, and she had to clench her hands together to try and still them as she fought for composure.

The chiming of the hour startled her, breaking the spell that held her captive.

What shall I do? Pelham is waiting for me, but he will know something is wrong the minute he looks at me, she thought. Ten to one, I should blurt out my disgust and he'd know I'd been eavesdropping!

The baronet's cruel remarks only strengthened her determination not to marry him, but something warned Sophie that it would be most unwise to cross him in his present mood. He sounded quite desperate, she thought, pushing aside the unwelcome suspicion that she'd been unwise to dismiss Kirk's advice to stay at the farm.

I must go home, Sophie decided, all her instincts screaming that she was in danger. But how the devil was she to achieve such a thing, when the baronet commanded all forms of transport?

Idiot, worry about that later, she castigated herself. First of all you must pretend you are ill, to give yourself time to think of a plan.

"Why, Miss Sophie, what are you doing back here? I thought you were seeing the baronet."

"There's no time to explain now, Nancy," Sophie said, rushing into the room and flinging herself down at the elegant writing-table. "I want you to take this note to Sir Pelham, and if he asks you must say I am too sick to receive him."

Nancy's plump face looked bewildered. "But, Miss Sophie—"

"Quickly, Nancy." Sophie thrust the scrawled note into her hand. "Then hurry back and help me to pack. We are going home."

"Pack?" Her maid repeated the word helplessly. "I don't understand."

Sophie bit down hard on the impatient reply that sprang to her lips. "Be a dear and just do as I say," she begged, giving her maid a little push towards the door.

Nancy hesitated. "I hope you know what you are doing, Miss Sophie," she said doubtfully, watching Sophie snatch open the clothes cupboards that ran the full length of one wall. "Your uncle won't be too pleased if you offend the baronet."

Sophie shook her head wildly. "I'll tell you everything later," she cried, grabbing a handful of dresses and tossing them on the bed.

She peered into the bottom of the cupboard. "Damn, where are my portmanteaus? There is only one small valise in here."

"They were taken to one of the store-rooms, of course." Nancy flapped her hands in consternation. "Miss Sophie! You are creasing everything!"

"Never mind. We can't take much anyway. This will have to do," Sophie declared, snatching up the valise and starting to stuff clothes into it willy-nilly.

"Miss Sophie, have you run mad?"

"Oh, do stop wasting time, Nancy, and please hurry with that note."

"Oh, very well, but I don't know what on earth your uncle is going to say," Nancy grumbled.

Even as Sophie heaved a sigh of relief there was a sharp knock at the door.

"No, don't open it—"

But it was too late.

CHAPTER ELEVEN

"WHAT? ROSE, I DON'T find this amusing. Now where is she?"

"I told ye. She's gone, Kirk."

Kirk stared speechlessly at Rose. He felt as if she had punched him hard in the gut.

Gone! Sophie had left him without a single word of farewell! An unbearable sense of loss seared through him.

"Of all the senseless, stupid things to do!" he roared, unable to contain the rage that filled him. "Why the devil couldn't she wait for my escort?"

"Because she knew ye would lose your temper with Stanton and make matters worse," Rose retorted, giving him a sharp look.

"I don't understand. She cannot still intend to marry that scoundrel!"

"Mebbe, mebbe not. But what's it to ye, Kirk Thorburn?" Rose demanded crossly. "I reckon it's about time ye decided who comes first with ye."

Kirk paled beneath his deep tan. "Rose!" he growled warningly.

Rose planted her hands on her hips. "Nay, I'll have my say, Kirk Thorburn. Ye are a friend of mine and a good man, but right now I'm ashamed of ye. Ye've been playing fast and loose with that lass, and she deserves better. I know ye owe a debt to the dead, but if ye choose your brother's memory over a girl who loves ye then ye are a bigger fool than ye look!"

Kirk glared at her. "Damn all women," he muttered furiously and stalked out of the cottage.

Seeking refuge at Haraldsgarth, he tried to find forgetfulness in hard physical labour. Exerting the power of his splendid muscles, he cleared a satisfying pile of fire-blackened stones, but once his fury had cooled his conscience began to trouble him.

Perhaps Rose was right. Perhaps he had let his sense of duty outweigh all else. Perhaps it would have been fairer to explain to Sophie . . . Perhaps . . . oh, the devil take it!

Wishing he understood more about women, Kirk's brain whirled as he strove to make sense out of Sophie's defection.

Of course, Rose was wrong to imagine that Sophie was in love with him. Good God, they'd done nothing but quarrel! She probably thinks I'm a monster, he decided ruefully, a deep gloom settling over him.

His black mood was not improved by the unexpected arrival of Becky early the next morning.

"Will has thrown me out," she sobbed, casting herself upon his chest in a flurry of tears, almost upsetting the easel and the drawing he was working on.

"Becky, I told you yesterday that it was over between us." Containing his irritation, he gently loosened her grip and put her from him. "If it's money you want, I'm happy to advance you the sum I mentioned the other day." He stared blindly at the half-finished drawing of the new house he planned to erect. "However, I have no wish to try and rekindle old flames."

"You still hate me," she wailed. "You hate me because I ran away with Pelham."

"No, not any more." He shook his golden head wearily. "But we cannot resurrect the past. Too much has happened to both of us since then."

She sniffed and gazed up at him piteously. "You are in love with Sophie."

Kirk suppressed a groan. "Sophie Fleming has got nothing to do with it. I am well rid of the troublesome wench!"

"What do you mean? I asked Will where Sophie had gone, but he wouldn't give me an answer."

Becky's face was alive with curiosity, and Kirk realised she mustn't have overheard yesterday's quarrel after all.

"It's no mystery," he said shortly, unwilling to reveal Sophie's secret. "She has merely returned to her friends."

Something in his tone convinced Becky it was futile to keep on trying to lure him back into her arms. No matter how he protested, he had the look of a man in love.

Swallowing a brief pang of jealousy, Becky shrugged philosophically and decided to make the best of it.

"I'll take your money, Kirk, but only because I know you won't miss it," she said with a return of her usual acumen.

"Where will you go?"

"Back to London. Here, there is always the possibility that I might encounter Pelham in some quiet spot, and I think I would grab the chance to knife him!" Becky's violet gaze hardened and Kirk knew that she was free of Stanton's spell at last.

Becky's expression cleared. "Will you give me a ride into Keswick? If I remember aright, the mail-coach runs today and I might be lucky enough to secure a place if I hurry."

"Of course," Kirk replied, trying to hide his relief.

They made good time and found that there was one single inside seat still available.

"Goodbye, Kirk, I doubt if we will meet again," she said to him as she prepared to board the coach after they had eaten a hasty meal.

A smile lit her perfect features.

"Perhaps it is better this way." She patted her reticule, where his bank-draft lay safely stowed. "I should have driven you mad."

"You'd have been bored within a week," he agreed with a grin.

Laughing, Becky stretched up to kiss his cheek, and he handed her into the vehicle.

Her expression sobered as she leant her head out of the window. "Take care, Kirk," she whispered. "Pelham is dangerous."

He started at this unexpected warning.

"What do you mean?" he demanded hoarsely.

"Just that I know what Pelham is like. Need I remind you I was his mistress for many years?" Kirk's expression hardened and she carried on hastily. "Never mind my morals. Remember what happened to Ingram when he tried to cross him."

"Do you have any shred of evidence to back your suspicions?" he asked eagerly.

Hating to disappoint him, Becky shook her head. "He never confided in me, Kirk, so I have no proof. All I know is that just before Ingram's death he was suddenly in funds. Not that it lasted, of course."

She paused and then added abruptly, "Did you know he plans to wed? Some heiress who will restore his fortune."

Kirk frowned grimly. "Aye, I knew."

Long after the coach had pulled away he stood there turning the problem over in his mind . . .

Sophie had rejected him, but he could not abandon her. She would brook no further interference on his part and he could hardly blame her, considering how ineptly he had handled matters in Watendlath, but perhaps she would listen to her oldest friend.

Calling for his horse to be saddled, Kirk strode across the innyard, a look of grim determination on his handsome face.

"REALLY, MY DEAR, you will have to learn to be more punctual. I dislike to be kept waiting." The baronet brushed Nancy aside, ignoring her gasp of surprise, and strolled into the centre of the room.

"I do not recall inviting you in, Pelham," Sophie said coldly. "Please leave."

He shrugged. "It pains me to have to point it out, but this is my house, my dear."

His cold gaze turned to Nancy. "Out."

Nancy's eyes widened. "Sir—"

"Out or I'll have you whipped for disobedience, you stupid hag."

Sophie felt her anger return in full force. "How dare you speak to my maid in such a manner?" she snapped.

"Oh, I shall dare more than that, my dear." The baronet laughed unpleasantly. "Now tell her to leave or I'll have one of the footmen throw her out."

The baronet's voice was quiet, but Sophie sensed the anger simmering in his well-fleshed frame.

"Do as he says, Nancy."

For an instant it looked as if her maid would dispute the command, but then she nodded.

"I think we have something to discuss," the baronet announced grimly once Nancy was gone.

Sophie ignored him. "What is the meaning of this outrage, Pelham?" she demanded haughtily, attempting to stare him out of countenance.

He laughed shortly. "Don't play the fool, Sophie."

His glance fell upon the disordered bed. "Packing? And in such haste too."

Sophie frowned. "I have no intention of talking to you, sir, until you apologise for your disgraceful behaviour," she announced. "I am astounded that you should neglect the civility you owe to me, and I demand—"

"It won't work this time," Sir Pelham interrupted bluntly. "You managed to bluff your way out of answering any questions yesterday, but I will have the truth now. The fact that you were planning to leave only confirms my suspicions." He fixed her with his cold gaze. "What exactly did you overhear?"

Shaken by the barely veiled menace in his tone, Sophie played for time. Moving gracefully to her dressing-table, she sat down, settling her skirts slowly.

"What do you mean?" she asked, carefully avoiding his gaze. "What should I have heard? You are talking in riddles, Pelham."

She picked up her silver-backed hairbrush and began to rearrange her disordered curls. "Are you angry because I kept you waiting just now? It wasn't my intention to do so, I assure you, but on my way downstairs I realised that I had forgotten my fan, so I came back to collect it." Sophie strove to inject all the conviction she could muster into her voice. "Unfortunately I could not find the yellow one which matches this dress, hence the mess. There is no need to imagine that I was packing! I would have kept our rendezvous if only you had waited another few minutes for me."

"Very good, my dear. You almost have me convinced. Almost, but not quite." The baronet laughed unpleasantly. "Now let's try again."

Sophie's dark eyes glared at him through the mirror.

"You have no right to question me like this," she said hotly, trying hard to think up a plausible denial.

"Come, enough of this nonsense," he baronet snapped. He produced a lace-trimmed handkerchief. "I found this just now outside my study door."

Recognising the dainty scrap of lawn he held out, Sophie paled. It must have fallen from her pocket, and she'd been too upset to notice its loss!

"What, nothing to say for yourself at last?" The baronet gave her a taunting smile. "You were eavesdropping. Admit it!"

"Go to hell!" Sophie's precarious hold on her temper snapped. She slammed down her hairbrush and whirled round to face him, her expression defiant. "I won't answer your stupid questions!"

"You little shrew . . ."

Before Sophie could guess his intention, he grabbed her by the wrist and jerked her to her feet with such cruel force that a shocked cry was startled out of her.

"Don't make me angry, my dear." He twisted her wrist savagely. "I am not an easy man to cross."

Sophie choked back a gasp of pain. "You want the truth? Very well, you shall have it, you bully! I wouldn't marry you if the King commanded it! You disgust me!"

"Damn your infernal impudence!" The baronet thrust her violently from him with a growl of rage.

Flung off balance, Sophie fell against a small tripod table. It gave way and she crashed painfully to the floor. For an instant she was too shocked to move, before her fighting spirit revived and she struggled to her feet.

Sir Pelham made no attempt to assist her, but stood staring at her with cold distaste.

"I had hoped to avoid unpleasantness, but since you now know the truth about my debts there is no need for pretence. Get this through your head—you are going to marry me whether you like the idea or not."

"Never." Sophie spat the word at him. "You are a liar and a hypocrite." She had guessed he only wanted her for her money, but she had never dreamt he might be Becky's mysterious lover, and she couldn't forgive him for the misery he had caused. "You can't make me marry you."

"Oh, but I can." His smile was silky with menace. "Here at the Hall I have a private chapel, so we can dispense with the necessity of a public ceremony. You will stand at the altar with me if I have to drag you there by the hair. And don't think you can defy me. There will be no guests to listen to your protests. No one will help you."

"No parson would consent to such vileness," Sophie gasped. She was shaking and her legs felt like water, but she held her head defiantly high.

"You think not? Then you are a fool, my dear. Men will do anything for money, and I know a certain cleric who would be only too happy to oblige. Not that it need come to such a pass. There are drugs which I can use beforehand to render you docile."

Sophie stared at him in disbelief. Impossible as it seemed, he really meant what he was saying!

"Oh, yes, I intend to go through with it, my dear." The baronet smirked, amused by the look of horror on her expressive face. "What's more, the arrangement won't take long to complete. You see, I've already taken the precaution of obtaining a special licence, so we ought to be able to hold the ceremony within the next day or two."

He bared his teeth at her in another taunting smile.

"Perhaps you ought to choose a dress to wear for the occasion—if you can find one that you haven't crushed too badly, that is."

Goaded by this deliberate mockery, Sophie flew at him, but he was too quick for her. He fended off her raking nails and held on to her hands, his grip savage.

"Temper, temper! You'll have to learn to control yourself better when we are wed," he jeered, panting a little.

In answer, Sophie kicked him hard on the shins, but since she was wearing flat kid slippers she knew it did little good.

"Hellcat!" The baronet released her and, thrusting her aside, swiftly extracted the key from the door. "You won't be needing this." He glared at her. "No one will come to release you, whatever happens, but if you are foolish enough to annoy me by making a fuss you'll get no food or drink until the wedding breakfast."

The door banged shut behind him and Sophie heard the key turn in the lock. She was a prisoner!

"MR. THORBURN, ma'am."

"Thank you, Jane." Maria Strickland nodded dismissal to the parlourmaid. "This is a pleasant surprise, Mr. Thorburn. However, I'm afraid my sister is not here. She is dining from home this evening."

"Actually, I came to see you, Mrs. Strickland." Kirk bowed politely.

Maria's dark brows rose. "Pray be seated, sir. Do you wish to wait for my husband? He will be down shortly."

Kirk shook his head. "I think it is better I speak to you alone." He shifted awkwardly in the satinwood chair. "I have come to ask for your aid."

Maria's fan fluttered in surprise. "Perhaps you had better begin at the beginning, sir," she murmured.

Kirk coughed. "You may find my story shocking," he warned.

Maria smiled. "I am rarely shocked, Mr. Thorburn."

Kirk's well-cut mouth thinned.

"I hope not, ma'am," he said drily.

"So you see," he ended his explanation, "Sophie has rejected my advice."

Maria strove for composure. "What you have to say is most alarming, sir." She surveyed her satin skirts for a moment and then raised her head. "I must admit, I have been anxious myself. Sir Pelham's behaviour while we were his guests was most odd. He showed no respect for Sophie and no regard for her wishes."

"Then will you add your persuasion to mine and beg her to return to Kendal without delay?"

Maria's fan fluttered in agitation and Kirk's expression grew impatient. "I know I have no right to ask you to break off your holiday—"

"My dear Mr. Thorburn, curtailing our stay here is of little importance," Maria interrupted. "You suspect that the baronet might make Sophie a dreadful husband, and I agree with you. For that reason alone, I am inclined to think that the betrothal ought to be broken off, but I do not understand why you think there is such need for haste."

"Once they are wed he will gain control of her fortune. I fear that he may have been cast into a panic by her absence and use the opportunity presented by her friendless state to bring the wedding forward."

"You think he would coerce her?" Maria gasped, turning pale.

Kirk nodded, and Maria's hand flew to her mouth in a shocked gesture.

"Shall I ring for your maid, ma'am?"

"There is no need." Maria recovered her composure. "Pray forgive me. I am not usually given to the vapours." She fanned herself vigorously. "It seems fantastic to imagine Sir Pelham a murderer!"

"Whether or not you accept that the baronet had a hand in my brother's death makes no odds," Kirk replied tightly.

"What matters is that you persuade Sophie to leave Stanton Hall before it is too late."

Maria bit her lip. "I do not like to interfere."

Kirk's hands clenched on the arms of his chair.

"But in this case I think I must," Maria continued slowly. "Thomas Fleming entrusted his niece to my care and I must fulfil that obligation. Whether or not you are correct in your suppositions, Mr. Thorburn, there is certainly cause for concern."

She gave him a direct look.

"I am grateful to you for coming all this way to warn me, Mr. Thorburn, but may I ask why you are taking such a close interest in Sophie's affairs?"

He coloured beneath her scrutiny. "I think you have already guessed the reason, ma'am."

Maria nodded, satisfied, and Kirk rose to his feet.

"Must you leave, sir? It is late, and I know my sister would ask you to remain as our guest for the night."

Kirk thanked her, but refused.

"Won't you at least stay and dine with us?"

Kirk hesitated and then shook his head. "I have already bespoken a meal at the inn at Ouse Bridge," he replied. "A friend of mine was kind enough to loan me his yacht to speed my arrival here. I intend to set sail on the return journey at first light and so must be up betimes."

"In that case, sir, I shall not seek to detain you."

Maria rose to her feet in a rustling of skirts and escorted him in person to the front door.

"You will let me know if I can be of any further assistance?" Unconsciously Kirk twisted the brim of his hat in his hands.

Maria nodded. "Of course." She smiled at him. "I am sure Sophie will wish to get in touch with you herself, sir, once she is safely home again."

Kirk politely returned her smile, but his heart remained heavy.

He should have made his feelings clear to Sophie while he'd had the chance, but he'd bungled it. The devil alone knew what women thought—*he* certainly didn't—but somehow he had the feeling that Sophie wouldn't forgive him for putting duty before love.

"OH, MISS SOPHIE, my head's all of a whirl!"

Nancy gazed open-mouthed at her young mistress. "Who would have thought it?"

"But you do believe me, don't you?" Sophie asked anxiously.

"Aye, that I do!" Nancy affirmed stoutly.

Sophie heaved a sigh of relief.

She had been kept solitary all day and once her first fury had worn itself out she had sunk into a dismal depression. Over and over again she had replayed the events leading up to her confrontation with the baronet, tormenting herself with the thought that she ought to have managed better.

Why hadn't she realised earlier that Becky's lover was the baronet? Good heavens, but it was so obvious that she must have been blind not to see it! Becky had even known that Haraldsgarth was ruined, in spite of frequently declaring that she hadn't kept in touch with anyone from Watendlath!

Yet even if I had known, would I have behaved any less stupidly? Sophie wondered dismally. Kirk kept warning me about Pelham, but I was too stubborn to listen to him. Too stubborn, too proud...and too desperately in love to think straight!

She had rejected all Kirk's advice, and look where her obstinacy had led! He must think me a fool and be glad to be rid of me, she thought sadly, her depression deepening.

Nancy's arrival with her supper-tray had been a welcome surprise, and Sophie's spirits had begun to lift when she realised that her maid was to be allowed to remain.

"Eat up your supper, Miss Sophie, and then we'll talk," Nancy had insisted.

Sophie had obeyed, realising that her maid had been badly shocked and was trying her best to preserve some semblance of normality.

But as soon as the meal was finished Sophie had made Nancy sit down.

"It is time I told you the whole story," she had confessed.

Recovering from her surprise, Nancy smiled with cheerful determination. "Never you fret, lass. There's many a slip 'twixt cup and lip, and that villain's plans don't deserve to prosper." She shook her greying head. "I never thought to see a gentleman behave in such a way!"

"Do you think we should attempt to escape? It will be difficult, but what other choice is there? I feel I must at least try.

I can't sit here meekly waiting for that brute to force me up the aisle!''

"That you can't, my lamb!'' Nancy nodded vigorously.

"One of the footmen will come soon to bring fresh fuel for the fire,'' Sophie said thoughtfully. "Perhaps we could distract him.''

Nancy eyed the brass poker by the hearth. "Aye, it might work at that, Miss Sophie.''

Sophie followed her gaze. A shiver ran along her spine as she realised what her maid was thinking, but she crushed her reluctance. "We have got to get out of this horrible place!''

"Where will we go once we are free?'' Nancy asked with a calm practicality that soothed Sophie's strained nerves.

"Keswick. It isn't very far and we won't get lost even in the dark if we keep in sight of the lake.''

"But won't Sir Pelham think of looking for us there?''

"I don't intend to remain in the town, Nancy. I have plenty of money—Uncle Thomas was very generous—so we don't have to rely on the stage. The landlord of the George has a carriage for fire, and there must be others. Travelling post will be both quicker and easier.''

"Oh, but I shall be glad to see Kendal again!'' Nancy exclaimed fervently.

Sophie nodded, but it occurred to her that it might be safer to head for Cockermouth, where they could beg the Stricklands' protection. The journey home to Kendal was far longer, which made the risk of Sir Pelham catching up with them proportionately greater.

She felt sure that the baronet would chase after them. He is desperate to get his hands on my dowry and he dare not let me spread the story of his perfidy, she thought, but decided not to add this anxiety to Nancy's other worries.

Instead, she concentrated on remembering the road to Keswick, pouring out aloud all the details she had noticed in the hope that talking about it would enable her to recognize their way in the dark.

"Shall I see if I can sew your purse into the hem of a dress, Miss Sophie?'' Nancy enquired when they had finished discussing their route.

"What a good idea!'' Sophie exclaimed. None of her gowns possessed deep pockets. "We shall have enough trouble without carrying bags.''

Nancy helped her select a redingote dress. It had a dark wine-coloured overskirt in a warm corduroy material, making it the most suitable in her wardrobe for the night ahead, but Sophie rejected the matching buckled ribbon sash.

"I don't want anything that might catch the light."

"Then you must wear a hood over your hair," Nancy cautioned.

Nancy swiftly completed her alteration to the gown, but Sophie decided to wait before putting it on.

"The footman might notice and think it odd I am wearing an outdoor gown so late in the evening," she explained, and Nancy nodded, impressed by this foresight.

"I think that's everything." Sophie's brow creased in concentration. "Since there are no more preparations we can make, shall we go over our plan again?"

They perfected their simple scheme and sat down to wait.

The house grew quiet and Sophie began to be alarmed that she had been forgotten and that no one would come to replenish the fire.

By the time the tap came at the door just before eleven she was so keyed up that she jumped. Quickly signalling to Nancy, she grabbed her book and sat down in the armchair by the fire.

"Enter!"

The youngest of the ornately liveried footmen, a callow youth who seemed overawed by his position, came scurrying in.

Looking up from West's *Guide to the Lakes*, she said in her most haughty voice, "What an age you have been! Pray attend to this wretched fire at once."

The footman glanced at the fitfully smouldering flames and then over his shoulder at the door, which he had left slightly open.

"Beg pardon, ma'am, but I was told not to linger," he said, setting down the bucket of seal-coal which he carried.

"Good heavens, you don't expect me to get my hands dirty, do you?" Sophie demanded with a petulant pout borrowed from Becky's repertoire. "Stop dawdling at once and get on with it, man."

Recognising the voice of authority, the footman succumbed and knelt by the hearth. Keeping his gaze fixed on the heap of coals he was carefully placing on the embers, he said, "Where is the poker, ma'am? I need it . . . ah!"

"Here you are!"

Nancy brought the poker down hard on his bewigged head and he slumped forward.

"For one awful moment I thought you were going to wait too long in the dressing-room," Sophie gasped, leaping to her feet. She began to rip off her loose robe. "Is he all right?"

Nancy bent over the footman. "Aye. His wig helped protect him." With deft efficiency she made him more comfortable, straightening his limbs. "He'll suffer naught worse than a headache when he wakes."

Sophie clambered into the wine gown and they both donned their cloaks, the plainest and darkest that Sophie owned. At the last moment she remembered to throw the hood up over her bright, revealing hair.

Their plan was to try and slip out via the servants' quarters, but first they had to traverse the richly furnished upper halls. Sophie's mouth was dry with fear as they crept from her room, but they saw no one.

A maze of drab passages and back-stairs led downwards towards the service area of the house and its rear exits, and Sophie stood back to allow Nancy to lead the way, knowing she would have been lost within moments if she'd been alone.

Giving the kitchens a wide berth, they slipped into the deserted laundry-room.

"There's a small door. I hope it's not been locked up yet," Nancy whispered.

It yielded to her touch and they found themselves in the grassy plot used for clothes-drying.

"I think we go this way, through the herb and kitchen gardens," Nancy whispered.

Sophie nodded and they set off at the fastest pace they could manage. Unfortunately this part of the grounds was not as well kept as the formal areas and Sophie cursed as her elegant leather-soled boots slipped on the wet grass and muddy paths, unlike Nancy's outdoor clogs. Nancy had removed them to creep downstairs, lest the iron caulkers shod over the alderwood soles made a noise, but now they gave her a secure footing that Sophie envied.

Sophie also began to wish ladies' gowns aped the more sensible shorter length worn by servants, for her skirts soon became uncomfortably damp and heavy as they worked their way round the side of the house.

They were barely in sight of the long gravelled drive when the elegantly high heel of Sophie's boot caught in a tussock of rough grass. She slithered, wrenching her weak ankle, and could not prevent a little gasp of pain.

"Are you all right, Miss Sophie?" Nancy asked anxiously.

Sophie nodded gamely, ignoring the fire in her ankle.

"We'll have to head for the main gates," she said. "I don't know the way through the park and we can't afford to waste time getting lost."

"We'll never get past the gatekeeper," Nancy objected.

"The wall is low. We can climb it."

Nancy wasn't sure she shared her mistress's confidence.

"Eh, Miss Sophie, but I'm too old for all this gallivanting," she muttered.

Sophie chuckled softly. "Nonsense," she whispered. "You are tougher than any of us."

Nancy gave her an answering grin, but their good humour abruptly vanished when someone shouted, splitting the silence.

"They must have discovered our escape!" Sophie gasped.

The noise increased and light blossomed from the direction of the house, illuminating the darkness.

"We cannot have more than a few minutes' lead on them. They'll catch up with us for sure." Sophie came to a rapid decision. "You must go on alone, Nancy. Hurry, I'll stall them for as long as I can. It's me they are after anyway."

Nancy gazed at her in horror. "I can't leave you, Miss Sophie!"

"You must! You have to get word to the Stricklands." Sophie's voice was harsh with anxiety. "Maria will help me, but I shan't be able to delay the marriage long."

Nancy nodded reluctantly, her face crumpling. She threw her arms around Sophie and gave her a brief fierce hug.

"God keep you, my lamb!" she sobbed.

For an instant Sophie lingered, watching her melt away into the darkness. Then she turned and began to walk resolutely back towards the house.

THE WIND BLOWING across the lake struck chill as Kirk Thorburn stood at the rail of the *Western Star*. He stared unseeingly at the grey water, willing the small yacht to greater speed.

"I've made some coffee for ye, sir. Will ye come below and drink it?"

"In a moment." Kirk smiled mechanically at the sailor, one of the permanent crew Mr. Farrington kept on board.

The sailor nodded and disappeared, shaking his head over this strange passenger.

Kirk barely noticed him go.

Harry had readily agreed to loan him the boat he kept on Lake Bassenthwaite. They hadn't seen each other in years, but they had been firm friends once and Kirk had been willing to risk a rebuff to his pride in order to save time in reaching Cockermouth.

Kirk stirred uneasily, raking a hand through his tousled hair.

His visit to see Maria Strickland had been fruitful, but he could not rid himself of the disquiet which had been haunting him ever since he had discovered Sophie's absence.

"Damn it, I swore I wouldn't interfere in her affairs again!" he muttered aloud and stamped below deck to consume his coffee.

His unease grew stronger as the morning passed. Kirk ignored it. By thunder, he had his pride and he'd be damned if he'd lay himself open to any more insults from that little baggage!

By the time he left the boat his mood was foul. Electing to dine in Keswick, it didn't improve his temper to find the yard of the George deserted.

"Ostler! Ostler! What the devil is going on?" he demanded when the groom came running to take Sultan's reins.

"Beg pardon, Mr. Thorburn, sir. Only there's a madwoman abadgering Mr. Fletcher. She came running in here not ten minutes ago, hollering fit to burst. Mr. Fletcher, he told her to go, but she marched into the parlour as bold as brass. She's demanding all manner of things, so I've heard, and Tom says Mr. Fletcher is likely to go off in an apoplexy!"

Kirk grinned sourly. It seemed that the landlord, who was noted for his bull-headed character, had met his match at last.

Tossing the ostler a coin, he decided to go and watch the entertainment while he waited for his dinner.

A crowd of giggling servants clustered around the entrance to the parlour, but, recognising him, they respectfully parted.

A small, thick-set woman stood firmly planted in the middle of the room. Her greying hair hung in wild disarray and her servant's attire was torn and splashed with mud, but nothing in her dirty face suggested that she was mad to Kirk. In fact something about her plucky stance stirred his admiration, and on impulse he stepped into the room.

The landlord was shouting in an angry voice, but he fell silent when he spotted Kirk.

"Can I do anything to help, Fletcher?"

"That you can, Mr. Thorburn, sir. You can tell this . . . this harridan to leave my inn before I set the law on her!" the landlord gibbered.

"Thorburn?" The woman's sharp eyes fastened on Kirk's face. "*You* are Kirk Thorburn, sir?"

Kirk nodded, vaguely disturbed by the intensity of her stare. He was just beginning to wonder if he had made a mistake in getting involved when she burst into noisy tears.

"Well, don't just stand there, man!" Kirk bellowed at the landlord. "Fetch the lady some cordial."

The landlord backed away in alarm.

"And you may bring me some brandy while you are about it," Kirk called after him.

Gingerly he put an arm around the woman's shaking shoulders. "Come and sit down, ma'am," he invited gruffly.

"Thank you, sir," his protégée sniffed.

To Kirk's relief, she stopped crying almost immediately.

"I'm sorry," she said. "I should be rejoicing that I have found you, not snivelling like a ninny."

This remark puzzled Kirk, but before he could ask her meaning the landlord came hurrying in with the required refreshments.

His protégée took a swift sip at her wine.

"Let me introduce myself. I am Nancy Nelson, maid to Miss Fleming." She gazed at him beseechingly. "She spoke of you as a friend, sir, and God knows she is in sore need of a friend to help her now."

A muscle by Kirk's well-cut mouth jerked involuntarily, but his voice remained creditably calm when he replied to this startling announcement.

"Where is Miss Fleming? I take it that she did not accompany you here."

Nancy shook her head vehemently.

"We planned to leave Stanton Hall together, but our escape was discovered. Miss Sophie bade me leave her and fetch help.

She told me to go to Mrs. Strickland, but that fool of a land-lord will not listen to my pleas. He refuses to hire out his gig without payment in advance, and I haven't a farthing on me!''

Kirk turned cold. ''Why did you use the word 'escape'? Is the baronet preventing Miss Fleming from leaving the Hall?''

''Aye, sir. He wanted to bring the wedding forward and locked Miss Sophie up when she said she would not marry him.'' Nancy quelled the sobs that threatened to rise in her throat and added in a choked voice, ''He plans to force her, you see, sir.''

''The devil he does!'' Kirk's intensely blue eyes began to blaze. ''Do you know when the ceremony is to take place?''

''Today, I reckon, from what Miss Sophie told me.''

''Then it is already too late to hope Mrs. Strickland can intervene.''

Rapidly Kirk explained about his mission to Cockermouth. ''But I fear they will not arrive until tomorrow, since they are travelling by road,'' he finished.

Nancy chewed her lower lip frantically. ''My poor lass said she would try to delay the wedding.''

''I think it is too risky to pin our hopes on her succeeding,'' Kirk answered gently.

''Oh, sir!'' Nancy blinked away a tear. ''What shall I do? I should never have left her!''

Kirk patted her hand in an awkward gesture.

''You have done all you could, Mrs. Nelson,'' he said firmly. ''I'm sure Sophie will be proud of you. Now you must recover from your exertions and leave the rest to me.''

''To you, sir?'' Nancy shot him a hopeful look.

''To me,'' Kirk repeated and rose purposefully to his feet. ''I have a score to settle with Sir Pelham Stanton, and what better time than now?''

''I WON'T SIGN.''

Sophie glared at the baronet across the width of his walnut pedestal desk. On its surface lay an impressive-looking legal document, the formal contract stating the marriage terms she had agreed to in Kendal.

Sir Pelham's thin mouth twisted in a mocking sneer.

''Very well, my dear, continue in your obstinacy. After to-night it will make no odds.'' He laughed cynically. ''If necessary, I can always instruct Conrad to forge your signature. He is remarkably skilled in such useful arts."

Sophie paled. She was very tired after a sleepless night spent pacing the floor of her gilded prison, but her voice was firm. "You won't get away with it. My uncle—"

"Bah! The old fool will have to accept accomplished facts. I will have the marriage-lines, and, make no mistake, I shall bed you whether you are willing or no! There will be no annulment, no claims of non-consummation!"

A shiver ran down Sophie's spine. The thought of his pale hands upon her body made her feel sick.

Her revulsion showed on her expressive face and the baronet threw down the pen he was still holding out to her with an angry oath.

"Do you think I wish to marry an ugly, ill-bred cripple?" he asked venomously. "Believe me, I would never do so if it were not for the fact I need your dowry."

The look of hatred in his eyes made Sophie recoil.

His nature is twisted, she thought, with a flash of sudden understanding. His over-weening pride and selfish ambition have driven out all finer feelings. He doesn't care whom he hurts so long as he gets his own way!

Fear curbed the retort that sprang to her tongue. Once he had control of her fortune, what was to prevent him arranging another little "accident" to remove *her* from his path?

"The ceremony will take place as soon as the parson arrives. He should be here within the hour." The baronet fixed her with a cold stare. "Wear the cream silk gown and tidy your hair. You look like a village slut."

Sophie was still wearing the wine redingote she had donned for her escape, and it had been stained and torn during the struggle to drag her back into the house.

"How am I to dress without the assistance of my maid?" Sophie taunted him, recovering her courage.

His frown deepened. The fact that the older woman had got clean away irked him, but he consoled himself with the thought that even if she managed to persuade anyone to believe her story it would be too late to affect his plans.

"I'll send one of the housemaids up to you, but heaven help you if you try any more tricks," he snarled, turning to tug savagely at the bell-pull to summon Conrad, who was waiting outside the study.

The baronet conferred in a whisper with his secretary and the fleshy young man departed with an obedient bow.

"I have sent him to fetch the drug I spoke of yesterday," Sir Pelham informed Sophie.

Her great dark eyes widened.

"It is a potent draught." Idly the baronet pretended to examine his well-manicured fingernails, but he was watching her like a hawk. "You'll be able to walk and talk a little, but nothing more."

Sophie could not repress a shiver, and she stared in horror at the glass of dark brown liquid which the secretary brought in.

Coming out from behind his ornate desk, the baronet thrust it beneath her nose.

"Smells vile, doesn't it, my dear? What a pity you dislike taking medicines." He smiled mockingly at her start of surprise. "You see what a devoted husband I shall make, since I can remember even your lightest remarks!"

His glance flicked towards his secretary. "Here, Conrad, hold her."

"No!" Sophie retched. "Take it away, for pity's sake!"

Sir Pelham laughed and set down the glass.

"Am I to assume that you will behave yourself without this little inducement?"

Sophie nodded silently.

"Do I have your word?"

Again she nodded and, satisfied, he waved Conrad to remove the sedative.

Sophie was trembling. Her reluctance to swallow his disgusting brew was quite genuine, but she had exaggerated her fear in order to convince him that she would honour her promise. Naturally she had no intention of doing so. Pelham had forfeited all rights! She would take any chance to escape that presented itself, and for that she needed to keep her wits about her.

The secretary shut the door quietly after him and the baronet said, "Now shall we discuss the matter of wedding gifts? I'm sure you'll be able to persuade your uncle into forgetting his disappointment at missing the ceremony. I have a fancy for something generously large and splendid."

Sophie regarded him with scorn. "What a despicable creature you are, Pelham!"

He raised his fist to hit her and then let it fall. He would not risk marking that white skin of hers before the service. There would be plenty of time to teach her obedience once they were wed.

"Watch your tongue," he snapped. "I don't find insolence amusing."

He tugged at the bell-pull again and, while they waited, delved into the pocket of his elegantly cut satin coat.

Sophie stared hard at the snuff-box he pulled out.

"It is pretty, is it not?" The baronet preened beneath her gaze and flicked open the lid. "French, of course, in *quatre-couleur* gold. Still, I suppose you would know that. Your uncle is a connoisseur of sorts."

Sophie's mouth had gone so dry that she could only nod.

"It is new." The baronet's gloating expression faded and he sighed. "I had another, very similar, but even finer. Unfortunately I lost it somewhere."

"Perhaps one of the servants stole it," Sophie managed to whisper.

"Don't be stupid!" The baronet glowered at her. "Do you think I would allow my staff to cheat me? I am not so gullible! It went missing last spring after a night at my club." He shrugged irritably, annoyed by the memory. "I was celebrating my return to London. A man must drink on such occasions, but carelessness led to my pockets being picked on my way home."

He patted the little box possessively. "I shall be more vigilant in future. It took my goldsmith months to find this one and adapt it to my wishes."

"Is that your initial?"

"So you have noticed it! I was beginning to think you had no appreciation of art!" Sir Pelham threw her a pleased look. "It is my own design."

The entrance of Simon Conrad saved Sophie from having to think of a reply.

Numbly, she allowed the secretary to take her arm and escort her to the door.

"Until later, my dear. And don't forget to smile as you come up the aisle."

Sophie did not hear the mockery in her betrothed's farewell. All she could think of was the last time she had seen that intricate golden S, when it had decorated the snuff-box on the counter of her uncle's shop, the snuff-box that had been found in Ingram Thorburn's dead hand.

CHAPTER TWELVE

A SUDDEN FLASH of movement caught Kirk Thorburn's eyes. There was someone in the marble pavilion that overlooked the flower-garden.

A faint curse escaped him. He had been counting on the fact that the grounds would be deserted at this hour. Desperately he racked his brains to think of another way of gaining access to the house, but he didn't know of any other secret entrance.

Not that it was truly a secret entrance, of course. That was just the name Ingram had christened it years ago. Its secluded door gave on to a series of passages, one of which led up a backstair to Pelham's boyhood room. Another, if he remembered aright, branched off in the direction of the chapel.

Kirk's plan was simple. He intended to conceal himself in the chapel and, at the appropriate moment when the parson asked if anyone knew of any impediment to the marriage, he would stand up and declare that Sophie was being forced.

If that failed, well, he was armed.

A swift glance at the sinking sun reminded him that it would soon be dusk. There was no time to stand here dithering like an old maid!

Resolutely putting aside the worry eating into him that he might already be too late, Kirk decided to run the risk of being seen. Taking a firmer grip on the crowbar he carried, he slipped cautiously from his hiding-place in the shadow of the cypress hedge.

At the exact same instant a frail figure emerged from the pavilion and began to walk towards him, head bowed as if in prayer.

For a moment Kirk thought she might not see him, but then she looked up and almost staggered back in shock.

"Mrs. Stanton. Don't be alarmed. I won't harm you."

"Kirk?" she gasped. "Kirk Thorburn!"

The old lady peered up at him. She'd been too surprised to let out a scream of fright, and now she had recognised him she knew that there was no need.

"Kirk, you must leave," she ordered in a quavering voice. "If Pelham discovers you are here there will be trouble."

Kirk's mouth set in a grim line. "The fact that you seek to warn me proves you suspect your nephew of villainy."

The gathering shadows could not hide her guilty blush.

"Kirk, you were always a good boy. Please do as I ask," she pleaded.

He shook his head. "It's too late, Mrs. Stanton. This time you can't prevent the truth from coming out. Pelham's gone too far."

She hugged her fur-trimmed cloak tighter about her tiny body. "I know," she whispered. Tears began to trickle down her wrinkled cheeks. "Oh, Kirk, I know about your brother!"

Kirk's fingers clenched on the cold iron of his crowbar.

"I wasn't sure at first that Pelham had been involved," his aunt continued shakily. "I suppose I didn't want to believe it. When I finally taxed him with it Pelham only laughed. He told me not to worry, that no one would ever find out."

Kirk handed her his handkerchief and she dabbed at her eyes.

"I think this fever for gaming has turned his brain. I have begged him to desist until I'm hoarse, but he won't listen. He's even mortgaged the Hall."

"So that's why he is desperate to marry a fortune," Kirk breathed.

Mrs. Stanton did not deny it. "He has chosen a Kendal heiress, a Miss Fleming. She is a sweet girl."

Kirk's heartbeat quickened.

"Have you spoken to her recently?"

Another sob shook the old lady. "Pelham will not let me see her. He says she is willing for the ceremony to go ahead this afternoon, but Kirk, I fear he is lying!"

"I know he is," Kirk replied firmly. "That's why I'm here. You see, Miss Fleming is a friend of mine and I'm going to put a stop to this wedding one way or another."

Her eyes flew to the sword he wore.

"Do you intend to tell Pelham I'm here?"

His demand made her tears fall faster, and Kirk felt a fleeting pang of sympathy for her predicament. She had always adored her nephew.

"I cannot condone what he has done," she whispered. "I came out here into the peace of the garden to pray for guidance, and God has sent you to me. My nephew has become a monster. He must be saved from himself before he hurts anyone else."

"Then we must hurry," Kirk said, taking her arm.

They approached the door.

"I have the key. There is no need to use that thing," Mrs. Stanton informed him with a shudder.

Once inside the house, Kirk had additional cause to be grateful for the old lady's assistance. The twists and turns of the numerous passages were more complicated than he remembered, but with Mrs. Stanton's help he swiftly found himself outside the chapel.

"I think it would be better if you waited out here until the service is under way," Pelham's aunt announced thoughtfully. "There is little concealment in the chapel for a man of your size."

Kirk nodded. All eyes would be on the altar; no one would notice him slip in later.

"Will you attend the ceremony?"

"Pelham requested my presence, and in his present mood I did not dare refuse him." She glanced at the diamond-encrusted little watch which decorated the sober neckline of her gown. "It is almost time." She wiped her eyes with a resolute gesture. "I must go in and take my place."

Her hand crept timidly to find his sleeve.

"I know I have no right to ask it of you, but say that you will not hurt him!"

He removed her hand gently.

"I'd be a liar if I made you any promise," he answered quietly. "I have sworn to bring your nephew to justice and, if Pelham resists, then be it on his own head!"

Her shoulders sagged and she turned away without another word.

Kirk watched her go and frowned. Could he trust her not to betray him or would the habit of protecting her nephew prove too strong?

Shrugging the thoughts away, he took up the position Mrs. Stanton had suggested behind one of the thick, ornately carved pillars that decorated the archway leading to the chapel doors.

After a few moments he heard the sound of approaching footsteps.

"My aunt must have already gone inside. Her maid said she left her room some time ago."

The baronet's voice sounded unnaturally loud in Kirk's ears and his jaw clenched involuntarily.

Another man answered in mellifluous tones.

"Indeed, go on ahead, sir. You must wish to familiarise yourself with the altar. I shall join you in a moment when my secretary arrives with Miss Fleming."

The other man, who was obviously the parson, quipped, "What? Will you risk bad luck by seeing your bride ahead of time, Sir Pelham?"

"*I* am not superstitious." The baronet's tone was reproving.

His remark provoked a flurry of apology, followed by the sound of the heavy chapel door shutting.

Kirk tensed. It was so quiet that he could hear Stanton breathing.

Suddenly all the frustration of these long months of inaction came boiling to a head, and Kirk knew he couldn't endure to wait another moment. Without pausing to consider, he stepped out of his place of concealment.

"A word with you, sir."

Stunned, the baronet stared at him, his mouth falling slack with disbelief. "Thorburn! What . . . How . . ." He stammered over the words, his shock rapidly turning to dismay.

Kirk slowly unsheathed his sword. The long, fine blade glinted in the candlelight that illuminated the corridor.

"You murdered my brother," he said softly.

"Prove it!" The baronet had turned a sickly grey colour.

"Don't worry, I shall."

"Hah, there is no proof! You are bluffing, Thorburn. No magistrate will believe you."

Kirk took a step nearer, raising his blade.

"Let's go and find out if you are right, Stanton."

The baronet's eyes rolled wildly.

"Don't be absurd, man. I'm not going anywhere. In a few moments I am going to be married."

"Wrong again, Pelham." Kirk shook his head.

A look of fury replaced the fear on the baronet's face.

"The little bitch! *You* were the one she met in Watendlath!"

"Leave Miss Fleming out of this," Kirk replied tersely.

"Ah, I see. Smitten by her rustic charms, are you? Or is it her dowry that impresses you, Thorburn?" The baronet gave a jeering laugh.

"Don't judge everyone by your own standards," Kirk retorted. "Unlike you, I have no need of Sophie's money."

Sir Pelham blanched, and it was Kirk's turn to laugh.

"The game's up, Pelham. I know all about your debts, and I'm not the only one. Soon your disgrace will be on everyone's lips." His smile hardened, his blue eyes cold. "Still so sure that the magistrates won't believe me?"

"Fiend take you!" The baronet had begun to sweat. "You'll never carry this off, Thorburn. I've a dozen servants—"

"But none within earshot," Kirk interrupted. "You gave them all leave to make merry in the servants' hall."

"How the devil did you know that?"

"Your aunt told me."

This simple reply seemed to rob the baronet of any further speech, and in the sudden silence they both became aware of the sound of footsteps.

Automatically, they both turned. Simon Conrad was approaching. At his side, her face as pale as her silk gown, walked Sophie. In her reluctant hand hung a posy of hothouse flowers, a bridal tribute.

"Conrad! Here, to me!" the baronet cried desperately, backing away from Kirk.

The iron grip on Sophie's arm slackened and she wrenched free.

"Kirk!"

She began to run towards him, but the secretary grabbed her, hauling her back.

"Never mind her, you fool!" Sir Pelham screamed. "Get Thorburn!"

Obeying, Conrad flung Sophie to one side and advanced on Kirk, drawing his light dress sword.

After one agonised look to check that Sophie had not suffered any harm, Kirk tried to concentrate his attention on this new threat.

The secretary was surprisingly good for a man of such fleshy appearance. Kirk had the superior reach, but his swordsmanship was of the plain variety; he preferred pistols. Unfortunately, never dreaming how matters would turn out, he had left his behind when he'd set out to escort Becky to Keswick.

He had borrowed this sword from the landlord of the George, who had acquired it in payment for a debt. It was a fine blade, but within moments Kirk realised that he had never learnt the dirty tricks that the secretary had mastered. Only his quick wits and natural strength enabled him to counter the flashy sword-play employed against him.

Sophie watched anxiously as he was gradually forced back, her joy at his miraculous arrival turning to fear for his safety.

"Don't worry, you'll be a bride yet!"

Unnoticed, the baronet had crept to her side, and Sophie flinched as he pinched her arm, emitting a vicious little laugh.

"You miserable swine!" With all her strength, she slapped his face, and his squeal of pain caused the distraction Kirk needed.

Abandoning the niceties, he lashed out with his fist, catching Conrad unawares. The blow landed directly on his jaw and the secretary crumpled into an untidy heap and lay unmoving.

"My dear sir, what is the meaning of this outrage? Have you no shame? How dare you brawl on the doorstep of the house of the Lord?" cried a mellifluous voice.

The noise of the fight had filtered into the chapel, bringing the parson and Mrs. Stanton hurrying.

Ignoring them, Kirk whirled to face the baronet, but Sir Pelham had already seized his chance.

"Let her go, damn you!"

The baronet laughed shrilly and tightened his savage grip on Sophie, who was struggling frantically to free herself.

"Keep still, you bitch!" Sir Pelham snarled, burying his free hand in Sophie's curls and yanking viciously.

Tears of pain spurted from beneath Sophie's eyelids, and with a growl of rage Kirk hurled himself towards the baronet.

"Come one step nearer, Thorburn, and I'll break it," he warned, forcing Sophie's arm up behind her back.

Kirk halted, and a thin little smile touched the baronet's mouth.

"That's better," he gloated.

"Pelham, please! Don't do this!" His aunt began to sob.

He glared furiously at her. "Be silent, ma'am!"

He tugged at Sophie's arm. "Walk!" he ordered.

"No!" Sophie spat the word at him, but when she tried to resist he increased the pressure on her arm.

"Do as he says, Sophie."

Kirk's anxious voice seemed to reach her through a mist of pain, and she nodded giddily.

Sir Pelham began to back away down the corridor. Half dragged along in his wake, Sophie sought frantically for a means of escape, but the baronet's grip never wavered.

Kirk followed, careful not to cause alarm by coming too close. He did not trust that wild look in those cold hazel eyes. One wrong move and Stanton would panic, forgetting everything but his own fear, and he had Sophie!

They had reached the grand staircase, and for the first time the baronet halted, uncertainty flickering over his narrow face.

A glimmer of hope lit up Sophie's distress. He's worried now that there's room for Kirk to spring on him. He can't defend himself and hold on to me at the same time!

"Let her go, Stanton," Kirk said quietly.

"Not until it suits me!" cried the baronet, but his voice quivered.

"Let her go and I'll leave here quietly."

"No!" Sophie protested, unwilling to be the cause of Kirk's defeat.

"Be quiet, Sophie," Kirk pleaded. "Release her and I give you my word that I will allow you a clear start of three days before I come after you."

"How do I know I can trust you?"

"The parson here can bear witness." Kirk gestured to the cleric, who had followed them at a discreet distance, accompanied by Mrs. Stanton. "All I ask is that you let Sophie come away with me now."

"Pelham, do as he suggests." The old lady spoke up. "Be sensible, boy! The truth is bound to come out. This way at least you have a chance. Don't make things worse."

The baronet hesitated, and in that instant his grip on Sophie's arm eased.

Seizing the opportunity, Sophie drove her unfettered elbow into her captor's ribs as hard as she could. Sir Pelham gasped, involuntarily slackening his hold on her other arm.

Instantly Sophie wrenched herself free and took to her heels.

"Good girl!" Kirk flung a comforting arm around her shoulders and gave her a quick hug before turning back to face the baronet.

"Come on, Pelham," he murmured softly. "Let's see how you defend yourself now you can't hide behind a woman's skirts!"

"Get away from me!" Gibbering with fear, the baronet stepped backwards.

"Look out, you fool!"

Kirk's warning came a second too late.

In his panic the baronet had forgotten where he was standing, and one high-heeled shoe slid over the edge of the top stairs, throwing him off balance. His arms wheeled up as he tried desperately to regain his footing, but it was no use.

His elegantly clad body tumbled backwards and, bouncing from marble step to marble step, came to rest spread-eagled on the cold stone below.

"MISS FLEMING! A word if I may."

Sophie reined in her newly acquired chestnut mare.

"Mrs. Birkett." She acknowledged Caroline's greeting with a slight nod.

"Will you dismount and enter?" Caroline gestured towards the house a little further down the street. "We could take tea together."

"No, thank you." Sophie eyed the parcels Caroline held. "I would not wish to interrupt your shopping."

"I have just finished." Caroline smiled. "It is such a warm day. I'm sure a little refreshment would not come amiss."

About to refuse, it occurred to Sophie that Caroline must have other matters than the unexpectedly mild April weather on her mind.

"Very well, but I cannot stay long. My uncle expects me home from my riding lesson," Sophie explained.

The groom, whom her uncle insisted attend her at all times, helped Sophie dismount.

"My servants will show you where to go," Caroline murmured to him, beckoning Sophie to follow her into the neat terraced house that was her home.

After the glare of the streets, the little parlour seemed deliciously cool.

"Pray remove your hat and sit down," Caroline invited.

While she rang for tea Sophie cast a surreptitious glance around her. It was a very feminine room, charmingly decorated in the exact blue of Caroline's eyes.

A wry smiled touched Sophie's generous mouth for an instant.

"You look a little pale. Would you like something stronger than tea to revive you? Some sherry perhaps?" Caroline asked solicitously.

Sophie shook her head and refused politely. Her uncle had purchased a horse for her, a pretty little chestnut mare named Jasmine, and she'd had several lessons. She was still rather nervous, hence her lack of colour, but she was determined to succeed in becoming a good rider, as she explained to her hostess.

"I see," Caroline answered. "Only I couldn't help wondering if you were still feeling the effects of your shocking tragedy. After all, it is only two weeks ago that Sir Pelham met his death."

Sophie gritted her teeth.

"I am perfectly well, thank you."

Her evasive answer caused Caroline to hesitate, but after their refreshments had arrived she said bluntly, "Forgive me if I offend, but you don't seem in the least bit broken-hearted."

Sophie tensed. "I find public displays of grief distasteful," she announced with perfect truth.

Caroline set down her tea-cup.

"Of course. Everyone must deal with bereavement in their own way, but I'm surprised you are not wearing mourning." She eyed Sophie's riding-habit, a dashing affair in fine royal blue cloth, its severe lines softened by military-style gold frogging. "And you left Stanton Hall before the funeral."

"I . . . I longed to get home," Sophie stammered.

"And Mr. Thorburn escorted you, did he not?"

Sophie nodded unwillingly.

It had been a dreadful journey. Old Mrs. Stanton's screams seemed to ring in her ears long after they had left the Hall behind and rejoined Nancy.

Maria's arrival at the George Inn had helped Sophie recover from the shock, but they were not free to leave Keswick until they had given evidence about Pelham's death to the local magistrate. Despite the fact that everyone involved, for varying reasons of their own, had agreed to say the baronet's fall was a sheer accident, Sophie found the interview a dreadful ordeal.

She had still been feeling shaken when they finally reached Kendal. Uncle Thomas, appalled by the news and distressed by Sophie's wan appearance, had ordered her off to bed, and when she had awoken the next day it was to discover that Kirk had already left.

The disappointment had been crushing. The brief letter he had left behind for her had merely stated that he had several urgent matters to attend to. Even worse, it made no mention of when he would return.

"It must have been terrible to actually witness the accident."

Caroline's probing remark broke the awkward silence that had fallen.

Sophie agreed warily. Her uncle had cautioned her to say nothing about the true events that had taken place at Stanton Hall.

"Whether the truth comes out is up to Kirk, lass," Mr. Fleming had announced. "I know he has to think of his brother, and I won't try to hide the facts if I'm asked, but there's nothing to be gained by letting the world know what an old fool I've been!"

He had shuddered, heaving a deep sigh. "When I think of the danger you were in! Eeh, lass, but the gossips will have a field-day if they ever find out Stanton had you imprisoned in that place of his! I could kick myself when I think of the damage this whole business might do to your reputation! Won't you wear black at least for a few weeks? It might stop some talk."

Sophie had shaken her bright curls. "I will not play the hypocrite, Uncle," she had said flatly.

He had heaved another sigh, too worried to try and persuade her. "Stanton's treachery has brought it home to me how much you need a proper husband to look after you, lass. I'm getting too old for the job."

Sophie had denied it, adding, "I'm not sure I want to marry anyway, Uncle."

"Hey, now, what's this? You've had a bad fright, lass, but you are only young yet. There's plenty of time to find the right man."

Sophie had coloured, and something in her expressive face warned him that his niece had already done so.

"So it's young Thorburn you've set your heart on, eh?"

Sophie's blush had deepened.

Thomas Fleming had stroked his chin thoughtfully, but to Sophie's relief he hadn't pursued the subject.

She had been too grateful at not having to explain about her tangled relationship with Kirk to wonder at his lack of curiosity, but, thinking about it now, it occurred to her how odd his attitude had been. It was almost as if he knew all about it, and yet that was absurd!

"And your betrothed's death coming so close to the wedding!" Caroline's voice was continuing relentlessly, forcing Sophie to abandon her thoughts and concentrate on the present.

"It must be hard for you not to dwell on the fact that the ceremony should have taken place next month."

Sophie repressed a shiver. She had ordered Nancy to burn the cream silk gown she had worn that fateful day, but her memories were not so easily eradicated. Nightmares still haunted her sleep.

"More tea?"

Caroline reached out to refill her cup, but Sophie shook her head.

"I heard a rumour the other day that you had returned your betrothal ring to old Mrs. Stanton. Didn't you wish to treasure it as a keepsake?"

"What are you hinting at, Mrs. Birkett?" Sophie demanded, tiring of the inquisition.

"I'm sorry." Unexpectedly, Caroline apologised. "I know I shouldn't ask, but what I am trying to discover is whether you truly loved the baronet or not."

"Loved him? I detested the man!" Sophie snapped, innate honesty getting the better of discretion.

"Thank goodness for that!"

"I don't understand." Sophie gazed at her in confusion.

"I will try to explain in a moment, but first I think I owe you an apology. You once accused me of being in love with Kirk Thorburn and I denied it, but I was lying." Caroline chewed her lower lip. "I would never be unfaithful to my husband, but I find Kirk very attractive."

Jealousy seared through Sophie, but she managed to say levelly, "Your private emotions are none of my concern. You don't have to justify yourself to me."

"But I do. Unless I miss my guess, you love Kirk, and I fear my infatuation has done him a disservice!" Caroline fixed her limpid blue gaze earnestly on Sophie's face. "Kirk is not attracted to me. I think he would be horrified if he realised how I felt! He is entirely blameless!"

"Why are you telling me all this?" Sophie asked.

Caroline sighed faintly. "Kirk came to pay a brief courtesy call on me before he returned north. I could tell that he was unhappy. He would not discuss it, but I think he is in love with you. However, I sensed there was something causing a rift between you."

Sophie tasted blood as she bit her lip. Bitterly, she reflected that Caroline was right. No matter how he felt about her, it was Becky Kirk had chosen!

"I just wanted to make it clear to you that I am not your rival," Caroline continued doggedly. "Even if I so far forgot myself as to disregard my marriage vows, Kirk would never consent to betray James."

"You must care a great deal for Kirk's happiness to risk telling me this," Sophie murmured.

"Above all else, Kirk is my friend." Caroline nodded. "That's why I wanted to know how you felt about the baronet. If you had been in love with Stanton...well!" She shrugged expressively. "I don't want to see Kirk hurt."

"The boot is on the other foot!" Sophie cried hotly. "Kirk must have guessed how I feel, but he left Kendal without a word."

"Then you *are* in love with him?"

Sophie couldn't deny it.

"I hope things sort themselves for you," Caroline said awkwardly. She paused and then added in a rush, "Will you keep my secret?"

"I won't breathe a word to anyone," Sophie affirmed, and Caroline let out a gasp of relief.

"I must go." Sophie rose swiftly to her feet, anxious to be on her own so that she could think over what Caroline had said.

"So soon?" Caroline prepared to escort her to the door. "I was hoping that perhaps we might start to become better acquainted."

"I should like that, but my uncle will worry if I don't return. He is even more nervous about my riding than I am!"

Caroline acknowledged this remark with a smile, but then her expression grew serious.

"There is one other thing I ought to confess. When Kirk first came to Kendal I'm afraid I rather exaggerated the extent of his fortune."

"But I thought his plantation was to bring in an enormous profit?" Sophie exclaimed.

Caroline coloured. "Kirk told me in confidence that its value would be affected by an attack of chenille bug, which apparently lowers cotton yields. I ignored him. It seemed to me that people would take more notice of his claims if they thought him to be a rich man." She shrugged defensively. "I did it for the best."

Sophie refrained from making the obvious comment that Caroline's meddling had placed Kirk in an awkward position.

"I'm sorry, I seem to have made a complete hash of things," Caroline sighed, leading the way into the hall.

Once upon a time, not so long ago, Sophie would have thrown Caroline's apology back in her face, but recent events had taught her not to be so hasty. She would always be hot-tempered, but she had acquired a little more tolerance, and kindness wasn't to be despised.

"I never thanked you for attempting to warn me about Pelham," she said slowly. "It was good of you to try, especially as I behaved like a spoilt brat."

Caroline's face brightened. "You have changed!" she exclaimed.

Sophie smiled faintly. "So my uncle informs me," she replied with a humourous inflexion in her voice that made Caroline laugh and say,

"Come again soon."

Sophie promised to do so and they parted on good terms.

ON THE RIDE HOME Sophie's thoughts were in a whirl.

She had assumed that Kirk had left Kendal in order to return to Becky's side, but Caroline's assertion seemed to contradict that idea.

But why had Kirk left in such a hurry? Could the dread of being thought a fortune-hunter have driven him away? He was a proud man, and Sophie knew he would hate being tarred with the same brush as Pelham.

It was another reason to hope that the real facts about the baronet's villainy never got out, but Sophie was aware of the flaw in her argument. If Kirk didn't broadcast the truth, which included Pelham's motive for marrying an heiress, of course, how was he to avenge Ingram's murder?

Sophie bit her lip. Was Kirk worried about her reputation? He had once accused her of being spoilt and selfish, but surely he couldn't think that she would rate gossip more important than a debt of honour?

Oh, why had he left without a word? If only she could have spoken to him she could have reassured him that she was prepared to endure the spiteful talk his revelations would undoubtedly bring.

She was on the point of dismounting from Jasmine's back when it suddenly occurred to her that her uncle was the last person to have spoken to Kirk before he left. Uneasily, she remembered how concerned Uncle Thomas was about the possibility of gossip, and he was very old-fashioned . . .

"Oh, no!" she breathed, almost breaking her neck as she scrambled down.

Leaving her groom tut-tutting his disapproval, she ran into the house. Pausing only to cast her whip and hat on to the hall table, she marched into the parlour.

"Uncle Thomas, I want to— Oh!"

Kirk Thorburn uncurled his great length from the armchair and rose politely to his feet.

"Your uncle is in the wine cellar," he informed her.

Sophie nodded wordlessly and collapsed on to a red-velvet-cushioned settle.

"May I join you?" Before she could frame a coherent reply Kirk had sat down next to her.

Recovering her breath, Sophie demanded, "Why didn't you let us know you were coming?"

"I did," Kirk replied coolly.

"But...but my uncle said nothing!" Sophie gazed at him in bewilderment.

"Ah, I'd rather hoped he might have changed his mind."

There was a rueful note in his deep voice, but Sophie scarcely heeded his cryptic remark. Her first astonishment over, a fierce joy had taken possession of her as her starved senses drank in his nearness.

He looked immaculate, in a smart grey coat over his pale lemon silk waistcoat. Cream-coloured pantaloons encased his long legs, their fashionable tightness defining the strong muscles in his thighs, and his boots were so highly polished that they almost glittered.

Sophie's mouth went dry. How blue his eyes were! They were smiling at her with that devastating charm she remembered so well, setting her pulses racing!

A little shiver ran through her. Suddenly every nerve in her body seemed to have come alive. She wanted to lay her head against his broad shoulder... She wanted to twine her fingers in the thick mass of guinea-gold curls that clustered at the nape of his neck... She wanted to feel his lips on hers... She wanted... oh, dear God, she wanted *him!*

"Did you receive my note, the one I left for you before I departed?" Kirk asked carefully.

Sophie's euphoria vanished in a twinkling.

"Indeed I did, sir." She glared at him. "Thank you for sparing me so much of your time when you were obviously in a hurry."

To her surprise Kirk merely grinned at her.

"Do you know," he said in a conversational tone, "I was beginning to think I had come to the wrong house, but now I feel at home."

Sophie flushed. Her gaze dropped to survey the somewhat dusty hem of her riding-habit. Damn, she had meant to keep her unruly tongue under control!

"Oh, Sophie, don't start aping those polite little drawing-room manners." Kirk tipped up her chin with a gentle hand. "I prefer you the way you are."

Sophie's heart skipped several beats, but she managed to say coolly, "And pray, what is that, sir?"

"Truthful, courageous and loyal," he replied with a sincerity that shook her to the core.

She swallowed hard. "Kirk, I—"

"No, wait. Let me finish." He touched one long finger to her lips. "There are many qualities about you that I find endearing, Miss Fleming, but most of all I admire your honesty."

A blur of tears almost blotted out his smile, and Sophie had to sniff hard before she could say, "You are very kind, sir, but sadly mistaken, I fear! I'm not in the least bit honest. If I possessed even a quarter of the attributes you so flatteringly accredited to me just now I would never have accepted Pelham's offer, which would have saved everyone a great deal of bother!''

Kirk suppressed a groan. ''Must we discuss Stanton right now?''

''Yes!'' Sophie almost shouted the word at him, her composure in shreds.

Kirk hesitated. He ached to enfold her in his arms and finish what he was trying to tell her, but a sense of caution prevented him. Her unguarded expression of delight on seeing him was encouraging, but he had no right to take her love for granted.

''Very well. I suppose you want to know what happened when I returned north.''

Sophie nodded. ''I won't have any peace until you tell me,'' she said simply.

''I went to see old Mrs. Stanton. The Hall is mortgaged to the hilt, but everything else is to be sold to try and pay off his debts.''

''I guessed as much,'' Sophie breathed. ''Does she have anywhere to go?''

''She has a small income from her late husband, barely enough to live on.'' Kirk coughed awkwardly. ''I offered her one of the properties I own in Cockermouth, but she has decided to live with a cousin in Derbyshire. That's where the Stantons originally hail from, if you remember.''

His generosity made Sophie want to hug him, but the expression on his handsome face curbed her impulse.

''Kirk, what else did she say?''

''I should have known I couldn't fool you,'' he muttered.

''She pointed out that there would be a scandal when Pelham's guilt was revealed, didn't she?'' Sophie persisted.

Kirk regarded the toes of his leather boots. ''Aye,'' he admitted at last.

The old lady had been vehement.

''My nephew is dead, sir! What good will it do to rake over old grievances now?''

Clad in black, she had faced him across the resplendent grandeur of the gold salon, her lined face ravaged by tears, but her head held defiantly high.

''Without your interference, Pelham would still be alive. Oh, I know he deserved punishment, but must you pursue him beyond the grave? It won't bring Ingram back. All it will do is cast a shadow over the reputation of Miss Fleming.''

Kirk had stared at her, unable to deny her angry claim.

"Can't you be satisfied with the fact that he is dead, Kirk?" she had continued more quietly. "You never used to be unreasonable. You were always a kind boy.''

She had paused and then added, "Stanton Hall and all its treasures will be sold. The house in London is already on the market. There is nothing left! Soon everyone will know that my nephew died a ruined man.''

When Kirk still hadn't answered she had fixed him with a stern eye.

"You owe me something, Kirk Thorburn. Against every family feeling, I helped you that day. Promise me that you won't hound Pelham now! Revenge is a bitter dish and you'll rue ignoring my advice, believe me!''

Kirk had refused to give his promise, but as he had ridden away from the Hall he had pondered her words.

If he revealed Pelham's guilt the scandal would rock society, and the gossip would reach new heights if he then went on to marry the baronet's betrothed!

Old Mr. Fleming had been cool when Kirk had approached him. He would run a dreadful risk if he exposed Stanton, but was honour satisfied by the mere fact of the baronet's death?

This dilemma had given Kirk sleepless nights, but, gazing down into Sophie's vivid little face, all his doubts suddenly vanished. He couldn't face the prospect of losing her. She meant more to him than anything in the world!

"You're right, the old lady did warn me," he said, finally answering her question. "However, I don't intend to reveal Stanton's guilt.''

Sophie's eyes widened. "But why, Kirk?" she breathed.

"Because of the way I feel about you," he said abruptly.

For a moment Sophie couldn't believe her ears.

"Me? But what about Becky?" she demanded.

"Becky?" Kirk's brows drew together in a puzzled frown. "What the devil has Becky to do with it? I haven't spoken to her in weeks. In fact I doubt if we'll ever see her again.''

Sophie gulped as the truth hit her. "Oh, Kirk, I've been such an idiot!''

"You didn't imagine that I had fallen under her spell again, did you?" Kirk demanded indignantly.

"You were very kind to her," Sophie countered.

"I felt sorry for her!"

Realising he was shouting, Kirk took a deep breath and unclenched his hands.

"Sweetheart, don't let's start quarrelling!" he begged.

Sophie began to giggle helplessly. "We always do so! Oh, Kirk, I'm sorry, but she told me . . . well, never mind what she said. I should have heeded Rose's warning and remembered that she was skilled at manipulating people."

"Rose sends her love." Kirk carefully steered the conversation away from the tricky subject of Becky. "And she asked me to thank you for the gift which accompanied the return of her dress."

A smile touched Sophie's mouth. Choosing that pretty rattle for Rose's baby had been one of the few pleasant moments in the last couple of weeks.

"I'm glad Rose was pleased," she murmured. "I like her."

"She would be one of your neighbours if you came to live in Watendlath."

Sophie swallowed hard. She hadn't misunderstood him!

"Work has started on the restoration," Kirk said quickly, afraid of her silence. "But we wouldn't have to live at Haraldsgarth. I own several other properties. You could choose whichever you preferred."

Astonishment made Sophie blurt, "Other properties? You mean you are wealthy in spite of what happened with your plantation?"

"My father invested in several diverse schemes. I inherited a tidy sum." Kirk suddenly grinned at her. "I can still afford to keep my wife in comfort, if not the luxury she is accustomed to!"

Sophie blushed. She had misunderstood Caroline's confession! "I thought you would be worried about being taken for a fortune-hunter," she admitted.

"That idea did cross my mind," Kirk replied drily.

"Did my uncle say anything to you before you left Kendal?" Sophie asked, plucking nervously at her skirts.

He nodded, looking faintly uncomfortable. "I asked him if I might pay my addresses to you and he told me to go away while he thought things over."

"Oh, I knew it!"

"Sweetheart, don't fly up into the boughs!" Kirk caught her restless hands and held them. "You can't blame him for being cautious. I don't give a damn if he wants to have my finances investigated."

"He said that?" Sophie gasped indignantly.

Deciding there was nothing to be gained from this conversation, Kirk drew her firmly into his arms.

"Darling, Sophie, how much longer do you intend to make me wait for an answer?"

Sophie's hands slid up around his neck.

"I wasn't aware that you had asked me yet, sir," she retorted with a saucy grin.

"Minx!" Kirk's grip tightened. "Damn it, do you want me to go down on one knee like some milksop?" he growled.

"Of course," Sophie laughed.

Kirk gazed down into her dark eyes, and his answering grin faded.

"My darling girl, I adore you," he whispered hoarsely. "I know I am no good with words, but I think I fell in love with you that evening in Maria Strickland's conservatory. It wasn't just because Stanton was a rogue that I hated the thought of his marrying you. I would have felt the same if he'd been a saint! I want you for my own!"

His golden head dipped to hers.

"Say you'll marry me, beloved!"

In answer Sophie sought his mouth, and as their lips met a joy more intense than any she had ever known shot through her.

I've died and gone to heaven, she thought incoherently, the thud of his heart loud in her ears.

The tenderness of his kiss slowly deepened into passion and waves of exquisite pleasure swept over her, intensified by the deliciously familiar masculine scents of his body and the forceful strength of his arms.

"Oh, Kirk," she breathed when at last he released her. "I'll marry you tomorrow if you like."

They gazed into each other's eyes and desire sparked between them anew.

"The sooner the better, I think," Kirk agreed with a gruffness that couldn't conceal his feelings.

Sophie shifted to rest her head on his shoulder with a sigh of pure happiness, and he held her tightly for a while in silence.

"Are you really sure about your brother?" Sophie said, stirring in his embrace as her conscience pricked her. "I have positive proof of Pelham's guilt, you know. He had another snuff-box decorated in exactly the same way as the one found in Ingram's hand. I saw it."

"The man I had on the trail in London wrote a few days ago to tell me he had found the jeweller who engraved them both," Kirk admitted.

"Then we could go to the magistrates. I wouldn't mind the gossip, truly I wouldn't."

Kirk shook his head, his expression sombre. "No, Sophie. Old Mrs. Stanton was right. There is a difference between revenge and justice. Pelham paid for his crimes with his life." His mouth twisted. "Anyway, I suspect people will remember how Ingram claimed he'd been cheated once it gets out that Stanton died a pauper, and they'll wonder about the fire. But I won't heap further shame and sorrow on that old lady's head."

A faint sigh of relief escaped Sophie. "I'm glad you have changed your mind," she confessed.

"My debt to Ingram has been paid." Kirk's deep voice was firm. "It's time to put the past behind us. My brother was a kind, gentle man. He would have been the last person in the world to want to sour our happiness."

He gently turned her to face him.

"You once told me that I put Ingram's memory above my feelings for you. It may have been true then, but I swear to you that it will never happen again. I love you more than anything, Sophie. More than honour, more than my life!"

Gazing into his vivid Viking eyes, Sophie realised he spoke the truth, and as he enfolded her into his embrace she knew that their future together would be all that she could hope for. They would quarrel and fight—that was inevitable—but nothing would ever divide them again.

"And I love you, Kirk," she replied simply, her dark eyes shining.

Their lips met in another tender kiss and, lost in a world of their own, they didn't hear the door opening.

Thomas Fleming hesitated, the bottle of champagne in his hand.

Then, with a little smile, he quietly withdrew.

Harlequin Romance ®

AVAILABLE IN OCTOBER—A BRAND-NEW COVER DESIGN FOR HARLEQUIN ROMANCE

Harlequin Romance has a fresh new eye-catching cover.

We're bringing you an exciting new cover design, but Harlequin Romance is still committed to bringing you warm and contemporary love stories that are sure to touch your heart!

See how we've changed and look for these fabulous stories with a brand-new look:

#3379 Brides for Brothers
by Debbie Macomber
#3380 The Best Man
by Shannon Waverly
#3381 Once Burned
by Margaret Way
#3382 Legally Binding
by Jessica Hart

Available in October,
wherever Harlequin books are sold.

Harlequin Romance ®—
Dare To Dream

MILLION DOLLAR SWEEPSTAKES (III)

No purchase necessary. To enter, follow the directions published. Method of entry may vary. For eligibility, entries must be received no later than March 31, 1996. No liability is assumed for printing errors, lost, late or misdirected entries. Odds of winning are determined by the number of eligible entries distributed and received. Prizewinners will be determined no later than June 30, 1996.

Sweepstakes open to residents of the U.S. (except Puerto Rico), Canada, Europe and Taiwan who are 18 years of age or older. All applicable laws and regulations apply. Sweepstakes offer void wherever prohibited by law. Values of all prizes are in U.S. currency. This sweepstakes is presented by Torstar Corp., its subsidiaries and affiliates, in conjunction with book, merchandise and/or product offerings. For a copy of the Official Rules send a self-addressed, stamped envelope (WA residents need not affix return postage) to: MILLION DOLLAR SWEEPSTAKES (III) Rules, P.O. Box 4573, Blair, NE 68009, USA.

EXTRA BONUS PRIZE DRAWING

No purchase necessary. The Extra Bonus Prize will be awarded in a random drawing to be conducted no later than 5/30/96 from among all entries received. To qualify, entries must be received by 3/31/96 and comply with published directions. Drawing open to residents of the U.S. (except Puerto Rico), Canada, Europe and Taiwan who are 18 years of age or older. All applicable laws and regulations apply; offer void wherever prohibited by law. Odds of winning are dependent upon number of eligibile entries received. Prize is valued in U.S. currency. The offer is presented by Torstar Corp., its subsidiaries and affiliates in conjunction with book, merchandise and/or product offering. For a copy of the Official Rules governing this sweepstakes, send a self-addressed, stamped envelope (WA residents need not affix return postage) to: Extra Bonus Prize Drawing Rules, P.O. Box 4590, Blair, NE 68009, USA.

SWP-H1095

Become a *Privileged Woman,* *You'll* be entitled to all these *Free Benefits.* And *Free Gifts,* too.

To thank you for buying our books, we've designed an exclusive FREE program called *PAGES & PRIVILEGES™*. You can enroll with just one Proof of Purchase, and get the kind of luxuries that, until now, you could only read about.

Big HOTEL DISCOUNTS

A privileged woman stays in the finest hotels. And so can you—at up to 60% off! Imagine standing in a hotel check-in line and watching as the guest in front of you pays $150 for the same room that's only costing you $60. Your *Pages & Privileges* discounts are good at Sheraton, Marriott, Best Western, Hyatt and thousands of other fine hotels all over the U.S., Canada and Europe.

Free DISCOUNT TRAVEL SERVICE

A privileged woman is always jetting to romantic places.

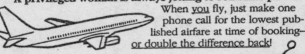

When you fly, just make one phone call for the lowest published airfare at time of booking— or double the difference back!

PLUS—you'll get a $25 voucher to use the first time you book a flight AND 5% cash back on every ticket you buy thereafter through the travel service!